"For this is the unicorn creed:
She must be a maiden indeed,
Completely straight-laced
And thoroughly chaste,
Who'd ride with the unicorn breed."

With leaf-scattering abandon the unicorn galloped to Maggie's side. When he saw Colin, Moonshine's slender legs stiffened and he tossed his mane aggressively. The distinguished little white goatee under his chin quivered with indignation.

"Maiden, a man comes with you. Does this mean you have betrayed me? What have I done to offend you? I who am your servant in all things, I who would give my life if you but asked, I who—"

"Dry up, darling, won't you please?" Maggie begged. "Of course you aren't betrayed. You remember Colin from before. He was with me when we met."

Moonshine approached cautiously, curling his lips back from his teeth and flaring his nostrils, sniffing elaborately. "No. No odor of chastity," the unicorn pronounced, nudging the now-nervous minstrel's leg in a rude gesture that brought the rapier tipped horn alarmingly close to a treasured portion of Colin's anatomy. . . .

Also by Elizabeth Scarborough

SONG OF SORCERY

and published by Bantam Books

THE
UNICORN CREED

Elizabeth Scarborough

BANTAM BOOKS
TORONTO · NEW YORK · LONDON · SYDNEY · AUCKLAND

THE UNICORN CREED

A BANTAM BOOK   0 553 17283 2

First publication in Great Britain

PRINTING HISTORY

Bantam edition published 1987

This books is set in Times

Bantam Books are published by Transworld Publishers Ltd.,
61–63 Uxbridge Road, Ealing, London W5 5SA,
in Australia by Transworld Publishers (Aust.) Pty. Ltd.,
15–23 Helles Avenue, Moorebank, NSW 2170, and in New
Zealand by Transworld Publishers (N.Z.) Ltd., Cnr. Moselle
and Waipareira Avenues, Henderson, Auckland.

Printed and bound in Great Britain by
Hazell Watson & Viney Limited,
Member of the BPCC Group,
Aylesbury, Bucks

For Marnie, Peter, Roger and Colin Cornwall for their encouragement and friendship, for my fellow unicorn fanciers, Pat Monaghan, Jean Jett, Rachel and Joanna Wulpert, Judie, Darcy and Panika Gumm, Gretchen and Mary Anne Walker, Heather Jett, Jocelyn and Colin Reed, Robyn Russell, Cathy Saunders, Naima Dickensen and Elizabeth, Roy, Jean and Ron English. Also, with fond admiration for lively memory of the late William D. Berry, wildlife and fantasy artist extraordinaire.

Many thanks to Professor Dean Gottehrer of the Journalism Department at the University of Alaska for his help with the manuscript, to my dear friend Jean Jett for her valuable comments and criticism and to Karen Haas at Bantam for her suggestions. I am also indebted to Dr. Thomas Johnston, professor of ethnomusicology at the University of Alaska, for his enlightening comments on magic and music.

PROLOGUE

When Colin Songsmith arrived with the royal party at Fort Iceworm, he scarcely recognized the place. Indeed, he scarcely could *see* the place, once he and the rest of Their Majesties' entourage had passed within the huge log gates, for it was crammed ten deep with people everywhere. Even now, in midsummer, when crops needed tending, animals needed herding, and peasants needed supervising, and in spite of Fort Iceworm's remoteness from Queenston, Argonia's capital city and center of both population and enterprise, no one wanted to miss the royal christening.

From all corners of the realm and the known world, the guests had already gathered—kings and statesmen, queens of faery, wazirs and wise men, gypsies, an unusually large number of assorted unattached noblemen, plus other noble people, ignoble people, were-people, half-people and even a few non-people. All had assembled to christen the baby Princess Bronwyn in the hall of her grandfather, Sir William Hood.

What portions of the castle's structure were visible were layered with silken banners of every color, bearing every crest in the realm, fluttering less with wind than with the comings and goings of the throng. The meadows separating castle and village from the vast forest were strewn with guest pavilions, like huge overblown summer flowers, crimson, azure, golden and green of every shade and tint. From the topmost turret of Sir William's keep flew the King's own crest, a rowan leaf on a field of scarlet. Directly below it, as was proper, flew Sir William's own banner, an iceworm, blue, on a field of white. Pennants bearing both emblems were hawked through the streets by enterprising peasants. Every cottager and holder for leagues around lodged at least twenty people in his small home, and at all hours elaborately clad servants came and went from the humblest of village dwellings. Never did the smell of cooking food, nor the sound of laughter and song, abate, for the entire week of festivities preceeding the christening.

It was a good thing that His Majesty was so tall. Otherwise Colin, whose duty it was as chief minstrel to always be at the King's right hand, chronicling his regally witty remarks on the marvelous occasion, could never have found either the King *or*

1

his right hand. Fortunately, His Highness was descended from frost giants, and was thus of conveniently outstanding stature.

Colin had less luck locating the other person he most wished to find at the christening, his old questing companion, Maggie Brown, Sir William's bastard daughter and Queen Amberwine's half sister. He knew where she was well enough—or where she had been, at any rate. It was Maggie's special talent, her hearthcraft witchery, which kept the entire christening from being a greater domestic disaster than it was. Hers was the power to perform all household tasks in the twinkling of an eye, and wherever she went she cut a swath of fragrant cooking fires, clean rushes, whitewashed walls, clean dishes, hot food, cold drink, emptied chamber pots, fresh linen, kindled torches and tidied beds. It was not an unpleasant trail to follow. Nevertheless, Colin had hoped for a more personal confrontation—a bit of a reunion, as it were—a chance to sing her his new songs, to tell her of his life at the castle, and perhaps to strut for her a bit in the rich apparel the King had given him. But somehow he never seemed to be free of his duties at the same time she was free of hers in the same room. Once he almost collided with her as he was coming in from a party at Sir Oswald's pavilion, but without looking up she'd brushed past him in a brown blur, automatically mending a small tear and cleaning a wine stain on his sleeve in passing. He was, for once, speechless, and after that had no more opportunities to seek her out, preoccupied as he was with his own duties of observing, chronicling, dancing, singing, entertaining and being entertained by his fellow guests.

So it happened that, although she was the first person he'd looked for, he never really saw her properly until the actual christening had begun and he took his favored place, slightly behind and to the left of Their Majesties' makeshift thrones inside the cow yard, which was the only area large enough to hold even the noble part of the assemblage.

King Roari and his queen, the exquisite Lady Amberwine, were flanked on one side by the most important of the royal guests, and on the other side by a smug and beaming Sir William, an equally proud Granny Brown, Maggie's irascible witch grandmother, and by Maggie herself. She was still dressed in her brown woolen skirt and tunic and manure-spattered wooden clogs, her apron splotched with a fresh grease stain, neglected in the excitement, her brown eyes darting restlessly around the courtyard, as if looking for tasks that still needed doing. Only her shining otter's pelt of brown hair was clean and neatly

2

braided, and bespoke personal preparation for the historic moment about to take place.

As the Mother's Priestess lifted Princess Bronwyn from Queen Amberwine's arms, and carried her gently and ceremoniously to the mound of christening mud heaped high upon the white-silk-covered table in front of the throne, Maggie caught Colin's eye and grinned at him. It was her old grin, and full of relief, though somewhat nervous. He grinned back at her, trying to think how to signal her to wait for him after the ceremony, but then there was no time. The baby had stopped howling in the priestess's unfamiliar arms, and now gurgled happily as the woman tenderly smeared the small body with the Mother's life-giving mud.

The congregation cheered as the last of Bronwyn's shining pink flesh was blessed with another gooey glob, and the small Princess was borne away into the castle to be bathed before the gifting began.

Colin thought then he might step over to one side and snag Maggie before she disappeared again. But before he'd taken a pace, King Roari lifted his hand slightly, and the royal herald, standing just to Colin's right, blew a loud, whinnying blast on his trumpet. Colin winced.

The King rose majestically—he was very good at being majestic, being so large—and the trumpet-silenced assemblage knelt; not an easy task, since a kneeling person took up more room than a standing one, and the cow yard was already packed.

Colin hoped His Majesty would have the good sense to make it short, whatever he had to say. The noonday feast awaited them and he, for one, was hungry.

"Noble friends and loyal subjects," King Roari began in his most dignified version of his booming hillman's brogue, "I shouldn't like it noised about that I'm a man forgets 'is debts. The queen and me and, aye, our wee baby too, all of us owes where we are today, that is together and able to be servin' you from the throne of our great realm, to the courage and loyalty of them as saved m'lady and child from certain unscrupulous sorcerers with whose names I will nae sully this grand occasion."

Ah, now wasn't that thoughtful? His Majesty was publicly going to thank Maggie and himself for rescuing the then-pregnant Queen Amberwine from the clutches of deluded gypsies and Maggie's deranged uncle, the wizard Fearchar Brown. It wasn't necessary, naturally. That was the sort of thing one had to expect on quests, but since the King evidently had made up his mind to make a fuss, Colin dusted off his own tunic and prepared to look humble and grateful when he was thanked. Maggie'd started the

3

whole thing, of course, but he'd gone with her as friend and protector during the rescue (well, usually he'd protected her; sometimes it was the other way around). He tried to catch her eye again, but she was staring at the King with a mixture of pleasure, apprehension, and what appeared to be impatience to be out of the cow yard and elsewhere.

"As ye all may know from the fine song m'minstrel Colin here has written about the quest, 'twas m'wife's sister, Maggie, took it on herself t'go tae m'lady's rescue. I've thanked her personal before, and Colin too, for t'great boon they've done us, but it's been pointed out tae me that though Maggie is, so far as I'm concerned, the noblest lassie in a' t'kingdom except for m'lady Amberwine, she has nae lands nor title o' her own. It also happens, y'know that I've nae blood relations, we Rowans bein' a notoriously careless lot with our hides, as ye may've heard."

The throng laughed politely. Maggie, kneeling, looked like she was preparing to sprint off down the hill and out the gate. Beside her, her grandmother and Sir William turned to see the King more clearly and Colin beheld the big, self-satisfied smile on Sir William's face. The reason for it was evident when the King spoke again.

"So it come to me that the thing for me to do—the thing for me to do is to adopt this woman, Maggie—Magdalene?" Sir William nodded his head. "Magdalene Brown, m'wife's half sister, tae be sister tae me as if she was born that way, and so a princess of the realm."

And without waiting for her to come to him, the King strode down off the throne's platform and in one giant step stood over her and clapped a silver circlet on her head. She looked up, startled, and the circlet slid down over one ear. She caught it and shoved it back up again.

"That's all I've got to say," King Roari said. "Let's eat, before the giftin' starts."

Whatever reward Colin had expected the King to bestow upon Maggie, a princess's coronet was the last thing he would have imagined. Her baffled expression was almost as funny as the sight of her; plain, earthy Maggie with grease on her dress, chimney grime on her elbows, and a crown on her head, princess of the realm! Ludicrous! Ah well, she'd give the court a few lessons in plain speaking, no doubt. Perhaps she'd even bring usefulness back in fashion. Choking back heartfelt but unseemly laughter, he wiped his eyes and tried to look decently, soberly pleased as he hastened forward to congratulate her.

But though she hadn't taken a step, she'd disappeared again.

4

Where before had been a clear space in front of her for the priestess to move about, now was a solid wall of the backs of eligible princes, dukes, counts and earls, each vying with the other to introduce himself in the loudest and most flowery tones, managing overall to sound very like the villagers hawking their souvenir pennants.

Sir William's grin spread across his face like jam on bread.

"Look at the bloody fools!" Granny Brown hissed. "You'd think they'd never seen a pretty girl before!"

"Now, Mother Brown," Sir William replied slyly, "It's only fitting a girl her age should have a few friends."

Colin thought the suitors seemed less like friends than like a pack of hounds tearing apart a doe, and he waited as long as he could to make his way through them to speak to her. But though he missed the feast entirely, and was almost late for the gifting, he never got near enough for her to hear him. Just before he turned to go, however, the composition of the cluster around her suddenly shifted, and she surfaced, like a drowning woman, and shot him one wild, despairing look before being swallowed up again, to be swept past him to the gifting tables.

He found a place near the Queen, behind a lady in an astonishing broad-winged purple cap with several yards of veiling attached. The first gift was just being presented. He didn't see Maggie there, nor her suitors—but he did spot one lone fellow who seemed to have missed out on the courting, an insolent looking gray haired chap clad in silver, down at the end of the reception line. Colin thought at the time that the fellow's sneer was inappropriate to a christening, but put it down to indigestion.

As was customary at christenings, the intangible gifts were presented first. These were bestowed by the magically endowed guests, each in accordance with his or her specialty. From Maggie's aunt, the seeress Sybil Brown, the baby received the gift of insight. From Queen Amberwine's faery kin, beauty and kindness to all natural things. From Granny Brown, whose witchcraft allowed her to transform things, the baby received the power to make the best of a bad situation. It went on and on like that—beauty, loyalty, courage, understanding, generosity, wisdom and other qualities a princess would need to live an exemplary life, along with certain wishes, spells, and enchantments for her protection from such baby's banes as diaper rash and colic. The King himself concluded that portion of the gifting by bestowing on her his own name day present, a bright red miniature shield with the Rowan crest carved into its wooden surface and painted by his own hand. Though Queen Amberwine looked up at her husband rather oddly, no one had the heart to tell the King that it was a peculiar sort of gift to give a daughter.

After that, everyone turned to the table where the more material gifts were piled. Some of them were mere toys, though others were amulets, talismans, medicine bundles or charms. These gifts were already unwrapped, and each in its turn was publicly admired and exclaimed over, after which the particular benefits of each and the donor would be noted by the Court Rememberer and ceremoniously explained to the by-now cranky baby, who clearly, from the smell of her, wanted changing.

Normally a model of poise and serenity, the queen rapidly lost her regal composure under the squirming weight of her child. Like many rituals, christenings were hardly designed for the comfort of the persons being honored. Desperate to find a gift gaudy enough to please her undignified daughter's unsubtle eye, Amberwine skipped over rattles, blocks, dolls, and magic stones.

The gilt box emblazoned with crimson jewels fairly leapt into her hand. She seized it and held it in front of Bronwyn's face, bathing the child playfully in the dazzle from the gems. The baby chortled and stretched out her chubby arms to snatch it. The queen allowed her to gum it for a moment or two before turning it over to see who had sent it. She shook her pretty head, shrugging, and handed it to the Court Rememberer to examine.

"Look, ma'am, where it was," her young lady-in-waiting suggested helpfully. "There's a bit of parchment there, with pictures and writing and all. Perhaps that says." But the parchment's drawings and runes were all indecipherable even to those of the court who could read. Finally, the King, always a man of action, tucked the parchment into his jerkin and took the box from the Court Rememberer.

"We'll just have a look, then," he said, lifting the catch, "There'll be a crest inside t'thing, of course."

But there wasn't.

The lid sprang open, and the crowd near the royal family gasped as a hideous gremlin popped from the box and bounced into the baby's face. "You're a dirty liar!" it shrieked at the little princess. "You're a dirty liar!"

Unlike the crowd, baby Bronwyn did not merely gasp. Taking the matter deeply to heart, she emitted a bellow that drowned out gremlin, crowd and all, for some time to come.

It was the baby's howl that first alerted Colin that something was very wrong and that the gift, which was concealed from him by the remarkable headgear of the lady in front of him, was in any way unusual. Up until then, he had been rather bored with the whole affair, preoccupied as he was with the amusing if rather alarming idea of Maggie Brown as a princess, and thinking to himself that a royal christening was not so very different from the more prosaic country ceremonies he was used to in his home village of East Headpenny—only the magic available to the royal child was of a higher, more powerful quality than usual. The bad as well as the good, so it now appeared.

Since he'd missed so much of what had gone on at first, he stepped forward to inquire of the lady in front of him. But before he could tap her on the shoulder, she jumped backward past him with a little squeal, evidently to make way for the Queen, who was fainting into her lord's arms. As the King caught the Queen, Colin caught the Princess, rolling from her mother's slackened arms.

No one challenged his right to lay hands upon the royal child, except perhaps the royal child herself, who was still lustily screaming. In the midst of the chaos, with the ladies screeching and noblemen cursing, the King roaring his concern over his wife like a mother bear with an unaccountably limp cub, and everyone pushing at the table, chattering like a lot of forest animals who have suddenly sensed the presence among them of a large predator, Colin's only coherent thought was to quiet the baby.

He began to sing for her *his* christening gift, a most soothing lullaby, though he feared, practically having to shout the song into her ear as he did, that his voice would sound anything but soothing. Fortunately the tune was undemanding, musically, being essentially a chanting of the higher reaches of the multiplication tables. The baby apparently found mathematics as enervating as Colin found less complicated christenings, for her mouth stopped quirking, and formed a tidy little "O," drooling small moist bubbles, and for a time she regarded him from round blue eyes, before they closed and she snuggled against his chest.

Perhaps the lullaby had had a calming effect on the adults present as well, or perhaps it was only that he had been singing longer than he realized, but when he looked up from the sleeping child, the Queen had revived enough to reclaim her, and the King had disappeared—though only visibly; Colin could hear the royal roar in the background, ordering his soldiers to prepare for an immediate return to Queenston. Closer to hand, those gathered around the Queen were arguing.

"Well, of course, it's some sort of a curse," said the lady who had jumped aside when Amberwine fainted. "You don't

7

suppose for a moment that sort of thing is a BLESSING, do you?"

"It has that look about it," the Grand Wazir of Babacoola commented. "Only a villain would play such a dastardly joke, and villains are unlikely to bestow anything *except* curses."

"What do you think it means?" Lady Althea, the Queen's nubile young handmaiden, asked. She was busily fanning Amberwine and the baby with a silken kerchief.

Granny Brown, across the gifting table from the rest of them, grunted. "Means she'll grow up a liar, no doubt. Pity no one thought to give her the gift of honesty. Now the damned thing's sure to stick."

Amberwine looked peaked and distraught, her eyes flitting from one speaker to the next, apparently in hopes that one of them would say something encouraging. The lady in the ridiculous hat was as fast with wit and tongue as she had been on her feet when the Queen was fainting. "Now, now, milady, don't you fret," she said, laying a kind hand on Amberwine's emerald satin sleeve. "I've been at court for many years now, and believe you me, if only the truth were known, *any* family of any real consequence has at least one little curse attached to it somewhere."

"That's so," nodded the Court Rememberer.

"Why, my dear," added the Dowager Queen of Wasimarkan, "From what *I've* seen of court life, I'd say that this curse could easily be the most useful gift your daughter's been granted yet."

"To be a liar?" Amberwine cried, and began to yawn. Colin noted the yawn with dismay. Having had the honor previously of rescuing Her Majesty from dire peril, and a dragon to boot, he was aware that the Queen, gentle and sensitive lady that she was, had the unfortunate habit of handling crises by napping for the duration while someone else dealt with the problem. Though she made a valiant effort at maternal protectiveness, rocking her persecuted child tenderly in her arms, the Queen was more affected by the rocking than the already sleeping baby. The more Amberwine rocked, the wider her yawns became, until finally they would not cease and she couldn't help nodding. At the last moment, she relinquished Bronwyn to the lady nearest her, and knelt peacefully at the table with her head cradled on her arms among the christening gifts until servants carried her to her bed.

But five days later, when the royal party was already a good third of the way back to Queenston, Colin found that what preyed on his mind wasn't the baby's curse, nor the Queen's continued somnolence, nor even the King's threats of war against whoever had cursed Princess Bronwyn. He was plagued instead by a niggling forboding centering on Maggie, and on the trapped look on her face when last he'd seen her. Funny as it had seemed at the time, it gnawed at him now, and so, when he'd sung Bronwyn to sleep for the hundredth time since the christening, he sought out the King, and begged his leave to return to Fort Iceworm.

CHAPTER 1

"Sorry, sir," the tower guard said. "No one allowed in Princess Magdalene's cell but family members." He jerked a dirt-creased thumb toward the tower door. "Her old man's in there chewin' 'er out right now."

"Oh, it's quite all right, I assure you," Colin replied, fumbling through pockets filled with penny whistles, bells, drumsticks and guitar picks until he found the crumpled piece of parchment with most of the Rowan Royal Seal still intact. "You see?" He waved the paper triumphantly. "I have a pass from the King."

The guard squinted down the considerable length of his crooked nose, just as though he could read what was written on the parchment. He couldn't, of course, or he would have seen that the pass was actually entitled "Master Songsmith to procure from the Royal wine cellar whatsoever brews and spirits he deems necessary for the entertainment of the King's Company." What the guard did recognize was the royal seal. His aunt had been sewing the blasted thing on those little flags for the last six months. He snapped to attention, or, at least, he snapped to his idea of attention.

A real guard would know about such things, but then, Bernard wasn't a real guard. He was only the cook's nephew, filling in while Sir William's militia honor-guarded the royal party back to Queenston. Well aware of his lack of professionalism about such matters as guarding and standing at attention, he endeavored to redeem himself in the eyes of this important gentleman by volunteering some inside information.

"I wouldn't go in there just yet, sir, if I was you, seal or no seal," he confided from behind his hand. "But if you was to put yer ear to the door, careful like, you might hear when 'is Lor'ship's leavin', an' manage to be out of 'is way, if you take my meanin'. 'Course," he shrugged. "You bein' a King's man and that, you mayn't wish to avoid 'is Lor'ship, but I should, sir, if I was you. Proper ogre he is these days, Sir William is, sir, if you take my meanin'?"

Colin took it. In a land where so much of the lore passed from tongue to tongue that even the archives were sung into seashells, any minstrel worth his salt knew full well the value of the oral tradition. He knelt and pressed his ear to the door, as suggested.

Sir William was just warming up.

"Don't you think I don't know what you're up to, you ungrateful girl!" the Lord-High-Mayor-Knight-Protector-of-the-Northern-Territories (-And-Surrounding-Villages) thundered. Colin could just imagine the old knight's face flushing the glorious eggplant color it always did when he was vexed. He sounded very vexed.

"You can't fool me with your witch's tricks, me as has brought you up by the sweat of my brow all these years and done my best by you, knowing full well I'd probably never marry you off decent, thorny thing that you are."

"*I* never asked you to marry me off," Maggie pointed out. "But since you insist, *I* must insist on doing it correctly." The thump and rattle of her loom continued rhythmically as she spoke, answering her father in a calm, reasonable tone calculated, Colin was sure, to drive Sir William into a fit of apoplexy. "As I've already explained to you, Father dear, before a hearthcrafter marries, she must spin, weave, and sew her own wedding gown, *and* it must be perfect *and* done without the benefit of magic. Surely you want me to look more presentable for my wedding than I did for my coronation? Now that I'm a princess, I'll have certain standards to maintain, you know. Oh, dear!" she gasped a maidenly little gasp and the loom treadles clattered. "I do wish you wouldn't distract me so, Daddy dearest. Just look at what you've made me do now. I've an error two rows back I didn't even notice, you're upsetting me so! I can't think what's the matter with you, railing at me like this! Haven't you heard that we princesses are delicate creatures, not to be yelled at or balked?" Her voice dropped to a growl closer to her usual husky register.

"Now, leave me be, while I fix it. You've had your way, gotten the King to give me a title and those poor sods out there to make fools of themselves proposing to me. Now I'll have mine. Why don't you send that lot of dandies down to Queenston to plague your granddaughter if you want to marry off a princess?"

"She's much too young for that, as you very well know, while you, my dear, might be considered a trifle overripe. Besides, Winnie's daughter can't inherit my post here. She's got the Kingdom to consider. By the iceworm's snores, girl, why won't you be reasonable? Princess or not, you've no lands of your own, and you can't inherit mine, not without a husband. Women can't BE Lord-High-Mayor-Knight-Protectors and so on—too rugged a job for 'em. I'm getting no younger, Maggie, NOR is your Granny, yet here you sit twiddling at this bloody loom when all the Lords of the realm are filling my coffers with useless baubles for you while they empty my forests of game and cry in the beer they swill from my kegs!''

"I'm sorry about that, I'm sure." Maggie's voice was as condescendingly patient as if she spoke to a particularly dimwitted cow. "I know how it must trouble you to have your precious game preserves invaded. But you've only to see reason, you know, and let me out of here, and I'll expand the food supply so no one will have to hunt."

"Not until you've chosen a husband and sent the rest of them packing," Sir William replied stubbornly.

"I couldn't possibly as yet. There's my hearthcrafter's wedding tradition to be fulfilled, as I believe I HAVE mentioned."

"How can the bloody thing be traditional?" her father demanded. "You're the only hearthcrafter in these parts, and the first one to marry that I've ever heard of."

"Probably there'd be more marriages among us if this weren't such a difficult tradition," she said with a suspiciously heavy sigh. "The Mother only knows how I hate to weave without magic. But that *is* the rule, and since I am, as you say, the only hearthcrafter in these parts, I'm afraid you'll simply have to take my word for it."

"But the suitors—"

"Why don't you tell them to go away and you'll let them know when I'm ready? At this rate, with you shouting at me every hour on the hour, I should only need another twenty years."

"I'll tell you what I bloody well *will* do, you snooty wench! I'll send them all out to do the most dangerous deeds they can do—that should take care of some of the wretches—and bind you to the first man among them who returns victorious and in one piece. You'll marry him whether you will or no!''

"That," Maggie said, "strikes me as a really dumb idea. If these fellows are such important Lords of the realm, don't you think asking them to risk life and limb on my behalf is going to be a bit hard on the national leadership?"

The thwack of a fist striking wood was followed by a howl of pain and a string of knightly obscenities from Sir William. After the hasty clatter of a loom bench being swiftly evacuated, Maggie asked, "Hurt yourself?" Her tone was a model of daughterly concern.

"You impudent wench! By the worm's rancid steaming bloody

13

breath, you'll marry the first fellow who comes back with a dragon's head or—or—an army of bandits in tow, see if you don't!''

''Naturally, m'lord Father, I'll have to do your bidding. You've *spoken*, haven't you? *And* the King?'' Her voice was frankly angry now. ''Who am I, your bastard and a simple village witch, to question your mighty will? Never mind that witches needn't marry and I'd be happier single, when you've taken it into your head that marry I will. But I WILL make my preparations according to the prescribed customs of my mother's people, and I won't budge before! And—why, goodness me, just look there!'' She lapsed back into sugary sweetness. ''A threading error. Excuse me, please, father, but this is very serious indeed. It may take me DAYS to fix this, but my dress really must be perfect so I'll be lovely as the May for the lordly dolt my beloved father picks for my groom. I shall have to take it all apart and do it over.''

The door swung open so quickly Colin had to jump backwards and down a step, hugging the wall to avoid being knocked over as the purple-faced and fuming Sir William stormed out the door and down the stone steps without even seeing him.

The tower room was bare of furnishings except for a straw cot and the loom and spinning wheel sitting on the stark stone floor. Behind the loom and in a pile near the wheel lumped bag after bag of silk, both spun and unspun. Beside the loom bench an unglazed dish held congealed porridge.

Maggie stalked the room, her cheeks blazing burgundy and her dark eyes smoldering like molten iron. She looked to Colin very much like a hungry brown lioness, her braids lashing tail-like in her wake as she prowled her cage.

Colin cleared his throat and she whirled, looking at once glad to see him and annoyed at being interrupted in the midst of a rage.

''They'd better never let me out of here or so help me I'll commit *treason*,'' she announced fiercely. ''I'll kill that bloody Rowan for putting me in this spot after all we did for him! What's the matter with your nosy King, anyway?'' she demanded. ''Why couldn't he just mind his own business?''

Colin shrugged and sat down on her loom bench. ''I suppose he thought you'd want to actually. You've never been backwards about speaking your mind before. If you *didn't* want to be a princess, why didn't you just say so?''

''What did you expect me to do in front of all those people?'' she asked. ''Shove the circlet back at him and say, 'sorry, Sire, I

14

never wear jewelry.' Oh, I suppose you're right. He meant well. It's just—just—''

"Just what?" he asked. To his surprise, he saw that her chin was trembling and a large teardrop was winking from it. "Oh, really, Maggie. You mustn't take on so. The King wouldn't have made you unhappy for the world. He honestly thinks he's done you a great turn. It was the only thing about this whole mess that pleased him, paying you back that way. All this business of tower prisons and mandatory marriage is your father's rather heavy-handed way of handling his domestic problems, not Rowan's. I'm sure if he and the Queen could have stuck around instead of having to rush right off to clear up this curse thing, none of this would have happened to you."

"I wish the rest of those ninnies who're hanging about acting so important would have rushed right off as well," she replied with a return to her former heated intensity. "They've been after me every minute since the christening, one bunch or the other. I've not had a moment's privacy. It was bad enough during the festival, not getting a chance to speak to you or walk out to the woods, but since then it's been impossible. And when they're not dogging me, they're rooting through the forest, killing Dad's animals, which I think is half of why he's so eager to be rid of me." She had been staring out the tower's narrow window as she spoke, and when she turned to him her face was both wet and anxious. "Oh, Colin, I just hope Moonshine has enough sense to keep clear of the castle. I haven't gotten to go see him since that evening you caught me slipping through the gate. If he comes looking for me, one of my gallant admirers is apt to think it clever to kill him and present me with a unicorn horn for a wedding present. Wouldn't Dad think that a heroic deed!" Turning back to the window, she buried her head in her hands and began sobbing with the same ferocious singlemindedness she brought to everything else.

"Of course!" Colin clapped his hand to his head. "I forgot all about the—" He bit off his sentence, remembering that Bernard liked to be a noncontributing party to his prisoner's conversations. Rising, he tiptoed to the door. As he opened it, the guard stumbled backwards, smiling at him foolishly.

Returning the smile with every evidence of man-to-man good fellowship, Colin joined him on the landing, closing the door softly. "She's taking all of this pretty hard," he told Bernard in an exaggerated whisper.

"Well, sir, I expect for an honest, hard-working wench like our Goodwitch Brown this princess business takes a might of

15

getting used to," the guard allowed sympathetically. "My old auntie always did say that politics was no profession for a decent woman but *I* say that Sir William's the Lord and the King's the King and a man has to have a job and . . ."

"Exactly," Colin agreed hurriedly. "I knew you were a compassionate sort of chap the moment I laid eyes on you."

"I does my best, sir," Bernard replied, flushing with pleasure at being complimented with such a large word, whatever it meant. "And say, if there's aught I can do to help . . ."

This was the opening Colin had been angling for. "As a matter of fact, old man, what with all this boohooing and so on, my handkerchief's gotten soaked, and my throat's quite dry from all the 'there-there'-ing, if *you* take *my* meaning, not to mention that it was a long, dry trip riding back here."

He looked around as if there could possibly be anyone else in the corridor. Finding the absolutely isolated stairway predictably empty of all but himself and the puzzled but enthusiastic Bernard, he dug in his pockets again and drew forth a silver coin, which he surreptitiously slipped into the other man's palm. Bernard, being no fool, had naturally had his palm already outstretched and waiting.

"Now, sergeant," Colin continued in his stage whisper, "If you could see your way clear to fetching the lady a towel to blow her nose on and a bit of refreshment for the two of us, I'll be happy to make sure she doesn't go anywhere in the meantime."

"Needn't ask me twice, sir," Bernard winked, pocketing the coin, "I reckon what with you bein' a King's man and all, it'll be well enough. And I'm obliged to be able to do somethin' to show the goodwitch I bear her no ill will. She's a hard worker and takes care of 'er own, she does, and my auntie says there's no nattier housekeeper in all the kingdom. A good woman and a good witch she is, even if she ain't exactly princess material, I say. Between you and me, I think it's a cryin' shame to keep 'er locked up like this, but no one asked me, you understand, and I need the job, and it's an easy one, even if it is a might dry, if you take my meanin', sir."

"How thoughtless of me!" Colin apologized, companionably setting his hands on the man's shoulders and giving him a friendly push toward the foot of the stairs. "Naturally, you'll need to refresh yourself before you climb back up these wretched stairs. And do try to make it a nice, clean, soft sheet you find for Maggie. Her nose is pretty raw from all that crying."

Bernard waved his version of a salute and bounded down the steps.

Seven giant black swans bore the wizard Fearchar Brown aloft in his magic chariot, up from the valley and across the glaciers, to cross the mountains dividing Argonia from Brazoria. Watching the ascent of the swans from her cliff castle's icy outer ledge was Princess Pegeen Ashburn, known commonly as Pegeen the Illuminator, only daughter and sole surviving heir of the last King, Finbar the Fireproof, and up until recently holding the satisfying rank of Royal Princess, Retired. Pegeen couldn't honestly say she wasn't glad to see Fearchar go—even if only for a short time. She hadn't had a moment's peace since he first sought refuge with her, and immediately set about making *her* sanctuary *his* stronghold.

As soon as he was gone, she fetched her drawing things and sat on her favorite spot on the ledge, intending to push from her mind, for the morning, at least, her trepidations about her lover. Today, when the glacier-rimmed valley was flooded with sunshine for a change instead of mist and rain, she would simply relax and enjoy the rare good weather and a chance to practice her own special illuminating magic. On warm days like this, drawing inside was out of the question anyway, since her cliff castle was carved in one piece from the ice at the edge of the great glacier which reared up behind it, and warm days meant drippy walls, which in turn meant running inks and spoilt parchments.

She would do as she used to on days like this, basking in the sunlight and enjoying the dizzying view from the ledge, watching the ice glitter and the prisms dance from the curiously slitted glacier across the valley to the iceworm-riddled glacial maze behind her castle. She would listen to the nonsensical gabbling of the Blabbermouth River's jade waters as they gossiped their way across the valley, and wish to her heart's content for an ink to match the deep cobalt of the glacial clefts or a green to match the lime of the valley's tender new grass, while admiring the picturesque decay of the ruined village sprawling beneath her perch.

She'd so hoped, when Fearchar first sought refuge with her, that he would enjoy sharing these quiet pleasures of hers. But he had no eye for the view at all, and no mind to share anything but his own plans for overthrowing Roari Rowan. She tried to tell him that sitting on a throne was no great joy—she had had more than enough of it, just watching her father rule, and when her brothers were killed attempting feats of magic beyond their skills (she had always been the talented one, actually) she had made

17

her decision and declined her place in the line of succession. Fearchar threw that up to her often enough, but, gracious, she'd had no idea she'd meet such a brilliant, ambitious man just before her father's demise—it had rather begun to look, in fact, as if King Finbar would outlive her, and the question of kingship would not arise in her lifetime. But it had, and Roari Rowan had been chosen her father's successor, a position Fearchar had been counting on rather more heavily than Pegeen had realized at the time.

She'd humored him, naturally, thinking he'd get over it, but instead of calming him down, her acquiescence had had the unfortunate effect of encouraging his rather outrageous plans. She should never have let him sell her jewels and the tapestries and furniture she'd brought with her to her hermitage, but he had been so excited about outfitting his new army (who turned out to be nothing but a lot of Brazorian brigands recruited with the help of a very questionable-looking young woman he'd met out in the woods somewhere), and had promised that when he won back the throne and she shared it with him, she'd get everything back anyway. Never one to place much value on objects other than scrolls and books, Pegeen had let him have her things. He had thanked her so sweetly, holding her hand and gazing into her eyes and speaking to her in that lovely plummy voice of his until she was quite unsure what she had promised him he might have and what she wished to retain.

Now, surrounded by his so-called soldiers at every turn, and even forbidden to smoke by an uncharacteristically solicitious Fearchar, who claimed her habit was dangerous and unhealthful, she was beginning to realize he would never come around and that it was she, in fact, who was being humored.

She did hope Roari Rowan would be able to read the message she had encoded at the bottom of her christening gift, the horoscope she'd sent little Bronwyn. Perhaps he'd come then and put a stop to all of this nonsense. She'd been most alarmed at Fearchar's gift—though he claimed the jack-in-the-box was a harmless joke, she was magician enough herself to know it for what it was, however convincingly he told her otherwise. She tried not to feel like a traitor to Fearchar because of the note to his enemy, but really, enough was quite enough.

And this latest scheme of his to boost the manpower of his ragtag army—unnerving. So unnerving that she reached without thinking into her pocket in search of her smoking materials. But an unmelodious blast from the tower to her left stopped her. The lookout was lowering his horn and pointing into the valley for

18

the benefit of his foreshortened compatriots infesting the village at her feet. Pegeen shaded her eyes and scanned the valley.

A thin trickle of movement stirred the trees along the river near the foot of the slitted glacier. As she watched, figures began to emerge from those trees, several men, and then the white that unmistakably marked, even at this distance, Fearchar's female "lieutenant," the silly little nymph who had affected that awful jest for a name. And behind her, another, nonhuman, figure, moving awkwardly, as if bound.

An involuntary groan of dismay escaped Pegeen's lips. He meant it then, and more to the point, he could really do it. Fearchar, with the help of that wretched young woman, actually meant to—actually HAD, unless her eyes and the distance deceived her, actually had captured a unicorn, would capture others, and use the mystical beasts' healing magic to make that miserable little army virtually unwoundable. Pegeen gave an unladylike curse on finding her smoking materials missing from her gown pocket. Guards or no guards, forbidden or not, she simply HAD to have a smoke.

CHAPTER 2

As Colin re-entered the tower chamber, Maggie jumped up from the loom bench where she'd sat sniffling, and dried her eyes with a furious swipe of her tunic sleeve. Giving him a quivery grin and a swollen-eyed wink, she began popping small objects from beneath the piles of silk into her medicine pouch.

"Nobly done, gallant minstrel, nobly done," she congratulated him, producing a brilliant silk gown from beneath the piles. "I take it all back. Never has a princess been rescued from a tower with a more commendable display of craft and guile. I do believe your time in court hasn't been a total waste after all."

"But I didn't—" he began. "I mean, I was only trying to get that nosy guard to go away so you could talk about Moonshine. Say, you DID have your wedding dress made all along, didn't you?"

"Why talk about Moonshine when I can see him?" she asked, pulling the silken robes on over her brown homespun. "And no, I didn't waste my time making this flimsy thing. Winnie gave it to me to change into for the christening, only I never got the time, so I stuck it in my pocket. It'll make a good disguise, don't you think?''

She finished adjusting the dress and admired as much of her somewhat lumpily overdressed self as she was able by looking down, then said firmly, "It will be very simple. All you have to do is pretend I'm one of those serving women who are helping my suitors eat us out of keep and castle.''

She turned to the window. Colin hadn't noticed before the black and white cat dozing in the sunlight slanting through the deep, narrow aperture. The cat, sensing itself the center of attention, stretched and yawned.

Maggie tickled the animal under its chin. "Well, dearie, now's your chance to be a hero like your sire,'' she said.

In reply the cat rolled onto his back as if to invite her attentions to his underside. When the solicited pattings were not forthcoming, he purred for awhile in a friendly sort of way, flopped back on his side, curled his tail around his nose, and slept again.

"He takes after his mother.'' Maggie shrugged, apologetically, though she needn't have worried on Colin's account. Though he had forgiven Granny Brown's familiar cat, Chingachkook, for trying to eat him when Granny, in a fit of pique, had turned him into a mockingbird, and had been glad of Ching's ability to converse with large animals, particularly dragons and bears, on more than one occasion, he had found Maggie's seemingly one-sided conversations with the cat disquieting. He was just as glad not to have the kitten of Ching and the Rowan barn cat to contend with.

"If you're bent on seeing your unicorn and becoming a fugitive from matrimony, we'd better flee,'' he advised. "Your guard could be a fast drinker, for all I know.''

Afternoon sunlight filled the center of the grimy, debris-filled courtyard outside the tower. Colin and Maggie slunk furtively around it, keeping close to the shadows near the walls. Maggie stepped in a pile of horse manure and snorted disgustedly, remembering how less than a fortnight before she had magically shoveled the paving stones free of cowflops and chicken doo in preparation for the christening.

Now the stones were filthy again, and the grass and flowers trampled. The splintery outbuildings, only recently feathered with their gay banners, were no more than splintery outbuildings again, decorated solely with new arrow punctures inflicted during her suitors' archery practice.

Maggie led the way inside the long, manure-fragrant stable,

since she was familiar with it and didn't need to wait for her eyes to adjust to the dimness inside. She ducked behind an empty stall while Colin fetched his horse, but she needn't have bothered; the groom, like the other servants, seemed to be taking advantage of her incarceration to let her father's property fall into rack and ruin.

"Your man didn't even unload Roundelay, much less feed and water her," Colin complained.

"About time the lout did something right," Maggie replied. "We'll take care of her when we've found Moonshine. Here, give me a leg up and hand me some of your gear to carry, so there'll be room for you behind."

Colin complied and mounted behind her. Though Maggie's presence made necessary some alterations in the delicate balance of his loading procedure, at least people were so used to seeing him with a horse full of instruments that the addition of one measly girl in the middle of it all would hardly be noteworthy.

Maggie kept an eye out for Ching as they passed her grandmother's cottage. He liked sunning himself on the roof, but today, fortunately, he seemed to have taken himself off, perhaps to supervise Granny while she brewed another emergency batch of ale at the tavern. They must be going through ale rather quickly now that she, Maggie, was no longer around to expand existing supplies. Well, let them stew. Granny, upon whom of all people Maggie had counted for support, had been no help at all when Maggie had tried the first few times to explain to her father that she didn't wish to marry.

No one challenged them as they rode down Fort Iceworm's one street and through the gate in the outer wall, which could be closed at night to protect the town from marauding enemies, had any enemies been foolish enough to want Fort Iceworm. The wall was mostly used to keep the moose out of vegetable patches and the bears out of the garbage, and was of no use whatsoever keeping out the salamanders, who crawled over it and into the thatched rooves, starting nasty fires.

The gate opened to the southwest, and the road led from it into a field of brilliant crimson fireweed and pink wild heather awash in a ground of green. The wildflowers were taking a beating this year from all the retainers' tents pitched in the field and from the jousting contests the guests insisted on indulging in, but Maggie relished the dazzling hues and tangy fragrance. It was good not to be cooped up in the tower any longer.

Beyond the meadow, forest stretched back as far as the eye could see, open only where fields along the road had been

21

cultivated. Above the forest the horizon was serrated by mountains almost exactly sky-colored and sharp as the tips of fat icicles.

Maggie strained forward in the saddle, searching the nearest trees for a glimmer of white. She was both relieved and disappointed to see none.

Colin felt edgier every minute, and hungrier and more tired and put upon. He was beginning to wish he'd told his sense of forboding to go forebode elsewhere, or had at least gotten a taste of the ale he'd sent Bernard to fetch. Maggie hardly seemed to realize he was there, and after all the trouble he was going to on her behalf, endangering the favor he enjoyed from the King by helping her elude her high-class suitors.

"I say, Maggie, after you've warned the unicorn, you DO intend to make some decision about all those chaps who want to marry you, don't you? I can certainly see your father's point, after all. It puts him in an awkward position, having his daughter refusing the greatest lords in the land. Makes him look as if he's gotten a bit grand for his station."

"I wouldn't know about that, but I've gotten entirely too grand for mine, and no one seems to mind but me," she replied wryly. "I've felt a proper dunce, I can tell you, having all those high mucky-muck men who've never laid eyes on me before declaring their undying love and worshipful devotion and so on. It's nice to hear people say flattering things about oneself, but what I've been hearing lately has nothing to do with Maggie Brown. Limpid eyes and lily white skin indeed!"

"It's amazing what political connections can do for a girl's complexion," Colin agreed. "But if you don't want to marry any of them, I don't see why you didn't just use your magic and walk out of there."

"Didn't you notice that big iron padlock on the door? Magic doesn't work on iron, you know, not mine or anyone else's. I even have to scrub iron pots by hand; hearthcraft won't touch them. And during the day there was good old Bernard. Gran gave him an amulet to protect him against *me*."

"Your grandmother helped keep you locked up? I'd have thought she'd be on your side. She—er—does know about you-know-who, doesn't she?"

Maggie sighed and searched the woods again. "She knows, but she doesn't like it. She says unicorns and witches have no business together, that unicorns are only for women who have all their power in their—well, I won't repeat *that;* it was rude. And

22

quite untrue. Magic gives Moonshine and me something in common." Colin thought she added the last rather defensively.

In a cautious, pacifying tone he said, "Perhaps your granny's afraid he'll steal your affection from her." He could see how that might happen, how the unicorn's unqualified admiration and undivided attention would appeal to Maggie. Her hearthcrafting enabled her to be the best-qualified to handle anybody's problems, take charge of all situations, and manage any possible difficulties for everybody around her, but it did not make her tactful or popular. It no doubt never occurred to her that people around her might prefer to make their own decisions and solve their own problems.

She considered his remark. "No," she said finally. "It isn't that. I think it's because, although witches don't have to marry, Gran says we need to mate after a certain age to reach our—um—full magical potential. She's quite inconsistent on that point—all these years she's watched me like a hawk to make sure I didn't mess about with any of the local lads, but now that she's been so successful that Moonshine's chosen me to be his maiden, she's put out about it. NOW she's going on about how my powers are going to need supplementing or some such nonsense. Perhaps she *is* just jealous, and making that bit up because she knows unicorns are only supposed to associate with maidens. But what's really bothering her, if you ask me, is that I'm the last of the Brown witches. If I stay a virgin to please Moonshine, there'll never be any *other* little Brown witches scurrying about, carrying on the line. Gran truly doesn't feel a witch should care about anything beyond her clan and her craft."

"You do a good job of that," Colin said ruefully. "I hope you realize how much trouble you're getting ME into."

Maggie swiveled in the saddle and flashed him a sudden, fond grin over the harp in her lap. "That's what happens when you go getting sentimental over old friendships with witches. If you didn't want trouble, why did you come back?"

"Well, I, er, that is—His Majesty wanted me to write a song about your courtship, immortalize your incredible beauty and goodness," he improvised finally. "And a bloody lot he knows about it, I might add."

Maggie was enchanted. "Oh?" she asked, looking back at him again when they'd turned onto a narrow trail leading up a hill and through a starchy stand of birch. "Go on, pray. Tell me more. What kind of song?"

"Oh, you know. The usual sort; your sparkling eye, your ruby lips, etc., etc."

"And have you thought of one?"

"Well, I was just going to use the old standard," he replied, giving his beard a thoughtful tug. "The one I sing to all my court ladies. I just change the hair and eye color a bit, you know, to fit. But what with you being a princess and a unicorn maiden and all that, it didn't seem—er—suitable."

She laughed. "You mean it was so bawdy you were afraid Gran would turn you into a mockingbird again!"

He winced. "Quite. Do you know, to this day I avoid all those ditties that begin with 'if I had the wings of a bird'?"

"I can well imagine," she said. "And it wouldn't do you any good to write one about me glorifying me to my suitors, either. I've no intention of sticking around so they can compare your song with the subject matter."

"I was afraid of that. Very well. What DO you intend to do?"

"Do as you said I should have in the first place. I'm going to ride to Queenston and ask Rowan if I can remain his sister but give him back the coronet. I'll tell him it's too much bother to keep it polished, and can't I please have a nice big bag of gold or a magic carpet or something useful instead."

Colin laughed. "Now THAT is worthy of a song," he said. "I don't think there's a single one about a quest to *return* a crown. It's my clear duty as a royal minstrel to accompany you and chronicle the event. Besides, until further notice, you ARE still the princess and I," he gave as good a bow as he could on horseback, "your humble servant, madam."

Fearchar's swancar glided back across the glaciers from the northwest and into the valley. The wizard enjoyed riding in the sky chariot as much for the prestige as for the mobility it afforded him. Though soaring above the haughty peaks might have been a thrill for ordinary men, to Fearchar the ride was by now merely one of the commonplace annoyances of building an empire.

True, he experienced a warm feeling when he skimmed the breast of the sprawling forest blanketing most of Argonia and knew he could say without fear of contradiction that any portion of woodland not currently under his control soon would be. But satisfying as it was to sit like a fur-wrapped god while his swans glided high above the ice-coated crests, the pleasure he obtained from mere riding was a trifling and solitary one.

He'd much preferred the other end of this journey, when his swans had spiralled downward toward the streets of the opulent Brazorian capital, only to shift slightly at the last moment,

24

lighting gently upon the second broad tier of the temple dominating the city with its triangular massiveness.

The passersby in that city had been awed, yes they had, at the sight of this obviously mighty enchanter, cleverly disguised as a modest pilgrim, descending to honor their city with his presence. But Fearchar had not wasted his time and magical resources to honor passersby, of course. He'd come to the temple for one reason only, and that was to confer with a priestess of great wisdom. Or at any rate, a priestess whose wisdom he had need of.

The priestess Helsinora was the greatest living authority on unicorns and their various usages. Fortunately for Fearchar the lady was, like his own Pegeen, a cloistered scholar, susceptible to his magnificence. In exchange for certain promises, she'd lent him her life's work, a series of scrolls containing every known and conjectured use for the enchanted beast, its feeding, mating and migratory patterns (conclusions from field observations collected and compiled by the priestess decades ago—unicorns were now even scarcer in Brazoria than they were in Argonia). The only problem was that the document was written in ancient Brazorian runes, and would need to be translated. But with Pegeen's help, he had no doubt he would soon be privy to all its secrets.

With the scrolls under his arm, he climbed from his chariot onto the cliff castle's outer ledge and strolled jauntily into the throne room. Pegeen jumped up quickly at his entrance and hid something in her dress. Ignoring the hint of smoke in the air and the guilty expression on her face, he laid the scrolls before her, carefully, on the seat of the throne, which was the driest spot in the castle.

Scorning false modesty, he told her how he had gained the confidence of Helsinora, who obviously recognized a superior mind and will when she saw one.

"Fine," Pegeen said, giving the document only a perfunctory glance before probing his face with suspicious blue eyes. "What does she look like?"

"Who?" Fearchar asked, carefully rerolling the scrolls before a threatening cluster of droplets forming on the canopy overhead could spoil them. Really, Pegeen had certainly allowed her once sumptuous and cozy hideaway to run downhill since he'd arrived. Even princesses, he supposed, were apt to get careless once they thought themselves sure of you.

"This Helsinora woman is who. Come now, Fearchar, you
25

know perfectly well what I mean. Is she beautiful? Slimmer than I? Has she any disgusting vices?"

"My dear Pegeen," the sorcerer replied loftily, "I scarcely noticed. Such considerations are entirely subordinate, as I see it, to making certain our land is delivered from the usurper of your throne." He looked wronged and wounded, primarily because she had failed to recognize the importance of his latest acquisition.

She mistook his expression for unappreciated devotion, however, and laid her hand contritely on his sleeve. "I'm sorry, dearest. But as *I* see it, such considerations are *most* pertinent."

She turned away abruptly and sourness edged her voice again. "That so-called recruiting officer of yours has brought an entire army of panting bandits with her. They await you below."

"Tsk, tsk, my lady, your manners are slipping. It's considered ill-bred, is it not, to keep guests waiting without?"

"Hired brigands can scarcely be considered guests," she countered. "And this castle woefully lacks a service entrance. Besides, I had no idea where to put the unicorn. The stables belonging to this castle melted years ago."

Though Maggie had convinced Colin to cooperate with her plans, she had yet to convince Moonshine.

Shortly after Colin's horse topped a hill beyond which the castle's turrets were no longer visible, they reached a glade. Pillared in birch and carpeted with moss and wildflowers, it was a perfect setting for the wide silver pool in its center, crystal clear and mottled with leaf shadows.

Maggie swung her leg over the chestnut's neck and hopped to the ground. Throwing back her head, she uttered a long ululating cry that seemed to come at once from her abdomen and from the roof of her mouth. It sounded like nothing human Colin had ever heard.

"That's the cry of the silver-spotted sea serpent," she told him proudly as the sound died away. "I learned it from one of the crew of the *Snake's Bane* last fall, before we left for Rowan's castle."

"But there *are* no sea serpents, silver-spotted or otherwise, around here," Colin reminded her. "It's too far inland."

"I know," she said. "That's how Moonshine knows it's me and not a real one."

Hooves thundered through the forest and Moonshine burst into the glade, his mane flying behind him like seawater curling in a ship's wake. His horn was a glittering lance, and his coat

26

dappled mist and smoke—very possibly, Colin thought, like that of a silver-spotted sea serpent.

With leaf-scattering abandon, the unicorn galloped to Maggie's side, more in the manner of a young puppy than one befitting the mystical enchanted beast Colin had barely glimpsed a year before, when Maggie and the unicorn first met.

When he saw Colin, the unicorn's slender legs stiffened and he tossed his mane aggressively. The distinguished little white goatee under his chin quivered with indignation.

Edging closer to Maggie, Moonshine rested his head on her shoulder and nickered in her ear, while his mind questioned hers.

"Maiden, a man comes with you. Does this mean you have betrayed me? What have I done to offend you? I who am your servant in all things, I who would give my life if you but asked, I who—"

"Dry up, darling, won't you please?" Maggie begged. "I have heard entirely too much of that sort of thing lately. From beings less sincere than yourself, true, but it wears one down anyway. So please stop." She sank to the ground and spread her skirts on the grass so he could rest his head on her knee. It seemed safe enough here, where they'd met so often before, and she was tired of riding. "Of course you aren't betrayed. You remember Colin from before. He was with me when we met."

The unicorn rolled one amythest eye in the minstrel's direction and Colin smiled ingratiatingly and wiggled a few fingers at him. Moonshine rolled the eye back toward Maggie. "*He* is a man. And NOT a maiden," the unicorn informed her.

"I heard that," Colin replied. "And I should *hope* I'm not a maiden. I went to a very great deal of trouble managing not to be, just recently."

Maggie was regarding Moonshine with surprised puzzlement not unmingled with hurt. "I thought only you and I could converse. I didn't think you could understand anybody else."

"Nay, maiden. I have the gift of human understanding and can discern all that is said by your kind—it is only that there are few among them who have the gift of unicorn understanding. *No* men that I've ever heard of." He rose to his hooves again and walked closer to Colin, who stood by his horse as she grazed and drank from the pool.

Moonshine approached cautiously, curling his lips back from his teeth and flaring his nostrils, sniffing elaborately. "No. No odor of chastity," the unicorn pronounced, circling the now-nervous minstrel and causing the chestnut mare to shy and dance sideways. The unicorn took no notice, but continued to sniff in a manner at once menacing, suspicious, and disdainful.

Colin was remembering all the stories he'd heard, not of the unicorn's wonderful healing magic, but of the beast's ferocity in battle and predilection for skewering any unwanted objects or persons bold enough to invade its territory.

"Are you *sure* you're not a maiden?" the unicorn asked finally, nudging the minstrel's leg in a rude gesture that brought the rapier-tipped horn alarmingly close to a treasured portion of Colin's anatomy.

"Absolutely not. Ask Lady Abigail," Colin answered. "Ask my mare, Roundelay. Maybe it's her you smell. I don't ask her what she does with her spare time."

"Moonshine, don't be so personal," Maggie reprimanded. "Colin has been a great help to me today. Maybe he understands you because he's my um..." she searched for a term that would fit into the unicorn's conservative and somewhat archaic view of human relations "... because he's my champion, I suppose you might say. Dad locked me up in the tower and was going to force me to marry, but Colin got me out of it. That qualifies him, doesn't it?"

But Moonshine was paying no attention. Completely reversing his arrogant stance, the unicorn now knelt supplicatingly at Colin's feet, left front hoof, horn and right front leg all touching the ground in front of the dumbfounded minstrel.

"Gallant sir, forgive this unworthy beast, I pray you. I tested you, knowing not that you championed my fairest Maid Maggie and freed her from frightful peril. As I am bound by the Creed to offer my friendship only to those most worthy, I naturally never thought to be befriended by a human man. Indeed, I have no instructions whatsoever regarding men who would befriend rather than slay me. I suppose I shall just have to consider that any friend of Maggie's must be a corollary to the portion of my Creed covering the unicorn's relationship to his maiden." And he recited, limerick fashion:

> "For this is the Unicorn Creed
> She must be a maiden indeed
> Completely straight-laced
> And thoroughly chaste
> Who'd ride with the unicorn breed."

Colin reassured the contrite unicorn that anyone would be confused about correct unicorn behavior given the same Creed

28

and the same circumstances, and that he quite understood, but hadn't they better flee?

As soon as Maggie was upon his back, Moonshine asked in a business-like manner, "And we are fleeing—whither?"

"To Queenston," Colin replied.

"Whither lies Queenston?" Moonshine asked. "By the great river or with the freezing winds? To the rising sun or to the setting sun?"

"Er—um—uh," Colin said, stumbling as he tried to calculate which natural phenomena would set them on a southeasterly course.

Maggie solved the problem. "That way," she said, pointing.

CHAPTER 3

It came as something of a disappointment to Fearchar to find that unicorns weren't so dreadfully ferocious as he'd been led to believe. Only twenty men, instead of the reputed one hundred, were required to restrain the beast. Of the twenty, only one was killed. No more than four sustained even mildly debilitating injuries.

"Are you sure this beast is in good health?" he demanded of his lovely lieutenant. She knelt before him, radiant as always in her diaphanous white wrapper and leafy tunic, which shed leaves in the most fascinating places every time the girl turned into a whirlwind.

"Oh, yes, Dark Pilgrim," she answered with a grave meekness which always gave Fearchar patriotic flutters on behalf of his own cause. His persuasive magic had worked wonders with this formerly disgruntled and disillusioned nymph. She was now a woman with a commitment—to him, and to the cause, naturally. Thank the Powers. He wouldn't like to see the fire in those green eyes turned against him.

"The beast walked of his own accord all the way here and insisted on bearing me on his back," she said with just the slightest hint of complaint. "I shall be sore for weeks, and will be very happy, I assure you, to make the return journey in my whirlwind."

"Your sacrifices in the name of the cause do you great honor, my child," Fearchar said. "Later, perhaps, I shall inspect and treat your wounds personally. It's the least I can do. But for now,

29

while our loyal followers hoist the animal into our stronghold, I will hear your report."

Rising gracefully, the girl ticked off completed tasks on her fingers. He found to his great joy that her intelligence was such that she required few detailed instructions if those he gave were liberally infused with attitudes harmonious to the best interests of the cause. If he could convince her, she could convince the bandits. Her magic, the natural, irresistable glamourie of all nymphs, was very like his own special powers of enchantment, which enabled him to imbue even the most absurd falsehoods with the credibility of irrefutable fact.

"As you have bidden, Dark Pilgrim, I have begun establishing a relay system of informants prepared to aid our cause. My brother's wife in the hamlet of Little Darlingham should prove particularly useful, as she has already in the past. She, like all of the faithful, is thrilled to hear of the rewards in store for our people when we triumph. I have spread the news of your great discoveries to every follower of the cause so each may rejoice that your wisdom has found eternal youth, health and beauty, benefits we may all glean by assisting in your work."

She smiled a dazzling smile, full of joy that she was able to share such news with her brothers-at-arms. Her slightly tilted eyes brimmed, burning with enthusiasm. "You are so wise, Dark Pilgrim, to share the fruits of your studies with the faithful. I now have more reports of unicorns available for capture than I shall ever be able to pursue."

"I'm sure you'll manage, my dear. Go on. What of these new men who came with you today? And this unicorn?"

"These are the men who followed Wulfric the Were, Dark Pilgrim. Though Wulfric prefers a solitary life on the whole, for love of me he has guided these men to the cause, and sends them freely to you, to help with your great work. It was he who found the unicorn as well, since he is wiser even than myself in the ways of the woods."

"Where is this fellow?" Fearchar asked. "I would thank and bless him and bespeak our cause to him personally." If the were was as good as Sally claimed, Fearchar wanted to make absolutely sure he fell under the wizard's own personal spell.

The nymph, sensing reprimand in her leader's tone, trembled prettily and dropped her gaze. "I—I took the liberty of bespeaking the cause to him myself, Dark Pilgrim, as I did his followers. You did say I was to do so, to be your right hand and the extension of your own tongue?"

"Still, dear child, one mustn't exceed—" Fearchar began, but the nymph rushed on, hastening to regain his approval.

"You see, I had this little idea of my own, for the good of the cause. It was a spur-of-the-moment inspiration, and I had so hoped you'd be pleased."

"I'm sure I shall be pleased, my child," the wizard replied as smoothly as was possible through clenched jaws. "Just tell me what it is you did with this man."

"When I went to trap the unicorn, Dark Pilgrim, I found Wulfric and his men had just slain a party of wealthy travelers. The lord of these travelers somewhat resembled Wulfric in his man form, and this lord protested, before his throat was slit like his fat purse, that his party was under the King's protection. He wore a brooch with his own seal and the usurper's wrought upon its surface, and he said it was his invitation to the christening of the Princess Bronwyn, the same christening to which you wished one of our followers to convey certain gifts, Dark Pilgrim."

"Ah!"

"When I learned of the dead man's errand, and noted his resemblance to Wulfric, I took it upon myself—"

"I would I had been there!" Fearchar cried, clasping his hands together prayerfully. "I would have commanded Wulfric to disguise himself as the dead lord so he might deliver my gifts and stay to spy on the christening and on my faithless relations at Fort Iceworm."

The nymph nearly swooned with ecstasy. "Oh, master! That's exactly what I did! I did well, then?"

"You did exceedingly well, my child," he replied beneficently. Then they both looked up as, with a final heave on the great thick ropes forming a man-powered pulley, his soldiers hauled the still-struggling, bundled unicorn even with the cliff's edge. From there they easily pulled the beast over onto the castle's outer ledge, and the feebly kicking cloven hooves vanished from view.

Fearchar smiled to himself and took his disciple's arm, steering her through the shrubbery at the cliff's base and into the secret entrance to the slippery irregular staircase leading into the castle's heart. The passage was his private discovery, an exit unknown even to Pegeen. "Come now, my valiant child, and allow me to tend your injuries while you tell me more of this remarkable friend of yours. We won't be disturbed in my study."

Prince Leofwin (Patebreaker) Longstaff, aspirant to the throne of the Duchy of Greater Frostingdung, was prepared this time.

As he predicted, the warlockish Count chap had done it again. Completely disappeared in the midst of the hunt, so that now, as before, the falcons flew in crazy, confused circles while the hounds whimpered and slunk about with tails between their legs, refusing to leave their masters' sides.

Leofwin had had enough of that kind of pig pox. He meant to do something about it this time. As commander of his father's troops in countless campaigns against the real or imagined foes of Greater Frostingdung, Leofwin knew how to deal with slippery foreigners.

Spurring his horse to a brutal gallop, the prince crashed through the woods, heedless of the branches slapping his face and arms, determined to overtake that sneaking fellow and have it out with him exactly what was going on.

For there was something bloody awful queer about the lizardy wizard. Leofwin had thought so from the beginning, even before the first time the man joined his hunt. The good Count was too tall and too quick and too keen of nose and sharp of eye to be the sedentary administrator of Brazorian lake island estates Leofwin's spies had reported him to be. Leofwin always made it his business to know who he was rubbing elbows with. And none of the reports he'd received told him the wealthy Count's elbows would belong to a man with such a lean, unfed expression, such a crafty glint about the eyes, and such a canny way of not speaking until everyone else had commited themselves. Nor had the reports mentioned the man's mysterious hunting habits.

Today was the third day in a row that the Count had started out with them, then simply disappeared. On the previous two days, the man had reappeared within an hour, and immediately set the hounds on the scent of game; a buck the first day, a boar the second, which he'd helped to slay with a bloodthirsty glee that Leofwin's soldier's heart could not help warming to.

But, good hunter or no, the Count would need the aid of all his gods if he intended to use the same trickery to steal the dowdy brown princess away before Leofwin could make his own move.

Leofwin needed the wench to wrest the title of Crown Prince of Greater Frostingdung away from his brothers. Not that he needed that particular wench for the job. Any wench would do, as long as she was a princess. Marrying a princess before his brothers did was the only way Leofwin could establish a superior claim to the throne.

In most countries, being eldest would have sufficed. But the Grand Dukes and Duchesses of Middle Frostingdung had for

j

centuries been in the habit of begetting litters of babies rather than producing their children singly, which naturally made for political complications since many of the little princes and princesses looked so much alike no one could ever keep track of who was born before whom. Leofwin was one of a set of identical triplets.

Of course, he could always assassinate his brothers—or he could try—and marry whoever he chose. But his brothers were his equal in ruthlessness and ambition, if not temperament: Whereas he would be apt to bash them with his sword and have it over and done with (and very likely get himself bashed in turn by the Grand Duke, who frowned on that sort of thing), Leofrig and Leofric were far more likely to poison him or lock him in a remote storeroom to starve. Fascinating fellows, in their way. Leofwin would hate to have to kill them even if he thought he could pull it off; he was fond of them. And a fellow had to marry somebody, so why not a princess?

Leofrig and Leofric were too busy keeping their eyes on each other to venture far enough from home to find a bride. Leofwin thought he might solve two problems at once by looking for a likely girl while he led campaigns against his father's enemies and the enemies of anyone else who cared to engage his services. The difficulty with that plan was that everyone at one time or another wanted him to fight everyone else, and by the time he'd conquered each in turn for a neighbor, none of their daughters were of appropriate rank anymore, since they automatically became slaves when their fathers' houses were brought down. His skill in battle had thus greatly enriched and enlarged his father's domain, but hadn't done him a bit of good at finding a bride.

Also, he'd temporarily run out of foes, having conquered everybody from the wastelands to the sea. To get out of having to stay at court and wait for his brothers to slip something in his soup, he'd agreed to attend this silly baby's party. He'd thought it very hospitable of Roari Rowan to create a new princess, as if the Argonian King had known that was just the kind of party favor Leofwin needed to take home with him. Now all Leofwin had to do was win the wench.

And he wasn't about to let some sneaking count circle around him while he was out hunting and make off with her. Leofwin had seen the peculiar gleam in Jivemgood's eye when he watched Princess Maggie. He strongly suspected the thoughts prompting the gleam corresponded to his own ideas about just how much wooing should be necessary before one threw the

33

wench over one's shoulder and rode off with her to one's own castle.

No one was going to beat him to it.

Suddenly an odd, furred figure sprang onto the trail ahead of him. Leofwin reined in so hard he nearly flew over his steed's head. The horse reared and screamed, fighting the bit so that for a time Leofwin was preoccupied with keeping his seat and calming the animal.

By the time he had the leisure to look again, the furry creature was gone, and in its place stood Count Jivemgood, a slight mocking smile on his face.

Leofwin was angry. "What the griffin shit are you up to, scaring my horse like that? Where'd that animal go?"

The man continued to smile at him, more broadly now, which was a mistake. Leofwin drew his sword and advanced with every intention of whacking the wretch in two.

"You think you're too bloody good to hunt with us, eh? Always sneaking off, aren't you? Well, let me tell you, you skulking slackard, if you don't give a good account of yourself at once, I'll see to it you never sneak again."

Leofwin was snorting like a bull by the time he'd finished, and had the vague feeling he'd made a fool of himself, had shown his hand too soon. He'd let the Count's silly sneering grin back him into a position he'd have trouble getting out of without a bloody sword and the need to make a hasty exit.

But slowly, with what seemed considerable effort, Jivemgood banished his grin and yielded, kneeling in the trail, soiling his fine silver breeches in the dirt and old leaves.

"Good and noble prince," he said in a voice which always reminded Leofwin of priests on tithing day, "Have I not said I would lead you to bounteous hunting, the like of which you've never seen? Now, behold, after searching these three days I keep my word."

"Speak plainly, man, before I find the sight of your blood more tempting than your conversation."

But Jivemgood's smile had returned, bland and pleased. "Unicorn tracks, great prince. Not less than a quarter-day old, by the spoor."

"Unicorn? You mean the animal whose horn can protect a man from poison?" Just the trick to protect him from his brothers, Leofwin thought, and maybe to impress that dowdy brown piece into swooning for him as well.

"That magic they can do, and much more besides, great prince."

34

"What are we waiting for, then? After him. But if I lose sight of you, you'd best not let me see you ever again, or I'll make you rue it."

Moonshine managed to evade the first two hunting parties.

He heard the hounds from the first group well before the hunters were anywhere near. Stepping across a stream and into the shadows, he took his friends far back into the woods until the baying of the dogs faded and the rumbling hooves of the hunters' steeds no longer made the earth tremble.

With the second party they had even less contact. The only sign they saw of it was a goshawk circling a hapless duck. They were well away when they heard the faint sound of the falconer's call signalling his bird to return.

When the danger seemed passed, Maggie twisted around on Moonshine's back and muttered what sounded like a rhyme under her breath. Dust and leaves began swishing from side to side, all the way through the woods, along every path Moonshine had taken.

"What are you doing, exactly?" Colin asked.

"Covering our tracks with a sweeping spell, in case some hound has his nose set on unicorn instead of boars or rabbits."

Late in the evening, they had reason to be thankful for Maggie's sweeping spell when they met the third party.

Considering the length of time the fugitives had been traveling, they hadn't made much progress. They were only a few leagues from where they'd started at midday. Not that Moonshine wasn't swift, nor Roundelay able to keep pace.

But every time they came to any body of water, Moonshine stopped to dip his horn into it. Then, to make up for lost time, he'd gallop at top speed until he reached the next waterhole.

The second time Roundelay's front end collided with the unicorn's back end, flipping Colin forward on his horse's neck, his instruments twanging and crunching alarmingly as they jumbled forward with him, the minstrel complained. "Is it really necessary to do this *every* time?"

Maggie, who had barely avoided a swim in the creek when Moonshine skidded to his lightning stop, was at first too busy catching her breath to answer.

Moonshine looked back over his shoulder with a martyred air and dipped his horn in the stream a second time. Just so the minstrel wouldn't miss the point that unicorns did with streams exactly as they saw fit. With that, he casually switched his tail and trotted across the stream.

Maggie had regained her composure by that time and smiled apologetically at Colin. "You'll get used to it. I have. He *does* have to do it. It's part of that—whadayacallit, Moonshine, that little verse?"

"'Twould verily be a boon to me, Maiden dearest, if you would refrain from referring to The Creed as 'that little verse.' It is the doctrine of my race, handed down from dam to foal. The passage under attack by our esteemed companion, however—"

"But I didn't attack—" Colin protested. From Moonshine's tone he suspected that no amount of championing or any other kind of good deed on the part of a non-maiden truly compensated for his lack of virginity or excused him for unprecedented and no doubt illegal possession of the gift of unicorn understanding. Never mind what Moonshine had sworn to the contrary.

"The passage goes," Moonshine continued, ignoring the protest.

> "This too is the Unicorn Creed:
> 'Tis ever the unicorn deed
> With the horn we possess
> All water to bless
> So its purity be guaranteed."

"A noble thought," Colin said, "Though rather mediocre verse, if you ask me. I still wish we could have taken the highway." He glanced uneasily about him. The woods was deeper and the shadows thicker than earlier in the day. Only occasionally did a trilling birdsong interrupt the plopping of hooves, the flitter of leaves, the more or less rhythmic muffled noises of his instruments in their hide bags, slapping gently against Roundelay's sides.

Colin didn't like the deep woods. His boyhood home in East Headpenney was full of meadows, with the forest trimmed well away from the village. As a minstrel, he traveled mostly to settled communities, entertaining people, seldom venturing where people were not. He didn't feel, on the whole, that he'd been missing much. He wasn't partial to shadows and silence and chilling gusts of wind.

"Stop worrying," Maggie said lightly. "Moonshine knows these woods well, particularly the waterways."

"I noticed," Colin answered, unmollified.

"Colin, we can't travel on the highway, and that's that," she said firmly. "It's hardly going to do me a lot of good to flee if I have to stop and say hello to every one of my father's freeholders between here and the Troutroute River, will it? And I won't exactly be inconspicuous, riding a unicorn.''

They followed a path winding along the side of a steep hill that was a sheer climb above, a sheer drop below. The path was broad and it grew gradually broader, leading gently down toward what seemed to be a slight thinning in the alder thicket dominating this section of forest.

Since no streams had crossed their path for the last half hour, they'd made good time. Then all at once Moonshine's ears cocked forward and he thudded to another jarring halt.

"What are you doing, darling?" Maggie asked.

"Yes, I can't imagine," Colin said. "There's not even a mud puddle near."

"Harken, maiden," the unicorn replied. "Do you not hear the hounds and hooves?"

Colin took the liberty of harkening too, and immediately heard what Moonshine referred to. He heard voices, though he couldn't tell from which direction. But the hounds and hooves were distinct now, and close behind them on this nice, wide trail. "They're after us! Run!" Colin cried, and sensibly made haste to follow his own counsel.

Maggie swiveled on Moonshine's back and chattered her sweeping spell so fast that only years of long practice kept her tongue from twisting. As the unicorn sped after Roundelay, the whole trail seemed to shake itself like a wet dog, sending a thick vibrating veil of dust, leaves and twigs flying from the ground to the treetops.

Besides covering their tracks, the chaos created by the sweeping spell provided cover while they plunged into the woods ahead. They could hear sneezes and coughing above the hounds and hooves, sign that the spell was distracting the hunters in an even more personal way than Maggie had anticipated.

But she had no time to congratulate herself. Suddenly Colin turned Roundelay around, almost impaling her flank on Moonshine's horn, and rode her into the willow thicket beside the trail.

Maggie caught only a brief glance of the hunting camp which had altered his course; crimson pavilions, men piling branches onto a conical arrangement of sticks for a campfire to roast the hind other men were dressing out on the far side of the camp, hounds gobbling the hind's entrails. No more than that was she able to see before she heard someone sneeze close behind her and Moonshine dived after Roundelay into the thicket.

The dust and leaves had barely settled to the ground when the hounds burst past her heels and into the open camp. Close behind them rode the sneezer, the red-faced, bandy-legged prince who had tried to amuse her with his impersonation of a recently captured enemy begging for his life.

One of the men building the fire looked up. Maggie recognized him as Lord Boarsbane. He looked more like a boar himself than like someone who was the bane of boars, in her opinion. "What tidings, Patebreaker?" he hailed the prince. "Did you find any of those unicorns you were seeking?"

Maggie stiffened, and felt Moonshine shrink beneath her. Neither of them had any inkling that anyone knew of Moonshine's presence in the woods—and they both knew for a fact that there were no other unicorns in the vicinity.

"I did not," answered the prince, and sneezed again before dismounting. Drawing a wineskin from his saddlebag, he swigged a long, thirsty draught, then passed the flask to Boarsbane, who did likewise. The servant who had been assisting Boarsbane with the fire lit it, and the spitted hind was fixed above it.

Leofwin allowed a boy to tend his horse, while he settled himself on a log drawn near the blossoming campfire. "Jivemgood was so sure he saw sign of one, and once or twice, before I lost track of the slippery devil, it looked likely to me too, I'll be flogged if it didn't. Where *is* Jivemgood anyway? Did he come in ahead of me?"

"Where do you think this hind came from?" a thin, ascetic-looking young nobleman asked. Maggie recalled him as the author of perfectly awful sonnets in her honor. He'd kept wanting to rhyme her despised full name, Magdalene, with words like "tambourine," "jelly bean," and "wolverine," with a predictably unflattering result. Though she had rather liked the one line which rhymed her with "poison green."

The would-be poet now turned to Lord Boarsbane. "I win my wager, by the way, old darlin'. The mysterious Jivemgood triumphs again—leading our Leofwin on a wild unicorn chase and still managing to bring home the bacon, if I may mix my metaphors, in time for tea."

"You may win your wager and lose your head if you can't keep a civil tongue in it, Lordling," Leofwin growled. The hard futile ride had done nothing to improve his disposition.

Maggie's eye was caught by a rustling of leaves among the trees farthest from them, beyond the camp. A man stepped out of the leaves and into the clearing. She could not remember having spoken to him, or place who he was, but she had seen him among the suitors. He was clad in a silver-gray silk suit that beautifully blended with his shock of fashionably shaggy silver-gray hair and his full gray beard. She couldn't see the color of his eyes, but in the deep shadow still surrounding him they seemed to glitter like an animal's.

"There's our crafty Count now," the skinny young lord said. "Come, Jivemgood, join us. Prince Leofwin has been pining for you."

Leofwin's tone was calm at first, but the tension in his back told Maggie he was holding himself under tight control. It almost seemed as if the prince feared the man who faced him. "Where the deuce did you slink off to this time, Jivemgood?"

But Jivemgood paid him no attention.

The Count's eyes really did glitter, Maggie could see that quite clearly now. He was staring straight into their hiding place. His nostrils, broader and flatter than she had ever seen on any man, flared even wider, as his head snapped up and he sniffed the air. He had caught their scent.

Had Wulfric still been in wolf form, he would have wagged his tail. He fought to restrain himself from licking his lips. What a delicious smell the beast had! The other scents were there too, though partly masked by the reeking hunters. A woman and a strange man and a horse. The woman smelled familiar, and he could not be sure, but he thought she was the Dark Pilgrim's female kin. He'd caught her scent only once or twice before.

Such scents, once identified, could be traced any time. He turned to the blustering young warlord, and curled his lips in a smile of submission. But only mock-submission. If the young warlord wanted his share of the beast's magic, he would have to pay Wulfric's price.

The bow-legged prince grabbed him and shook him and threatened him with his fist. "Answer me, you smirking he-witch!" the prince demanded.

Wulfric kept smiling, thinking how pleasant it would be to drop into wolf form and scatter His Highness all over the forest, but he restrained himself and put on his tail-wagging voice instead.

"Cast no blame on my shoulders, great prince," he whined, "for did I not track the beast yea, even unto this glade where now we stand? Hear me, oh great Lord. The beast is wily and surpassing swift! Many times have I pursued him, and many times has he escaped me also. But he is near, great prince, and you shall have his horn for your cup if you help me capture him."

Not that he had need of Leofwin to capture this unicorn or any other. He had only to drive the beast to Her, and She would accomplish the capture. But She valued fighting men as much as unicorns, and he would make Her a present of this one, whom the other men feared and named The One Who Made Greater Frostingdung Yet Greater. He was a fierce warlord, and though Wulfric did not like him, the man had the same hungry feel to him as others Wulfric had won to the cause. He would be good. She would pet Wulfric and make much of him when he delivered this wicked-tempered warrior to Her.

"Why should I help YOU capture him?" Leofwin growled, taking another swig from his flask. "What would you want with him after I take the horn?"

"Maybe he wants to give it to the Princess for a saddle horse!" Boarsbane laughed.

"Or give her the flayed skin for dress material," the poet said. "Lord knows the poor girl could use a new outfit. I once won what was supposed to be a belt of unicorn hide in a dice game. Scroungy-looking thing. I'd never have wagered for it, but I was carried away by the spirit of my wine cup. Lucky for me I won, too. In my sorry state, I bet my seven-league boots against it. The thing was undoubtedly the hide of some sorry white nag, but the chap who lost it to me claimed it had the power to protect him in battle. He'd have done better to carry something that had the power to protect him at dice."

"That's why you need to win the Princess, isn't it? Because you lose at dice so often?" Boarsbane asked. "I saw you gambling on your expectations of her dowry with that dwarf the other day."

"You wrong me, sir. I was winning. But as I was saying, I can well understand how the excitement of chasing such a—shall we say *novel* beast, could have its appeal. Such sport will be a happy consolation prize in what must be a demoralizing situation for you who lack my well-bred finesse and have no hope of winning the royal witch."

"Well-bred finesse my eye!" Boarsbane scoffed. "All you have is a well-bred mama and papa who want you well-connected with the King in case he takes it into his head to annex your piddlin' lands and turn them into a parade ground."

"While you, on the other hand, have something more practical to offer her? Your thirteen half-troll children by three dead mothers and a great moldly castle sitting in the midst of a marsh full of serpents and will o' wisps?"

"It's not a marsh, it's undrained agricultural property. And I'll thank you not to slight my home, youngster. It's simple, true, but at least the mortgage is paid. And the children do need a mama.''

"What for? Lunch?''

"Ah, great lords,'' Wulfric sighed, tearing a half-raw chunk from the blistering hind and devouring it whole. "Can you not see that the possession of a unicorn is preferable to the possession of any woman? Can you not see that the possession of such a beast is preferable to any treasure, or to any reward you might gain by capturing him? Have you not heard the legends of his life-giving properties? Of his marvelous horn? Of the wondrous elixir of which he is the single ingredient?''

"Hah!'' Boarsbane laughed. "A princess in the keep is worth two unicorns in the woods, I say. Leofwin, old boy, don't you know when you're being had? The Count is making merry with you again! Unicorns! Bah! I tell you there are no such things! No one in MY family has ever seen one, and my estates include leagues and leagues of wild country.''

"I understand the beasts are not supposed to be partial to marshes and wasteland,'' the young poet said superciliously. "They are, rather, beings who prefer to inhabit dreams and enchantments, and are said to be visible only to beautiful young girls. But for all that, they're no more solid than the ones my Lord's family has never seen, I fear.''

"Is that true?'' Leofwin demanded, and grabbed Wulfric by the throat.

"Gurgle glook,'' Wulfric replied. Leofwin loosened his grip and the disguised were resisted the impulse to snap the Prince's jugular with his teeth. Instead he replied meekly. "No, great prince. The beasts exist as surely as you and I. Have none of you ever seen the magic cups that protect the drinker from poison?''

"Ah, everybody knows those are fancy carved cow's horns,'' Boarsbane scoffed. "Probably enchanted by some witch to keep the poisons from working. I tell you, there are no such animals. I've never seen one, and neither has my father, and neither did HIS father.''

"Perhaps you should have asked your mothers and grand-mothers, great Lord?'' Wulfric suggested. He would have enjoyed seeing their faces if he had suddenly uncovered the unicorn's hiding place, but he knew that they would never capture the beast in that fashion. They needed Her, or the cooperation of the maiden with the beast now, and that they did not have. Besides, these simpletons were unworthy to see the unicorn. They probably didn't believe in weres either. Such men would undoubtedly refuse to believe their own eyes. They were rich and comfortable, and preferred to make dens of their own choosing, to deny the laws of the forest which suited them not. They were the oppressors and royal lackeys of whom She spoke. They were not fit for the cause, as they went on to prove.

"My dear Jivemgood," the young one yawned, "You're a superlative hunter but I fear you have been deluded by poetic metaphor. The unicorn is nothing more than a symbol for unattainable purity, an idea obviously conjured up by the fairer sex to heighten their allure and enhance the illusion of their spiritual superiority. I, for one, intend to retire to dreams of some sweet young thing with none of those burdensome accoutrements."

"Now that's the first sensible thing you've said all day, young Greystraw," Boarsbane agreed. "I, too, intend to take to me bedroll here and now, Prince Leofwin. If you like, I'll be happy to help you chase wild geese in the morning. At least I know *they* exist." And he drew out his knife, gouged out a huge hunk of meat to gnaw on in bed, and lumbered off to his pavilion.

Leofwin's cold blue eyes locked with Wulfric's, and held, as if trying to see through him. His gaze never faltered as he made his meal of the meat, before sharing it out among the servants and sending them away.

When he'd chewed his last mouthful, the prince said slowly, "But they do exist, these unicorns, don't they, Jivemgood? I've seen the horn, you know, and it was no carved cow's horn. It was in a treasure chest I captured in some seige or other, though I was more interested in gold at the time. I regretted my oversight when I learned what it was, but by then it was too late."

"Of a surety they exist, great prince," Wulfric replied.

"And there's one around here, you say? You've seen it?"

"Close by, great prince. I've not seen it. Sensed it, rather."

"What are you waiting for man? Lead me to it!"

"Such haste, great prince, is of no help capturing unicorns. As the meatless young one has said, the unicorns must be captured by a woman's hand. I know a woman who will help us, but we must travel many days to find her."

"By that time he'll be gone!"

"I think not, great prince. But even if he is, there are many others nearer the woman."

"Humph, seems like a lot of trouble to avoid getting poisoned! I'm better off to keep avoiding the company of poisoners instead!"

"There are—other benefits, my lord. The secret elixir made from the beast's other parts grants immunity from ills and wounds of all sorts. And boundless male potency," he added the last to sound like an afterthought, but as he'd expected, the warlord leaned forward eagerly.

"How do we get this elixir, then?"

"Through the woman of whom I spoke, great Prince."

"Eh? Is that so?" Leofwin scratched his chin, considering. Wulfric wondered if he should not now reveal the hidden unicorn, to convince the Prince. But no, instead of being convinced, Leofwin would try to capture the beast himself. If he failed, he would rouse the countryside in his search for it, and Wulfric would have the whole of Fort Iceworm to compete with for the beast, and lose the man to the cause. And if Leofwin succeeded, Wulfric would lose both man and beast. For what man save Her Dark Pilgrim had need of more than one unicorn?

So Wulfric merely nodded, and waited.

While Leofwin thought, and weighed, and finally yawned. "Sounds lovely to me, old man. But d'you think it can wait a bit? There's something back at the castle I need to attend to first."

Wulfric smiled as if he understood, though he didn't. He would not tax himself by trying to comprehend what caused men to act as they did.

"Are they asleep?" Colin asked. The campfire still glowed, but when the Prince and Count had drifted over to the tents, the whole camp had sunken into quiet.

"They can't be," Maggie said. "He saw us. I know the Count saw us."

Moonshine quivered. He'd felt the Count's eyes on him too.

"Could you hear what those two were saying at the last?" Maggie asked Colin. "I'm sure they were talking about Moonshine." Colin's excellent ears were part of his inheritance from his mer ancestors, who had also bequeathed to him his musical ability.

"I only heard part," Colin replied, sending this thought, like the others, to Moonshine to relay to her. "They didn't talk about Moonshine in particular, but that Count said a lot of wild things about unicorns."

"Horrible things," Moonshine shuddered. "I heard it all. The man must be mad. He speaks of one who bottles unicorns to cure men's ills."

"Yuck," Maggie said. "That's disgusting."

"It takes all kinds," Colin said. "But let's get out of this place before he popularizes his ideas."

"I would I knew where he obtained them," Moonshine fretted.

"I thought you said you could understand anybody's thoughts," Maggie said, eyeing the quiet camp for any sign of movement.

"Not his," Moonshine said. "He has a strange mind—I would not say a human mind, though that is strange enough. But the other—the Prince—maiden, we must leave this place quickly. His thoughts about you were VERY unchaste."

"I can well imagine," she replied.

They slipped past the camp without incident, though once one of the hounds, an odd one who more closely resembled a wolf, seemed to stir and lazily watch them. Colin, in a voice quieter than his thumping heart, murmured the lyric to the most potent lullabye he knew, the Keynote Address of the Hostess at Her Majesty's Royal Baby Shower. The wolf-dog stretched its front paws, laid its muzzle along them, and seemed to sleep once more.

Three streams and a small pond later, Moonshine stopped and sniffed the air. "Surely now our enemies are behind us, Maiden. But I fear me greatly that I have become lost. I know not whither Queenston lies. In my haste, I've become disoriented and have forgotten the exact pointing of your fair finger."

"Never mind," Maggie said. "I've changed my mind."

"What?" Colin almost fell out of his saddle. "You mean you're NOT going to see the King? Where do you intend to go? Surely you haven't changed your mind about wanting to marry one of those gallants? If you're escaping, you'll have to escape TO somewhere, you know. That's the way it's done. And you haven't got any friends abroad—except maybe the gypsies, and who knows where they are?"

"There is one other person," Maggie reminded him. "And with that loud-mouth Jivemgood blabbing it all over Fort Iceworm that there's a unicorn loose in the woods, before long someone's going to believe him and we won't be able to turn around without running into hunters. And that's not even counting the ones Dad will have after me! We need special help if we're going to make it as far as Queenston. So what do you say we head south for a bit until we cross the Troutroute?"

"To your Aunt Sybil's?" Relief poured over him. "Of course! She's just the person to help us. Why didn't I think of her?"

So they broke into a trot and headed south. And across the pond by which they'd paused, a lean gray figure rose and stretched, and wagged its tail smugly, and padded back through the shadow-haunted woods to a camp full of sleeping huntsmen.

CHAPTER 4

Passing by the royal armory on his way to the royal pantry for a midnight snack, the Chief Archivist and Central Headquarters Dragon Liaison Officer, Sir Cyril Perchingbird, stopped suddenly. Footsteps, slow and measured, clanking with a weary hollowness, treaded close to the closed, iron-bound door, then paced away from it.

Now which of the royal palace's assorted apparitions was wandering tonight, Sir Cyril wondered.

Perhaps it was the Lady Drucilla, executed during the second reign of the House of Strongheart for messing about with the King in plain sight of Queen Ethel, a wild fierce woman if ever there was one. Sir Cyril fervently hoped the shade was not that of Queen Ethel herself, who later died of a mysterious stomach ailment. He took comfort from the fact that he had never heard any report indicating Ethel was in the habit of bestirring herself posthumously.

And anyway, the steps sounded as if they belonged to a masculine spirit. They practically marched; as well they might, coming from the armory. They could scarcely belong to one of the poor young Ashburn princes, in that case. Neither lad had ever taken the slightest interest in warfare. If they'd spent more time in the armory, in fact, and less attempting to practice the sophisticated parlor magic even their royal father was capable of performing only in his heydey, they mightn't have died before their times. Perhaps one of them would be reigning now.

But he was being nostalgic. They was always the possibility that if the princes had lived, Argonia would now be embroiled in civil war. No doubt things had happened for the best. Roari Rowan filled the throne well enough. And he, Cyril, had the good fortune to correspond with the remaining Ashburn heir, the Princess Pegeen, a brilliant historical mind and undoubtedly the most learned woman in the kingdom.

Wouldn't this ghost business be a fascinating tidbit to add to his next packet to Her Highenss? He hoped the ghost was one of her more interesting ancestors, so she'd be sure to reply quickly. He hadn't had a message from her in six months.

Now if he could just manage to peek through the door without frightening the shade away. Torchlight spilled forth; not much, just enough to see from the two torches burning high on the stone walls that the intriguing footsteps belonged to no ghost.

King Roari, clasping what seemed to be a small animal to his massive chest, stalked his own armory.

Sir Cyril opened the door wider. The King stared at him as if the Chief Archivist himself were a ghost. Hastily, Cyril bowed. "Your pardon, Majesty. I heard your footfall and thought to investigate."

The King nodded tiredly. Even in the wavering torchlight, Sir Cyril saw the worry lines creasing the King's broad freckled face above his beard, and the red webs around his blue eyes.

"May I be of some service to Your Majesty?" he asked impulsively, though in the King's acceptance of his explanation there had also been dismissal.

His Majesty started to shake his head, then looked down at the animal, which Perchingbird now saw was no animal at all but a baby wrapped in a fur blanket. "I don't need you," the King replied. "But maybe ye c'n help her. Do ye ken what babes like? Winnie's still a-sleepin' and Bron sets up a terrible howl when any of t'ladies touch her. I've been nursemaidin' her ever since we left Fort Iceworm. T'only other person she'll have aught t'do with was young Songsmith, and he's deserted me, th' scamp."

It just so happened Perchingbird knew a great deal about babies. His parents had whelped so many there were never enough servants around to tend them all. Sons and daughters in great profusion had trailed through their castle, most of them finding their way out into the fields of his father's rich agricultural estates, where they worked right along with the peasants. His father believed in starting from the ground up, literally.

Sir Cyril was the odd one, gifted with a peculiar magic talent which his parents, though they didn't understand it, encouraged from the start. ('("Though you understand it doesn't come from *my* side of the family," his sunburned father had protested when his mother approached him about little Cyril's gift. "Never mind, dear," Mother had replied, "He has your eyes.") Cyril was allowed to make the queer letters from spoken words, to codify the stories his grandparents told him, and the servants' grandparents. He was allowed to pump mercilessly any wandering minstrel hapless enough to wander into their home, begging the bard for more tales of the exploits of Finbar the Fireproof, Argonia's colorful King at that time. Later Cyril entered King Finbar's service, but that was after the King was an old man, his sons dead, his daughter in self-imposed seclusion. While he was still growing up, Cyril earned his right to practice his craft by making himself useful with the little ones, which he could do indoors, instead of helping out in the field. He'd become quite a hand with children, as adept at feeding and changing them and making them laugh as his mother and sisters.

"The young princess is what now, sire? About nine months old?" he asked.

"Um—Aye, that's right," the King said, pulling the wraps back from the baby's wet pink face as if to check his facts with her.

"Porridge," Perchingbird pronounced, and confidently led the way to the kitchen.

The King, though mystified, followed.

"Porridge?" His Majesty asked, just to make sure he'd heard correctly, while his Chief Archivist pulled ingredients from bins and cupboards in the royal pantry.

"Yes, sire. Porridge. Just the thing to stick to her little ribs. See now, she's awake already, but she knows we're looking to her needs. There, there now, little Sis." He paused between counter and table to chuck her under the chin. "We'll have you a nice mess of porridge in no time." The baby tracked him across the kitchen, and for the first time in many days, her eyes were dry.

An untidy hour later, the princess slept again on her father's lap. Porridge was smeared across her cherubic face and stained her pink velvet gown, but she cooed in her sleep, hiccuping contentedly now and then.

Rowan leaned back in his chair, combing the porridge from his flaming beard, a thoughtful expression on his face. Talking to a bright lad like Perchingbird would be a better way to spend the evening than pacing the armory. The stone floor there was hard even on feet used to marching long distances over hilly terrain, but it had been the only room in the palace where Rowan felt at home. Kinging was tougher than soldiering, and the former border lord sometimes yearned for his sword in his hand and his shield before him. He didn't quite have a grasp yet on the subtler weapons needed to defend himself, his family, and his kingdom against the forces aligned against it.

Perchingbird was a good man. He'd figured out how to talk to the dragons, Grizel and Grimley, while everyone else stood around shaking their heads. Rowan had originally recruited the dragons through the magic cat who accompanied Maggie Brown when she and young Songsmith saved Winnie. Problems arose when the cat had to return home to Fort Iceworm to serve his mistress, and Rowan's regime found itself in possession of a

Royal Air Force consisting of two dragons no one could address. "Try Sir Cyril, the archivist," someone had finally suggested. "He speaks all manner of heathenish tongues. Writes 'em, too." And sure enough, after a brief, heated discussion with Grizel and Grimley, Perchingbird had managed to master the rudiments of dragonese, and so became the Liaison Officer between the crown and its dragons.

Generally Sir Cyril stayed put down below with his conch shells and scrolls, however, and only occasionally emerged from his quarters in the records hall when he was needed to interpret for his exclusive fiery acquaintances.

Ah well, Rowan thought, there was no sense to having sound men like Perchingbird serve under one if one never asked their advice. He'd talked this curse thing over with practically every other so-called adviser in the kingdom. Why not with a man who at least had the wit to know which end of a bawling baby wanted attention?

"So, Cyril," he said casually. "What do you make of the box and that piddlin' bit of paper that's cursed my little lass here?"

Perchingbird turned from wiping the dishes. Rowan's cook from Castle Rowan had taken over the palace kitchen, and she was a most particular woman. Sir Cyril had no wish to offend her and risk losing his kitchen privileges. He smiled politely and encouragingly, but blankly for all that, and asked, "What box is that, Sire?"

"You don't KNOW?" Rowan's voice started to rise to its usual roar, and the baby whimpered and wriggled. "You mean to say you really don't know?" the King repeated, whispering this time. "Some blackguard gave Bron a wicked toy at her christening. We think it's cursed her. I know for a fact it's cursed her mother. I never thought t'be sae anxious t'get m'lady OUT of bed in m'life. She's been asleep these three weeks past and won't rise."

Perchingbird was no whiz at protocol, but he knew enough to skirt *that* particular royal complaint. "You said something about a parchment, Sire?"

"Aye, a parchment. Come under the cursed box. No one knows what it means. D'you mean t'say none of that pack of advisers of mine even asked you about it?"

Perchingbird shrugged. "There *are* others in the palace who read, sire. Usually documents don't come to my attention unless they're at least a decade old."

"Worthless lot o'lamebrains," the King growled, and dug inside his clothes, carefully, so as not to wake his daughter. He

48

pulled out a soiled, much-creased, besmeared and flattened scroll, which he tossed across the table to Perchingbird.

Sir Cyril's eyes glanced swiftly over the document, then stared back at his King with an expression of incredulity. "*This* accompanied a curse, Sire?"

The King nodded. "'Twas underneath the wretched box." His eyes narrowed as he waited to see what the one man in his court who obviously knew how to help him but hadn't been asked had to say.

Sir Cyril shook his head and scanned the scroll again. "That's impossible, Sire. I know this hand, these illustrations. This is nothing more than a christening gift from Her Highness, the Princess Pegeen the Illuminator."

Reaching an arm the length and breadth of a medium tree across the table, Rowan snatched back the document, stared at it with no more comprehension than he'd had before, and tossed it back to Perchingbird. "Hmph," he said.

Sir Cyril reexamined the scroll. "Yes, sire, this all seems perfectly innocent. All the Princess Pegeen is doing here, really, is translating the standard horoscope for an upperclass lady born under your daughter's moon into ancient Drumclog runic, an archaic written language in which the noble lady is most proficient."

Rowan sighed and nodded. His only hope of finding the sender of the curse was lost.

"Wait," Sir Cyril said suddenly. "What can she mean by this?" His intelligent round face sharpened with concentration. "Oh, dear. I must be mistaken. No, surely not. That rune has two meanings and they both—Your Majesty?"

Rowan's weary red-rimmed eyes snapped to attention.

"I'm afraid I was slightly mistaken. This document is not a simple horoscope, as I thought at first, though it's meant to look like one. The Princess Pegeen has carefully encoded a message, sire, in the last portion. I don't know exactly how to translate it back into the Argonian tongue, but what it essentially says is that unless you make haste to the Princess's home at Worm's Roost Castle, not only is your child cursed but your entire reign, and possibly the kingdom, is in jeopardy." Perchingbird glanced once more at the document. "And though it doesn't say so, sire, I very much fear from the manner in which the Princess chose to warn us that she is also in grave danger."

Even the Queen stirred from her sleep as Rowan's roars echoed through the castle all the rest of that night, waking his generals, his admirals, his administrators, and his advisers.

Leaving his daughter with her yawning mother, the King harangued his cabinet about the need for speed. The arrangements, he was told, would take several weeks, while the army was called back from its various outposts. Armies could not be gathered up just like that, didn't he know.

Once more it was Cyril Perchingbird who had the practical suggestion. "My Lady Pegeen writes only of the need for speed, Sire, not striking power. The fastest route to Worm's Roost is by sea, a fortnight's journey in good weather, compared with a month overland." The Chief Archivist was also keeper of Argonia's somewhat sketchy maps, which contained details of matters like time and distance.

Another adviser, eager to make up for not thinking of Perchingbird's idea himself, added, "That little ship Your Majesty is so fond of, the *Snake's Bane*, is in port now. A serpent hunter like that is far faster than our naval vessels."

The man had a good point. Serpent hunters were built in Ablemarle, where the shipbuilders understood the necessity for outslipping serpents. The naval shipbuilders native to Argonia had never quite got the hang of building their ships, which were largely used on missions of state anyway, as light, fast or maneuverable as vessels like the *Bane*.

"Right you are, man. Bring me the *Bane's* Captain Seagarden and ask him before he meets me here to have Bosun Pinchpurse ready the ship to sail on the next tide. You seem bright enough to serve me, so get ready to come along yourself." He turned to another lord, who hadn't said much but had at least kept quiet. "You too, and you," he said to another.

From behind him, Perchingbird intruded diffidently. "Sire, I would like to serve you also on this journey, if I may. And perhaps the Royal Air Force would be a boon?"

"So be it," said Rowan. "Tell me, Sir Cyril. Is there anything in the archives tells what kind of armor a man's supposed to wear on shipboard?"

CHAPTER 5

They crossed the Troutroute river by the middle of the day following their encounter with Leofwin's hunting party.

Colin looked forward to seeing Maggie's Aunt Sybil for

several reasons, not the least among them the excellent taste and generous size of her gingerbread shingles.

Sybil Brown was in her garden when they broke through the woods, into the little clearing containing her gingerbread cottage. The cottage was Sybil's inheritance from a late unlamented ancestress who was fond of children—in the culinary sense—and used the cottage to entice them into her clutches. Sybil was as different from that long-gone semi-ogress as a sword was from a spindle. Far from gobbling the local children, she was inclined to let any of them who were adventurous enough to visit her literally eat her out of house and home. Or had been, before Maggie had helped her repair her home, and had placed a heavy preservative spell on it, making it less than palatable. Now visiting children had to eat their gingerbread the dull way, from a cookie jar.

Sybil straightened as her visitors approached, and braced her hands on the small of her back, beaming, surrounded by vanquished weeds and pampered pansies. "My, that didn't take you long at all," she said, pushing back the broad brim of her garden hat. A sprig of lilac dipped jauntily over the edge of the brim, bouncing close to her left eyebrow.

"You've been keeping track of me again," Maggie accused affectionately, sliding from Moonshine's back to embrace her.

"Sure I have, child. You're the only grand-niece I have, you know. And *Colin*, my boy, how sweet you are to visit an old lady again!" Colin kissed the proffered cheek and returned the sprightly sorceress's smile. "You can rest your beasties now," she told them. "It's quite all right. Those hunters left the forest early this morning. I checked after breakfast. They've all returned to the castle."

That was one of the other reasons Colin was glad to see Aunt Sybil. Her magic, the art of seeing the present even when she didn't happen to be present where it was occuring, was extremely useful at times. This particular time it was also reassuring.

He removed Roundelay's saddle and bridle and unloaded all of his instruments, then began to rub her foam-flecked back with a brush and rag from his saddlebag.

Moonshine was still fresh and frisky, but Maggie rubbed him down too. Although he didn't need it, he liked it. Sybil lifted a hand and stroked the unicorn's nose. He nuzzled her palm enthusiastically. "What a lovely creature *you* are," she said. From her pocket she drew a crumb of gingerbread and offered it to him in a courtly manner. He accepted it in a greedy manner.

Sybil laughed. "Eat all you want here, Noble Unicorn. If the cookie jar isn't entirely to your liking, there's always the flower bed. I'll mourn my delphiniums sorely, but someone as lovely and special as you are surely can't graze on mere grass.''

"You are most gracious, Goodwitch," Moonshine replied, dipping his horn low in a courteous genuflection. "And I am properly grateful for your offer. But delphiniums would not agree with my digestion, I think. However, if you happen to have any of those long orange things—" He eyed the vegetable garden covetously, and Sybil obligingly pulled up her carrot patch for him. "Ah, excellent," he said when he'd sampled one. "And your grass looks delicious as well. I beg your leave to dine, Maiden?"

Maggie ruffled his forelock and kissed him at the base of the horn. "Certainly, darling. But don't be a pig. I'm sure Roundelay likes carrots too."

"I suppose you'll have to scold me too," Maggie said, wiping her mouth with her napkin and leaning her knife against the edge of her empty plate. Colin continued tucking away trout in honey sauce and cauliflower casserole.

"Now why would I do that, dearie? Even if you do wait too long to come and see me, I love you, Magpie, and I'm very proud of you. You should know that." She patted Maggie's hand soothingly, but her sharp brown eyes were bright and inquisitive as a bird's. Sybil closely resembled her sister, Maggie's peppery Granny Brown, except that she was rounder and kinder and of a sweeter disposition than either Maggie or her grandmother. Maggie used to think, when she was small, that Sybil was so sweet because she lived in a house made of cookies and candies. But that theory hadn't borne up under adult scrutiny, since the house's building materials had apparently had no noticeable influence whatsoever on the personality of Grandma Elspat, the child-munching ogress.

"I ought to have known I could count on you, Auntie," Maggie said. "Everybody else is ready to have me drawn and quartered because I don't want to go along with *their* plans for *my* life."

"I know, dearie, I know." Sybil kept patting her hand. "I've been watching. And I know you wouldn't ever do anything you didn't feel was right, whatever Maudie and your father and the King think. I only wonder if it's really wise to put off your future for the sake of your unicorn? Don't get me wrong." She held up a hand to stave off the retort Maggie's mouth was open to make. "Moonshine is a marvelous creature, and you'd be a fool not to enjoy his company. And, of course, you're quite right about our witches' tradition being rather against marriage to unmagicked men. But times are changing, child. Magic is wearing thinner with each generation, and if strong witches like yourself don't breed it'll soon be out at the heel altogether."

"YOU never married," Maggie said. "And Moonshine likes you, which means you probably never even—"

"Don't be pert with me, Maggie Brown," Sybil snapped. "No, I never have, if it's any of your business, Miss, but if you must know it's because of my powers. Gentlemen callers don't care for a woman who can check up on them as I can. And I—perhaps I know just a little too much about the goings-on of other folks to let me work up the kind of notions about a man I'd need to have to mate with him."

She turned thoughtful. "Though there was *once*, mind you. But it's not *my* future we're talking about here. Weren't there any of those young men you could've married, just to please your father? Someone who'd let you keep Moonshine?"

Maggie shook her head. "Only one old widower, Lord Feeblydon, who came to the christening on a litter. He's in his nineties, I believe, and blind. I offered to marry him. I thought he might enjoy a little looking after, and wouldn't interfere with Moonshine and me, but Dad said he wasn't about to call any ninety-year-old relic 'son'."

"Unreasonable man, your father," Sybil sympathized, shaking her head.

Maggie nodded glumly. "And the thing is, Aunt Sybil, even if it weren't for Moonshine I wouldn't care to marry any of those men. They all know I'm base-born on Mama's side, and most of them have a wretched attitude towards witchcraft. That whiny warlock you may have seen with Prince Leofwin was the only one among them with any magic, and he makes my skin crawl. But I wouldn't even mind that except they all make fun of me behind my back. I know they do. For all their flattery, I didn't feel like one of them even *liked* me."

"I was going to talk to you about that, Maggie," Colin put in. "The thing is, see, you don't know how to gussy yourself up and talk like a real lady. That's what those fellows are used to. Why, you're a very attractive girl, if one likes the type, and all you have to do is—"

He choked on his last sentence, ending it with a cough as he caught the force of her glare.

"Just where do you suggest I start to make myself pretty for your kind, Master Songsmith? Shall I start by bleaching my hair and skin, or will it do if I just make myself a couple of inches taller?''

Colin blushed. He hadn't realized his own preference for willowy fair ladies was so obvious to her.

"You can start, niece," Sybil said severely, "By apologizing to your friend. If he hadn't liked you well enough to come back and help you, we'd have nothing to argue about here. You'd still be locked up in the tower.''

Maggie flushed bright magenta, and said in the smallest voice Colin had ever heard from her, "Sorry.''

Colin shrugged. "Perfectly all right, old girl. I only meant you should really try to wear a nice dress sometimes, maybe fix your hair up like the ladies in court, put a bit of scent behind your ears. I know you can do it," he said encouragingly. "You washed up rather well that time you danced for the gypsies. How's anybody supposed to know you well enough to like you if you bark at them all the time and perfume yourself with last week's goose bastings?''

She lowered her eyes and clenched her hands till they were white-knuckled in her lap, but her chin was still set stubbornly. "Why should I want to know them anyway, people like Leofwin and that silly Earl Greystraw with his awful sonnets?''

Sybil shook her head. "You young folks are so quick to trounce each other. Poor Robbie Greystraw. It's not his fault about the sonnets, you know.''

"PLEASE don't tell me it's mine for inspiring them," Maggie groaned.

"No, but I will tell you you were wrong about none of those boys having any magic. Poor Robbie's just one of those unfortunates whose magic is so watered down it's almost invisible. He comes from a long line of transformers, powerful as your Granny Maud in their day, I hear. And one of Robbie's sisters is a reasonably adept spinner who can change straw into fine linen. But the family has married in with regular folks so many times for wealth and rank that now there's not much magic left to Robbie. The closest he can come to transforming anything is saying, 'your lips are like a rose.' Though I can't think at all why he'd want them to be, since that would make kissing very prickly.''

"Very well, then, I'm sorry for him," Maggie said. "But his sonnets still stink, and I still won't marry him." She shot Colin another defiant look. "And I won't marry anybody who only wants me because I dress up fine or because I'm all of a sudden a princess.''

54

Colin lifted an eyebrow. "Do as you like then, witch. You do anyway. But I personally don't see what's so much worse about a man wanting to marry a pretty woman because she's a princess than a unicorn making friends with her because she's a virgin. If you hadn't been, you know, he'd have gored and trampled you to death. So the legends say."

Maggie jumped to her feet, tipping the table so that it rocked dangerously. "That's not true."

Colin repeated, "It's what the legends say."

"I'll just see what Moonshine has to say about *that*," she challenged, and flounced angrily out of her aunt's cottage.

Colin felt vaguely ashamed of himself, but also felt she had it coming for being so superior about the whole thing. Just because she was a powerful witch and the Queen's sister and a princess into the bargain, she thought she was better than everybody else. Let her prefer unicorns to men if she liked, but one had to hold up the side. Even if the side contained such unsavory specimens as Prince Leofwin and Count Jivemgood.

Still, it hadn't been a very nice thing to do. He stole a shamefaced glance at Sybil. She winked at him, broadly. "Play us a bit of a tune, won't you, dearie? To cheer a lonely old lady?"

The lynx, Myrrll and Pyrrll, were enjoying their evening drink for the first time since the two-legged had come to their territory and taken away the mighty one-horn, Eagledown. After that, their water started tasting odd, smelling bad.

They left that place before the rot came and soon they found another place, with good water, where a one-horn was and other lynx were not.

This evening they decided to wait beside the stream, to thank the one-horn and to warn her of the two-legged, no more than a day's easy loping towards the mountains.

But no sooner had Myrrll finished drinking and sat down to groom herself than Pyrrll gave a warning growl.

Two-legged. Many large hairy ones and one small smooth one—the female with the scent of magic about her, she who had lured Eagledown to her lap while the others bound the helpless one-horn with a long vine.

Did the two-legged female come for lynx this time? To wrap their dead fur around her, perhaps, so she would not have to be smooth any longer? The young cats, ears back and hindquarters twitching, spotted fur bristling along their spines, backed into the cover of the trees.

The two-legged female paid no attention to them. She sat beside their new stream and waited. The lynx waited, too. They wanted to see what would happen. They were cats, and therefore curious.

Soon the one-horn female came to bless the stream. She was old, but her horn was good, and she dipped it, banishing impurities only she could detect in the stream's crystal waters. Then she sniffed, and raised her head, and sniffed again, scenting the two-legged female who waited, downstream.

Myrrll growled. She had no wish to move again so soon. She liked this place and this water. Pyrrll yowled his warning cry to the she one-horn, but the beast was trotting toward the two-legged female, enchanted by her scent, and already singing her praise. Pyrrll's cry dissolved into an angry growl. He did not wish to move again either.

Myrrll gathered herself into a ball, and sprang. Her spots blurred to blotches as she soared across the forest floor, covering the distance between herself and the one-horn with a single leap. Another leap, and she was atop the one-horn, riding her, sharp claws bared. This was not the thanks the cats had meant to offer, but perhaps this thanks would save the one-horn. Pyrrll sprang too, landing in front of the one-horn's chopping hooves.

The angry one-horn pawed and stamped the ground, wielding her horn with great fierceness, but Myrrll's claws were very strong and Pyrrll was very swift and flexible. Pyrrll shuttled between the one-horn's legs, tangling her feet so that she could not rear and could not move forward.

The two-legged female sat, waiting still, not seeing the one-horn, not seeing the lynx. The trees were many between the two-legged and the lynx's tangling tawny bodies.

Long did they worry the one-horn, driving her back, away from the two-legged. The one-horn was very fierce, but she was old, and tired quickly. The lynx herded her to their new lair, a warm hole against a hillside, with shielding trees and bushes.

Three nights passed, and each evening Pyrrll went to the stream and saw the two-legged waiting, and left again, thirsty. On the fourth evening the two-legged was not there, and Pyrrll raced back to his sister and to the one-horn to get them to join her in refreshment. But the one-horn would not speak to them and would not rise. All they heard from her that night and long after was praise and song for the two-legged female who had gone.

Maggie stood in front of the unicorn, her fists balled against her hips. "Well, is it true or isn't it?" she demanded. "Surely

56

you can tell me that. Would you really have gored me, or is that just a story?"

Moonshine continued chewing with his head down, his horn tip tracing thoughtful little patterns in the grass. "Why ask such a question, Maiden? You are pure and have never had anything to fear from me."

Maggie's bravado collapsed and she sat down, suddenly too tired and discouraged to stand. "Then it must be true."

Moonshine stopped grazing to nuzzle her cheek comfortingly. "Don't fret, Maiden. That part of the Creed applies only to false virgins. It has naught to do with you and I."

"You mean to say that if I hadn't been a maiden when we first met—" She was unable to leave the subject alone.

"'Twould have been my duty to slay you," Moonshine affirmed.

"Whew," she said ruefully, "Lucky thing for me I could outrun the baker's boy when I was fifteen."

"Oh, maiden," Moonshine pleaded, "I probably would not have done so. I can't remember all that part—the details of the verse escape me. But I'm certain I would have been lenient with *you*. My dam did not say, in her teachings, that a unicorn could not be merciful to the good and beautiful."

"Where's your dam now?" Maggie asked. "I'd like to get this thing cleared up."

"She was taken from me before she was able to complete my education."

"Pity," Maggie said.

"Indeed," Moonshine agreed.

"Well, did she tell you what if say, now that we're *already* friends, what if I was to marry somebody—for instance, somebody very nice, very pure in lots of ways, I mean, somebody you really liked a lot. What I mean to say is, what would become of you and me if I married this very nice person and sort of, you know, lost my maidenhood? If I married or met somebody, a man, for instance . . ."

"An excellent choice for someone of your species, Maiden," Moonshine nickered, showing his large white teeth as he plopped down beside her to rest his head in her lap.

"Is that a joke?" she asked. "Because if it is, it's rather to the point. Not that I want to do anything like that now, you understand, but if I ever did want to mate—"

Moonshine rolled a soft violet eye at her. "Maiden, would you forsake me then?"

Maggie ran her fingers up under his mane and let it trickle

through them like streams of milk. "No, of course not, darling, not willingly. But don't you see? Unless I could acquire enough of your lovely habits to remind Gran of a unicorn so she could change me into one, providing she would, of course, and believe me, there's little chance of that—"

"Good," Moonshine said. "I fear you are not unicorn material, Maid Maggie."

"Well, I don't know about that, but even if I was, Granny's changes are only temporary, so that wouldn't work anyway. Sooo—unless maybe you're really an enchanted prince?"

Moonshine rose in a huff. "Certainly NOT! I am a bona fide, genuine, authentic unicorn and have never been anything else! I had a unicorn dam and a unicorn sire to prove it, before they were taken from me. And now—" he folded back down again, resting his head again on her knee. "And now I have only you. Pray forgive me, gentle Maiden, for waxing wrathful, but I should be sorely loath to lose you."

She sighed, running her finger along the spiral of his horn. "I'd hate to lose you too, darling. But I don't see why we'd have to part over something like mating with our own kind. Surely that Unicorn Creed you're always going on about has some provision in it somewhere for old friends who are no longer maidens? What if you were to meet some nice unicorn filly and wish to mate with her yourself? Would I have to trample and gore *you*?"

Moonshine blew a long, forlorn breath through his velvety nostrils.

"It just seems to me that it'd be a singularly silly way to do things," Maggie continued. "Your Creed tells you what you may and may not do about almost everything, but leaves out the important parts. When you consider what it DOES tell you to do, from what you've explained to me, I wonder that there are any of you left! You're supposed to put yourselves in the hands of any girl at all—now correct me if I'm wrong—any girl at all, no matter what she's like otherwise, if she's a virgin, you're supposed to go with her. Is that right?"

"I-I think so. That's not how the verse says it but—" the sing-song of the Creed whirled in Moonshine's head, confusing itself with Maggie's argument. The verses he could remember seemed similar in content, if not spirit, to her disgruntled interpretation, but somehow he didn't feel the Creed was supposed to mean what she suggested.

Now she had another question. "Doesn't the Creed even tell you to ask for references from your maidens?"

"Oh, NO, Maid Maggie. We can tell, you see, by the sweet odor of chastity that surrounds the true maiden, and a special, wonderful feeling that comes just from being near—"

"Can't say I think much of it then," she said and unceremoniously but gently dumped his head from her lap and stood. "As soon as I talk to the King about not being a princess any more, we'd better see if we can't scare up another unicorn—one with some experience in these matters—and continue your education, and mine, about this Creed of yours. It's quite bad enough to be bound to such an impractical system to begin with, but really, it's just plain unthinkable to be ignorant of ALL the ins and outs of what you *do* have to work with." Brushing her skirt free of grass and a few of his loose chin hairs, she strode purposefully back to the cottage, relieved to have made up her mind on the matter of Moonshine's bothersome Creed. As soon as they'd dispensed with this princess business, they would settle Moonshine's problem once and for all.

Moonshine wasn't so sure of that.

Strains of fiddle music danced through the cottage. At Sybil's table, Colin sat with his fair head bent over his fiddle, the fingers of his left hand jumping like grasshoppers while his right hand sped the bow over the strings. Across from him Sybil sat, hands folded demurely around a teacup, ankles primly crossed beneath her chair. But her cheeks were pink with pleasure and her toes tapped sneaky time to Colin's tune.

The song ended as Maggie took the empty chair beside her aunt.

"Have a little bearberry wine, Maggie dear," Sybil offered, already pouring a cup of clear garnet liquid from the uncorked jug on the table. "You look like you could use it."

Maggie drained the cup in three swallows. To forestall having to discuss Moonshine's revelations, and also to keep from having to admit that Colin had correctly recalled his unicorn lore, she asked, "What was that tune you were playing when I came in?"

Questions about music could always put the minstrel off any other subject.

But it was Sybil who answered. "Your friend was just playing me the ditty he's composing about you for the King's Grace, dearie. It's very clever. Sing it for her, laddie."

"It's an instrumental, actually," he said. "A reel. But I thought up a verse or two for it." He picked up the fiddle, hesitated, set it down again and refilled his cup, then Maggie's—Sybil's was at her lips, only partially concealing the twitch at the

59

corners of her mouth. "You still look thirsty, Maggie," Colin prompted. "Drink up." And he emptied his own cup in one swallow.

He pretended to tune until her cup was almost empty again. Then, when the focus of her eye was no longer as piercing and the set of her jaw had softened, he began. He knew very well the value of preparing one's audience ahead of time. After a lively introduction on the instrument, he lifted his chin from it long enough to sing:

> "Is your life too peaceful, Lord?
> Too drearily serene?
> Then harken, sir, and take to wife
> The Princess Magdalene.
>
> As gentle as the hunting hawk
> As docile as the dragon,
> She'll fix your supper, fix your bed
> And then she'll fix your wagon."

He stole a glance at the object of his dubious flattery while he tucked the fiddle back under his chin and played another rollicking chorus. She stared into the bottom of her wine cup, seeming to find within its depths something of absorbing interest.

> "Sweet Maggie is the bride to wed
> To have men deem one bold
> For she's as shy as conqu'ring hordes
> A-swooping down on gold."

A final flourish and he ended the tune, and met Maggie's lugubrious face.

"Why, Minstrel Songsmith," she fluttered. "I didn't know you cared. That's the nicest thing you've ever said about me!" And she flicked the dregs of her wine into his face and broke into a laugh that was half maidenly giggle and half witchy cackle. "I only wish you'd thought to sing that ditty before my worthy admirers began to press their suits. You'd have no doubt saved me a lot of trouble!"

He bowed gallantly and saluted by touching his fiddle bow to his forehead. "What can I say, milady? Riding with you these past few days has provided me with new inspiration."

"Pickle it, minstrel," she grinned. "I don't suppose anybody

60

around here would be interested to know what I've decided to do about this whole situation?"

Sybil had started clearing the table, but now she interrupted seriously. "Maybe you'd best wait till I've taken a few sightings before you jump one way or the other, dearie."

Maggie sobered and apologized quickly. "Of course, Aunt Sybil. I was going to ask. Please, could we see what the hunters are doing now? And also—do you suppose you could find out if there are any other unicorns in the forest Moonshine could talk to? And maybe, if it's not too much trouble, perhaps we could see about Winnie and the King and the baby?"

"Yes," Colin agreed, "I'd like to find out how all that curse business is going."

Sybil nodded and smoothed her skirts beneath her, situating herself comfortably before her ball. "Let me see now," she said, placing one hand carefully on each side of the crystal and gazing into it. "I think we'll do the palace first. I'm dreadfully concerned about the baby too, now that you bring it up. Ball," she addressed the globe in tones that brooked no nonsense. "Show us the King, please, and what's going on in the royal family quarters."

"If it's not too embarrassing," Colin added, earning himself harsh looks from both women. He continued to stare with wide innocent eyes into the crystal.

Shattering rainbows splintered themselves around the room, green, sapphire, pink, orange and red, harlequining the people with polychrome spangles of light and gilding the floor and walls before clearing.

The royal nursery, a room as cold and stony as any other castle chamber, was softened by screens of gilt and rose pink, tapestries depicting insipid-looking big-eyed animals, including a particularly unrealistic dragon. Beside a gilt cradle carved with all manner of hearts and flowers there stood a sturdy table, currently occupied by a large pink baby with hair like copper wire and a voice like a choir of banshees.

Queen Amberwine, more distressed and less well-groomed than Maggie had seen her look in her entire life, leaned over the child, attempting to free a lock of her long golden hair from the baby's sticky grasp. A platoon of ladies-in-waiting fluttered ineffectually, offering suggestions and comments, but no help.

"Why, she isn't wet at all, the little minx!" the Lady Elise announced after visually checking the appropriate portion of the child's body. "And she doesn't want anything to eat. I think she's just crying for attention, milady. 'Tis best not to spoil children."

"Dearest Elise," Winnie said, "I shall be only too glad to hear your views on child rearing AFTER you have helped me convince my daughter she is not a hair ornament. Please remove her. This hurts."

Aunt Sybil shook her crystal experimentally. "That's very good, ball. We're happy to know the little darling is dry and well-fed, and that Amberwine is awake again. But what about the curse? And where's the King?" To Colin and Maggie she commented, "One has to be firm, don't you know. Even the finest crystals can be erratic at times, and think you'll settle for just any old vision."

Colin stared thoughtfully into the ball as it rearranged itself, its picture dissolving into colored clouds which dissolved into the rainbows again before dissolving for a brief moment into clear crystal. "Do you suppose the curse can have started already? Lady Elise sounded angry at the baby."

"Some people are always angry," Sybil answered, carefully not looking at her niece. Another shower of rainbows jigged around the room. From the center of the crystal, waves broke outward, threatening to crash onto Sybil's best linen cloth.

Then, as suddenly as the waves had rolled to the fore, they receded, leaving behind an image of the sea serpent hunter, *Snake's Bane,* wallowing in calm seas backed by the purple tinged peaks of a distant mountain range.

"I think my crystal is showing off," Sybil said, tapping it with her fingernail. "I get company so seldom; it likes to put on a good show for a sighting. But we've no time for that today, dearie," she said into the ball. "Now, be a good thing and show me King Rowan, if you will."

At that, the ball blurred a sulky gray, then focused slowly on board the ship. Roari Rowan's orange-maned head towered above everything on deck except the mainmast.

"I say, I wonder what Sir Cyril Perchingbird's doing at sea?" Colin said. "He's the chief archivist at the palace. You wouldn't believe what he knows about lullabyes."

"And *I* wonder what the King's doing at sea," Maggie said. "How am I supposed to give him back this crown if he won't stay put? I certainly don't intend to swim after him."

The King was having difficulties of his own. 'I should have known better than to get aboard this thing," he roared. "Infantrymen don't belong on ships! Anybody knows that!"

"Ah well, yer 'ighness," said a wizened little man Maggie

recognized as Colin's friend, Bosun Ned Pinchpurse, a former pirate, " 'Tis unusual weather we're 'avin.' "

"Unreliable if you ask me. At this rate it will take us two MONTHS by sea instead of two weeks. We could travel cross-country in half the time."

Sir Cyril's oiled serpent-gut slicker, worn to protect him from nonexistent spray and wind, crackled as he paced the deck. High above the *Bane*'s decks, the dragons Grizel and Grimley indulged themselves in loop-the-loops and aerial acrobatics as they circled the ship, occasionally dipping low enough to cause the slack sail to flap fitfully. Perchingbird examined a battered scroll, sighing and shaking his head as he did so. "It clearly shows right here that if we come up on the sea side of the glacier—" he pondered aloud.

"It doesn't take a learned man to see that the journey's shorter by sea in good weather, m'lord Archivist," one of the other lords answered loftily. "But the fact is, sailing ships happen to need wind for their sails or—"

He fell to the deck as a red-and-gold scaled missile the size of the King's stables zoomed past him. Grimley still enjoyed watching humans cower once in awhile. The force of the dragon's passing caused the ship's timbers to quiver in the best nautical tradition.

"Blow me down!" swore the sailor who was helping Bosun Pinchpurse uncoil a line.

"Nearly did at that, didn't 'e?" Pinchpurse winked in the direction of the fallen lord, then looked up, shielding his eyes with the flat of his hand while he watched the crimson dragon fly belly-up against the sun while his blue-green mate flew figure eights around him. Then, looking away, the bosun squinted at Sir Cyril, who was trying to maintain his balance on the uncooperative deck.

"Hey, there, m'Lord. You talk to yon critters, doan't you? Like young Songsmith's pussycat used to?"

"Not exactly," Sir Cyril answered. "I use their own sound. The cat apparently communicated on a more supernatural level."

"Whatever. Why doan't you ask 'em if they'd be so kind as to stop messin' about up there and put their lazy tails to work makin' wind for this vessel?"

The image faded in another splatter of color.

"Well," Sybil said. "It looks like you're going to have a bit of a wait for the King, dearie, if he's to be gone all those weeks."

"No matter," Maggie said. "We can use the time to find

another unicorn and get this maidenhood business cleared up—it would be nice to have that out of the way, anyway, just in case Rowan proves difficult.''

She outlined for them her conversation with Moonshine, ending with the solution that had occured to her.

"Very sensible," Sybil said. "But had you considered that by binding him to you and taking him all over the countryside you're putting Moonshine in grave danger? No matter where you go, there'll be people—and from what you've told me, I should think there'll be unicorn hunters all over the woods. You can disguise yourself if you like, though once you're away from here I doubt you'd be recognized anyway. But a unicorn is always very obviously a unicorn.''

Maggie's face fell. As her aunt had pointed out, the major problem still faced them. Whatever she did about finding other unicorns or giving back crowns, the woods would still be full of huntsmen. Moonshine was as elusive as the wind on his own, but hampered by her he wouldn't be easily able to slip from the hunters' clutches. He would need her help, and she wasn't sure even that would be enough. Though her magic could be turned to self-defense if she used a lot of ingenuity and concentration, she could scarcely count on it to defend both herself and Moonshine— and Colin Songsmith wasn't any more a warrior than she was.

Sybil patted her shoulder and gazed into the crystal again. "Don't you fret about it, child. I have a little idea. But first, we can just have a look, now can't we, and see where those young men are? Then you and Moonshine and young Colin can simply avoid that part of the forest.''

Humming Colin's tune about Maggie under her breath, Sybil called for a vision of the hunters.

The requisite rainbows again wheeled around the room, the glass cleared, and a walk-in fireplace at the tavern at Fort Iceworm formed in the crystal's center.

"Bother," Sybil said, using her strongest invective. "This isn't what I wanted at all. Must have been some interference from my humming your song, Colin.''

The glass showed Sir William and Granny Brown standing beside Granny's ale-brewing cauldron. Granny stirred the mixture in the kettle with slashing swipes of her wooden paddle. "Don't you raise your voice to ME, Willie Hood," the old lady snapped. "Or you'll likely spoil the brew.''

Maggie grinned and drew her chair closer to the table. "Let's keep this vision anyway," she said. "I want to hear how they're getting along, now that they've driven me away. I'll wager the whole castle is a complete shambles by now.''

Sybil smiled to herself and held the vision.

The foreshortened figure of Sir William said, ''Your pardon, Mother Brown. But she's had her chance. I told those lads that the one who came back with proof of the most valiant deed would win her hand and I mean to bide by my word.''

''He didn't say anything about unicorns,'' Maggie remarked, puzzled.

''He probably doesn't know. We ought to have realized Leofwin and Jivemgood wouldn't mention it. If you were a unicorn hunter bent on taking a rare beast like Moonshine from the lands of a lord with your father's temper, would YOU tell him about it?'' Colin asked.

''I only helped you, Willie,'' Granny Brown's words snapped off like icicles, ''to teach the girl that it isn't good for a right-minded witch to stay in the company of a—to avoid her responsibilities. I wasn't trying to help you marry her off to any of those noble numbskulls. They're as worthless a lot as I've ever seen in all my born days, and I advise you to send out our village lads to round them up and bring them back so you can send them packing.''

Sir William's face turned eggplant-colored, and he drew himself up to his full insignificant height. ''I am lord of this castle, Goodwitch, and my word is law. I have said that the most valiant deed done by one of those numbsk—noble gentlemen—shall win my daughter and indeed it shall. And for your information, I let them know that for MY money, I held the most valiant deed ANY of them could accomplish would be to bring Maggie back.''

''My Lord Son-in-Law,'' Granny said with sugar-coated nastiness, ''how would you like to spend some time being even more bull-headed than you already are?''

Sir William's mouth dropped open and the glass clouded.

''Drat,'' Maggie said. ''I wanted to see that.''

''Where are Maggie's admirers?'' Colin asked.

Sybil concentrated on her ball again but this time it refused to focus. A blur of green and brown that seemed to be forest bounced within the globe for a moment, before the ball caught in quick succession several wraith-like, bewildered-looking figures on horseback, wandering around in another blotch of green and brown.

''Gracious,'' Sybil said. ''It simply won't work properly at all some days unless one can give it specific places or people.''

"Try Prince Leofwin," Maggie suggested. "He's the worst of them."

But no matter how Sybil concentrated, she received only the image of bouncing greenery.

"Then how about Count Jivemgood?" Colin asked. But the crystal wandered aimlessly through hazy forest scenes before it finally settled in seeming desperation on the running form of a lean gray wolf, from which it stubbornly refused to budge.

Maggie tried again. "If it can't show us unicorn hunters, maybe it will show us the nearest unicorn we can talk to about Moonshine's Creed?"

Sybil brightened. "Oh, yes, I'm sure it can manage that. Ball, show us the nearest unicorn."

After its usual prismatic display, the ball revealed Moonshine searching Sybil's lawn for bits of uneaten carrot.

"Not THAT unicorn, you foolish bauble!" Sybil cried, exasperated. "Do you suppose I need *you* to be present in his present when it's my garden he's dining on? We want to see the NEXT nearest unicorn."

But none of her further instructions or entreaties were sufficient to produce another clear image within the crystal, which resorted to flipping from Moonshine to the wolf to the bouncing greenery and back again in such rapid succession that soon everything was a uniform green and gray striped pattern.

"Bother," Sybil said.

"I suppose we'll just have to find another unicorn ourselves," Maggie sighed. "I don't guess you could lend me that little silver mirror again? The one you had shown me three visions so I could find Winnie and the gypsies?" Without Sybil's mirror, Maggie and Colin would have had a difficult time locating Winnie, much less rescuing her.

But Sybil was shaking her head. "No, child, I'm afraid not. As you can see, my powers are a bit erratic today. They don't get a workout like this very often, you know, and the ball is temperamental sometimes. Even under the best of circumstances, it's hard to lend the same magic out twice. Three wishes are three wishes, even for family."

Maggie's face fell, and Sybil hugged her, adding more cheerfully, "Chin up, dearie. With all that forest around you and the hunters AND the unicorns, how would you know where any of you were, anyway?"

Colin reluctantly agreed. "I can see where in a magic mirror one tree might look pretty much like another. Landmarks probably wouldn't be all that easy to find."

"Well," Maggie said after the long silence that followed Colin's unfortunately perceptive remarks. "If you can't help, I suppose we'll just have to get on the best we can."

She turned toward the door but Sybil pulled her back down into her chair. "Don't be so hasty, girl. I didn't say I couldn't help at all."

Taking the ball from the table, she placed it carefully back on the mantle before opening a cupboard from which she drew a roll of ribbon-tied vellum. "I only said I couldn't give you MY magic. But I do happen to know someone else who can help you if anyone can."

Colin moved his fiddle and bow from the table, and leaned across the map Sybil unrolled onto the linen cloth. Maggie touched the vellum's surface with wondering fingers. Real maps were not common outside the archives. In a land with one main road, few journeys were undertaken requiring a chart. This map was exceptional even at that, however, for its surface was embellished with drawings of animals, trees, and something else that could not have been handier; streams, rivers, lakes and waterways of all kinds.

"Beautiful work, isn't it?" Sybil said proudly. "He made it himself. He's very clever at that sort of thing, quite aside from his prowess as a master of disguise."

"Who?" Colin asked.

"The man you must go see—an old beau of mine." Her cheeks glowed burgundy. "The mighty and mysterious, but really very nice, Wizard Raspberry. If anyone can help you, he can."

"I must not fail again, O Wulfric," the nymph said, clenching her dainty fist and shaking it for emphasis. "I must not disappoint the Dark Pilgrim. He *needs* the beasts for his great work, to ensure the triumph of our cause."

Wulfric whined agreement and insinuated his snout into her fist. He had finished feeding and had come to make his report, to find Her sorely distracted, pacing the hive-like base camp like a caged thing while Her comrades swarmed through the caves, lashing together fresh-stripped poles to gate the entrances of two of the caves. She planned that these should serve as corrals where more than a single unicorn could be held; she could thus avoid the arduous trip to Worm's Roost after each capture.

But She had not succeeded in capturing the beast She most recently sought to win for the cause, and blamed Herself.

Wulfric had retained his wolf form so that She might take comfort in caressing his fur and talking to him as She never did when he was in human guise. He hated changing into man form anyway. He did not enjoy having to walk on two legs, and losing so much of his sense of smell. He was a fine wolf, but a poor specimen of a man; the way other men treated him when he was one of them told him so. Even She liked him better as a wolf, as he knew from her behavior. So he waited to transform himself awhile longer, and licked her hand instead.

"I have a confession to make, loyal friend," she confided. "I know the reason I failed. The last unicorn was denied me—for she was *there*, I promise you—because I have spared, from foolish sentiment, another beast, she who purifies the stream I used to guard near the hamlet of Everclear. I have harbored a weak sympathy for the townsmen who know of the animal and depend on her, but now I see that neither my attachment for them nor theirs for the beast must interfere with our great task. If the townsmen seek to prevent us from taking the beast, they will have to be dealt with." And she smiled bravely down at him and tossed her golden curls back over her shoulders in a determined gesture.

With an excited whimper full of love for his mettlesome little leader, Wulfric began the process that altered his form, and in a few moments stood up beside her as the counterfeit Count Jivemgood.

"Ah, Sally," he said. "Am I not your faithful servant in all you would accomplish? I bring you great good news that will end your self-reproach and help you achieve all you desire." He had to tame his voice back down from an elation-escalated howl before he could continue. "For at that castle did I not meet a great and bloody warrior to help you win your cause? Even now does he not travel in seven-league boots to meet you and to help us capture beasts and to school our comrades in warrior ways? And did I not also see another unicorn coming this way, and on his back the female who is the reviled kin of the Dark Pilgrim? Will not the vanquishment of those two be pleasing to the Dark Pilgrim?"

Sally leapt to her feet and threw her arms around him, kissing his hairy cheek. "Oh, it *will*, Wulfric, surely it will indeed! You're a staunch companion if ever any girl had one! I'm certain the Dark Pilgrim will reward you by finding a way to release you from your affliction so you'll never have to turn back into a man again, even in broadest daylight.

"And, oh, I know you're very tired, but perhaps we could go together, I in my whirlwind and you in wolf form, to greet our new ally? I can show him the way back here, while you lure that other beast and the traitor-girl within reach of our band."

"It is good, your plan," Wulfric agreed, and dropped to all fours.

After a restless night and a good breakfast, Colin and Maggie stuffed their saddlebags full of fresh raspberry tarts; some for themselves and some a present from Aunt Sybil to the wizard. Adding to these two rounds of cheese, a loaf of bread apiece, and a cloth bag of salted seeds and nuts, they mounted.

"I'll keep a close watch in my crystal," Sybil promised, as Maggie leaned down from Moonshine's back to give her a final peck on the cheek. "If I see anything that could be useful to you, I'll send a message by Budgie." Budgie, Aunt Sybil's familiar, usually flew freely in the forest near the cottage, but was always available to carry whatever messages his mistress had to send. He trilled now from his perch at the windowsill, as if in affirmation that they needn't worry; he was on the job.

Thus reassured, the travelers set out. They journeyed for two days, following the wizard's map, and though they grew damp around the edges from fording so many streams, they experienced no serious catastrophes. Even the weather was fair. Overhead, lapis skies were frilled with only the most ornamental lacy white clouds. The forest smelled fresh, and its floor was carpeted with spongy emerald moss that made traveling pleasant and easy.

After Moonshine purified the streams they crossed, the water acquired a flavor that was so sweet and pure as to be almost intoxicating. Bright fish flashed across polished stones in the shallows, while deeper places drowsed in cool green shadow. Rabbits and squirrels, moose and fox crossed their path. Colin sang all the new songs he'd learned at court, leaving out only the lullabyes. Maggie sang too, in her husky, slightly off-key voice, and laughed until her sides ached.

Toward dusk of the second evening, they camped beside a wide, bubbling stream. Maggie conjured a smokeless campfire and settled down next to it.

"Court must be the most fascinating place," she remarked, her head still full of the songs he'd sung that day. "All those songs, all the music and dancing and feasting, all those people from different places with so many stories to tell. I expect you must be very anxious to get back."

Colin sprawled comfortably in the forked roots of a spruce tree, hands cupped behind his head, boots off, chewing contentedly on a blade of sweetgrass.

"Oh, I expect I can wait," he said. "It's very interesting at first, of course. There *is* all that music and dancing. But you must remember, I'm PLAYING the music much of the time instead of being entertained myself. And the people—I'll admit everybody seems very witty and charming and amusing, to begin with. Until you begin to understand that the jokes are often not meant to be funny, at least not to whoever's the butt of them. People aren't exactly over-scrupulous about confining their use of magic to authorized practice, either. Lady Janet Swanneck broke out in the most frightful warts, for instance, just before she was supposed to meet her husband-to-be. Which not only discomfited Lady Janet but also started the rumor that her suitor, who passed over Janet's elder cousin Maide to court her, was a transformed toad. You see how those things get out of hand?"

Maggie nodded, smiling, and turned over the cheese sandwich she was toasting in the fire.

Colin sighed. "One almost envies the generals. At least they get to wear armor to protect them from some of the backstabbing." He chewed the sweetgrass thoughtfully for awhile and continued. "Do you know, the song Rowan wanted me to compose for you wasn't the first one that's given me difficulty since I joined the staff."

"You? Having trouble thinking up songs? I don't believe it!" she scoffed. Ever since she'd known him, he'd practically exhaled a freshly composed verse with each breath.

"I just haven't had the time, what with following the King around and playing all of his favorites, altering the standard forms to fit his daring deeds—which so far have been confined to levying one unpopular tax and naming you princess. He hasn't many friends of his own in court yet, so he likes me to be there to listen to him when he wants to talk and drink with him when he wants to get drunk. And I can tell you," Colin rolled his eyes to convey suffering martyrdom, "when that whittled-down frost giant gets drunk, it takes me weeks to recover!"

"I seem to recall something about that," Maggie said, her smile deepening as she remembered Colin's first attempt to keep up with the King's remarkable capacity for strong drink. Colin had not fared very well that time, either. "And I suppose you're right about court. I probably wouldn't like it at all. I keep forgetting the only people who have time for all those balls and feasts are the ones who have someone else to do the work for them. With my luck, I'd be working while everyone else was dancing.''

Colin grinned at her forlorn tone, then said solemnly, ''I know just what you mean. I'm always much too busy to enjoy myself, what with playing and all of the other social duties that are expected of me. Wenching, for example.'' He sighed a deep, put-upon sigh, wriggling his toes luxuriously and shifting position, watching her reaction from beneath lashes lazily lowered to half mast. ''Now that takes a tremendous hunk out of my average day at court. An honest musician like me can scarcely get any work done at all for all the time and trouble it takes to keep the court ladies happy.''

Moonshine, grazing nearby, lifted his head and snorted, eying Colin severely.

''Beg your pardon,'' Colin half rose from his lounging position and bowed as elegantly as possible. ''I quite forgot there were unicorns present.''

Maggie gnawed reflectively on her cheese sandwich, then gestured with it, asking, ''And this lady you were telling Moonshine about earlier—whatsername—Adelaide? Adeline? Agatha? Al—wha—what!?'' she cried, leaping up, suddenly empty-handed.

The bandit of a raven who had swooped down to pluck her sandwich from her fingers flitted out of reach onto a poplar limb. He cocked his head sideways, after each peck he took at Maggie's sandwich, and regarded them with a look that said he found the food acceptable but was naturally used to more elegant fare.

He was still there the following morning when they arose. According to the wizard's map, they were not to cross the stream on whose banks they were camped, but were rather to follow it. It flowed in a peculiar fashion, counter to the southwesterly course of the Troutroute River.

''Well,'' Colin said cheerfully, when Maggie had replaced the map. ''At least we won't get lost. We even have a guide.'' The raven flapped in circles above them as they mounted and rode along the stream's bank.

Before long, however, they found the footing near the water's edge swampy and uncertain. Tall grasses hid pockets of water. Seemingly solid ground turned to mud that sucked the horse's hooves deep, making every step an incredible effort.

The twelfth time Roundelay mired a hoof in an innocent-looking patch of grass and sank to her belly in an all-engulfing

71

pit, Colin dismounted and led her forward, for approximately two steps. Then he too stepped into gentle green grass that on involuntary closer investigation turned out to be a minor channel of the stream. He swore, deeply and heartily.

Moonshine tsk-tsked, in spite of the fact that even he had been provoked into using one of the stronger unicorn oaths, when trying to tear the mud from his hooves with his horn.

Above them, the raven circled and cawed.

"You might pull that little trick you did last year out of your hat NOW, when it would really be useful," Colin complained, floundering for dry ground. "While I didn't care much for climbing into that oversized basket you made when I was expected to use it to rescue a dragon, I wouldn't mind having it to float downstream in now, instead of having to battle *this* muck."

Maggie glanced at the water dubiously. "You mean you want to ride on the water when we don't HAVE to?" Maggie disliked water. She remembered all too clearly the nightmarish story her Granny told her as a girl of a Brown ancestress who'd been melted in her own dishwater by a cagey enemy. Not that Maggie herself had ever personally shown the slightest tendency to dissolve, but one couldn't be too careful. Other than the scrub water necessary to work her magic and an occasional wash behind her ears, she generally avoided the stuff altogether. And in this case, even if she didn't melt, she could very well drown, couldn't she? It wasn't as if she was like Colin, who was descended from mer people and swam like a fish.

"If we keep on this way," he pointed out, "We're either going to be wet to our ears or we'll have to go so far from the banks to find solid footing we may lose the stream entirely. Then we'd never find your aunt's friend."

Against her better judgment, Maggie had to admit he was probably right. She found a slightly drier patch of swampy ground than the one Colin was sunk in, and dismounted.

While he gathered a huge mound of reeds and grasses, she plaited them together, faster than his eyes could follow. Before it should have been possible, the hillock of grasses had become a bowl-shaped basket large enough to accommodate two people. Moonshine watched the proceedings with great interest.

"I could probably make this large enough to hold you," Maggie offered, catching his eye. "But I have to draw the line at Colin's mare. She'd sink us all."

Moonshine quickly demurred. "Nay, maiden. It is given to unicorn kind to purify the waters, not to ride upon them. I will

72

journey with the horse and help her keep close by the bank, so that we do not become sundered, one from the other.''

"That's very decent of you," Colin said.

Then, in an unprecedented exhibition of bravery (for him, at least), he climbed into the basket-boat and held onto the bank by gripping a projecting tree root until Maggie persuaded herself to climb aboard.

Since they were going downstream, they saw no particular need for oars or paddles—or at any rate, they didn't see the need until the boat began to spin like a saucer.

Maggie shrieked and covered her head with both arms, and hugged the bottom of the boat as it sped down the sliver of silvery water, bumping the banks and flirting with low-hanging branches that threatened to sweep the passengers into the swift, shallow current.

The raven saw them ducking and grabbing at branches and seemed to find their activity amusing. He dived at them again and again, uttering gravelly cries and fanning them with his wings.

"Do you suppose he wants more sandwich?" Colin asked.

"I don't know what the cheeky thing wants," Maggie growled back up at him, "But he makes ME want a slingshot."

In spite of her brave words, she stayed determinedly huddled in the bottom of the boat. She didn't see the water rush so quickly past an upended log that the log seemed to be swimming toward them. Neither did she watch the long olive shadows stripe across the crystal waters, light, dark, light, dark, as the basket whirled between ranks of spiraling spruce. And she missed the otter who stared at them curiously for only a moment before apparently deciding they had a good idea and sliding into the water himself.

But Colin saw and felt everything, and lay with his feet on one side of the boat, his back braced against the other, arms outflung around the edges, reveling in it all. He breathed deeply of greenery-spiced air sweetened with the fragrance of the wildflowers which nodded in a neighborly fashion as the boat passed. As naturally as he breathed, and smelled, and saw, he started to sing. He sang just to sing, for the joy of it, imitating the birds and pipes and harps and fiddles, making nonsense sounds, singing lyrics only half-remembered, and slapping his legs in time with the companionable rhythm of Moonshine's and Roundelay's hoofbeats in the woods nearby.

From her vantage point at the bottom of the basket, Maggie stared dizzily up at him. "You're daft. You know that, don't you? We shall be dashed to pieces or drowned any moment now in this ill-begotten creation of mine and you're warbling away like an overblown relative of Aunt Sybil's Budgie.''

He bawled out his chorus before answering, and gave her sodden braids a playful tug. "Don't be stuffy. This is fun if you'll just relax. Look, why don't you join me in a chorus or two, and maybe you'll forget to be frightened.''

"I'm NOT frightened. I merely have no wish to face death sounding as if I'm on some holiday outing.''

"Just pretend a little. Come on now. I'm really *quite* a wonderful song leader, everyone says so, particularly on chanteys. Try this. Repeat after me: 'And it's hey-hi-ho and away to the rolling sea.' ''

That chorus cheered Maggie considerably. At least they were NOT on the rolling sea, merely a little stream. She sat up and flung her braids back so they streamed over the side of the basket, and favored Colin with a cautious, somewhat resentful stare. It was all very well for him. He *liked* water. The same mer blood that made him like water made him like to sing like a common siren, if without the usual disastrous results to seagoing vessels.

The boat tipped gracefully round again as his voice soared on a high note and sailed right up there for awhile. The harmony between the song and the boat's swirling, tilting onward rush caught Maggie too, and she scarcely knew when it was she started singing. Her voice blended with the raven's as much as with Colin's, but somehow everything around them made music; their voices, the water's swish and splatter, the clopping hooves running beside the stream, the dip and twirl of the basket, the raven, who not only contributed his voice but danced a crazy counterpoint overhead. Whether their voices drove him to keep his distance or he had simply tired of diving at them was impossible to tell, but he stayed in the sky and stopped annoying them.

They passed from stands of mostly small trees into vast overhanging canopies of large ones, from mostly purple flowers to mostly yellow and white ones, from muddy banks to sandy beaches, and from seeing nothing beyond them but dense trees to suddenly spotting through a break in those trees a glistening range of snow-capped mountains.

Colin, without missing a beat, pointed out an owl swooping across the stream far beyond them. Maggie whooped and nearly upset the boat when she spotted a tufty-eared lynx and her kittens drinking within touching distance of their basket.

Moonshine halted then, and before the mother lynx could be frightened away by Maggie's racket, diplomatically dipped his horn into the stream to reassure the lynx that they were interested in her welfare, not in harming her or her kittens.

Some time later they passed a beaver dam which spanned another inlet to the creek. The beaver popped from his lodge and slapped the water indignantly for silence. He was ignored.

They rode like that all day long, singing and laughing and talking and coming close to a soaking more than once. As darkness approached, they glided out of a broad meadow with a spectacular view of the Majestic Mountains. The range was so named, Colin explained, because the explorer who discovered them wished to honor the King, but Argonia happened to be between kings at the time and who knew but what the new ruler might not be a queen? So the explorer played it safe and simply labeled his find Majestic.

A short time later the boat swept out of the meadow and into a woods, and then a peculiar incident occurred which was to color the rest of their journey.

They heard a thump, as if some creature had fallen from the sky. Moonshine and Roundelay stopped, their ears pricked forward. The deep, webbed shadows cast by the tamarack and tall cedars appeared to gather themselves quickly together and leap— to splash suddenly downwards a short distance from their boat. For just a moment, Maggie had the impression of a booted foot and leg, but she had no time to see if the rest of the body would follow, since their boat chose that time to turn once more in the current. When they swung back again, the boot and leg had disappeared, the shadows were gathering on the other side of the stream, and then, abruptly, lifted. Once more the sunlight played among the trees as it had before.

All of them were shaken. Only Moonshine's presence kept the mare Roundelay from fleeing. Colin and Maggie stopped singing, and watched the mossy ground for other strange presences. The woods began to seem sinister—instead of a friendly carpet, the moss now smothered the ground, crept along tree roots and cloaked branches. Yet another variety of moss dripped down from the same branches, trailing from them like the long green hair of strangled sirens.

But quite apart from the unwholesome atmosphere, the waning light and the density of the trees made maneuvering more difficult, particularly since the banks were high and the stream was unusually broad at this point.

Seemingly bound for imminent collision, they snarled instead in a tangle of exposed tree roots. Grasping spectral fingers could not have been more unsettling or inconvenient. Maggie hastily began searching for a place to pull the basket out of the stream for the night.

She was still searching when they rounded the next bend. There, directly ahead of them in the very middle of the stream, sat the smallest castle either of them had ever seen. More cottage-sized than castle-sized, it nevertheless boasted the standard turrets, and sported a tower at each corner, and a drawbridge and a moat, into which the stream fed, circling the castle and making an island of it.

The raven, absent since the boat first entered the woods, suddenly reappeared, croaking and cawing in a triumphant, raucous voice.

And slowly, with a creaking as painful as bones breaking on an inquisitor's rack, the drawbridge lowered. Moonshine stopped in his tracks, and Roundelay nickered nervously. Colin and Maggie ceased breathing, while their eyes darted from bank to bank, seeking some handhold they might use to pull their craft from the water before it delivered them up to whatever dwelled within those mossy walls.

But the castle's occupant didn't wait for the boat. As Colin and Maggie watched with horrified fascination, a great, long snout appeared on the bridge, followed by revolting, shaggy forefeet with talons as long as knitting needles. Soon the rest of the monster lumbered onto the bridge.

They had no hope that it failed to see them, for it ogled them with enormous, popping red eyes, larger than dinner plates and alight with malicious glee. The snout hung below its disgusting, pendulous abdomen, and the entire fearsome apparition was coated with green slime and poisonous-looking growths, covering what looked like razor-sharp scales.

A slack, purplish tongue lolled from between fangs that would have done honor to the largest of bears. Its back was thronged with lethal spikes, and a thick ruff of stiff green hair wound itself around the monster's neck.

The boat skimmed ever closer to the bridge, and the monster reared, roaring with a voice like a forest fire, and clawed the air, as if limbering its talons to flay them as soon as they came in reach.

Moonshine trumpeted and pawed the ground, then, lowering his head, he made ready to charge. He sent a last cry to Maggie. "Fear not, gentle maiden! I shall protect you from harm if I die in the attempt!" And launched himself at the monster.

76

CHAPTER 6

Wulfric had ample opportunity to change from wolf form back into the guise of Count Jivemgood, for he heard Prince Leofwin swearing half a league before he smelled him.

"You certainly took your time," the prince complained when Wulfric detached himself from the night to stand before the nobleman's campfire. "I thought to meet you long before this— but, say, you must have passed me. How did you get here ahead of me? Even in this fancy footwear it's still taken me three days and a seven-league charley horse to make it this far."

The seven-league boots were propped against the log on which the prince sat vigorously massaging his shins. His feet were red and blistered—the poet's were several sizes smaller. Wulfric's lower jaw dropped in a human parody of his wolf-grin. Give him four fleet paws any night.

Suddenly the campfire flared as though in a high wind. Leaves hurtled themselves suicidally into the flames. And from the black woods behind the gray-haired were-man, a sigh brushed the trees. Nearer and louder, the sigh became the rattle of dry leaves, and the writhing of new leaves against each other. Stalwart trees quaked to their roots.

Then, with a final rush, the fire blossomed more brightly than ever before it was smothered with earth and wet leaves. Showering sparks as high as Wulfric's head, it flickered and all but died. Beyond its embers Leofwin saw a cyclone spin into his camp.

The whirlwind spun itself down slowly, until the debris that had formed its substance fell to the ground and Leofwin saw a beautiful woman pirouette gracefully on one toe until she faced him.

Leofwin knew the type. Water nixie. Nymph. Long blond hair, big green eyes. Body that wouldn't quit. They were all alike. He'd met plenty on his campaigns. He leered at her, the pain in his feet and legs forgotten. "Well, well, Count, old chum. What have we here?" he asked. "Kind of you to consider my needs—"

"On your knees, churl," Wulfric snarled. "Bow your unworthy head to the field marshal of our gallant cause, the battle maiden, Sally Forth."

* * *

77

"No, Moonshine!" Maggie cried, staring in horror as the unicorn charged the hideous moat monster. "Wait!" But already Moonshine was plunging headlong at the slimy apparition. Maggie hollered and gestured, rising first to her knees and then to her feet trying to attract Moonshine's attention.

"Don't!" Colin yelled, but by then it was too late. The basket boat tipped as Maggie stood, and flopped itself over, dumping both witch and minstrel into the frigid waters.

Maggie flailed and screamed angrily, "Hellp! Save me, dammit! Can't you see I'm drowning?"

Colin offered her his hand. "Try standing up," he suggested. "It's only knee deep."

Together they sloshed to shore. "Pah!" she spat the word out along with the water. "I knew I shouldn't have trusted a man who likes boats."

"And *I* never should have trusted a witch with no more sense than to stand up in one," he spat back, then nodded to where the unicorn and the monster stood, quietly, barely a cart length between them as they studied each other. "Look there," Colin whispered, pointing. "Isn't that curious, though?"

The monster made no threatening movements toward Moonshine, but the unicorn rolled his eyes and shook his mane nervously. "This thing smells odd, Maiden," he told Maggie. "Almost it smells—"

"Come on," Maggie pulled at Colin's arm. "Before that thing charges him."

But Colin pulled back, and when she turned around to give him a piece of her mind, he pointed to the monster's feet, shambling once more in an odd, blind, cumbersome gait towards the unicorn. "Look at that, will you?" Colin insisted, "At his feet, there, below all that shaggy stuff. I don't believe I can truthfully say I've ever seen a moat monster in its stocking feet before, have you?"

Maggie stopped sputtering and squinted through her dripping lashes.

Even in the waning light she could see that the monster was indeed wearing, under his monster feet, a pair of socks that seemed to be knit from the remnants of someone's ragbag. Indeed, they looked ready to return to the ragbag again, for the heel on one foot and the great toe on the other were worn through the pattern of variegated stripes. A moat monster wearing socks meant only one thing to Maggie.

"Well," she sighed with no small relief, "I hope Aunt Sybil's tarts haven't gotten mashed."

"Yes," Colin agreed. "Looks hungry, doesn't he? We'll just have to take your aunt's word for it that he's as benevolent as she said. She might have gone into more detail about that master-of-disguise business, though. I wasn't prepared for anyone so flamboyant."

Approaching the monstrous wizard and the still-skittish unicorn, they heard a soft, pleasant voice speaking from between the enormous monster teeth. "Verily, you are a handsome creature," it said.

An ordinary-looking human hand draped up the monster's pendulous stomach and stretched towards the unicorn's flaring nose. "I thank you very much for purifying my moat. Yonder ducks and fish would thank you as well, had your companions not affrighted them."

Moonshine nickered, "My *companions* affrighted them? What do you suppose you did? Think not to trick ME with honeyed words and a kindly scent, varlet! Maiden!" The unicorn appealed to Maggie. "This thing would parlay with me. What am I to do? I would bespeak this creature to save you, but already I have sullied myself and gone against my Creed by associating with your minstrel-champion. Now you see what has become of it? Having once lowered myself, I'm expected to chitchat with any sort of vile hobgoblin who cares to pass the time of day! Whatever shall I say to such a creature?"

"Try 'you're welcome, mighty wizard' for openers," Maggie said. "And don't be such a snob, darling. This particular vile hobgoblin is a friend of the family. Wizard Raspberry, I presume?" she asked, extending her hand somewhere towards the end of the monster's snout.

The thing attempted to bend over her hand as if to kiss it or bite it with his gigantic teeth—shreds of birch bark, she could see now. But as he leaned forward, his head began to slide off. Maggie caught most of it in her arms as it peeled away from the top half of a bony individual of her father's generation.

The man sported a bushy beard and shaggy gray hair which stood out in all directions from having the monster's head pulled off over it. His ears also stuck out at acute angles from either side of his head, and were distinctly pointed. A tattered gown embroidered with crude chainstitched astrological designs clothed the half not covered by the monster's bottom portion. Seemingly oblivious to his strange appearance, the wizard examined his guests with eyes as shrewd and curious as those of the raven, which now perched on his shoulder. He seemed to think THEY were the funny-looking ones.

Maggie wrung her skirt out between her hands before wiping her fingers on it, then re-extended her hand to the unprepossessing wizard. "Pleased to meet you, I'm sure. Wizard Raspberry, isn't it? This is Colin Songsmith, the King's minstrel and my traveling companion, and this is Moonshine, who's a unicorn, as any fool can see. I'm Maggie Brown, daughter of Bronwyn, daughter of Maude, daughter of Oonaugh, but most important, I suppose, from your point of view, niece to Sybil." She ended her introduction with a sniffle and a sneeze.

The wizard pulled a handkerchief out of her ear and handed it to her. "Of course you are," he agreed kindly. "I'd have known who you were straight away if Jack here hadn't insisted you were marauding bandits. That's why I greeted you in costume. But please, come, you're wet, and you must be tired and hungry."

When they were sitting wrapped in blankets while their clothing dried by the wizard's fire, Maggie asked, "You call the raven Jack. Is he your familiar, then?"

Raspberry smiled. "Oh, no. We're just good friends. Like all the others." A sweeping gesture indicated the squirrels, rabbits, chipmunks, martins, ermine and mice who nested in nooks and crannies throughout the room. Nesting materials were abundant, for the room was littered with piles and piles of bark and old cloth. The animals made full use of it all. The ones who weren't napping stared at the newcomers from eyes shining like sparks in the candlelit room.

"They seem to like you," Colin said conversationally.

"We have a working relationship. They shelter here and share my garden whenever they wish, and I, in turn, use them for models for my disguises and drawings." He smiled indulgently at the mother squirrel nursing three babies, all of them cuddled into an old robe stacked atop a mound of bark. "Also, they make excellent paperweights."

One of the squirrels scrambled to get a better position at his mother's breast, and his tiny legs churned out a piece of bark. Maggie picked it up and started to restore it to the pile, when she saw the drawing, a charming sketch of the spotted buck rabbit who was currently sniffing and hopping among the crumbs on the wizard's table. "He almost looks as if he's moving," she said, comparing the sketch to the rabbit.

The wizard nodded and looked amused. She began to examine other sketches. Most of them were of forest creatures, drawn with the same lifelike quality, in realistic poses and attitudes. Many were clearly the models for the heads adorning the wizard's walls. The heads were hung as hunters might hang

80

trophies, or warriors their shields, but the wizard explained they were only the top portions of his various disguises. The majority of them were realistic replicas of deer, moose, bear or dragon, but a few were as wildly imaginative and outlandish as the moat monster.

Among the sketches and masks were some drawings of elves and faeries, and even one of a troll. A fetching charcoal depicting a pointy-eared child with the wizard's wide enigmatic grin was tacked above the mantle, and caught Maggie's eye.

"Self portrait of the artist at an early age?" she asked.

"My daughter," he replied with what she thought was a trace of sadness. "But, come now, you didn't travel all this way to talk about me, nor just to swim in my moat, either, I'll wager. Tell me, what service may I render?"

Maggie outlined their problems for him, with an occasional assist from Colin and from Moonshine, who knelt contentedly in a pile of straw in one corner of the room and noisily crunched carrots from the wizard's vegetable patch.

"I see," was all Raspberry said when she'd finished.

"Can you help?" she asked.

He smiled. "Partially. I can't give you any pointers on indefinitely maintaining your chastity, though I'm sure I could think of something if a pretty lass like you was looking for someone to *relieve* her of the burden—"

Moonshine stopped crunching carrots and glared, and Maggie flushed a shade deeper and shook her head.

"But as for Moonshine, I can provide some assistance."

Selecting a long strip of bark from beneath a dozing red fox, Raspberry wet the bark, then rolled it into a tight cone. From an earthenware crock he drew a glob of amber goo, which he liberally smeared with a fingertip along the edges of the cone. "Extra-sticky tree sap," he explained. "Wonderful for sticking things together."

They nodded and watched while he finished the cone, holding it up parallel to Moonshine's horn and studying it critically. Then, with a satisfied grunt, he set the cone in his lap and began passing his hands across it in strange designs.

"Stand back," he warned, as both Colin and Maggie crowded close in their curiosity over the mysterious cone. "This part is simple, but the spell I'm about to invoke is dangerous. It's a spell of invisibility, which I'll apply directly to this cone rather than to Moonshine's horn. That way you can just take the cone on and off without making the horn permanently disappear. But the spell can waste you away to nothing if you get in the way. I have to shield against it myself."

His inquisitive guests hastily removed themselves to their former positions on the opposite side of the table.

"Here we go!" he said, and intoned in a ceremonially deliberate voice.

> "Celery and grapefruit,
> Lettuce, melon, eye of newt.
> Broccoli and cauliflower!
> Grow much thinner in this hour.
> Water only thirst to slake;
> Shrink as slim as garter snake.
> Thinner thin than onion skin
> Till the light can pass within.
> Stir well in a glass receptacle!
> Now the thing is imperceptible!"

It was, too. As they watched and Raspberry chanted, the solid bark cone in his hands thinned and thinned and grew first translucent, then transparent, until, with the final word of the enchantment, it disappeared utterly.

Gingerly, Raspberry bore what seemed to be air to Moonshine, who watched him nervously. "What have you there, mighty wizard? Hold! Hold, I say! Let me look—"

"You can't look, silly," Maggie said. "That's the point of it all. It's invisible."

"Just a bit of millinery work, noble unicorn," Raspberry answered soothingly, "to make your identity less obvious."

Steadying Moonshine's twitching neck with one hand, the wizard fitted the "o" made by his fingers and thumb over the tip of the unicorn's horn with the other hand and slid the nothingness in his palm down until his hand rested on the unicorn's forehead. While the hand was sliding downward, the horn above the fingers disappeared. Moonshine crossed his eyes trying to see his own forehead.

"Is it really GONE?" he asked.

For an answer, Raspberry found a silver-backed, only slightly cracked, lady's hand mirror, and showed Moonshine his reflection with the cone of invisibility in place. Then he raised the cone, before the unicorn became unduly alarmed, to reveal the familiar opalescent horn.

He had to repeat the sequence several times before Moonshine was mollified. Then, laying the mirror aside, the wizard jiggled the cone against the base of Moonshine's horn.

"It's a bit loose. Perhaps we might tie a handkerchief around it when you gallop, though you shouldn't have any problems otherwise. It's not as effective as making your actual horn invisible, you understand, but I thought perhaps you'd like to be able to show it, in case you should meet those other unicorns you're seeking."

"Assuredly!" Moonshine said. "I wouldn't want them to mistake me for a HORSE!"

"No," Maggie said, "But it will be very handy to have any other humans we encounter think you're a horse. You can cover your hooves just by standing in something that conceals them."

"Are you going to clip his beard?" Colin asked.

Moonshine rolled his eyes again and Maggie answered quickly. "No, of course not. If anyone asks, I'll just say he's a very OLD horse, and we grow them bearded at Fort Iceworm for warmth."

But Colin's question had upset Moonshine. Glancing again at his hornless reflection in the wizard's mirror, he began to tremble. Maggie quickly removed the cone and tied it up with her own handkerchief, so she could keep track of it.

"That was VERY impressive," Colin said. "I'd drink to that any time."

"Ah, yes, drink!" the wizard said. "What will you have? Ale, wine, mead, moose milk?"

"You have all that?" Maggie asked, for she could see no signs in the small keep of brewing facilities or wine stores.

"No. Actually, all I have is water. But you may have anything you like." He filled earthenware tumblers with water from a pitcher and set them before his guests. "Go on. Just say what you'd prefer."

Colin sighed. How sad it was that the very magically gifted were so often a little deranged. Even Maggie was watching the wizard warily. But the poor man *had* provided a very effective disguise for Moonshine, which was what they'd asked him to do. To humor him and to be courteous, Colin sipped his water, saying, "Actually, I'd prefer ale but there's nothing like a cup of wa—ale?"

He nearly gagged on what tasted like Granny Brown's finest dark ale. Lowering his cup, he peered into the clear cold moat water it still contained, then cautiously raised the cup to his lips again and took another sip. "Ale. But—"

"A simple disguise," the wizard shrugged and grinned a

83

mischievous grin that made his pointed elvish ears look more appropriate than ever. "I could disguise the look of it, too, if you wish. I don't usually take the trouble here at home, though. All I eat is fish and vegetables and an occasional egg now and then. Most of the animals hereabouts are friends of mine, and it doesn't seem neighborly to hunt them. But I can make fish or vegetable hash taste like venison or paté de fois gras if I feel like it."

"Lovely!" Maggie exclaimed enthusiastically. "May I please have some cider? Hot and spiced would be wonderful."

"You and Maggie should open an inn together," Colin suggested, joking. "You could make a fortune between you with your magic making eggs taste like venison and hers expanding it into an entire roast deer in savory sauce, all with none of the trouble or expense of hunting a real deer."

"To the best of my knowledge," the wizard replied with mock arrogance, "Royal princesses, even reluctant ones, have *never* become innkeepers, no matter how profitable the venture might be."

Maggie laughed and raised her pseudo-cider in a toast, clinking tumblers with the wizard's container full of ersatz Ablemarlonian wine—Old Executioner '47, a very good year, he gave them to understand. "I've had enough of innkeeping AND princessing," she declared. "And I daresay the wizard keeps himself to himself out here because he likes being alone."

Raspberry chuckled and winked merrily at her. "Not all the company one has in normal society is so enchanting."

"Still," Colin argued, "I should think it would be boring out here in these woods all by yourself all the time with nothing to do but draw pictures and dress in funny costumes."

"If I remember correctly," the wizard said, "they do much the same thing at court, except they don't draw pictures. Besides, that's not all I do; I have my little projects as well, you know, and my garden. And people do seek me out now and then to ask for a spot of magic. What they pay helps provide me with what I can't make for myself, which isn't much. Usually I charge some commodity that will help with my projects, though that depends on the client."

"What projects, master wizard?" Maggie asked. She hadn't thought about a fee, though she should have. Even among friendly magicians who extended a certain amount of professional courtesy to each other, some fee had to be charged in order for the magic to be worth anything. Granny Brown had told her that often enough. But Maggie realized Raspberry was too polite to bring the subject up directly, so she asked, "Do you mean you practice learning extra skills your magic doesn't aid you with? Like my Granny does healing and ale brewing, which have nothing to do with transforming, and like Aunt Sybil practices metalsmithing to relax her from gazing into the present?"

"Yes," the wizard nodded, "Precisely like that. And like you go on quests to provide diversion from hearthcrafting."

"It's not really like that," she protested.

"And like Colin here performs real heroics to give himself a break from simply singing about them," the wizard finished.

Colin looked up, startled and pleased. He'd never thought of it that way before but now that the wise and mighty wizard mentioned it, he supposed one *could* look at the quests he'd undertaken in that light.

"I don't do anything so practical myself," Raspberry confessed. "Mostly I just tinker with trying to make the things I draw work. Like balloons, for instance."

"Balloons?" Maggie asked. "That's a funny word. What does it mean?"

"Nothing—yet," the wizard answered. "Though it's supposed to be a sort of flying ball that keeps floating through the air after you've let go of it. I drew the first one before I left court many years ago. Even built my house here with towers so I'd have a good place to launch the things from, once I got them invented." He shook his head sadly. "So far, I haven't been able to make the idea work."

"I'd have to see a flying ball to believe one," Maggie said, settling back in her chair with her arms crossed under her blanket and a skeptical expression on her face. "Unless it's magic, of course, I can't imagine such a thing working."

"You're right, I'm afraid. Mostly it doesn't," the wizard admitted, rising and combing through the upended boxes which served him as cabinets until he extracted a triumphant fist full of small tan objects. These he rolled onto the table in front of Maggie. "So far, fish bladders work best. You can blow them up and sail them. They'll go as far as the edge of the moat with a good headwind."

He sounded so discouraged, Maggie tried to appear interested as she watched him puff one of the bladders to twice its normal size. It hung on the air for a moment, then dropped sputtering to the floor.

"They'd be wonderful toys," Colin said helpfully. "Children would love them at fairs and festivals."

But Raspberry shook his head. "They're too heavy, you see.

85

That's the problem. I'm sure one could get them to fly properly, if only one had enough air. And then too, what if they did catch on with children? What would happen to all the fish then? I hate making a toy out of part of a living thing."

Maggie picked one up. "I don't think you need to worry. They aren't very pretty or colorful. I doubt children would take to them anyway."

"But you want them to really FLY?" Colin asked. He was becoming intrigued with the idea. "Like dragons?"

"That was the idea. I'd hoped eventually to think of something one could do with them that would make them rather larger. I'd even thought, you know, that perhaps I might find a way to blow one up large enough to carry a man."

Maggie was still handling the bladder. "Colored silks would be prettier than this," she said critically. "Lighter, too."

"But one couldn't just knot a handkerchief, don't you see?" Raspberry protested. "All the air would get out."

"One could, however, sew it in the proper shape," Maggie said gently. It was clear from the ragged condition of his gown and the roughness of its embroidery that Wizard Raspberry knew very little about tailoring, however much he might know about the other aspects of disguise. "Then you could seal it, if it was to stay up a long time, by waterproofing it the way we do the seams of our snowboots."

"Wouldn't that make it too heavy?" Raspberry was as avid now as a hound with a scent.

"Not if you only did the seams," she replied. "Even that tree sap you used to glue Moonshine's cone should do."

Before she'd finished speaking Raspberry was sending squirrels and rabbits scurrying as he knocked over stacks of drawings and pawed his way under his bed. "I have a very large stock of colored handkerchieves somewhere," he said. "A friend of mine left them here, a performing magician, you know, one of those chaps who keeps pulling things out of the air. Taught me a few tricks in payment for some little thing I did for him, but then he persuaded some of my rabbit friends to join his show and didn't have room for all the—ah! Here they are!"

By the time Maggie curled up in the straw next to Moonshine and pillowed her head against his neck, she felt more at peace with the world than she had in some time. With her magic guiding the sewing and fine stitching, and the wizard providing the pattern for the balloon and the air to blow it up, they'd had several lovely toys bobbling around the room that very evening.

She smiled to herself, recalling how pleased Raspberry had

been. "I can scarcely wait to float them off the tower in the morning!" he said. "I'll wager they'll sail clear to Queenston!"

"At the very least," Colin had agreed. "We'll have a regular launching ceremony. I'm sure I'll be able to think of an appropriate song."

But the morning was to bring other, more pressing business. And guests.

Making inquiries of the other animals in the district, Wulfric soon learned that Maggie Brown and the unicorn were quartered in the castle of a well-liked wizard whose premises were considered locally to be inviolable without invitation. The woodland creatures carried on about the wizard in a perfectly disgusting fashion.

The foxes said how clever he was, the rabbits how kind, the bears how brave and the elk how fleet, while one particularly doting lynx went into raptures about the man's inquisitiveness and patience. When a porcupine started telling him how good-natured the wizard was, Wulfric growled that he had half a mind to find out if he could add to their testimony his own about how good the wizard tasted. He would have tried, too, except that the slavish devotion of the other creatures made him feel slightly off his feed. He settled for eating the rabbit, instead.

But that didn't solve the problem of how he was to pry the unicorn out of the castle. The solution didn't occur to him until after he'd eaten the rabbit. He thought how delicious the hare was after all the scrawny, sickly animals he'd been eating along the way, where Sally had already captured the unicorns. A deer had complained bitterly, before he'd gutted her, that he'd never have been able to catch her if humans hadn't stolen her friend the unicorn, leaving the water in the district to putrefy and her and the other deer too weak to run. That gave him his brilliant idea.

He howled victoriously at the sheer craft of his plan, then changed his howl to one of illness, pain and self-pity. By the time a few of the larger animals had gathered to see who would have the privilege of finishing him off, he had his story ready.

"Oh, my furry brothers and sisters, I want to thank you for coming," he gasped, crawling piteously on his belly toward the lynx, and allowing his tongue to loll. "I fear I'm a goner, for the blight is upon me! But I say unto you, it is not too late to save yourselves! Act now, before your stream is destroyed too, and your forest ruined, and all of you sickened by the evil acts of that EEEVIL man in yonder castle and the wicked wanton witch he shelters, yea, even in the midst of her foulest deed! Free yon unicorn from their wretched hands before you, too, fall prey to my terrible—cough, hack, gag—affliction." Here he rolled over on his back and waggled his paws feebly in the air.

"What's with him?" a raven asked from an overhanging branch.

"Too much wolfsbane is my guess," the lynx said. "Or maybe it's that full moon we've had lately. You know how wolves are about full moons."

"Just keep him away from my litter," the boar's mate grunted.

"Oh, bristly sister," Wulfric cried, allowing his voice to shriek to its most piercing. "Why, I would not harm a hair of your chinny-chin-chin. Oh, no. Far from it! I seek only to warn you. That evil woman lodging with your crafty wizard means to destroy us all! In all parts of the greenwood, our furry brothers are dying, I tell you, dying in agonies from water tainted for want of unicorn magic! It's purely dreadful, is what it is, brothers and sisters. I urge you, as a dying brother to you all, with my last breath, I beg you, storm that castle and free that unicorn! Let every beast here today among us apply his or her fangs, teeth, horns, claws, talons and thews to the task before us and free our forest once and for all of the human menace! Gasp-choke. I'm done for, brothers and sisters, but I will not have died in vain if you heed my words and save yourselves from the horror awaiting you." And with that, he performed a very credible death rattle and slunk convulsively into the shrubbery, just in case anyone had ideas about taking advantage of his nobly done demise to add variety to the menu.

From his hiding place, he heard them conferring, shuffling, snuffling, arguing, until at last the bear stood on his hind legs and looked around, saying, "I think ol' Rrraspberry has something to answer for here. That *she* is up to no good. I knew it all along."

"But the unicorn came WITH her," the lynx protested.

"Unicorns got no more sense than wizards when it comes to *shes*. Everybody knows that," the bear growled. "I say we makes jam outta ol' Rrraspberry and her with 'im."

Colin awoke to the sound of roaring. Unable at first to remember where he was, he tried to unstick his weary eyes as his mind wandered out of a dream of glittering ice caverns and beautiful women with expressions of frozen horror. Since it wasn't a particularly pleasant dream, he managed to convince his eyes to compromise and open half-way.

The icy walls of his dream thereupon turned to log ones, the icy floor to bark-strewn boards, and one of the frozen ladies turned into a bearded man who was hastily pulling on his socks. Ah, yes, the wizard. That explained that. But what was that damnable roaring? Colin rose on his elbow and considered the noise.

He initially decided it was the stream that fed the moat indulging itself in a midsummer flood, except the roaring wasn't a gurgly sort of roaring. It was rather a growling, hissing, squawking, mrowling, stomping, pawing kind of roaring. It sounded more like—he sat up abruptly as the wizard stepped quickly over Maggie and Moonshine and reached for the door.

"Wait, Raspberry!" Colin called, drawing on his own boots and breeches and reaching for the sword the King had given him all at once. "What's amiss here? It sounds as if every beast of the forest is converging on us. Have you invited them all to breakfast and kept them waiting?" He pulled on his shirt while he waited for his answer, stuffing flutes and whistles and picks back into his pockets.

"You're close," the wizard said, but didn't return his smile.

Maggie rose in a brown tangle from the crescent of Moonshine's neck. She turned her back as she drew on her tunic and skirt under the blanket. Her movement alerted the unicorn, who bolted awake.

"What ho, Maiden?" he asked, jumping to his feet. His ears pricked, then flattened as he sniffed the air. "I hear a most unseemly racket!"

Maggie shook her head and quickly slipped the invisible cone over his horn, in case the disturbance was of human origin. Then, heeding the impatient gestures Colin and the wizard were making, she and Moonshine followed them across the open courtyard leading to the drawbridge. Jack the raven circled them protectively as overhead flocks of birds, geese, gulls, and ducks as well as ravens, hawks and owls, wheeled screaming and honking in a sulky gray sky.

Colin swore and wiped a tangible blob of evidence of the birds' displeasure from his hair. At the gatehouse, he and Maggie crouched nervously behind Raspberry as the wizard grasped the handle of the drawbridge ratchet and lowered the bridge with a squealing clank onto the opposite shore.

With seeming nonchalance, Raspberry started to cross the moat.

At once the clamor dulled to an anxious grumble. The whole forest tossed fitfully, as in a bad dream, agitated by the wind.

The same wind whipped Raspberry's beard and Moonshine's mane and tail, and lashed Maggie's snarled hair about her face.

But it was difficult to say whether the wind or anger ruffled the pelts and feathers of the throng around the bridge. Foxes, otters, bears, lynx, deer, wolves and wild pigs faced them with a collective feralness focused so fiercely that hairs rose on the back of Colin's own neck. On the perimeter of the crowd, a small phoenix looked dangerously close to bursting into flame as it huddled close to its companion, a diminutive salamander. The wildfowl ceased their troubled aerial gyrations and settled on the end of the drawbridge, forcing the wizard back a step.

Hundreds of bright wild eyes glowered accusingly at the wizard.

Now Raspberry's pointed ears tilted forward and Colin saw him force himself to maintain his casual stance.

"What is it, friends?" the wizard asked in a tongue that, while it seemed to be Argonian, contained also something of the speech of each beast. "I smell no smoke, no great fire that would drive you forth in such numbers to seek refuge within my walls. To what do I owe the honor of this visit?"

A brown bear rumbled forward, growling low in his throat.

Moonshine, whose ears had also tilted forward, broke Maggie's hold suddenly and reared, shaking his mane heavily. "The bear lies!" he screamed.

"What about?" Maggie asked. But as she sought to lay a restraining hand on his back, another angry roar rose from the mob, and it began pouring toward them, sweeping Wizard Raspberry in front of it.

In one rabbity bound, the wizard leapt back behind the gatehouse and began raising the bridge again. Wildfowl exploded upward, shrieking, as the bridge clanged shut.

Mopping his brow, Raspberry sank back against the gatehouse. "This is serious," he said. "They seem to think I've betrayed them."

Moonshine snorted. "If you're in charge of this woods, good wizard, I suggest you make that bear take back his slanderous remark about my maiden immediately! Bears! Bah! They're such liars!"

"Would that I could follow your suggestion, wise unicorn," Raspberry replied with a faint suggestion of a smile, "but it isn't that easy, you see, to make a bear do anything he doesn't wish to do. Besides, Bonebelcher isn't the only one who thinks we're all unicorn-nappers."

"Unicorn-nappers?" Colin echoed, "But that's utter nonsense! We already *have* a very serviceable unicorn at our disposal. Or rather, he has us, and I must say for my part he's more than enough. The only reason I, personally, am wandering about out here in the woods like this is to do him a great personal favor at tremendous inconvenience to myself and considerable peril to my career."

Raspberry held up a restraining hand. "Hold, minstrel. *I* believe you. But *they* seem to think otherwise."

"I thought you were friendly with them," Maggie said, ducking gracefully aside as a load of goose guano plopped past her nose and onto the stepping stone at her feet. Raspberry opened the door to the gatehouse tower and they resumed their conference on the dark inner stairway leading to the tower's crenelated roof.

"Ordinarily, I *am* on good terms with most of them, even Bonebelcher," Raspberry replied in answer to her question. "Though he's always been a surly sort—comes from closer to the village and has had some close calls at being hunted, you know. But, though he has no use for men in general, I was beginning to hope he rather liked me and—eh?" he broke off as Jack, seated on his shoulder, began making low gargling sounds which Colin surmised from the way the wizard kept saying "uh huh—and then what—is that so?" constituted speech for the raven.

"Well, now. That is interesting," Raspberry said when the raven had finished. "Jack here tells me there's a strange wolf in the neighborhood. A sick wolf who's been stirring up the woodland creatures, telling them that the part of the forest where he comes from is dying, and all of its denizens with it, because human beings are kidnapping unicorns and leaving the water to go bad."

"That's awful!" Maggie cried. "Anyone who'd do a thing like that should be torn to shreds!"

"That's the general concensus," Raspberry said glumly. "And the wolf has convinced most of the animals that you and Colin are the kidnappers, with Moonshine as your latest victim. I'm supposed to be your accomplice, harboring you in my castle."

Moonshine butted the door open with his horn. "*I'll* tell them," he said, and pranced out into the courtyard with his head held high. "Kindly open your gate, wizard."

The raven squawked loudly and circled Moonshine's head.

"Your disguise!" the wizard said, chuckling to himself as he reached up to remove Moonshine's cone of invisibility. "No wonder the animals became so upset when you showed yourself. They must have thought we'd de-horned you.''

Once more the bridge was lowered, but this time the others kept well back while Moonshine trotted across it, tossing his head a little contemptuously.

"See here, you ridiculous beasts," he scolded, "I am a free unicorn, here on a perfectly normal quest with my maiden and our good friend the minstrel, and I'll thank you to—"

"You're the one who's ridiculous, 'corny,'" the boar grunted. "Letting those scoundrels lead you to the slaughter without so much as a fight while you forget your proper duty and let our water spoil.''

"I must say," a long-snooted moose sniffed, "I never thought I'd see the day when a unicorn lowered himself to become domesticated. I think it's just vile the way you're behaving!''

But the bear called Bonebelcher lumbered forward again and swiped at Moonshine's horn. "Come along, buddy, whilst we got 'em cornered in there, and you can get away. Take a little nap back there in the greenwood. We'll make sure she and her pals don't never hurt none of your kind again." With a great lunge, he grasped Moonshine's horn and tugged. The unicorn danced back, shaking his head angrily.

"How *dare* you! Let go, I say!" Moonshine cried as the bear dragged him forward.

"He can't do that!" Maggie exclaimed. "I'll throw a ring of fire around the castle this very minute and—" Colin grabbed her hair as she rushed forward.

"And start a forest fire that will burn the whole place down?" he asked. "That'd get rid of the wizard's friends alright. AND Moonshine. AND us. But I'll admit it would save them the trouble of tearing everything to pieces if you burn it all down first.''

Moonshine, feinting forward and with a quick lunge to the rear, caught the bear off guard and escaped, galloping at top speed back into the courtyard. Maggie stopped talking of burning things and snuggled protectively against the unicorn's neck, but the look she threw Colin was clearly calculated to singe.

Wizard Raspberry raised the bridge again. Catching the angry looks passing between the two friends, he intervened on Colin's behalf. "He's right, you know. *They* think they're just protecting Moonshine and themselves against the trouble the wolf told them of. If only they'd listen to us for a change.''

"Let down that bridge again and *I'll* make them listen to reason," Maggie snapped. "Those narrow-minded brute-brained

92

beasts ought to know better than to think any of us would be party to a scheme like that.''

"A few of them do understand human speech,'' the wizard said mildly, "But I doubt if they'll respond well to being called narrow-minded brute-brained beasts.''

"Oh, I won't say that,'' she said, reaching past him to lower the drawbridge herself. "I'll be sweet as pie, you'll see. But I won't be intimidated by a bear or two and a lot of walking fur cloaks.''

"Maggie—'' Colin began, but was drowned out by a deafening roar as Maggie strode out onto the bridge.

Moonshine leapt forward. "I'll defend you, Maiden!''

"Don't be silly. You saw how vicious that bear was,'' she called back over her shoulder. "If you're killed defending me all of this will be worthless, won't it?''

The roar grew until it shook the ground, and the animals surged forward, onto the bridge. Maggie didn't falter, and kept her expression calm, gentle and kind. Whether or not her voice matched it, or whether indeed she said anything at all, Colin couldn't have said, for he couldn't hear a thing over the roaring.

Bonebelcher growled and snuffled a challenge, and charged. Hot on his heels ran the boar and his family of wild pigs, while the birds pecked and plucked at Maggie's hair.

Above the roar, Colin heard her yell, "Just a cross-cursed minute, you beasts!'' and the bridge was suddenly laden with throngs of scampering, scurrying, charging, crawling beasts all trying to attack the witch.

Moonshine screamed a high, piercing scream and shot forward, his horn working like a scythe, cutting feathers and fur from his path to his maiden. Wizard Raspberry jumped into the fray too, and tried to pull Maggie away from her attackers, but was himself attacked.

Colin raised his sword, Banshee Bringer, and started forward, yodeling a particularly effective battle song he'd heard His Majesty singing while in his cups. To Colin's total amazement, his voice carried high over all the racket, and the animals began melting from the bridge in droves.

"Wha—?'' he stopped and saw Maggie, scratched and bruised but basically whole, being helped to her feet from beneath Moonshine's shielding belly by the wizard.

As soon as Colin ceased his song, the animals renewed their attack.

"Keep singing!'' Raspberry called. And Colin did, continuing the battle song and looking as menacing as he possibly could until they were all safely back within the courtyard with the bridge up again.

"This is getting monotonous," Maggie panted. "No matter what we try to say or who tries to talk to them they just don't listen."

"Aye. I'm glad you've proved that to your own satisfaction, witch, after almost costing us all our lives," Colin said. "I'm afraid my singing battle songs isn't going to improve their impression of us on any sort of permanent basis. They don't need any more ranting and yelling, that mob. They need to calm down a bit, before they tear this castle apart stick by stick."

"Perhaps another, more soothing song?" the wizard suggested.

"You must be jesting!" Maggie said. "Anything more soothing than a tribe of dragons in full flame would be lost on that bunch!"

"It's worth a try," Colin told her coldly. "My voice DOES carry rather well, so I've always been told. It's the siren blood, I suppose."

Maggie sniffed, and dabbed at a scratch on her arm with a spit-wet fingertip. "Well, unless you want to see your siren blood all over the ground, and ours with it, may I suggest from recent bitter experience that you conduct your serenade from the tower instead of the bridge?"

He knew a good suggestion when he heard one. "Right," he nodded, and headed for the door.

"Colin," she called after him. "Watch out for the birds, won't you?"

At first nothing seemed to happen.

Colin had decided to use a tin whistle to play a gentle air, rather than spend his voice on singing and risk having it fail him. He raised it, trembling, to his lips, and feared for a moment his breath would refuse to come. But after a vain puff or two, the music which was his magic took over from the frightened, mortal part of him, and he began to play—sweetly, liltingly, first the air, then a medley that became an improvised woodland rhapsody.

To his immense relief, his efforts weren't wasted on the beasts. An otter stopped throwing rocks at the castle after the first few notes, and the bear, after circling restlessly for a chorus or two, settled down grumbling and promptly fell asleep. The birds stopped circling Colin's tower almost immediately, and soon folded their wings, roosting on the tower's crenelations and joining in with their own thread of melody.

Colin played until the sun rose reluctantly into the sky and the wild mother pig had to stop listening to give suck to her piglets. By then it was so quiet that, except for the tune, all that could be heard was a woodpecker pecking time, his red head darting in the dazzling greenery as he added counterpoint to the rhythm dictated by the whistle.

At last, Colin stopped. "Thank you, thank you very much. You've been a wonderful audience but now it's time for a few words—" He was cut off by disgruntled growls from the bear and the boar, who rose as soon as he stopped playing. "All right, all right. I *love* encores—"

Wizard Raspberry and Maggie had climbed the tower stairs and now stood beside him.

"Softly, minstrel," Raspberry suggested. "Perhaps I can reason with them as you play."

Wulfric had watched from within the foliage as the animals descended on the witch and tore her to shreds. He couldn't linger any longer than that, for now it was day, and he had to spend a few hateful hours in man form, which meant he must flee this part of the forest before the animals turned on him, too.

But he felt well pleased with the report he could carry to Sally. With the humans out of the way and the Dark Pilgrim's treacherous she-kin destroyed, the unicorn was theirs for the taking.

He loped in wolf form as long as he possibly could, to the edge of the forest, thrilling to the bestial roaring and the witch's screaming.

He felt so good as he ran that he covered a great deal of ground long before he had to surrender to man shape overtaking him, as it always did at least once before the sun reached the middle of the sky. He covered so much ground, in fact, that not even his sharp ears could hear the minstrel's battle song or the whistle. Nor could he hear the voice of the wizard as he made peace with the neighbors Wulfric had schemed so hard to set against him.

CHAPTER 7

Leofwin decided he had almost missed his calling. The warrior prince business was dull and unstimulating compared with a career as one of Sally Forth's hooligans—or revolutionaries, as she called them.

Though so far there'd been little opportunity to collect spoils, all he had had to do to accomplish Sally's first mission was stand around the tavern and look fierce while she bamboozled the town's mayor into surrendering the local unicorn.

Between Sally's winsome way with an argument and the not-too-subtle hint of violence from the loitering bandits, the mayor's reluctance melted into a mealy-mouthed prayer that she wouldn't sack the town. To Leofwin's amusement, Sally said nothing one way or the other. She just smiled prettily.

Something buzzed past Leofwin's ear and he swatted at it, thinking it one of the pesky mosquitoes so prevalent in these swampy lowland areas. A faery the size of a bottle cork, dressed in a motley collection of what seemed to be well-used kerchiefs, escaped his swat and shimmered near the mayor's nose, fists balled on her fly-speck hips.

"I'm telling you, Fuller," she threatened, "You can't let them do it. I'm not going to let you let them do it."

The mayor swiped a cupped hand at the end of his nose, but the faery bobbed out of reach. Wearily, the man said, "More to the point, Little Woman, these good folk are not going to let us NOT let them do it. And excuse me, but they're a lot bigger than you are."

"Don't you give me that," the faery scolded, hovering in front of his nose again and shaking her small finger vigorously at him. "There's more grown folk in this town than *this* turncoat trollop brought with her." She jerked a tiny thumb at Sally Forth. "And you have three pretty good magicians and a damn good village witch besides. How much advantage do you have to *have* to defend Snowshadow, anyway? I suppose you've conveniently forgotten that it was the very unicorn you're dying to sell out who kept you slobs from fouling your own nests and dying of water poisoned by your own slops when her windiness there decided she was tired of guarding your stream and set off to be queen of the bandits."

"We have only your word for it that the unicorn Snowshadow does anything at all, faery," the mayor replied. "Does she ever come into town to get shod at our local establishment? No. Has she ever offered a lift to even one citizen of this fair village? No, again. All WE'VE known of her is that she warns the game away from the stream if any of us are so foolish as to try to hunt when she's around. As you do, you imp. Nastur—Sally, here, always made herself more than agreeable when SHE was our stream guardian. Prettied up the scenery, pointed out good places to hunt, rode at the head of the founder's day parade for the last ten years.''

The faery shook her head slowly and flew to the door. ''You're a dunderhead, Fuller. Snowshadow's been good to this town. She only does what unicorns are supposed to do, and whether you know it or not, idiot, that's exactly what this rotten burg of yours needs. I'm warning this town here and now. Send this pixilated strumpet and her outfit packing, or you'll be sorry!''

The mayor was no fool. He had the innkeeper chase the little insect out with a broom, and got down to negotiating how much valuable consideration the township could expect as recompense for the cultural, aesthetic and environmental deprivation they hoped to experience with the loss of their unicorn.

The actual capture was slick and easy, due again to the brains and beauty of their cute little leader. She sat herself down in the grass, looking so demure and delicious Leofwin could hardly wait until they'd bagged the beastie who very sensibly wandered out of the woods to lay its horny head in her lap.

But now that the capture was accomplished, and the beast docile as a saddle-horse in its specially prepared hobbles, Leofwin dawdled behind. The others poured back into the tavern for refreshment, and Sally lingered back in the woods, whispering sweet lies into the unicorn's ear to keep it calm. If only she'd stay put and not turn into a whirlwind before his comrades were out of earshot, Leofwin fancied he'd manage to find the life of a brigand very rewarding indeed.

With dragon-manufactured wind, the *Snake's Bane* made even better time than her crew had originally anticipated.

They rounded the Southern Arm and sliced through the Ablemarlonian Straits in four days flat, a record unheard of for any sailing vessel in the known world.

Now they hugged close to Argonia's easternmost shores. For the last two days and nights they'd seen nothing but the blue-white shelf of the Suicide Glacier, which was so called because it kept hurling bits of itself into the sea. It was believed by superstitious early explorers to be the last of the frost giants, slowly dismembering himself in remorse over some lost battle.

Sir Cyril was fascinated by the glacier, and by the sea otters lounging on the discarded pieces of its body. The slick-skinned creatures sported and called to each other, seemingly unconcerned by the huge chunks of ice plunging randomly into their playground. Perchingbird's only regret was that the weather didn't always permit him to observe the shoreline as closely as he would have liked.

By the middle of the first day his note-taking was interrupted by a fog settling heavy as a mourning veil around the ship, and allowing about the same visibility. Neither torch nor candle could penetrate the gloom to any helpful degree at all.

"Can't go on in this muck, Sire," the captain informed the King.

But when Perchingbird informed the dragons they'd have to stop for the night Grizel had demanded, "Whatever for? The light of MY life can surely throw a bit of flame forth to serve as a beacon for YOUR measly machine." She'd shot a tongue of flame from port to starboard to make her point.

"Not at the sail, if you please, ma'am," Perchingbird pleaded.

"Don't work yourself into a sweat about it, little man," Grizel's mate soothed. "You mustn't mind my little spitfire getting hot under the collar like that. Her time is near, and you know how odd females get when they're about to bear their young."

With that Grimley had flown forward of the mast and had sent a blast of flame across the gloom, piercing fog and darkness enough to help the navigator locate a landmark or two to steer by.

A short time later the King, on his way to get sick over the railing (His Majesty was an infantryman, and not a very good sailor) passed Sir Cyril and stared pop-eyed at the chief archivist. After relieving himself, Rowan turned back to Perchingbird and offered him the fur-lined cloak that spanned the royal shoulders. "If yer cauld, man, put on m' cloak, but for the love of us a' take that candle out of yer jacket."

Puzzled but ever obedient to royal command, Sir Cyril accepted the King's cloak and wondered if His Majesty's sea sickness was so far advanced that delirium had set in. Then, looking down to fasten the royal brooch at his shoulder, he saw what had made the King stare.

A soft but brilliant illumination glowed through cloak and jacket, just above Sir Cyril's heart.

"Ah, this. 'Tis no candle, Majesty," he reported.

"By m'shield and armor, m'lord," the King said, dropping with wobbly and unaccustomed piety to one knee, "But if that's no candle then I vow yer bein' sainted before m' very eyes!"

Teddy hastily knelt on the rolling deck and helped the King back to his feet. "Get up, please, Sire, and don't let anybody see you doing that! I'm no saint, or if I am, someone has very bad aim at bestowing halos. Look." He pulled the princess's parchment from beneath his wraps. Freed of his clothing, the elaborately drawn pictures and embellished script glowed with enough light to brighten a ballroom.

The King whistled. "They don't call Pegeen Ashburn the Illuminator for naught, do they?" he asked softly, staring at the scroll. "This'll provide light enough tae take us tae t' landing nearest the Worm's Roost."

"Odd I never noticed this quality to her writing before," Perchingbird puzzled. "But then, I never examined it in the dark before, either."

"Must be a handy talent, that. Saves her a royal ransom on candles, I'd think," Rowan agreed.

After that discovery the fog had been little problem, except that it impeded Sir Cyril from studying the glaciers as carefully as he would have liked. This was the third day of foul weather, and soon the *Bane* would reach the eastern harbor with Perchingbird knowing little more about the conformation of the icy cliffs than he'd known to begin with.

Otherwise things could hardly be better, he thought as he hummed a little tune to himself. The ship was making excellent progress. He was seeing new sights, singing new—songs? Now why should he be singing an unfamiliar tune just now? And come to think of it, how could any tune possibly *be* all that unfamiliar to the keeper of the archives? Certainly he'd never shown any musical improvisational ability before, and he was quite sure he was well acquainted with most of the predominating modes in the musics of the world of which Argonia was part.

Then he realized he was singing the song because milady Pegeen was singing it, urging him to come to her quickly.

Close off the starboard bow a sheet of ice plummeted into the sea, rocking the *Bane* even more severely than the rolling seas were already rocking her. Sir Cyril forgot the song and glanced around him, thinking to remark on the incident to whoever was closest at hand.

But all around him crew members and King's men alike stood stock still, staring out to sea, eyes straining toward the sound of Princess Pegeen's voice, which seemed to come from everywhere at once.

"I wonder what she's doing out there?" Perchingbird said to the gunner's mate, a red-haired fellow named Liam. He noticed that tears rolled down Liam's cheeks and, in a voice that sounded dreamy and far-off to his own ears when compared to the reality of the song, asked, "Why do you weep?"

"That's the lullabye she used to sing to me as she nursed me at her breast," the man said, not answering the question so much as murmuring in amazement to himself. "Lovely to hear it again. Faith! I haven't heard her sing it like that since she died, thirty years or so ago when I was a lad."

Swimming feverishly in the back of Perchingbird's mind was the notion that it was not possible for him to hear Princess Pegeen singing so many leagues from shore. It was not possible for Liam to hear his mother who had been dead for thirty years. It was not possible for Liam to hear his mother at all when Perchingbird heard only Princess Pegeen. It was not possible for the entire crew to stop work to listen to songs compelling each man differently but equally. Only by magic could such occurrences be possible, and only one sort of creature possessed such magic. But which creature that was he couldn't seem to remember, and really, he didn't care at the moment. He couldn't be bothered to catalogue magicks when he needed so badly to hear what it was that Pegeen was singing.

Neither he nor any of the others took note for some time of the other creature, the one who did not sing but who undulated through the waves towards them, circling their ship not once but more than a half dozen times. The same creature who, having embraced the *Bane*, began constricting rhythmically around it, squeezing the ship in a pulsing vise not entirely out of time with the sirens' songs which had taken control of the men's minds.

Colin managed throughout the first few days of the journey through the shadowy eastern woods to keep their spirits aloft by playing various dance tunes and the few marching songs he knew, but by the fourth day his repertoire had degenerated into murder ballads. One after another, he sang of the most gruesome crimes committed in history, until finally he ran out of even those.

"Are you sure that's all you know?" Maggie asked. "Perhaps you've overlooked some lesser offenses. Don't you know any fraud ballads, maybe, or perhaps a breaking-and-entering air? Or maybe a ghost song. This is just the place for ghost songs!"

"No, and it's just as well." He shivered under his cloak for though it was still late summer at Wizard Raspberry's castle, here in the mist-riddled midst of the giant cedars the air was dank and chill. "I'm making myself nervous enough as it is. And I seem to have frightened off Lyrrill and the kittens."

Maggie craned forward on Moonshine's neck, then settled back with a shrug. "She's just scouting ahead, looking for her grown cubs again, but I wish she'd hurry back." Maggie preferred that the party stay together, besides which she found the sight of Lyrrill reassuring. The lynx had come to the castle after the other beasts had accepted the explanations offered by Wizard Raspberry, Maggie and Moonshine and had dispersed. Lyrrill had found the wolf's news disquieting, she had told the wizard, not because she'd ever believed Wizard Raspberry guilty of betrayal but because her young ones from the previous year had established their territory in the lands where the wolf said animals were dying. She was going to find them, she told Raspberry, and if she found them well, there would be a unicorn nearby who might answer Moonshine's questions. If the cubs were ill when she found them, and there was no unicorn, then Moonshine's magic might serve to save them.

Normally the lynx ranged just beyond the tip of Moonshine's horn. Her young kittens rolled and bounced and tried their best to tangle her competent paws, but she kept an even pace, her furry pouch of an underbelly swinging rhythmically as they traveled through forest so smothered in moss that even birdsong was muffled.

Colin's most hair-raising songs were more cheerful than that strangled silence. At night, Maggie always made her fuelless magic fire, and it was lucky for them all she had that power, for the wood underfoot was soaked by a constant drip from lush green leaves. Underbrush was scantier, and trees larger, than near Sybil Brown's cottage, and the mossy groundcover, which had been cheerfully sprinkled with dogwood and saxifrage near the wizard's castle, began more and more to sprout mugwort, lousewort, fly-specked orchia, skunk cabbage, wax flowers and the deceptively demure pink bell-like blossoms of poisonous bog rosemary.

But what made them the most uneasy was the abrupt change in the character of the streams and rivers. Unlike the crystalline waters of the North, these flowed sluggish, clouded and murky.

Moonshine was appalled. "How long can it have been since a unicorn has serviced this area?" he asked Lyrrill.

The lynx waved her paw unconcernedly. "This is not the plight of which the strange wolf spoke, O Singlehorn," she told him. "The water has always been thus, for it is the tears which wash the face of the great frozen giant who weeps among yonder mountains."

"She means the glaciers," Colin explained when Moonshine questioned the information. "Apparently the lynx only knows the old legend about them. As we now know in this enlightened age, the glaciers aren't really suicidal frost giants at all. The best scholars agree that the real frost giants simply shrank in might and stature like the rest of our ancestors. Now the only remnants of them are more or less man-sized, like the King. What the *glaciers* are, actually, are the shields left behind by the frost giants. As the sun melts the ice on their surfaces, they shift positions and gouge great chunks out of the earth beneath them. I suppose that's what really makes the water dirty."

"Heartened as I am to hear a reasonable explanation," Moonshine said, "I must purify this water at once, or it will spoil my maiden's tea. Excuse me." With that he dipped his horn, sending ripples of clarity across the murk.

No simple natural or legendary phenomena could explain the stench pervading the forest by the end of the fifth day, however. All that afternoon they found dead animals; a bear carcass first, then hares, squirrels, foxes. All had lolling tongues, and lips rolled back over their teeth, paws outstretched and stiff and fur damp from the steady drizzle. Some were bloated already but none were even partially eaten. Those who hadn't had the strength to drag themselves away from their own excrement lay in it.

Lyrrill returned from her patrol. She seemed to droop from the tufts of her ears to the black tip of her bobbed tail. "Death everywhere," she reported to Moonshine, her voice audible to Maggie's and Colin's ears as a low, eerie moan. "I found one like myself, but not mine. She is ceased."

"Did you see no *living* thing?" Maggie asked, looking up from the tea she was boiling in a new-formed earthen kettle over her magic fire.

"None," the lynx replied.

Colin regarded the tea-kettle dubiously. "I hate to drink that stuff, even after Moonshine has magicked it."

"You do me a disservice, minstrel," Moonshine replied huffily. "How can you doubt me when my powers alone have preserved our company from the fate of these other creatures?" But the unicorn broke off soon, unable to concentrate even on defending his besmirched honor. He surrendered instead to the tremors that twitched the skin all the way down his back. He felt unusually skittish.

Colin noticed his uneasiness. "It must be these woods, I suppose, since if Lyrrill says we're the only living things about then we must be. But I can't help feeling we're being watched."

"Perhaps it's the mosquitoes," Maggie suggested, swatting

one. "They seem to have survived." She made a face and started to swat again when Colin snatched her arm down.

Tiny wings backflapped furiously and a small, greenish faery quivered before her eyes.

"I beg your pardon!" Maggie cried with real embarrassment, made particularly acute since the finger-high faery didn't look as if she'd survive the first swat. "You're the first living creature we've seen all day and I—"

"You call this living?" the faery demanded, then moaned, "Mouse-blood! I wish I were dead if it is! Mind you, my mother *warned* me not to drink the water."

She sank into a heap of vari-colored rags, which on closer inspection proved to be cast-off butterfly wings, settling herself on the edge of Maggie's kettle. Long strings of purplish hair were plastered against her small narrow skull, and she ran her tiny fingers through it repeatedly, lamenting, "It wasn't like I wasn't brought up well, or anything like that. 'Stick with dew and nectar, Trickle,' my mother always told me. 'Dew and nectar's the thing for faeries.' But let me tell you, it's not often a regular Little Person-type faery like me gets a chance at being a stream guardian. These positions generally go to the big girls. Nymphs and dryads, you know. I just happened to be here when that renegade Nasturtium took off to go revolutionize the kingdom."

Maggie, deciding the faery was delirious, held a flower-full of unicorn-blessed water under the tiny woman's chin. "Try a bit of this."

The faery spat—but feebly. "THAT'S the stuff that made me sick, and so quickly too." She wailed, "I didn't think it would work so quickly! Blasted mortals. Never believe a thing you tell 'em."

Maggie continued to urge her to drink. "It's all right. Moonshine fixed it. It'll cure you."

"Lady, I don't care what your horse did in that water, it won't—" the faery said, then sputtered as Maggie poured the water into her open mouth, almost drowning her in the process.

"He's not a horse," Maggie explained before the faery could dry off enough to come up with a whopping curse, which was the kind of thing Little People of all varieties were quite adept at. "Moonshine is a unicorn, incognito." Already Trickle's complexion waxed somewhat healthier, and her eyes gained luster, along with a certain malicious vengeful look that caused Maggie quickly to lift Moonshine's cone of invisibility. "See?"

"Now I've seen everything," the faery groaned. "First I'm half-killed through the plotting of a water nymph who'd rather be a bandit, and now I'm saved by a unicorn who'd rather be a horse. Don't tell me; let me guess. You're really a beautiful princess who'd rather be a witch."

"Something like that," Maggie replied, startled.

"I would NOT rather be a horse," Moonshine protested.

"Whatever you are, you've certainly done the trick," the faery told him, standing now on the kettle's edge and stretching luxuriously. "Why, I feel better already, and another knuckle high to boot! Sorry if I was a bit short with you, but you wouldn't *believe* what I've had to put up with these last few days. That this should happen to me on my very first stream! First, that good-for-nothing hussy who was here before me has the unmitigated GALL to show her face in MY territory again, then that idiot of a mayor was stupid enough to listen to her. I'm just about fed up, I tell you. If I hadn't been so sick, you mortals would have been in a bad way. I was just about to let you have it after I told you what I think of your kind and your stinking garbage. I suppose you're taking this poor unicorn off to market or wherever as well?"

The others were too astonished to answer, but lack of response didn't trouble the faery.

She continued. "I don't see what riches you can possibly gain that are going to make up for this mess. None of this would have happened if you stupid, greedy fatheads had stood your ground."

"She's still feverish," Maggie said, dipping for some more water.

Colin wasn't so sure. "We have no idea what you're talking about, faery. But it seems to be that if you're this stream's guardian it was your responsibility to protect it from whatever—er—polluted it."

"Whoever, you mean. A whole village, a crazy nymph and a swarm of bandits besides. Come on, big boy, give me a break! A guardian spirit can only do so much, I don't care what your stupid legends say. And let me tell you something, pal. I did my best to convince that idiot bureaucrat he should stand up like a dwarf and fight those poachers to his last breath. But he just shook in his shoes and fingered his gold and gave me to understand that he didn't take orders from any faeries smaller than a wine jug—and threatened to use me as a swizzle stick if I didn't beat it. What could I do?"

"You have magic powers," Colin informed her almost primly.

Her narrow-eyed look was scornful. "Like I said, I do the best I can. In this country faeries have no corner on magic. That little town had three second-rate magicians and a first-class witch, and the mayor was a dwarf blacksmith who could twist iron horse-shoes all around *my* magic. Besides, the poor sods seem to have done themselves in already without my help."

"You mean they're dead?" Maggie asked. "The whole village?" She'd heard rumors of villages wiped out by border raids or disease of one sort or the other, of course, but Fort Iceworm was remote from all that. A few older folk or sickly youngsters died each winter, a family was sometimes killed in a night fire, or a hunter who stayed too long in the tavern might freeze to death trying to find his way home in the snow. But death to a whole village was still the stuff of fireside stories to her.

Trickle shrugged sullenly. "How should I know? I couldn't stand to see them take Snowshadow away, so I went out flying around. I guess I lost track of the days. I took that drink without even thinking about it as soon as I got back, and since then I've been too sick to care about anything. But if they are dead, they had it coming, is all I have to say about it."

"If you were in sooth troubled for the safety of this Snowshadow," Moonshine asked, "Why did you fly away and not instead stay and seek to warn her? It seems to me you were as guilty of her abduction as those you accuse."

"If that isn't just like a pointy-headed unicorn!" the faery said, facing him. "Look, fellow, I'm about one hundred and three years old by human reckoning, and I haven't spent my WHOLE life guarding *this* stream. I've been around a little, too, you know. I've seen you guys when you meet your first girlfriends, and whatever you use to think with then, it isn't your brains. Snowshadow has a nose to smell with, or at least she did the last time I saw her. We'd been hearing of this gang of unicorn-nappers for a couple of weeks, and Snowshadow knew about Nasturtium, even though she'd never met her. I'd even told Snowshadow what the wicked trollop looked like. So that unicorn didn't need me to warn her, and I didn't need to get skewered for interfering in her social life, all right?"

Moonshine considered and finally conceded, "'Tis true I would have allowed no one to gainsay me the privilege of meeting my Maid Maggie. But that was a worthy and noble attraction of a true unicorn to a chaste maiden of the highest order."

The faery looked at him with her one-hundred-and-three-year-old eyes. "Sure. Aren't they all?"

Maggie studied Trickle silently for a moment. Something about the cynical little being reminded her very much of Granny Brown when she'd been up to really wicked mischief—like the time she changed a tinker who'd tried to cheat her into an earthworm and presented him to small boys bound for a fishing trip. Of course, one could be seeing similarities where in all likelihood none existed. Still . . . "Can you show us the way to this village?" Maggie asked. "Perhaps there are survivors yet. Moonshine's magic could cure them."

"Why would he want to use his magic to help them, knowing the way they treat unicorns around here?" Trickle asked.

"Yes, maiden, why should I?" Moonshine asked. "If my magic can do all that, should I not apply it instead to the innocent beasts of the forest, who suffer through no fault of their own?"

"Mainly because they're not suffering any more, being dead," Maggie replied pragmatically. "And if you apply your talents to the innocent beasts of the town instead, we may discover where the bandits have taken that other unicorn, and somehow be able to free her so we can get straight answers to our questions."

"Did I not tell you?" Moonshine trumpeted, bucking around in little circles like a frisky colt. "Did I not tell you, Small One, that my maiden is the cleverest as well as the most beautiful and kindly of all? What a marvelous plan! Let us hasten at once to implement it."

"Yes, let's," Trickle agreed. "At once. I feel another wave of nausea coming on."

"You really must take better care of yourself, my dear," Fearchar said.

Pegeen turned guiltily from her mirror of ice. She'd been trying to determine whether she was actually becoming fat or was merely pleasingly plump. To her dismay, she had discovered dark bags under her eyes, and a certain drawn quality about her mouth. Even her hands were no longer ladylike; their nails were chewed well into the quicks. "It's that unicorn, Fearchar. His screaming keeps me awake nights. He must be utterly terrified. Can't you release him and find some other way to solve your personnel shortage?"

Fearchar's arms slid around her waist, and his saturnine face appeared in the frozen mirror beside hers. "Take heart, my princess. The unicorn should be in much better spirits tonight. Sally has brought him a companion."

"Oh, dear. How many are you going to take? I'd hoped one would be quite enough."

"Gracious, no, darling. I hope to have over two hundred followers before I overthrow Rowan. Each of them must be equipped with the powdered horn, a belt of the hide, and a hoof

106

or two for luck. The elixir must be saved for the casualties that cannot be avoided by such magical prophylaxis. For it has to be bled fresh from the beast before each use, you know.''

"Surely you don't mean to kill them!'' Pegeen said, aghast. "Those beasts do nothing but good all over the kingdom. Fearchar, their loss would be a terrible blow to Argonia under ANY reign.''

"Calm yourself, pet. Nothing has to be done until I've gathered sufficient forces. And you'll be happy to hear that our valiant Sally has recruited another whole band of patriots to our cause. I'm keeping them here at the castle until they're fully indoctrinated. They can join the others who serve us and help guard the beasts.''

"Fearchar, I'm frightened of those robbers you call patriots. They may accept your pay for now, but they're ruthless, dangerous men. And—and you're so often gone.'' She looked down at her ravaged hands for a moment then turned back to him resolutely. "Not a one of them is worth a hair off a unicorn's hide. You mustn't sacrifice—''

"My dear girl,'' her lover said, drawing away and looking down his long, hawklike nose at her. "While I have always found your merciful disposition to be one of your more charming characteristics, I must insist that you allow me to handle this without interference. You have no need to be alarmed by our own revolutionaries. They are each and every one, like their brothers in the woods, under my personal spell. The very essence of that spell is that you are, like myself, completely sacred. They are instructed to die for either of us. Not one of them will ever touch the hem of your skirt except for your own protection and I, naturally, determine how and from what you are to be protected. So you see, you have nothing to fear.''

A coldness not caused by the room's icy drafts penetrated Pegeen's gown and heavy woollen shawl, raising goosebumps on her arms.

"As for slaughtering the beasts, do you know, my wise darling, you've given me food for thought. It may be, if we are very careful, we shall be able to remove the horns, necessary hide, and hooves, and, by virtue of the beasts' healing powers, have them regenerate in one another the missing parts, so that our supply of medicinal charms will be virtually limitless!'' He patted her arm and seemed not to notice that she flinched from him. "Why don't you forget all of this and draw some nice pictures, darling? Perhaps prepare our coronation address.''

But as he strode for the tapestry-covered door, Pegeen called to him once more. "Fearchar?"

"Yes?"

"You aren't going to harm those beasts now, are you?"

He stroked his chin, considering. "Helsinora's research specifies that the ingredients of the elixir must all be fresh to be most effective, as I've mentioned. But I'd still like to experiment with that idea of yours a little in advance of when we'll actually be needing the potions and charms. But, no, I'll tell you what, darling. Since you're concerned that I might wipe them all out, I'll wait until I have a couple of extra beasts in reserve, in case something untoward happens to the one I want to use to heal the first—er—subject. You see? I am moved by your gentle sympathies."

Two tears rolled down Pegeen's cheeks, and she mopped them away with the fringe of her shawl. What a fool she was! She ought to have known from her training as a princess that someone as ambitious as Fearchar would stop at no crime, no matter how heinous, to gain his ends. And she was powerless, at the mercy of his "protective" spell. She'd heard her ladies speak of being a prisoner of love before, but she'd never fancied she'd personally experience the phenomenon implied by the term in such an appallingly literal fashion.

She had to think, to plan. To that end, she gathered her inks and parchment and stuck them into her dress pockets. Then, taking an unlit torch from her chamber wall, she stepped behind one of three old, worn tapestries she'd been allowed to keep when Fearchar sold her finer furnishings. She was outlined against the threadbare fabric for only a moment by a faint, warm glow. Then the hanging flattened back against the wall, and the glow faded, leaving the ice-walled room once more in darkness.

Sir Cyril was brought to his senses by three occurrences, the first of which was the frigid sea water pouring over the splintering deck and into his boot tops. The second occurrence, which allowed him to become aware of the first, was the cessation of the enthralling song. And the third occurrence was that he suddenly heard the rippling of girlish laughter, and realized the cause of song and laughter and that the *Bane* was most certainly doomed, even as the laughter rose above the crunching and cracking of the ship's timbers, and above the pulsing sound emanating from the awesome beast that slowly strangled the vessel.

The dragons were nowhere to be seen. Nevertheless, Sir Cyril called out. His voice was frail against the sundering decks, throbbing beast, and malicious giggles. He hollered until his throat was raw, while waves washed over him from a hole in the center of the ship—a hole that yawned where once the mainmast had stood. It must have made a fearsome crash when it broke off and fell into the sea, yet he hadn't heard it. And only gradually did the other men onboard regain awareness of their surroundings.

"HolysaintedsacredMother, lads, we're goners!" Liam cried as he was swept to his knees by another wash of water. "The beast is takin' 'is revenge on us all for every snake we ever made into oil!"

"Aw, gar!" Neddy Pinchpurse slipped and slithered across the crazily sloping decks, avoiding boards that shot straight up into the air from the force of the serpent's caress. In his right hand he held a harpoon. "Where's 'is bloody 'ead?" he asked. "Ain't no slimey gonna take my ship out from under my very feet!"

Perchingbird stumbled up beside him and restrained his arm. "I shouldn't do that if I were you, bosun."

Pinchpurse turned on him. "Oh, you wouldn't, would you, Lor'ship? Well, just what would yer Lor'ship do?"

"I'd SCREAM!" Perchingbird screamed.

But Pinchpurse glowered scornfully at him only a fraction of a second before drawing back the harpoon and thrusting deep into the writhing, pulsing mass holding their ship together.

An arrow-shaped head rose, three tiers of twisted serpent distant from where they stood. As it reared from the sea, water sluiced back from its slitted eyes, flat and clear as glass. Almost in a yawn, the thing opened its cavernous jaws. Its fangs flittered in the steady light still emanating from Princess Pegeen's parchment. The head darted forward, straight for Pinchpurse. With the boom of an avalanche the jaws clamped together.

Ned screamed.

He was joined by every man still clinging to what was left of the deck.

The head snapped back suddenly, and tossed the harpoon it had plucked from its body far out to sea. Then, seemingly miffed by the hostile gesture the harpoon signified, the serpent began uncoiling itself.

"Oh, no!" the King's first admiral cried, "When it releases us we'll be thrown into the sea!"

"Aye," Pinchpurse said grimly, between screams. "They likes their feed moist and juicy-like, snakes do."

"Where's my flaming air force?" Rowan roared, and pitched overboard, still encumbered by his chain mail shirt, shield, and heavy leather armor. Fortunately, several coils of sea serpent still writhed between king and sea. Hacking out with his great broadsword, Old Gut-buster, Rowan sank the sword into the serpent's hide and pulled himself onto the monster's back. Then using the sword as a crutch, he attempted to stand and reach the ship again, bellowing battle cries and curses all the while he danced on the snake's slippery back.

Perchingbird clung for his life to a hatchcover, and wished just this once that he could cry for help without the use of his tongue, no matter how many languages it had mastered.

The serpent snaked yet another coil loose, rattling the ship like a pebble in a gourd.

"Whoops! Whoops! Whoops!" Rowan yelled as the beast slipped beneath him. "Whoa, beastie! Ye great slithering slime of a thing, hold still and feel my blade!" But the serpent continued to unwind, and the king's feet continued to juggle him about on the beast's twisting coils.

But his bellowing was not in vain. Now another noise joined the general melee, and the dragon Grimley flew into view, diving across the sea from over the glacier. A ball of flame burst from his golden lips, scorching the serpent with a hiss more hideous than that of a thousand snakes.

"Hold! You can't do that!" a high-pitched feminine voice squealed. "Make your dragon stop that!" Two mermaids popped out from behind the ice chunk which had concealed them, and began swimming frantic circles around the ship, monster and all.

The gorgeous green-haired siren broke off a piece of ice and flung it at Grimley. He was having a lovely time barbecuing the serpent, while the sea snake recoiled into a tight defensive cone around the ship, squashing in its coils all who couldn't manage to scramble toward the remaining mast. Only the King's sword remained in direct contact with the great snake now, and from its pommel His Majesty dangled, heavy not only in flesh but in several stonesweight of armor as well.

The siren's iceball flew wide of Grimley, who carried another length of snake. The serpent hissed and moaned horribly.

"Let him go, you awful things!" shrieked the green-haired mermaid's accomplice, a shapely semi-lady with lavender tresses and very healthy gills.

But Grimley struck again, and the serpent convulsed, washing them all in icy seawater as great waves broke over the shattered decks.

Sir Cyril saw the serpent's head rear high above his disintegrating sanctuary, and saw the King dangling from the monster's neck. Then, with a final mighty curse, Roari Rowan, sword and all, plunged straight for the bottom of the sea.

"Grimley, stop!" Perchingbird shouted. The dragon hovered, considering the best portion of the serpent to fry next.

"What's the matter, hot shot? Don't you like to have a little fun?"

"His Majesty is overboard. Force the mermaids to fetch him."

It didn't occur to Perchingbird at the time that dragons and mermaids probably had no common tongue, but as it turned out they didn't need to have. The mermaids had taken an active interest in the dragon's conversation, and understood readily enough what Sir Cyril's instructions to Grimley had been.

"I'm going, Lorelei!" the lavender-haired lass sang out, diving.

"No fair! You got the last cute mortal! I'M going too!" cried the green-haired Lorelei, who also dived.

It took both of them to haul the King to the surface and lay his body out on the first ice chunk they could find large enough to accommodate him. Then Lorelei swam back over to the serpent and ship and addressed Perchingbird. "We saved him, like you said. Now will you make that dragon let our Ollie alone so he can grow another skin?"

"Only if you'll help transport the rest of us to safety," Sir Cyril replied. "When your serpent uncoils again, we'll all drown."

"Well, I don't see what's so awful about that," the mermaid pouted prettily. "You mortals are such sillies about getting a little damp."

"Madam," Perchingbird rejoined, mustering all of the dignity he could in his precarious position. "This vessel is on a mission of national importance. The man you just rescued is Lord King of All Argonia. We are joined with him to do battle with the evil sorcerer, Fearchar Brown, who has laid a deadly curse on the Princess Bronwyn, and whose evil machinations imperil our good country. As a patriotic citizen in Royal Argonian waters, you can easily understand, I'm sure, that it would be contrary to national interests for us to drown at this time, however much pleasure the sight might afford you and your companion."

"Well, gee, don't get huffy, sweetmeat," the mermaid said. "You should have said you were after that eel, Fearchar, to begin with. I have a few things to settle with him myself!" Diving back into the water, she swam to the serpent's head and instructed him in nautical rescue procedure.

* * *

111

The moon was high and white, providing light for the reluctant Trickle as she led them to the village. As Colin later remarked, they could have found the town anyway, without the moon, without a guide; indeed, with their eyes closed. For it smelled worse than the pit of a giant's privy tower.

So thoroughly befouled was the place that even the stream, though it had already been blessed with Moonshine's magic upstream, near their camp, was in this place slick with rot and excrement. Wind whipped leaves across its surface, and shook the naked limbs of trees, as gnarled and blasted as if they had finally succumbed to a hundred harsh winters. Dead moldy leaves scurried like rats down the muddy track that seemed to be the village's main thoroughfare. The road started at the stream and appeared to continue past the town, through the forest to the south and east.

By the sickly moonlight, Maggie saw flowers hanging dead over the side of their windowbox at the first cottage on the right. And on the left, the door of the third dwelling down hung drunkenly from one leather hinge, creaking back and forth in the soughing wind.

No lights burned, nor did smoke rise from any chimney, either for warmth or for cooking.

"Here it is," Trickle said. "The prosperous hamlet of Everclear; population, zero. Have fun, ducklings. Ta." With that, she flew away.

Colin gulped. Maggie took a deep breath to stifle the gagging in her throat and said to Moonshine, "The first thing, I suppose, is to cleanse this water."

"Stick my horn in THAT?" he asked, prancing from one hoof to another. "It's very nasty, maiden. I'll soil my horn."

"Is there an exemption in your creed that says you don't have to purify water so foul it will soil your horn?" she asked innocently.

"Not that I know of," he sighed, and quickly submerged the extreme tip of his horn in the swill-filled stream.

Clarity instantly spiralled from the point of Moonshine's horn, devouring the filth that had choked the stream. Before long they could even hear the difference as the freshly cleansed water bubbled around and over the stones in its bed.

Moonshine's face wore a vaguely gloating expression as he raised it, but he sniffed disdainfully saying, "Phew. Well, now that I have provided the potion for your ministrations, Maiden, good minstrel, I shall leave you for a time and undertake to remedy the ills of those beasts not yet beyond the power of my horn.''

"Very well," Maggie said, giving him a farewell pat on the flank. "But do be careful. There are unicorn-nappers about."

With a toss of his foamy tail to show exactly what he thought of such dangers, the unicorn galloped off down the street, then turned into the darkness at the rear of the hovels on the right.

A wolf's howl rose on the night wind. Colin stared around him, his eyes probing shadows, his hand on Banshee Bringer. Maggie took another deep breath and knelt beside the stream, filling their two water skins until they were swollen full of the bright, healing liquid. She handed one of the skins to Colin. "It'll be faster if we split up. I'll take the cottages to the left, you take the ones on the right. If you find anyone who seems to have the least spark of life, just pour this between his lips."

Colin licked his own lips nervously. "But what if—I mean to say, I'm not much good at telling." He didn't care to be separated from the others to go mucking about among dead people, either. The very thought of it depressed him, made him feel helpless and, if not actually frightened, at least sensibly worried.

But Maggie was impatient to start, and answered rather sharply, "Then give it to all of them. It can't hurt." So saying, she marched boldly into the first cottage on the left. There was nothing for Colin to do but start his own rounds.

The first two cottages Maggie checked were empty, and she discovered the probable reason at the third, where six adults and two young boys lay slumped across the table. They seemed to have been dining together. When her eyes had adapted to the faint moonlight slanting in through the unshuttered window and her nose had adjusted to the smell of death sufficiently that she could breath again, she took her own advice, and doggedly pried one head after another up from its resting place, searching staring eyes for any signs of life. Even though she saw none, pity moved her to dispense a few drops from her flask across each set of grimacing lips.

Emerging from that house, she stood for a moment wiping her eyes. Betrayers of a unicorn the people within might be, but they looked very much like her own neighbors at home. She felt embarrassed seeing in such undignified extremity people she'd never gotten to know as human beings, as if she'd caught them bathing, bereft of the trappings with which they disguised their imperfections. She forced herself toward the next cottage.

Across the road, Colin timidly knocked on the door that

already stood ajar. "Is anybody alive in there?" she heard him whisper hoarsely before he entered.

Smiling slightly to herself, she stopped at the doorway of the middle cottage on her side of the road, gathering her own nerve. She heard the cries just as she put her foot on the threshold.

At first, they seemed to come from within, but her rapid search of the premises revealed no one at all in the cottage. Puzzled, she stepped back outside. Colin had disappeared by now, and in the distance, above the gusting wind, she heard the pounding of Moonshine's hooves as he conducted his own errands of mercy. But she also—yes, very distinctly now—heard a pain-filled moaning.

Walking toward it, she followed the mud-mired road a bit past the last cottage, down what seemed to be a well-traveled cart path. The road crooked abruptly, and meandered into the forest. Looking back, she could see that she was still well within sight of the town, but the moaning was louder than ever now, and she hurried on until she came to a long, low building. This was most certainly the inn from its size and its position, easily accessible yet well-removed enough that revelers would not keep townsfolk awake nights. It was from this building that the miserable survivor still keened what sounded like his death agonies.

But at least someone yet lived who might tell what had actually happened to the unicorn and her captors. Maggie breathed a prayer of gratitude to the Mother, along with one of hope for the preservation of at least this one inhabitant. Perhaps this man would be one of the wizards of whom the faery had spoken. For now, listening closer, Maggie could make out strange words amidst the moaning—possibly some magical spell.

As she opened the door to the inn, she realized that the moaning was not, after all, just moaning, nor was it any magical spell, but a song of some sort, and very badly sung at that. Chiding herself for being as over-critical as Winnie always accused her of being, she reminded herself that a very sick person such as this one obviously was could not help slurring song words.

She rushed through the door and toward the voice, bruising her shins on an overturned bench. Swearing through her teeth and rubbing her shins, she listened more intently, using the sound to help her locate a path to the singer. To her disappointment there was nothing remotely wizardly or even particularly helpful about the words of the mysterious song:

"Where is me bed?
Me jolly, jolly bed?
Awwwwwwwllllgonnne for beer and tobacco!
For I lent it to a whore
And now it is all wore..."

When her magic had lit one of the torches on the wall nearest her, Maggie saw that the voice belonged to a disheveled heap of soiled and stained, though formerly elegant, garments. The heap was sprawled at the end of a long table in a dark corner near the hearth, which was set into the wall farthest from the door. Maggie pulled the torch from its socket and made her way to the singing bundle. From the sound of him, the man had to be in terrible pain.

"Are you quite all right, sir?" she asked, bending over him. His head was collapsed on his wrists, and all she could see was the bald spot on the top of his head shining in the torchlight amid a mad scattering of tankards and jugs. The bald spot, she thought at first, was in roughly the same place a pilgrim's tonsure should be.

But it was no pilgrim who raised leering, reddened eyes in answer to her question. Nor was it with brotherly love that he grabbed her wrist and pulled her, torch, flask, and all, into his lap. Prince Leofwin's breath was so strong it not only knocked her own breath from her, but totally overpowered the charnelhouse smell of the village as well.

"Ah, little wench, there you are! You took long enough at fetching that drink!" He snatched at her flask. She snatched it back. He peered at her closely. "Eh? What's t'matter with you? What've you done to yerself—you've gone and gotten all sooty. I thought you were golden-haired. Been cleanin' the chimney, have you?"

"Don't be an ass!" Maggie snapped, attempting to reclaim her arm and finding to her dismay that he was much stronger than she, even in his current condition. "Let go of me at once!"

Instead, with one hand he pulled her face down into his own, nearly smothering her, while he fumbled up her skirts with his free hand. Her magic jerked the threads of her skirt so that they pulled it modestly down again.

His porcine eyes grew sly. "Oho, not only sooty but snooty, are we? Like that little unicorn-loving nymphie thing? SAVING yourself for your cause, are you, dearie?" He poked her chest painfully with a squat finger. "Well, you mind me, little honey,

115

and forget about unicorns and causes, if you know what's good for you. Causes are for men fool enough to believe in them and unicorns don't care for YOUR kind of girl." He chucked her under the chin and she bit viciously at his finger. "Now, now, enough of that." He pulled the torch from her hand and, without releasing her, stuck it in the wall socket above him.

Then he pinioned the arm that had held the torch to her side, along with the one still holding the flask. "You don't need to play hard-to-get for old 'Fwin to like you, little one. I've something to comfort you. How would you like to receive the favors of a real live handsome prince?"

He puckered up for her kiss, and at the same time relaxed his grip on her as he waited to receive her gratitude. Maggie broke his grasp and jumped to her feet.

"Bugger off, your highness. I've had a long, hard day. If you can't do anything to help us save these people or rescue that poor unicorn—" she looked at him suspiciously. "Say, how come you're alive when all the village is dead from the poisonous water?"

"Water?" he scoffed, rising from the bench into a semi-crouch and stumbling towards her. "Never touch the stuff. Ale and wine alone are fit for the innards of warrior princes like me. Now come here, little honey, and stop being so blasted coy. And so sassy. Where do you think an ugly, bad-tempered, ill-favored, swarthy little number like you'll ever get another chance at any man, much less a prince?"

"You'd be surprised," she said, backing into another bench and knocking it over. Awkwardly, she hopped backwards across it. Her foot caught, and she fell sprawling on her back.

Leofwin landed, whoofing, on top of her. "You're uncommonly lacking in a seemly show of gratitude, my girl. Let me tutor you in some manners."

Maggie gave her best magical cow-moving shove but the prince was very heavy and lay grinning down at her, highly amused and no little pleased with himself.

"Look here, you idiot—your Highness," she said. "I'll have you know you're not the only royalty around here. I've lately been made princess myself by King Roari Rowan, as I trust you'll be mortified with shame to remember if you look at me closely. I'm sure His Highness won't like it at all that a foreigner such as yourself, illustrious lineage or no, is running around OUR country molesting OUR maidens when there are loyal subjects who badly need his help."

That made the prince sit up. Maggie smugly congratulated

herself on appealing to his instincts of regal responsibility and international diplomacy.

Planting a hammy hand on each side of her face, he studied her closely. "*You're* the Princess Magdalene, for whom I've been facing deadly peril and braving unspeakable dangers from which, I can tell you, I've barely escaped with my life—if not my property, since those blackguards took my seven league boots that I won fair and square cheating at dice!"

"That's me," Maggie acknowledged cheerfully.

"What a remarkable piece of luck!" he cried, and shoved her back down again while trying once more to ruck up her skirts. "Here I've been going through all this silly questing when all I needed was this opportunity—and well-earned it is, too, I might add! Now I'll simply despoil you, and your king will be certain to give me your hand to go with the rest just so I'll take you home and make an honest queen of you. As THE Prince of Greater Frostingdung with THE bona fide princess in his possession, I can spare a unicorn or two. For, with you in tow, my dear, I'll not only win my own kingdom but your undoubtedly substantial dowry as well."

"Uh oh," Maggie said, and began wriggling more furiously than ever, wrestling with the prince, who was fairly agleam with drunken glee.

"This is MOST opportune," he chortled.

"This is most IGNOBLE, is what it is," Maggie complained, batting angrily at his busy hands. "This is no kind of behavior for a gallant prince at all, if you ask me."

Leofwin chucked her forcibly under the chin with one hand and recaptured both of her wrists with the other. Though Maggie was no weakling, neither was she a match for Leofwin. He was an unusually hefty sort of prince.

"You've been listening to too many romances, little honey. You seem to think that witches like yourself could turn into REAL princesses, who, as everybody knows, are so fragile they'd break if one were to jounce them around like this—"

"I do NOT listen to romances and whether I shatter or not, my *ribs* are certainly not going to hold out much longer if you don't get your knees out of them!"

But now the prince was bent on giving her a speech.

"Gullible people like you, you see, believe that old myth that nobility is an asset in noblemen. Let me tell you, sweeting, it's no great help in the prince game at all. Rape and pillage of foreign villages is *my* specialty. It's what I'm good at," he concluded without false modesty.

117

Maggie groaned. "I was afraid of that. There are people out there who need our help, and you're—stop that, now! Unhand me this instant, or you'll regret it!" She clawed and bit and began screaming words he couldn't quite make out as he was disarranging their garments for his convenience.

"You can't fool me, lovey. That hot temper of yours is all flaming passion, isn't it? Don't worry about those sods out there. They're done for, and OUCH!" as she bit him, "I'll put you out as well if you don't cease that caterwauling and be goo—" He lifted his arm to strike her as she let out another bellow. But before he could strike, he felt a distinct, uncomfortable warmth growing at his backside.

"Sic 'im!" Maggie shouted so loudly that dust and cinders jarred loose from the rafters.

Mercifully for Colin, most of the cottages he entered were empty of people, living or otherwise. At the fifth, a smithy, he found the mayor, the dwarf blacksmith of whom Trickle had spoken, lying across his anvil as if broken, moonlight glinting grotesquely off his empty eyeballs.

The sight was too much for Colin, who succumbed to a prolonged period of intense vomiting before forcing the body onto its back. He mechanically poured the unicorn water through the dwarf's teeth, though of course the halfling just continued to lay there, still staring.

Dumping the body none too tenderly back onto the floor, Colin trudged on to the next cabin, and the next, now finding more people, matrons, men and children, mostly little boys, though one or two lifeless infants were female.

When he'd finished his row of cottages and Maggie had still failed to appear, he began to search her row, adding an extra drop of unicorn water to the bodies in the cottages for good measure, in case she hadn't gotten as far as he had. It might have been his imagination, but he fancied that some of the bodies in her row looked somewhat less dead than those in his own row, if such a thing were possible. Telling himself he was an idiot to think one corpse could possibly feel warmer than another, he hurried on to look for Maggie. She might have found a survivor. Of course! That had to be what was keeping her.

But he began to be perplexed when he had searched all but the last cottage without locating her. Ducking back out into the wind-ruffled night, he suddenly stopped cold, his anxiety turning to alarm as he heard screams from back down at the end of the road.

He ran, pelting down the muddy track, slipping on leaves and falling in the sucking mud, but righting himself and running all the faster.

The screams rang louder and louder, deafening him to the slow, slurping footsteps shambling in his wake.

Moonshine was disappointed when the dogs and cats and horses he touched with his horn failed to respond immediately. He'd hoped a spark of life remained in at least one of them. For surely the animals of the village would be more inclined than the people to answer his questions about the other unicorn.

Animals would be clever enough to be grateful and candid to one who saved them.

Though if those silly beasts who'd turned against the wizard and had dared to attack his maiden had been any indication of the quality of the beasts hereabouts, perhaps he was wrong. Still, for some reason, perhaps because his wonderful maiden seemed to think it was the right thing to do, he was willing to try to save them. He was therefore not surprised when he suddenly remembered a portion of the Creed he could have sworn he'd never known to begin with. It just popped itself into his head and sang itself to him. He was sure he'd never learned it at his mother's withers, but nevertheless it sounded right and clearly pointed out his duty:

> "For it is the Unicorn Creed
> To offer the horn to the need
> Of beings infected
> With water-connected
> Afflictions. We rise to the deed."

It ended oddly, compared to the other passages, but that was undoubtedly because of its essentially activist character.

He was relieved that the Creed substantiated Maid Maggie's idea, which was, as were so many of her ideas, unconventional. Like insisting that he associate himself not only with her but with minstrels and ersatz moat monsters.

But she was a very *good* maiden, nevertheless, he was sure of that, and very pure. Somehow her ideas always seemed to turn out right; the minstrel had saved them at the wizard's castle, and the wizard himself, contrary to first impressions, was a well-bred elf with exceedingly good taste, who appreciated the beauty and wisdom of unicorns.

Above him, the wind raced through the trees, and a cloud whisked across the moon. Once he thought he heard Lyrrill's hunting cry, and another time a wolf howled, seemingly nearby, and Moonshine quaked, just a little, wondering why that particular wolf should be alive when all else throughout the woods was dead.

The entire situation was eerie, was what it was. Normally, Moonshine didn't mind eerie. There were those, in fact, who considered HIM slightly eerie. But tonight, with the reek of all those dead things still haunting his nostrils, he minded the eeriness a great deal. It simply wasn't wholesome.

He wished Maid Maggie and the minstrel would hurry. He'd run out of cats and dogs and horses, and was reluctant to start on pigs and goats and chickens.

Back by the stream, Roundelay nickered uneasily, and Moonshine cocked his head to hear what she was saying.

That was when he heard the first scream.

Colin raced into the tavern and skidded to a halt. The screams were multiple and mingled, both male and female. By the bright light of a fire that streaked like lightning around the tavern floor, he saw that some of the screams, the wrathful, offended ones, came from Maggie, who was on the pointing end of the fire. The other screams, the pained and frightened ones, came from Prince Leofwin, who was on the receiving end.

Brandishing Banshee Bringer, Colin leapt from table to bench to table until he reached the corner where Maggie's fire had corraled the prince.

Noting the sword in Colin's hand, Maggie dowsed her fire before it could climb the Prince's pant leg. "It's about time you got here," she said. "My finger and my voice were getting very tired."

"That was CRUEL, witch!" Leofwin complained, rubbing his hindquarters as if inspecting for damage.

Maggie shrugged. "I thought I heard you say something about wanting flaming passion, but in my line of work, the best I could come up with was passionate flaming."

"Keep that in mind, varlet," Colin said sternly, looking down the length of his blade at the seated and sweating nobleman. "Trifle with the Princess Magdalene and you're playing with fire."

"Oh, Mother," Maggie moaned. "You sound like the dragons now."

"It's a good thing you didn't maim me," the Prince said pettishly. "Half the ladies in this part of the world would never forgive you."

120

Colin danced about, thoroughly enjoying himself, threatening the Prince, who had sat down next to his own heavy battle sword. This was what gallantry was all about, defending one's lady from black-hearted princes, just as Sir Osgood the Good did in the ballad of the same name when he defended the Lady Corisande from the vile and lecherous Sir Cuthbert.

But evidently Sir Cuthbert had not been the swordsman Prince Leofwin was, for before Colin knew it, the Prince raised the great iron weapon and with a leisurely whack shattered Colin's blade to irretrievably small pieces. "Get lost, hero, and let the lady and me continue our conversation. She's beginning to fancy me. I can tell." And with that Leofwin swiped a brutal slash where Colin's head was formerly.

By then, however, Colin had crawled beneath the table, and on hands and knees was trying to reassemble the shards of Banshee Bringer.

"You broke my sword," he accused Leofwin, who loomed menacingly above him. "The King *gave* me that sword, and you broke it."

"Never mind, warbler. You won't have need of it again when I'm done with you." He started to duck down under the table low enough to reach Colin with his blade, but stopped in mid-stoop.

Moonshine exploded into the tavern, spraying bits of clattering crockery and fragmenting furniture behind him as he flew to the rescue. Flying behind him was Trickle, hanging on for dear life to the end of his tail.

Rearing mightily, the unicorn stopped before them.

"You screamed, Maiden?" he asked.

Prince Leofwin had joined Colin under the table when Moonshine first appeared, but now the Prince crawled far enough out to shake his sword threateningly at the unicorn.

Maggie concentrated very hard, telling her magic she needed to chop onions with the largest knife available in the immediate vicinity. Leofwin's blade wrenched itself from its owner's hand and began making short, harmless whacks at the earthen floor. The whacks were harmless enough, at least, until the Prince tried to regain his blade and it mistook his fingers for onions. He drew his hand back speedily.

But by then Moonshine had spotted him, and was making rapid thrusts and lunges with his horn under the edge of the table. "Come forth, villain, and prepare to be skewered like the wild pig you are!" the unicorn shrilled to the Prince, who understood only the angry whinny and the rapier horn. "Despoil MY maiden, will you? Take that!"

"Let him be, Moonshine." Maggie grabbed a handful of mane. "For now." She found the outline of his disguise in her pocket and slipped it over his horn. "This is the kind of filth it truly *would* be a shame to soil your horn with."

"Ah, but one false move," Colin cautioned as he scuttled out to join his friends, "And she'll sic your own sword on you. If I were you I'd come away from it." Leofwin followed his advice, looking chastened and pensive and suddenly sober.

"Whew! Am I glad *that's* over!" Trickle said, extricating herself from Moonshine's tail and collapsing across the rim of an empty flagon, her skinned knees and dirty legs draped over one edge—head, shoulders, and small, sinewy arms over the other. "Because we've got a *real* problem approaching—" she looked over her shoulder, toward the door. "Correction, here."

Colin stared. Maggie hugged Moonshine tighter. Even Leofwin's jaw dropped.

From the gloomy night, blown in on the rainy wind and heralded by their unlovely fragrance, shuffled three of the men Colin recognized as among those whose dead lips he had wet with unicorn water. They didn't look a bit better walking than they had looked splayed in various morbid poses around their cottages. The dwarf blacksmith was still sooty and starey-eyed. Against the color of last year's fall leaves, the cobbler's pockmarks blazed like live coals. Mud caked the potter's hair, and smeared across his face and down his tunic. He'd apparently succumbed to the poison while working with his clay, since Colin had found him collapsed over a squashed pot. The dark smudges only made his dead skin look more waxen, his eyes more like stones under shallow water.

Oblivious to everything but their goal, the three grisly figures lurched their way to a table and sat, elbows bent, eyes staring at nothing.

Soon these apparitions were joined by a fourth, one of the men at the table of six first treated with unicorn water. The fourth paid no attention to his fellows, but walked straight past their table to the shelves behind the long table that served as a bar. He pulled down three clean flagons. These he held under the open spigot of the nearest keg until he had filled all three. He might have seemed to be going about his daily business except that he failed to shut the spigot as he shuffled to the table of his fellow townsmen. Brew gushed onto the earthen floor, turning it muddy and wending a shining trail between table legs and under bench seats. Mechanically, the innkeeper smacked the pints down in front of his customers and shuffled off again.

"They must have good credit," Colin mumbled under his breath, exchanging wary looks with Maggie. "He didn't even take their money." Maggie's face was closed, her eyes narrow and suspicious. She still felt some trickery unconnected with Prince Leofwin was taking place under her nose. She smelt the sorcery, but she wasn't sure where the spell was coming from.

Moonshine's eyes rolled so far back in his head that only the least glimpse of violet was possible.

Leofwin fainted dead away.

"The water seems to have worked," Colin finally remarked with an optimistic smile as pallid as the newcomers. "They—er—do seem to be ambulatory, even if they're not very sociable to outsiders. But that's not so strange. I've been in many a town where the folk are like that. Usually they just need warming up. A little song, perhaps and—"

"Shhh," Maggie said. "Something *is* wrong. They're not just unfriendly; they don't even know we're here. And they were *dead* before, I tell you."

Moonshine recovered himself enough to protest. "Something is *wrong*, you say? With MY magic? Nay, Maiden, you're mistaken." He sniffed tentatively, then flared his nostrils boldly wider. "Smell. The odor of death has departed."

With considerable difficulty, Trickle struggled up from her lounging position inside the flagon, dried her wings on the hem of a bar towel, and flew to the table full of moribund drinkers.

She fluttered at their eyes, ears and noses, but no matter how annoying she tried to be, none of them paid her any attention whatsoever. After a short general tour of inspection, she flew back, lighting on Moonshine's nose. "What a bunch of deadheads," she said. "I could have flown in one of their ears and out the other and they'd never have known the difference. But you can relax, 'Corny. Nothing went wrong with your magic. It's just that not quite enough went right.

"The way it looks to me is, your horn managed to put the bodies of these rascals back in business—enough so they can go through all their old habits like eating and drinking and fouling up my poor stream." She paused to scratch her head and glanced again at the townspeople. In the flickering light of Maggie's torch, the faery's tiny lips almost appeared to wear a brittle little smile. "But as for what's inside of them, if indeed anything ever was, all of THAT's still out to lunch. Nobody's home inside

123

their eyes at all. I'm afraid, gallant heroes and heroines, you guys with your mighty magical meddling have created a whole village of zombies."

"How sordid!" Moonshine said.

"Surely you're mistaken," Colin laughed nervously. "Only evil magicians can do that sort of thing."

"See for yourself," Trickle said, beckoning him with a mocking waggle of her pin-sized forefinger to follow her to the door.

Maggie followed too, and together the three of them peered through the splintery doorway out into the road, where silent villagers wandered in aimless pantomine of their daily lives. They were heedless of the fine rain which now veiled the woods, heedless likewise of the mud churning under their stumbling feet, and heedless as well that they walked abroad not in daylight, but in the water-riddled moonlight. They seemed scarcely more alive than their own shadows.

CHAPTER 8

"*Very* good, Ollie. That's it," the mermaid Lorelei prompted. "In, out, in, out, squeeze, release, squeeze, release. Eureka! He's coming around!" She did a backflip in the water, and surfaced facing the group of cold, wet sailors and soldiers who huddled together on the narrow strip of rocky beach between the great forest and the cold gray sea.

Sir Cyril was fascinated by the mermaids and their lengthy pet, and his fascination must have showed, for Lorelei dimpled prettily at him. He smiled back—guardedly. However fascinating and helpful the mermaids were now, on their best behavior, Perchingbird knew from his conch-shell-preserved lore that most members of their species were essentially nothing more than appealing, sea-going chowder-heads with alarming necrophiliac tendencies. That is, most of the female members of their species fell into that relatively (if one didn't count the odd shipwreck or drowning) harmless category. The males were very much worse. So bad, in fact, that the females preferred human males (preferably drowned) or selkies, the were-beast sea faeries who were seals in the sea and men on the land. The archives held several recorded cases of lineages born of alliances between the merwomen and the selkies. Young Songsmith, the King's minstrel, was said to be descended from such a mating.

What was so interesting about these particular mermaids, besides the fact that they were the first of their kind Sir Cyril had ever seen, was that they were altering their usual habit of drowning mortals and with great professional skill were directing their sea serpent in his exertions to revive the King. True, both mermaids and serpent were performing under some duress, but now that they'd gotten used to the idea, they did the job relatively cheerfully.

Lorelei had persuaded the sea beast to beach the last few cubits of his tail, a length sufficient to coil several times around the King's massive chest. Under her direction, the monster expanded and contracted his tail in a gentler version of the pulsating rhythm with which he had wrecked the *Snake's Bane*. Each bellows-like squeeze forced geysers of water from Rowan's mouth.

Perchingbird answered Lorelei's smile with an inquiring expression. He was beginning to understand the gurgly musical language passing between her and the serpent, and they seemed to have abandoned the idea of drowning the *Bane*'s survivors, at least for the time being. Lorelei actually seemed pleased at his interest, and nodded encouragingly to him.

He left the clutch of half-drowned men, and waddled forward to observe the rescue proceedings more closely. His legs ached, and his knees still wobbled from the terrifying ride he and his shipmates had endured astride the slippery unsinged portions of the uncomfortably rotund serpent. Though he knew the monster had not taken nearly as long as it felt like to ferry them from their ship's wreckage to the beach, the journey through the blinding fog and ice-clogged sea had seemed endless. Sir Cyril still feared that the delay would cost the King his life.

But even as he approached the monster-wrapped King, he saw Rowan's arms begin flailing weakly.

Lorelei's dimpled smile deepened, and Perchingbird complimented her. "Wonderful work you're doing there, Miss. And a very good idea you had using your—er—pet—to revive His Majesty. I doubt any of us could have applied sufficient pressure to get the sea water out of His Royal Highness by ourselves."

The mermaid flirted her irridescent tail in a pleased way, and said, "If you silly clams had just let us *know* you were after Fearchar and weren't just *any* passing ship, Cordelia and I wouldn't have allowed Ollie to play with your boat to begin with."

"Of course not," Cordelia agreed. She sat on a rock a little off shore, and flipped her long tresses back over her bare shoulders with a little shimmy of her human torso that sent a gasp of admiration through the ranks of the castaways, momentarily stilling the collective chattering of their teeth. With a fond smile of acknowledgement to her admirers, Cordelia continued. "You can't imagine how distressed I was to find Lorelei here in my waters in the state she was in after dealing with that horrid wizard! She and I schooled together, you know, simply ages ago, and although she was *much* older than I, I have always considered her a dear, dear sister. Ollie found her, actually, on an ice chunk not far from this very beach. By the time I answered his summons she was a perfect wreck, all dried out and wrinkled from being out of the water too long, and her voice nothing but a hoarse croak."

"I daresay I can't have been THAT bad," Lorelei replied edgily. "But I was upset, as any self-respecting siren would be. That Fearchar sailed out of our gulf like a greased eel. After the conversation I had with a descendent of our people, a certain minstrel, I began to doubt Fearchar ever intended to keep his promise to join me. I only wanted him to give up that split-tailed princess he'd been seeing, and come play with me as he always said he would." Her full lower lip quivered, whether with indignation or hurt Perchingbird couldn't tell. "But he had those big ugly swans of his attached to his boat, and used magic to get away from me so quickly I had to use all my energy to swim! Before I could sing the tiniest little note, he landed his boat and disappeared into the woods without even saying goodbye."

"She might have died on that rock if *I* hadn't saved her," Cordelia said. "But we've been having such a lovely time since then, playing with Ollie and all of the little fishing boats from the windside shore."

Perchingbird thought she must mean Brazoria. Argonia was, to his knowledge, relatively uninhabited on this coast. Most Argonians had settled in the southwestern regions, near the capital of Queenston and the Gulf of Gremlins. Better that Ollie and his friends posed a threat to Brazorian maritime activity than to Argonians.

The silver-spotted sea serpent relaxed its tail, and the King spat out the last of the seawater. Rubbing a wet, whiskery cheek against the monster's scales, His Majesty snuggled deeper into the coils. "Your skin's a might rough, darlin'," the monarch murmured to the monster. "But, ah, don't I love a lass with a firm grip!"

126

Lorelei leapt from the shallows like a porpoise, and twisted in mid-air, slapping Ollie's tail smartly with her own. Then, with a graceful flip, she arched herself so that she dived into the deep waters further off shore, where she resurfaced and calmly swam back to the beach. Shaking the water from her long green locks, she pouted. "You mustn't give Ollie all the credit, sweeting. *I'm* the one who saved you."

Cordelia slapped her shimmering tail and flung down her comb. "Remember, sister dear, whose waters you're swimming in. Ollie is MY pet, and though I'm glad to share my territory with you when you're not yourself, all mortals in these waters are mine and—oooh, lookie there! Doesn't he have LOVELY hair, though? Just like coral!" She stared admiringly at the King's suddenly fully revealed form, including the coral-colored hair, as Ollie's last coil unwound and slithered out to sea, leaving His Highness to fall flat on his royal backside. "Oh, no, sister. I really think I must have that one back."

With a great smack of her tail, which not entirely by accident splashed water over Cordelia's freshly dried and groomed coiffure, Lorelei flung her upper half onto shore and clasped the felled King's boot with a possessive hand. "You're NOT going to take him back, and never you mind his hair. He's MY ally, and it was MY information about Fearchar that helped put him on the throne, wasn't it, angelfish? I'm not about to let you drown him after all the trouble I've been to!"

"What a lot of bilge you're talking, sister Lorelei," Cordelia sniffed, tossing her newly soaked lavender hair, her alabaster assets aquiver with indignation. "Some guest YOU turned out to be. See if I ever share my salvage work with you again. To think you would turn on me for the sake of a coral-haired mortal! Haven't you learned anything from your experience with your precious Fearchar? These men have no honor at all—that's why I prefer the company of a real snake like Ollie!"

Lorelei was firm. "I'm sorry, sister. It's just that this is more important than mere salvage work. Can't you see how damaging it will be to our mer mystique if mortals think just anyone can go around enticing mermaids to beach themselves simply by ignoring us? I know I've been an awful silly, and *that's* why I can't let you drown these men right now. They're going to catch Fearchar for me at last, aren't you, little blowfish?" The last remark, Perchingbird realized, was directed at him.

He answered quickly, in his most conciliatory tone. "Yes, Miss. Er—at least, that's part of our mission. If you or Mistress

Cordelia would just be so kind now as to tell us where we are so we could be on our—"

"You're on the beach, silly," Cordelia snapped. "Where you were put by my dear Ollie, whom you almost murdered, as you very well know. Now you'll all just have to excuse me, for I really can't be bothered any further with your ridiculous problems. I have a dear friend who has been badly injured by certain cruel humans, and I must attend him." Her long gilt eyes accused them all, lingering longest on King Rowan, before returning to Lorelei, whom she addressed in a tone that showed she still stung from what she considered Lorelei's defection.

"Lest you make the same mistake again, sister dear, I advise you not to trust these men so completely. If I were you, I'd insist they bring that shark of a magician to this very spot, and throw him to you with an anchor 'round his ankle, in payment for their lives." Cordelia paused for a moment to allow her suggestion to sink in, then smiled sweetly at the crew. "I don't suppose any of you boys would care to join a lady in a little swim?" In spite of the wistful expressions lingering on the faces of a few of the men, there were no takers, and the disgruntled mermaid dived into the sea and swam rapidly towards the last few loops of still slightly smoldering seasnake.

Lorelei watched thoughtfully until both Cordelia and the snake were well out of sight, then turned back to Perchingbird, her eyes slitted and glittering with a strong emotion Sir Cyril couldn't name. "Never mind her. She's only trying to spoil my fun because she's jealous of me. But she does have a point, doesn't she? I mean, you boys DO owe me a great debt for saving you, don't you? Now, I don't know if I really want you to *drown* Fearchar exactly, when you find him, but as for that split-tailed princess—"

Ah, yes! Now he knew. The emotion so prominent in her expression was greed. Though she had played the benefactress well enough until now, Perchingbird knew that, considering the avaricious and amoral natures of mermaids, he oughtn't to be surprised that she was attempting to use their plight to her own advantage. Not only did she plan to seek vengeance on Fearchar, she was apparently even more interested in disposing of Princess Pegeen, her rival, as well.

The King was still regaining his senses, and when he did, the honor of the throne of Argonia would compel him to obey any demands imposed on him by the lethal, beautiful being who had saved his life, and whom he would be obliged to serve. The best thing for all concerned would be if Lorelei never formally voiced her ideas as demands at all, if she were subtly but gently reminded that although the castaways were shipless and largely without weapons or provisions, they still had considerable power at their disposal. Perchingbird could think of only one way to present an argument sufficiently timely and convincing to dissuade the determined siren.

"Oh, Dragon Grimley, sir!" he called to the heavens in general. "Might I have a word with you?"

Several sailors instinctively jumped into the sea as a spurt of flame shot out of the woods. Perchingbird took an involuntary and very hasty step backwards himself as Grimley poked his head through the trees.

"Didn't mean to scare you, hotshot," the dragon said affably. "But I couldn't see a flamin' thing in this fog. Thought I might come down to earth, so to speak, and pick up a nice morsel of moose or wolverine for the missus as long as I'm in the neighborhood. Couldn't find a single cow back at the castle. Guess it's just too flamin' foggy to do much huntin'. By the time I see my dinner, I've burnt it, if you see what I mean. What can I do for you this time?"

At the sight of the dragon, Lorelei had let out a girlish shriek and had dived into the cold gray waves.

"You're done it already, sir, thank you," Perchingbird replied. "Unless, of course, you could tell us where we are?"

Grimley scratched one of the red scales along his spine with a sharp-taloned foot. "Let me see. I'd say you were about—the castle is—uh—well, there are two mountain ranges and another big ice between the sea and—"

Perchingbird listened patiently, but soon realized that although the dragon might know perfectly well where they were, and could undoubtedly fly himself away in the direction of the castle at any time, he didn't know how to communicate his perception of the time and space involved to the earthbound and much slower people.

Frustrated, Grimley began to belch smoke from his nostrils and his eyes glowed red with vexation.

"Never mind, sir," Perchingbird said quickly, not wishing to add dealing with an overwrought dragon to his other problems. "I'm sure it will come to you. Perhaps Lady Grizel could—er—shed some light on the situation."

"That's what's got me so steamed up, hotshot," the dragon replied. "Grizel can't come, and I've got to get back to her. I only came back to tell you you folks are going to have to continue without us. While you and the others were getting all wrapped up in that long wiggly fella and listening to those fish-girls sing, the missus started cookin'. I think she's going to pop our little bun out of the oven any time now within the next moon, and I have to get back to hunt for her while she's hatchin'.''

"What's all this, Cyril?" the King, who had revived, demanded in a booming voice that quieted any concern anyone may have harbored about the recovery of his lungs from their dousing. His Majesty was surrounded by the rest of the crew now, and must have been sitting, since the top of his head wasn't visible above the others. "Is that Grimley? Ask him to be a good fellow, will you, and fetch us up a fire? The men are going to perish of t'chilblains if we don't warm 'em soon."

"Your pardon, sir," Perchingbird said to the dragon, and joined the cluster around the King. Rowan looked somewhat paler than usual, but was busily burnishing the metal on his armor, drying it with a torn piece of someone's cloak. Perchingbird conveyed the dragon's message.

"Well then, that's all right," the King said. "Their new dragon cave is near m'family home, Castle Rowan. I've a wee garrison there. Just gi' this tae t'captain o' t'guard." He slipped off his signet ring. "Have 'im meet us wi' horses an' arms. Surely t'dragon can show them how tae get t'where we are?"

"We'll hope so, Sire," Sir Cyril said. And though he carefully explained the King's wishes to Grimley, and attached a note to the ring, depositing both in his own purse and tying the purse around one of the dragon's claws, he had little faith the captain of the guard would understand either the dragon or the note. He could not draw pictures, as Princess Pegeen could, to enlighten others of their situation and the King's commands.

Watching the dragon's bright form vanish into the fog, Sir Cyril very much feared the mission, if not their collective existence, was doomed. Even if they managed to find their way back to Rowan's castle, could they possibly do so before their adversary had gained the strength he needed? If they met the wizard in the fullness of his power, while they were in their current depleted condition, could they even hope to prevent him from usurping the throne, never mind forcing him to lift the curse from Princess Bronwyn? And meanwhile, as they shivered on the beach and wondered where they were, in a condition unfit to save themselves, much less anyone else, the Princess Pegeen, one of Argonia's greatest ladies to Perchingbird's way of thinking, languished in the clutches of a ruthless, unscrupulous villain.

130

"I'd better never catch you doing that in sight of my innocent lambs," the woman snapped, watching Wulfric change to man form. "If you had any decency, you wouldn't perform such a disgusting spectacle in front of a respectable widow woman either."

But her slightly bulging black eyes watched avidly as she saw gray fur change to smooth human muscle and the tall, gray-haired man rise from his hands and knees to stand before her. "Really," she said, "I don't know what dear Nastur—excuse me, Sally, must be thinking of to send such a depraved creature as yourself to see her only sister-in-law when she knows very well I have three lovely chaste daughters who must be protected until a suitable match can be found." Her flat, nasal voice stopped as she ran the red tip of her tongue over her pointed teeth, smiling slightly in spite of herself. Her perfume was of such a cloying sweetness that for once Wulfric was almost glad to be in man form; the scent was enough to send his wolf nose into spasms of revulsion.

But he was on a mission for the cause, so he said politely, "I implore you to forgive this ugly carcass, noble relative of my gallant leader, but I bear an urgent message from Her. She would have you know that your opportunity to serve is nigh. Your beautiful daughters may well attract the beasts we need to accomplish our great purpose. There is at least one of these creatures loose in yon woods, though even now our Sally lays a clever snare for her. I shall watch for your signal, as you have arranged with Her. Be alert for strange beasts or men, and notify us of any who come nigh."

"Naturally," the lady replied curtly. "And don't you forget I'm to be rewarded. I've already done you one service, and I've yet to see my pay for that. I should be made at LEAST a duchess and suitable marriages arranged for all my daughters—it isn't easy for an attractive young widow like myself to manage alone with three tender blossoms to maintain in a fitting style. By the way," she curled a lock of brazen hair around a long sharp fingernail and gave him a sly look from beneath pale lashes, "I don't suppose you go through that distressing transformation because you're an enchanted prince, do you? Because if you are, I have several important connections among the sorcerous set who might help you if you were willing to pay . . ."

By that time, however, Wulfric had changed back into wolf form and leaped back across the stream which bordered the woman's garden. He bounded into the woods. But he was not going so fast that he failed to see one of the lady's "innocent lambs," a truly delicious looking sunny-haired young girl, seated by the stream bank among a varied flock of admiring beasts. Angrily recalling the woman's brutal remarks about his degrading transformation into man form, Wulfric slavered as he regarded the girl and thought it had been some time since he'd enjoyed lambchops.

He was gauging the distance between them and preparing to leap when he heard Sally's hunting horn.

Leofwin awoke while Colin, Maggie and Moonshine were discussing with Trickle what was to be done about the zombiefied villagers. After a few generally ignored preliminary groans, the Prince crawled to Maggie's feet and began kissing fervently the tattered hem of her skirt.

Maggie slapped his hands away. "Will you *please* stop pawing my clothing," she asked. "Here we are in the middle of nowhere with unicorn-nappers and zombies all around us, bandits on the prowl, the royal house cursed, the King Mother-only-knows-where on some quest or other, while a lot of addle-pated noblemen like you who are certainly no better than they ought to be chase us about trying to do brave deeds, and all you can do is attempt to launder my skirt by slobbering on it." She snatched the cloth out of his hand and started to turn back to her friends, but he threw himself prostrate and clasped her ankle, crying, "Forgive me, noble enchantress! I had no idea you were anything but another ravishingly gorgeous maiden. How was I supposed to know you control fire, can turn my own blade against me, command a unicorn and raise the dead? Most of the girls I've ravished don't even *have* hobbies. Spare my miserable life, I implore you, for surely you are as good as you are beautiful."

"Right," she said. "And you told me not long ago exactly what you thought of my looks. Never mind. Just get up, why don't you, and tell us how it is you happen to be waiting for us here when we left you behind days ago?"

"That's easy," the Prince said, relieved. He plopped heavily down on the bench in front of his collection of empty flagons. Maggie noticed that he now seemed completely sober. His speech was no longer slurred, and his tone was relatively civil. "I won at dice with that simp, Greystraw, and took his seven league boots, family heirloom for the Greystraws, you know, seven league boots. They may be transformers through the male

132

line, but his mother's people were elf cobblers, every one of them, for all their pretensions of nobility."

"That explains how you got here so *fast*," Colin acknowledged, "But not how you got *here* so fast. One might think, Highness, you were in league with those unicorn-snatching rogues."

Leofwin wiped his hand across his eyes. "Not so fierce, bard, not so fierce. Have pity on a sick man, will you? You people have a rude way of ending a lovely binge. I'd planned to hunt unicorns, not abduct them. I only followed that crazy Jivemgood here with a mind to winning a prize worthy of the little lady." He nodded toward Maggie. "I don't know why the fellow had to take MY seven-league boots. He's lots faster than me—must either have his own pair or a magic carpet or something stashed somewhere. Normally I don't hold with that kind of hocus-pocus, you know. A man should rely on his own thews and good iron sword, to my way of thinking. But in this case, since what I was promised was at quite a distance and seemed just the trick to acquire a special trinket for my family and the little lady's hand in the bargain, I used the bloody boots. And let me tell you, my legs will never be the same again!"

"What exactly did Count Jivemgood have to do with the unicorn-napping anyway?" Maggie demanded. "We know that's what you were up to so you can stop all that hogwash about presents for me."

"He didn't have much at all to do with it that I could see, Your Bewitchingness. It was mostly that nymphy little bitch that was behind the whole thing, though they kept talking about a dark monk or a black pilgrim or something or other and about how they were going to start a new world right here in old Rowan's kingdom. My feeling was they wanted the 'corns for the general usefulness of the beasts—keep strategic cisterns pure, mend the sick, that sort of thing. There was some raving about an elixir from Jivemgood and, of course," he glanced sidelong at the zombies who continued bending their elbows and slopping brew down their fronts with chillingly automatic regularity, "if that horn water can do THAT sort of thing to people, I can see—"

"That wasn't intentional," Maggie said. "Tell us more about the woman you mentioned. You said she was a nymph but—"

"She IS a nymph," Trickle said bitterly. "A renegade. Used to have my bit of turf, down at the stream. Her name was Nasturtium then. I only met her once before—well, before now, but the animals didn't seem overly fond of her. She always

133

seemed to feel nymphing was beneath her, though she didn't mind flaunting herself in front of the townsmen when their wives weren't looking, according to what I heard. Thought she was above guarding streams and protecting animals. Looks like she's found someone else who thinks so, too, and got them to help her steal poor Snowshadow.''

Suddenly the faery flew over to Leofwin's ear, and with all her strength grabbed its lobe and gave it a vicious tweak. ''He knows where she's taken Snowshadow. Make him tell! I saw him cuddling up to that hussy!''

''Ow!'' the Prince cried. Colin grabbed his arm as he swung at the faery. Leofwin regarded the tiny woman ruefully and rubbed his ear. ''You didn't see enough to know what you're talking about, maggot. I had no chance to cuddle your friend before her pet wolf sprang from the bushes and tried to slay me. If it wasn't for my faithful sword, I'd be a dead man. I fought my way into a corner of this inn, and held them at bay until the girl gave the order to leave. I swear I don't know where they took the 'corn. Probably wherever they keep the others—back with this priest or pilgrim or whatever he is, I'd think. They took my boots and gear, and I was doing a fine job of getting drunk until everyone around here began dropping like slops flung out the window. It's been a heavy task, I can tell you that, trying to swallow down enough funeral libations to send each of the poor sods off to the next world.''

Trickle opened a bulging sack that had been tossed into a shadowy corner. ''Looks like you've been having a harder task yet looting the houses, haven't you, noble prince?''

''A man has to have some compensation for his trouble,'' Leofwin answered. ''I've lost my magic boots and gear.'' He looked sadly at the sword still chopping away at the ground. ''Even Old Spleen Splitter there, that you've got chopping mudpies out of the floor, has been turned against me, and after all we've been through together, too. I wish you'd stop it doing that, ma'am. That is a real genuine personally tailored sword of invincibility wrought for me by my own goblin granddaddy, and I hate to see it doing women's work.''

''In good time,'' Maggie said. ''I wouldn't be overly interested in that sword right now if I were you. It makes Moonshine nervous. He hasn't split a spleen yet this week himself, and he's wanting practice.''

Moonshine assumed an appropriately ferocious expression.

''Make him stop that, ma'am, won't you? I can't tell you

134

anything else. I was into my second jug before Sally and her boys were out of town."

"How long have they been gone, then?" Maggie asked.

Leofwin scratched his chin. "I couldn't say exactly. Can't even really tell you how long I've been here—I rather lost track of time after the fifth keg."

"I suppose we'll just have to try to find out about them at the next town then," Maggie said hopelessly.

"Yes, well, at any rate, we can't just leave these villagers wandering around like this," Colin said. "We'll have to report their problem to the nearest proper authorities."

"Perhaps kinsmen can care for them until my magic can finish its task, Maiden," Moonshine said. "I'm sure it will work—in time. I do so hate leaving a job half done."

"What's to be done with them in the meantime?" Maggie asked no one in particular. She personally didn't feel much encouraged that any amount of attention could help such pathetic-looking specimens, but one could hardly leave such a group lying about for the next unwary traveler to stumble over. Besides, she couldn't help feeling guilty that her interference had robbed these people of what little dignity death had left them.

"*I'll* look after them, Princess," Leofwin offered with a gloating gleam in his piggish eye. "It should be fun. I hear zombies will do anything they're told."

"Good idea," Trickle agreed. "We'll get them to move their privies and their garbage dumps to the other side of town, away from my stream, for starters and—"

"Hold there, half-pint," the Prince objected. "You'd not have a direct descendent of the goblin king, Gawdaufool, digging privies?" He reached for his sword, but it turned on him again, whacking remorselessly toward him, still under the influence of Maggie's magic.

The faery grinned. "I sure would, big boy. And you won't be needing your oversized frog-sticker, either, unless you plan to dig with it."

"It'd be a shame to ruin a blade like that with digging," Colin said. "I'll take it, if you can get it to cooperate, Maggie. He broke MY sword, after all, and I shall probably need one if we run into any of those bandits."

Maggie nodded and the sword sprang into his hand as if of its own accord.

Leofwin jumped to his feet. "See here, you can't just take my sword and leave me here digging privies with a lot of zombies! I won't stand for it!"

135

But before he could move, Trickle hopped onto his ear. Cupping her hands, she shouted directly into it. "NOW HEAR THIS, Big Shot. Behave yourself, or I will personally arrange for the biggest mosquito you've ever met to drive you totally out of your mind." She jabbed him hard with the needle-like tip of her fingernail. He clapped his hand to his ear, howling, but by that time she'd zipped to the other side of his neck and gouged him several more times. He swatted there as well but she evaded him, flying above his head and jerking a lock of his hair in a hard tug that caused him to yelp. For several minutes she continued to attack while the Prince pinwheeled like an infuriated windmill.

"STOP!" he bawled at last, sinking exhausted back against the table. Tears coursed down his ruddy cheeks and droplets of blood gleamed like small rubies where the faery had left her marks. "I—I can't take any m—more."

Trickle turned to Maggie and Colin. Her tiny face was full of grim satisfaction. "Very well. Now that His Highness and I understand each other, I think you people can go about your business. I'll see to it these louts eat and exercise and take whatever rest people in their condition will take. Don't worry about them. Just send some more mortals back for them, and try to find Snowshadow as quickly as you can."

Dawn marbled the sky with carnelian as Colin, Maggie, and Moonshine returned to their original campsite. Colin nodded sleepily against Roundelay's neck and Maggie yawned with every other breath.

Moonshine, however, pranced happily, head swinging from side to side. "Heard you, Maiden, how the dogs of the village barked again, and how the horses neighed? My magic made no half-creatures of those honest beasts."

Maggie leaned forward wearily and patted his neck. "No, darling, you healed them completely, true enough. Only the people aren't as good as new because of you. Which confirms what I've been thinking. There's some bad magic brewing behind this matter somewhere."

"And my horn dipping has improved the stream too," Moonshine continued, too enraptured of his own magic to heed her misgivings of bad. "See how even the little flowers lift their heads along the banks?"

"Aye," she agreed, yawning again. "I do seem to see a daisy or two sprouting amongst the mugwort this morning."

They breakfasted over one of her magic fires. Neither Colin nor Maggie were very hungry. Both still carried the death stench

136

of the village in their nostrils and the cold stare of the zombies in their minds' eyes.

"I'm going to look like the locals if we don't sleep soon," Colin complained, stretching hugely. "But somehow I feel disinclined to do it here."

Maggie shivered in the predawn chill, and pulling her woolen tunic tighter against her arms, moved closer to the fire. A thin mist danced above the stream. The moss underfoot was clammy with dew, which soaked through her soft skin boots.

A flutter of movement in the trees alerted Moonshine, who lifted his head and searched the forest. Soon, Lyrrill padded purring towards them.

"Looks as if she's found her cubs," Colin said.

Moonshine repeated the remark to the big cat, who licked her paw and groomed herself in a satisfied fashion. "Yesss," she replied. "And Lyrrill hass raissed no ignorrrant kittens. Not dead of poisssonss werrre *my* chilldrren! Norr crraven in theirrr dens while ssinglehorrrns werre ensslaved. Myrrill and Pyrrill live, asss doesss the sshe ssinglehorrrm they prresserrved frrrom wrretched hunterrss and fallsse sshe."

Moonshine's trot was a frisky little jig as he followed the lynx's furred paws across the dense forest floor. Deeper in the woods, the travelers began to notice more small animals still thriving among the trees. They could hear larger animals too. Colin thought this forest must be awfully full of wolves. He heard the same one, he was certain, as he had heard howling near Everclear. And hadn't Leofwin said something about the nymph unicorn-napper having a pet wolf?

Moonshine heard very little, for he was fairly chattering at Maggie. "Just think, at last, Maiden, I will meet one of my own kind who will know ALL of our precious Creed. How wonderful to be learned in the ways of my dam and sire! And I shall owe it all to the steadfastness and wisdom of you, my kind, beautiful, intelligent, gentle, witty, noble maiden, more caring and more loyal and—"

"Oh, leave off, won't you?" Maggie asked, blushing as she caught Colin's amused smile. She ruffled the unicorn's mane lightly. "I'll be as glad to clear this thing up as you will. We really must see if the King can't put a stop to these unicorn-nappings as soon as possible. Perhaps he'll grant me their heads as a boon instead of making me keep the coronet, eh? That would solve all our problems."

"Except the villagers," Colin reminded her.

"Yes, of course," she agreed "I hadn't forgotten them. But

137

surely there's somebody in this spell-riddled realm with the power to put them right again. It isn't as if they'd have to start from scratch, after all. Moonshine's already brought the Everclearians back to life—at least, almost.''

Colin pulled a wry face. "I'm afraid in cases like that almost really isn't good enough."

Lyrrill picked her way into a thicket of young cedar, and Moonshine followed closely. With great bouncing bounds, the lynx's youngest kittens tumbled playfully out of the underbrush, hissing, and brandishing small splayed paws. Beyond them, Lyrrill turned suddenly, flanked with what seemed to be two mirror images of herself.

Before Colin and Maggie could congratulate the cat on reuniting her family, a peevish voice from behind the three adult lynx said, "WILL you wretched furry beasts remove yourselves and stop lashing your nasty little tails in my face so I can look upon this kinsman you claim to have found!"

The lynx family scooted themselves farther back into the brush on either side of the path they had opened for Moonshine.

The other unicorn lay on a bed of flower-studded moss. Her coat was whiter than snow, and her mane and tail a tawny golden. Her horn was set rather lower on her face than Moonshine's, so that she always seemed to be looking down it, and it was also more opaque than his, shining with a soft ivory patina. Only the few nicks and scratches still gleaming through her coat lingered to remind her of her disagreement with Myrrill and Pyrrill and marred her perfection. Her eyes were the silver of winter water, and a few silvery hairs gleamed in her otherwise creamy muzzle.

But she was staring in horror at Moonshine. "Your horn!" she cried.

"My—oh, yes, this little device," he said, crossing his eyes to try to see the horn between them. "Maiden, if you'd be so kind?"

Maggie plucked off the cone of invisibility.

"Clever, isn't it?" Moonshine chuckled to the older unicorn. "A little something dreamed up by my clever maiden and her friends to protect me."

"Humiliate you is more likely!" the other unicorn sniffed. "Just as these nasty cats have humiliated me and kept me from my finest hour. I am Primrose. My dam was Dewdrop and my sire the magnificent Rosebriar, and I demand to be released from this ignominious captivity."

"Haven't you got it wrong?" Maggie asked. "The lynx twins rescued you. It's that other unicorn who was captured."

Primrose favored her, if favored was not too kind a term, with a glacial stare and a haughty sniff, after which she studiously ignored the witch, and asked Moonshine in carefully measured tones, "Whoever the person whom you so shamefully bear upon your back may be, kindly inform her that *I* speak with no human save only my own pure maiden, from whose side I was so rudely torn by these two overgrown bird-breathed mouse-catching fools. I decline to be addressed by other persons of the human persuasion, and must once again insist that I be released and reunited with my maiden immediately."

Moonshine backed up two steps, his rump pressing against Roundelay's nose. He had not the slightest inclination to argue with the severe older unicorn, but neither had he the slightest idea what she was talking about.

Primrose was not backwards about enlightening him. "All my born days I've tried to do the unicornly thing, waiting for just the proper sort of maiden to come along. Mind you, never did it cross my mind to accept just any mongrel-bred scullery maid." She cast a significant glance at Maggie. "Nor the kind of girl who might desecrate my innocent presence with the taint of a *male*," and her watery stare stabbed at Colin. "Nor would I consort with one, ever, who would dare to unhorn me with shameful magicks that would make of me a mere nag."

"I BEG your pardon," Maggie began to huff. But then, taking note of Moonshine's intense attentiveness to his kinswoman, she stopped herself, flushed with fury, and allowed Primrose to continue.

"No, more to my liking was the charming creature who came to me in my very own glade. A beauteous vision she was, hair as golden as my mane and skin as white as my coat, of rosey lip and cheek and eyes both bright and decorous at the same time. Ah, me, but her manner and mien showed me at once that a more unicornly girl I never before had beheld."

"Tell me this," Colin demanded. He hadn't liked the remark about him tainting innocent presences. "If you unicorns are supposed to love the first girls you meet, just how many girls had you beheld *before* that one, anyway, to know that she was so bloody superior?"

Primrose loftily ignored him as she kicked out to her left in an attempt to injure Myrrill, who sprang back. "I would have joined her blissfully but for these foul cats. They sprang upon me

139

and virtually tore me from the side of my dearest maiden before I could make myself known to her.''

"Only to protect you!'' Maggie said. "Why, we've been hearing horrible things about—''

But Primrose raised her voice above Maggie's and wouldn't hear anything she said. One after the other the unicorn recited the alleged virtues of her lost maiden, and the treacheries of the lynx and her demands for release. Graphically and categorically, she told Moonshine what she thought of lynx and of cats in general and of people and of Maggie and Colin in particular. She waxed eloquent on the subject of persons, lynx, and even fellow unicorns who would keep a devoted creature like herself from being with her chosen maiden.

Finally even Moonshine tired of listening to her and silenced her with a desperate whinny. "Enough! Enough! You're free, for pity's sake! You're free to seek any maiden you like—only make sure next time it's a maiden, indeed, and not some wicked nymph ensnaring you with glamourie instead of goodness. You're free to go wherever you like. Only please, first, tell me the rest of the Creed.''

"You don't know the Creed?'' Primrose asked, blowing derisively through her flaring nostrils. "You don't even know the Unicorn Creed?''

"Nay, lady, I do not. My dam was captured by hunters in my early youth and—''

"Hah! Did I not tell you? You should never trust these humans! Even your own dam was captured, and still you consort with them, you foolish foal!'' She trumpeted triumphantly as she rose to her feet, though she looked rather nervously at the family of lynx lying purring behind her, thoroughly absorbed in washing each other with patient swipes of great pink tongues. Reassured by her former captors' lack of interest in her, Primrose told Moonshine, "I haven't time to tell you the entire Creed, of course. But, since you've persuaded these feline felons to free me, I shall grant you the answers to a very few brief, specific, well-considered questions.''

Moonshine glanced back at Maggie. The witch sat with her arms tightly folded and her lips tightly clenched into a thin line. She nodded curtly in response to his inquiring look. "Go ahead. It's what you came for, after all.''

Turning back to Primrose, Moonshine blew and stamped for a moment or two before saying, "We only wanted to know, Lady Primrose, what becomes of the love between unicorn and maiden when the maiden—when the maiden is a maiden no longer?''

"You sully my ears with such filth?" Primrose screamed, and tried to bolt past him. But, though none of the lynx had appeared to be paying her any attention whatsoever, Myrrill casually laid a claw-studded paw against her flank. Primrose abruptly thought better of leaving. "Well, since you *ask*," she answered. "Of course, I'm not one to horn in where I'm not wanted, but since you *did* ask for my counsel, I think I must tell you that it's as plain to me as the horn on my face that that girl of yours is NOT up to standard. Any maiden who would even allow you to consider such an obscene question has something to hide. Obviously, she's harboring lewd thoughts about a *man* —and we needn't look much farther than the end of your own tail to see who that is, do we, since your little friend has even had the gall to force her paramour on you."

Overriding Moonshine's objections that Colin had actually proven very useful from time to time, Primrose continued. "Purity and goodness are the unicorn's manifest concerns, dear boy. One must never forget that. You have chosen unwisely. This girl is grimy, not immaculate. She is dark, not fair. Her tongue is quick and sharp, not sweet and gentle, and I can't say that I think that insolent look in her eye is at all in keeping with the properly ladylike spirit a unicorn maiden is supposed to exhibit at all times." Sniffing fastidiously, she added, "Furthermore, she very much resembles people I have observed from a sedate distance who are known to be witches. And I suspect she is an extremely ill-tempered one at that. You would be well rid of her."

"She's very pleasant to me, thank you, and she only works the most comforting and genteel sort of spells, I can assure you. And—and besides, she IS my maiden, and the first I ever met. It isn't her fault her people have made her a princess and wish her to wed." Moonshine finished what had started out as a heated defense quietly, staring down over his horn at the ground in front of his hooves.

"Her? A princess?" Primrose let forth a horse laugh that wasn't at all prim. "Really? You can't expect me to believe that!"

"It is so," Moonshine insisted stubbornly. "What says the Creed?"

"Before I tell you that, I must stress that the Creed could in no way possibly apply to this witch-wench of yours, whatever her political or personal status. She is simply not the least bit maidenly, never shall be and, I suspect, never was. She offends the very spirit of the Creed, dear Moonshine, and we unicorns must observe the spirit of the Creed even more stringently than the letter of the Creed, don't you see? But come. Have that hussy remove her disreputable rump from your back and come forth

141

with me a short distance. I won't desecrate the Creed by reciting it in her hearing."

Maggie dismounted angrily. As Moonshine and Primrose brushed past her and knocked Roundelay aside, Colin remarked, "Something tells me Moonshine's new friend doesn't care for you."

Maggie glared at him.

For a long time Primrose and Moonshine stood nose-to-nose in conference in the narrow glade beyond the lynx's hiding place. Then, abruptly, Primrose wheeled and galloped away.

Moonshine trotted back to Colin and Maggie, his head drooping sadly, his great amythest eyes so troubled that Maggie forgot her vexation and reached out to stroke his neck tenderly. "What did that old biddy tell you, anyway?" she asked. "I don't suppose I can even hope the Creed is in our favor?"

"Maid—or rather, Maggie, the Creed says only that unicorns may befriend none but true maidens. Primrose says I'm defiled beyond redemption already because Minstrel Colin has seen and conversed with me. And she also said she—I beg your pardon but she—" If unicorns were capable of blushing, Moonshine would have done so. "She doubts the sanctity of your honor."

"My honor's as sanctified as anybody's, thank you," Maggie replied, preparing to remount. "And I think we'd better forget all this nonsense for now until we see what can be done to prevent Primrose's sweet pure maiden from luring others of your kind into her nasty little snares."

But Moonshine could not take Primrose so lightly. Even if she had been fooled by the nymph, she was an older unicorn of considerable experience, and apparently of considerable knowledge. And nymphs, after all, were very like mortal girls, enough so to mate with men and fool other mortals. A nymph's charm could easily mask her with a semblance of mortal purity, quite conceivably convincingly enough to deceive even a unicorn. Her infatuation with the nymph notwithstanding, Primrose was the only authority Moonshine knew on correct unicorn behavior, and he needed to consider her words carefully. "Maid—Maggie, if you wouldn't mind very much, could you ride with Minstrel Colin for a time? I would seek solitude to ponder these matters."

Maggie's back stiffened, and she opened her mouth to speak, but instead clamped her lower lip to her upper like a snapping turtle and silently allowed Colin to help her up before him.

"I suppose," Colin said, "Now that we have found out what you needed to know about the Creed, we ought to go straightaway to the capital, and await the King to see what's to be done about the brigands—and your crown of course."

Maggie shrugged and didn't answer until a few minutes later when, straightening slightly, she replied in a careful, impartial tone. "I think by then it will be too late to do anything about the raiders. If we're to help the unicorns, we are going to have to do it by ourselves, even if it means we must deal with the brigands ourselves. And also we must, of course, let someone in authority know the plight of the village at once."

"'DEAL with the brigands'? What do you mean, 'deal with the brigands'? Really, old girl, I wish you would listen to yourself sometimes. It's always the same with you, you know. Rescue this! Rescue that! No wonder the King wanted to make you a Princess. You think like a bloody knight!" He realized that she was upset, and this was not a particularly good time to lodge a complaint, but he thought he ought to take advantage of her unusually subdued mood to get a word in edgewise. The sullen silence from both Maggie and Moonshine as they backed out of the lynx lair and trotted back down the trail through the woods gave him a perfect opportunity to express himself fully on several matters which had been irking him.

"First," he reminded her, "I helped you rescue a dragon so we could rescue your sister from that uncle of yours and ANOTHER dragon. Then nothing would do but what you had to go and get yourself locked up in a tower and the only decent thing for me to do was to rescue you from that. Now here you go again, wanting to stand against hordes of bandits and rescue unicorns who, for all we know, don't want rescuing any more than that prissy Primrose did. I'm fond of you, Maggie, and I like to think that I'm a patient man, and the Mother only knows I admire unicorns as much as the next person, but you never mentioned anything about another rescue when we set out on this journey. All you said was 'help me turn in my crown, Colin, so I won't have to part with Moonshine,' then it was 'Let's find us another unicorn and see what she says about Moonshine's bloody Creed, Colin.' Very well, now. I've helped you find another unicorn. And now, just because you don't care for what she said, you want to go traipsing about after a lot of very dangerous people who will more than likely damage us beyond all possible hope of repair, simply so you can rescue ANOTHER unicorn."

Encouraged by her lack of argument, he continued, "This time I'm not having it, I tell you. You seem to think I've nothing better to do than be your accomplice in all these silly schemes of yours. You forget, I'm responsible to the King for making songs, making people happy, for singing of history, not making it. His Majesty and your father will hold me to blame if anything happens to you. So this time we are going to do the clever, cowardly thing instead of the noble, numbskulled thing. This time we are reporting the *entire* problem, village, brigands, unicorns and all, to the proper authorities at the nearest village of—er—suitably healthy persons, and then we're riding straight for Queenston."

Moonshine's fog-gray form flickered in and out of the trees ahead as he led the way down the trail. Maggie sighed and slumped against Colin's chest. "Whatever you think is best," she said.

CHAPTER 9

Only Pegeen knew of the secret passage leading from her private chambers to the top of the maze. She and her brothers were children when she'd discovered the passage during a holiday with her family. Her father, King Finbar, had used the cliff castle for a summer retreat, a sanctuary from the demands of his court. Pegeen had found the passage while hiding from her brothers, lively little boys who thought teasing their sister was the best sport available when their father and tutors were too busy to take them gaming or help them play at jousting. The Princess was delighted with her find, and liked to imagine that her passage had been carved by the great worm for the express purpose of delivering her from her tormenters.

Not that she still believed that could be true. The worm's last great emergence had been decades before Pegeen first came to Worm's Roost. The passage was the trail left by the worm's great body and hot breath, and the thick substantial walls forming the maze were the residue of the glacier's original pre-worm surface. Legend had it that the worm still slept deep within the maze of turnings and looping paths it had carved into the heart of the ice mass sweeping up the mountain behind the castle. The servants had always tried to scare their small royal charges into submission with tales of the worm, threatening in low, whispery voices (they said it that way partly to sound like the worm and partly to keep Her Royal Highness, Mama, from hearing) that the worm would slither hissing and steaming out of his maze and into their very bedchambers if they weren't well-behaved. Secretly, she had rather wished it would. It would have been exciting to see that, and being the youngest and only Princess in the royal family was seldom very exciting.

When she was little, she had fearlessly walked upright along the edges of the wall closest to the castle. Snow drifting close to the castle's back wall had shored the maze's walls in places, making them quite thick, in places easily an arm's length wide. Of course, they were still slick and precarious, but although she was older now, and larger and less agile, she felt sure that with the aid of the light that was part of her illuminating magic, she could easily find the chamber where the unicorns were being confined.

Close by the rear wall, the half-snowfilled impressions left from the worm's undulations formed several good-sized culs-de-sac, icy rooms with only a single, easily blocked opening accessible from the door at the back of the castle. Three such chambers lay between her secret exit and the back door to the great hall Fearchar had turned into a barracks for his garrison. Beyond the barracks door on the other side were several similar rooms. Those particular rooms had once made convenient freezers for perishable foods. Pegeen had not been adverse to purloining a snack now and then from those stores in the course of her youthful adventures.

No one would see her, not even the guard on the tallest turret, since his post was in front of the castle and her route would be shadowed by the castle itself and the foot of the glacier where it met the back wall. Though that front guard post was a good vantage point for seeing the terrain clear to the sea on clear days, one could hear very little there of what went on inside and to the rear of the castle, because that topmost sentinel tower was situated directly above the noisy rushing waters of the Blabber-mouth River, which kept up an endless, senseless stream of chatter day and night. On the other hand, from the back of the castle one could hear almost everything said from the guard towers in the front, because the sound carried well from that height, and also because anyone speaking in that tower usually had to shout to make himself understood over the river. Pegeen had learned to differentiate between the river's noise and human sounds but Fearchar's new guards were still leery of the river. Many who had stood watch in that tower had had to be reprimanded for turning in false alarms and sending arrows into the noisy waters below. Now they were inclined to attribute all distant noises to the river, and trust their eyes alone.

Pegeen donned an old pair of woolen britches once belonging to her father. They were tight through the hips, but would keep her knees and shins warm above her kidskin boots. Girding her cloak above her knees, she crawled through the tunnel, whose entrance was concealed by the tapestry in her chambers, rolled the packed snow door with which she blocked the outlet away from the back wall of the castle, and crawled out onto the portion of the maze wall butting against her secret exit.

She'd come out here to smoke often lately, but had never tried to negotiate the walls since her girlhood. She searched for a moment the vast expanse of shadow and glittering ice before her. Oh, well. No time like the present.

With what she hoped was pluck and tenacity which would have made her father proud, she applied herself to the wall, left knee and hand followed by right.

She had a lovely night for a crawl. The moon was cooperatively bright and half-full, and for a change neither rain nor snow assailed the glacier. Even the wind was agreeably absent. In all, she needed only an hour to reach the former cold storage chamber.

The unicorns were exactly where she had expected they would be. What she had not expected was the wretched state in which they were kept. Dirty straw filled the bottom of the chamber, to keep them from freezing to the ice, and the little female lay quivering on a pile of old blankets, near the wooden trough set next to the man-made door barricading them from the main tunnel. Otherwise, the poor beasts had no protection from the biting winds and icy rains which plagued the glacier almost daily.

The male unicorn trotted in restless circles around the chamber until Pegeen feared he would fall over his own stumbling feet. His golden-spotted sides were flecked with foam and with ice crystals where the foam had frozen on his skin, and his mane and tail were matted with filth. Occasionally, he would back up to a rear portion of the wall where it curved sharply back, so that it was invisible from the entrance, and give it a disheartened kick with his back hooves. A powder of ice and snow showered from the wall, but otherwise the kicks seemed to make little impression.

The little female no longer watched his efforts. Her eyes rolled back in her head, and each breath heaved from her like a sob. Frost rimmed the beards of both unicorns, and their noses and mouths. But what most appalled Pegeen about the pair's pitiful appearance was that both of their horns were broken. The male's splintered a handspan from where the spiral tip should have ended, and the female's was no more than a jagged shard protruding from her forehead.

"Oh, my dears, I had no idea," the princess said, half to herself. But the female seemed to have heard, and lifted her head, managing with seeming difficulty to focus on Pegeen. An

146

indigestible lump rose in Pegeen's throat. "Fearchar said you were well taken care of! Well, never you mind, my friends. I shan't allow this disgraceful state of affairs to continue any longer. I—"

"Leave us, lady," the female sighed, and though she didn't really speak Pegeen could have sworn she did, which didn't exactly surprise the Princess, who had, after all, been brought up to rule a land where a good third of the populace possessed at least some magical talents.

"In the state you're in?" Pegeen replied. "Certainly not. I'll see to it somehow that you're released, as soon as I can speak to Fearchar alone. Meanwhile, isn't there something I can do to help you?"

"Leave us," the female repeated. "You can do nothing."

"Oh, yes she can," snorted the male, whose eyes kindled red in the moonlight as he, too, looked up at the princess perched above his prison. "She can come down here and let me give her a taste of hoof and what's left of my horn. If she's a maiden, I'm a donkey! Not that I'd pass up a chance to make mash of that yellow-haired tease who led us into this prison—"

"Peace, Eagledown. I feel her heart is good, but she must leave us, for she can do nothing."

"Her heart is good, her heart is good," Eagledown mocked. "Is that what you told yourself as they hauled you up here? That those townfolk who let you be taken had good hearts, or that demon's doxy who betrayed us both?"

"That doxy is my enemy too," Pegeen said. "She has completely subverted the character of the man I love. I can't understand how he could allow you to languish in such squalor, but I—"

She broke off. From the front of the castle, the guard's conch shell sounded the alert. She'd been discovered after all!

Footsteps clattered in the castle, and men cursed as they slipped on icy floors and fell. Pegeen twisted around on the wall, trying to crawl away again before she could be discovered. Instead, she lost her balance and slid down the wall, into the unicorn's pen. She was unhurt, her fall broken by the slight outward curve of the wall, but as she rose to her feet, Eagledown advanced on her, red eyes blazing.

"I beg your pardon. Clumsy of me," she apologized, and slid across the chamber, insinuating herself quickly between the female unicorn and the wall. "I trust you'll overlook my familiarity on such short acquaintance but under the circumstances—"

But now both unicorns ignored her, and were still, with ears

147

cocked sharply forward. From the front of the castle, voices shouted, and the unicorns' keen ears missed none of what was said. Pegeen found that by being still herself and paying attention to the unicorns, she, too, could hear every word spoken as if the sounds were amplified through the unicorns.

"WHERE did you see it, churl?" Fearchar was demanding. "How could you see anything at night?"

"It was the flaming, Dark Pilgrim. A great flaming dragon, it was, coming from the coast, I'd judge it, heading west-sou-'west."

"A dragon? From the coast. Aha! What color?"

"Ruddy, Dark Pilgrim. Like the ruddy one that went by earlier today with that big-bellied blue."

"A big-bellied blue, you say? Had she any green on her? And the other, was its red tinged with gold?"

"Aye, yer Reverence. They lit in the mountains, as I was bringing midday meal up to Jack on his shift. This red 'un went by just now looked to me as if he was headin' for the castle you told us to keep an eye on over past the mountains there. So I blowed me conch."

"Good lad! Though you should have reported the earlier sighting as well. Sergeant!"

"Yes, Reverence!"

"Send a scout to Sally Forth at once. She's to return here in force immediately."

"Yes, Reverence."

"And the ruins, are they fortified as I ordered? And does our reception committee know its task?"

"Yes, Reverence."

"Good, good. Post additional guards and drill the men four times daily. Sentry?"

"Yer Reverence?"

"Report all future movements of either dragon. They are treacherous beasts, who have betrayed me before. They aid the tyrant Rowan. Should the monster approach our stronghold, inform me at once and I shall preserve us with my magic."

"That's the bravest thing I ever heard, Yer Reverence, to face a dragon singlehanded to preserve us! May I say, sir, it's an honor to serve a leader like yourself. But, sir, what if the beast brings the garrison down on us, along with the King's men?"

"Which garrison is that, sentry?"

"The garrison Rowan keeps at the castle, Reverence."

"There no garrison there any more, sentry. They all were

discharged, by special orders, weeks ago, when our gallant followers visited the castle to relocate its supplies.''

Comradely laughter from the troops was followed by rattling weapons and clattering footsteps. Then once more all was quiet, except for the background noise of the river.

The unicorns relaxed and their ears stopped straining forward. Pegeen hugged against Snowshadow's back and avoided the baleful glare Eagledown turned on her.

"Distressing, isn't it?" she said conversationally. "I'm afraid it's looking rather more dismal all the time, wouldn't you say? I do hope neither of you will mind terribly, but I'm in the most dreadful need of a smoke.''

Sybil yawned and rubbed her eyes, and finished the last of her tea before turning her attention to her crystal ball. It looked as hazy as she felt. Budgie chirped and dug his little talons into her hair.

"Yes, dearie, I'm tired, too. We'll just have our evening sighting and then it's off to bed with us both. No, I quite agree. I'm not up to watching Maggie's suitors blunder about in Willie's wood any longer either. Such a timid lot! Not one of them save that nasty Prince boy and that horrid Count has had the gumption to wander out of reach of Willie's dining hall—and what a trial that's been for the help at Fort Iceworm, I should think, without niece to help! What shall we do? Watch the children, then? Ah, to be young again. I did so enjoy that evening young Colin took her for the lovely boat ride out to Raspberry's castle. But I don't suppose it would be very nice, would it, to spy on them like that. Let the Mother take Her course, I always say, don't I, lovie? But he's such a charming boy, and very good with Maggie's moods. Let's just do a bit of a scan now and see if we can't come up with a unicorn so the children can get all of this nonsense over and done with. There—something's coming—''

She peered closely into the glass, her face reflecting the rainbow sparks that preceded the picture. Then, as the crystal cleared, she stared hard, and gripped the ball between her hands. The picture changed of its own accord, as it had done only twice before in her career. The other two times had been during periods of great peril. Once, it had spontaneously showed the death of Maggie's mother, Bronwyn. The other time, the ball had zeroed in on brother Fearchar's secret island, when he had kept Maggie and Winnie prisoner there.

This time three visions followed, each close behind the other. Sybil's eyes burned with strain.

Budgie fluttered and chirped uncertainly. Gently, Sybil lifted him from the top of her head and stroked his feathers as she carried him on her index finger to the door.

"I know you're small and can't possibly make it all the way to the coast in time to warn the King, dearie. But perhaps you could find Maggie?" The bird whistled an agitated sort of whistle. "No, I realize you're not a crystal ball. No, no, forget it. It was too much to ask. But—ah, now you could make it as far as Wizard Raspberry's castle, could you not? Such a GOOD bird!" She flipped her finger into the air and Budgie winged away into the woods.

"Do watch out for owls, dearie!" Sybil called after him, and closed the door only when he was out of sight.

Hours after they'd left the lynx lair behind, Maggie continued to seethe. It was all so unfair! Of course, she couldn't blame Moonshine for wanting to think over what the old nag had said—that was perfectly understandable, what with Primrose being the first unicorn the poor dear had met in ages. Naturally, Moonshine would be inclined to give the older unicorn's spiteful words undue importance.

But the nerve of that horn-headed, dry-dugged old plowhorse! Imagine her judging someone on appearances like that! All Maggie had asked of her was a perfectly civil question, just to try to help. How perfectly filthy of Primrose to deem her unmaidenly simply because of her companions and her coloring. It was evil-minded, was what it was. Evil-minded.

She craned forward on Roundelay's neck to look for a glimpse of Moonshine's tail among the trees. Surely by now he would see that Primrose had absolutely no authority to tell him whether or not Maggie was suitable. Primrose was only one unicorn. There were bound to be other, wiser ones. Unicorns were commonly known to be exceptionally wise creatures, on the whole. Just her luck to venture into a stupid, narrow-minded one. It was hardly possible that all unicorns shared Granny's and Primrose's opinion that unicorns and witches didn't belong together.

Ahead, Moonshine halted to purify a stream. Maggie swung her leg over Roundelay's neck and slid down. Colin watched, looking surprised and vaguely troubled.

Moonshine raised his head and shook his dripping horn. Maggie offered her handkerchief to dry it. "Here, let me. How are you doing? Aren't you lonesome up here all by yourself? Colin thinks we should stop at the next village and ask for help to rescue the other unicorns. It seems like a good idea to me. What do you think? I mean, of course we'll lose time, but on the other hand we'll gain help, and I—"

She met his beseeching gaze, and realized with self-disgust that she was prattling wildly but seemed unable to stop herself, though she despised prattlers. She couldn't bear for him to turn his head away and trot on without her. Her hand trembled as she ran it down his silky neck. His skin leapt under her touch and she pulled back her hand as if he'd burned it.

"Of course," she continued, "I'll need to ride with Colin again when we get to the town. I don't think the disguise is good enough to protect you from a whole town, but meanwhile—"

"Maggie, my friend," he said, "I would not willfully say you nay, for whatever you may be to others you are beloved to me. But I cannot deny that Primrose's words trouble me sorely. I must ponder them further, and seek what truths may dwell therein."

"Oh, I *know*," Maggie cried, "Oh, of course, I know *that*. Certainly you have to think about it. In fact, I'd be very disappointed in you if you *didn't* think about it, and I'm sure when you do you'll see that—"

He looked away, shame-faced, and the words came tumbling out of her before he could go away from her altogether.

"Maybe I'm not pure in all the usual ways. I mean, I still am physically and all that, but in those other ways, well, I have my faults. But what I mean to say is, you already knew I was a witch!"

His sides heaved, and the eye nearest her flicked forward, and away again, watching her covertly. She slid her arms around his neck and hugged him, burying her face in his mane. "Oh, Moonshine, I thought you didn't mind that I wasn't perfect. I thought you knew me too well. I had no idea I'd shame you just by—being me. If I'd known—but never mind."

She straightened, and pawed at her eyes with the back of her hand, ignoring the handkerchief she'd offered him a short while before. "I suppose if I'm not suitable, I'm simply not suitable. If you'd like to meet the maidens in the next village, to find someone else, I'll help you. Colin will too. I'll ask him."

"There's no need—" Moonshine began.

"It's all right," she said, stopping him. "Granny's probably right. I did very nicely without a unicorn before I met you, and I'm sure I'll manage splendidly after you—get resettled. I . . . I'm

151

very fond of you. I want to see you happy. Only this time, be sure.''

He dipped his horn and walked slowly across the stream.

She took Colin's hand and remounted.

For a while they were all so silent that the birds' songs sounded raucous and ill-timed. They began gradually to travel through a healthier-looking terrain, ribboned with a twisting jade channel of the same stream that had flowed so sluggishly by Everclear, and other streams and ponds as well, and brightened with flowers and the scamperings of squirrels, rabbits, fox and deer.

Maggie sat stone still on Roundelay's shoulders. It could have been pitch dark for all that she saw. Colin was uncomfortably conscious of the tension in her back, and the set of her head made his own neck ache in sympathy. Still, it was a pretty day. In spite of himself, he began to hum a jig under his breath, and then to whistle.

Without further warning, Maggie collapsed in sobs.

"Here now." He took both reins in one hand and gathered her awkwardly against his chest with his free arm. "This won't do. You're shaking so hard you're frightening the horse."

"I don't c-care," she wept, but dried one eye enough to see if Roundelay was indeed affected.

He patted her tangled hair with his free hand and tried to see over her head to the path beyond. "Of course you care. You care about everything. That's just the problem with you. It seems to me, witch, that this unicorn business has had the most unfortunate effect on your disposition. I don't recall that you wept so much while we were battling dragons and wizards, and here in the space of two months you're twice weeping like a baby."

He'd hoped to provoke her customarily tart reply, but instead she cried all the harder, and the horse did begin to shy. Alarmed, he slowed Roundelay to a walk, and looped the reins around his wrist. Using both arms now, he held her close and kissed the top of her head and her forehead, which felt feverish, as he would kiss a child's.

"Please, Maggie, don't cry. Shall I sing you something? A nice murder ballad, perhaps, or a battle song to cheer you up?'' She didn't answer which was all right because he didn't much feel like singing then anyway. "Perhaps you'd like to snap out of it long enough to do a bit of magic, then? That might make you feel better. Shall I dirty a pot or two, or rip something you could mend?''

At that she threw her arms around his neck and wailed like a banshee. Roundelay was naturally used to peculiar noises, being in the employ of a minstrel, but Colin was sure she would not peacefully endure such a racket as Maggie was producing. There was no help for it. Dipping his head, he kissed her on the mouth, which stopped the wailing effectively, as he hoped it would.

But in other ways, the kiss surprised him. For one thing, she didn't bite him, but seemed to get right into the spirit of the thing, even forgetting momentarily to cry. In spite of the acid remarks it often produced, her mouth was as warm and sweet and moist as any girl's he'd ever kissed, though considerably saltier. And for a person with so many sharp edges and prickles about her, she was extremely soft and pliant-feeling. Quite a pleasant surprise, on the whole, but one which began provoking confusing and disturbing reactions within himself. He was both relieved and disappointed when she finally pulled away from him, mopped her face, and said, with a rather sheepish smile, "Maybe I do harbor impure thoughts, after all. But I wish that old nag would stick her wretched horn—"

"That's a good witch," he laughed. "Why not throw a really foul curse on her? Let's see, what could a hearthcrafter do to curse a unicorn? Turn all her grass sour so it would give her the bloat? No. I don't suppose that would be fair to other animals." He snapped his fingers. "I have it! We're working on the wrong unicorn. Why don't you just give a love potion to Moonshine?"

There was a subtle change in the quality of the smile she gave him. "Wrong kind of spell. I don't want *that* kind of love from a unicorn. Besides, Moonshine's magic would cancel out anything I did that involved a liquid, and I'd hoped—I mean, I'd rather not need—I never thought I'd need—"

She turned her head away, and he picked up a long tangled strand of her hair and joggled it playfully. "Bad idea. Forget it, witch."

She sniffed. In spite of how she felt to his touch and tasted when he kissed her, she was really alarmingly unattractive when she cried. Her eyes swelled and reddened, and so did her nose, and it ran as well. When the ladies at court wept they always managed to do so prettily, with a lace handkerchief and a minimum of unpleasant noise and secretion—save a nicely placed tear here and there on a flawlessly pink cheek. And they always insisted, of course, that their tears were for love of him. The girls he'd known in East Headpenney never cried at all unless they stuck themselves with a pitchfork or a cow stepped on one of their feet, at least none of them had cried in his presence since they were children. Maggie's crying was like a child's—heartbroken and angry at once, and terribly honest. He had to remind himself this child he was beginning very much to enjoy comforting was a powerful witch, a nobleman's daughter, and, for the time being at least, a princess.

So he unlooped the reins from his wrist and took them in each hand on either side of her in the friendliest possible manner, and hummed something soothing under his breath—he forgot what—a dirge, perhaps.

As the sun set and the cloud-swathed moon rose, Moonshine stopped. Beyond the wall of trees, a cart track ran parallel to the woods, then down through a meadow. In the midst of the meadow stood another, almost ornamental, grove of trees, joining the forest on the side farthest from where Colin, Maggie and Moonshine stood. Within the grove a stone tower was outlined against the last frail pink of the dying sun. A brook flowed out of the grove, around the tower and past it, and into the village at the edge of the grove.

Moonshine turned to Maggie. "I would don my disguise now, if you please, and accompany you to yonder town."

Maggie nodded, and silently slipped the disguise over his horn and started to knot her handkerchief at its base to hold it in place.

But Moonshine said, "Nay, Maggie, I would have it loose, so that I may remove it of my own accord when I deem it timely."

So he did intend to find another maiden in this town, one who would be more acceptable to Primrose and the Creed. Maggie gulped to swallow the lump in her throat, and said, "I could help you with it. Not that it's any of my affair, but invisible things are a bother to find once they're lost and your—first attempt—might not be—satisfactory."

Halfway to the tower a traveler overtook them and passed them from behind, which was remarkable, since the man was afoot while they were mounted. He walked very quickly, though he was so bent over that even when he turned towards them, tugging at the oversized cap he wore, they couldn't quite see his face. They could smell him, though. The ill-cured sheepskin cloak he wore over bare legs and feet reeked so badly that they had to avert their noses.

Colin asked as courteously as possible, for one with his nose in the air, "Can you tell us the name of yonder town, good man, and where we might find lodging for ourselves and stable for our mounts?"

The man lifted his head for a fraction of a second, giving him a startlingly wide yellow-toothed grin. "Why, traveler, you must

154

have strayed far not to know of Little Darlingham and its famous tower.''

"What's so famous about it?'' Maggie asked. "Who lives there?''

She had the impression that beneath the cap, the stranger's sharp eyes were darting from her and back to Colin, but lingered most often on Moonshine, who pranced nervously behind her as she pretended to lead him.

But the man answered quickly in a whining voice that seemed oddly familiar. "Ah, lady, have you not then heard of the poor widow woman who lives there with her three daughters whose beauty is known all over the land? And as for your question of lodging, do not even righteous widows and beautiful daughters have to eat? And in such a large tower, is it not likely such a woman would accept lodgers for a few pennies a night or the chopping of wood or the drawing of water or perhaps,'' his head turned slightly towards Moonshine, "the trade of an extra steed?''

"Er—thank you, good man,'' Colin said. "We'll give it some thought.'' But the fellow was already lurching down the road ahead of them, his hips switching as he walked in a manner that reminded Maggie of a dog wagging its tail.

"Oh, no,'' Colin said between mouthfuls of the widow Belburga's bread. "They were really quite dead, weren't they, Maggie? It wasn't a trance or anything like that, or anyhow I didn't think so, did you?''

"I don't see how it could have been,'' Maggie replied, wrinkling her nose in remembrance and pushing away the plate of food. She'd only been picking at it, anyway. "Trances don't usually smell that bad.''

The remembered smell of the village wasn't the only thing quelling her appetite. She didn't care much for the widow's lodging, either. The stable to which she'd led Moonshine and Roundelay was such a neglected disgrace that she could only bring herself to allow them to remain after she had vigorously applied her magic to cleaning and repairing the stalls. The tower was dank and cold, the bread hard, the stew tasteless, and the dishes greasy. A line of white clothing was strung down the middle of the circular room, from the spiral staircase disappearing into the ceiling to the diamond-paned window next to the heavy door by which they had entered. The fire in the hearth was dead.

Neither was the widow Belburga particularly warm in her welcome. The woman had been very prompt about taking Colin's coins, and very slow to feed them or tell them where the stable was. She had stared at Moonshine rather too sharply from under her preposterously long, pale lashes. Colin had begun speaking loudly of their adventures, stressing the desperate plight of the people of Everclear and hinting broadly at his own royal connections as a means of intimidating the good widow into treating himself and Maggie properly. His ploy worked almost too well.

Belburga was hanging on to every word, even adding coals to the brazier by the table and igniting a torch to supplement the stub of a candle inadequately lighting the table. Maggie could almost hear the woman's mind working behind the elaborate superstructure of impossibly brazen curls, which she kept patting, as if to reassure herself her head was still within them.

"And a prince, you say, was involved? What a coincidence!" the widow was saying now in her flat, nasal whine. Beneath the frivolous lashes her eyes were black and keen as a weasel's. She leaned forward, fanning her hand over her deep bosom, which she heaved at Colin in what Maggie thought was a rather disgusting fashion. Colin gave her his undivided attention. "My first husband, Harry, was a prince, you know," she confided. "He was the father of my precious Lily Pearl. Oh, I can see it shocks you, to see a gentlewoman like me living like this, but I haven't always been in such reduced circumstances, goodness no!" She smiled a bright, close-lipped smile. "And I do know a thing or two about *noblesse oblige*, too, being royally inclined as I naturally am from my days in court. That's why I think you really must, Master Songsmith, take it upon yourself to lead a few of our stalwart village lads—a little stupid, our boys, true, but steady—and bring those poor persons from Everclear back here where they can at least receive direction in leading useful lives, if they never recover themselves fully."

That undoubtedly meant, Maggie thought, that the widow felt some of the Everclear folk might make handy, unpaid servants.

"And, of course," Belburga continued, "You simply must bring that poor young prince back here to my tower where he can mix with folk of his own station."

"He's not really a very nice person," Maggie said.

Dame Belburga raised a thinly-plucked brow and favored her with a cool look, the first attention of any kind the widow had spared her that evening. "Princes, my dear young lady, are ALWAYS nice people. Those of the lower classes simply fail to comprehend at times the awesome burdens of royalty that set them apart from your average riffraff."

"Is that so?" Maggie asked, then thought better of saying any more, since she was very tired and had no wish to spend the night looking for somewhere else to stay, however unpleasant these present quarters seemed.

"Yes, indeed," Belburga assured her. "Of course, my Lily Pearl now, being of royal blood herself—did I mention Lily Pearl's father was a prince? Yes, well, Lily Pearl's nature is one infinitely suited to understanding such things—she is the epitome of sensitivity, delicacy and the *utmost* refinement. That's all quite aside, of course, from her astonishing beauty, which is, I hardly need to mention, already a legend throughout Little Darlingham and, indeed, through most of Argonia by now, I should think. You'll have to meet her, Master Songsmith. I'm sure you would love to write a song about her yourself, for singing back in court."

Colin gave her a half-bow from his seat. "I pine for the pleasure of doing so, Dame Belburga."

"Of course you do. But first, you really must bring that prince back. Then perhaps you might wish to commemorate their meeting. Right now all of my girls are far too busy developing their particular gifts in the privacy of their chambers to entertain paying guests." She sighed and dabbed at her lips with her handkerchief. "One really must be so cautious rearing one's children, mustn't one? It's so important they meet the right sort of people. One certainly wouldn't want such lovely girls as mine taking up with someone *common*, and acquiring unsavory habits." She looked directly at Maggie as she said the last and rose. "If you'll excuse me for a moment, Master Songsmith, I think I may have one nice bit of cake left for you from our own meager, but nourishing repast. I shan't be long."

"I don't seem to be popular today, do I?" Maggie remarked wryly, while the widow was out of sight behind the line of clothing.

"Perhaps a bath?" Colin suggested, and added quickly, "We probably both still stink of zombies, and are so used to it we don't smell it on each other."

She nodded, but dully, and stared into her plate.

Belburga bustled back to the table in a swirl of mended lace and rather odious pink velvet. "I was just thinking to myself, Master Colin—I MAY call you, Colin, mayn't I? You do remind me, a bit, of my third husband—but back to my point. I was just thinking that on your return you would undoubtedly enjoy meeting my second daughter, Ruby Rose. Now SHE is a girl of most remarkable accomplishments, and, it goes without saying, of course, incredible personal loveliness. Her father—my second husband . . . is, or was . . . a most marvelous wizard, capable of absolutely astounding feats of magic, and a very learned man as well. Ruby Rose is blessed not only with my looks but with her father's brains and talent. Purely a genius, the girl is. I'm sure you would adore her. You DID mention that you hold a high position in court?''

With what Maggie felt was shockingly poor taste, Colin proceeded to go into great detail regarding his position in court and his relationship with the King, leaving out any hint of Maggie's own royal associations, except to say that she was a witch from a powerful family.

Belburga was unimpressed, and regarded Maggie more coldly than ever.

"I had a great-uncle once who married into a family of witches—we always felt, in our family, it was his greatest misfortune. I personally feel one ought always to stick to one's own class of people, don't you agree, Minstrel Colin?'' Not that it really mattered whether or not either of them agreed. Belburga continued without pause to regale them with the travails of her uncle, who sounded pretty awful in spite of his niece's obviously biased account. When at last she seemed to be running down, she turned another peculiar close-mouthed smile on Colin. Maggie thought that for someone who talked as much as Belburga, she didn't open her mouth much. It gave her an odd expression—as if her teeth hurt her.

"But I suppose," the widow continued after such a short pause that Colin had no chance to recover enough to proffer a remark of his own, "that being a country-bred boy, and one with magical merman blood in your heritage, didn't I understand you to say? you might have much in common too with my charming, nature-loving youngest daughter, Daisy Esmeralda (Esmeralda's foreign for Emerald, you know, and sounds so much more genteel than *our* word, don't you think?). Not that she's at all affected—her sisters and I call her Daisy, because she spends so much time amid the flowers in her little garden by the stream, playing with all of her little animal friends, who naturally idolize her. She's quite made pets out of even the wildest among them. Simply everyone who's anyone will tell you that our Daisy is the kindest-hearted, gentlest, most generous and best-natured of maidens. Besides, of course, being the fairest in the land with the possible exception of her two equally beautiful sisters— though I must say Lily Pearl has always been popularly considered to be the *best* looking. But I'm sure you two would have a great deal to talk about, though Daisy is most shy and modest except with her animal friends. But then, you could undoubtedly win her over by singing her an animal ditty or two."

"Or maybe you could just act beastly," Maggie whispered to him behind her hand.

The widow, if she heard, ignored her, and reiterated the charms of her daughters for another hour or so, while re-emphasizing at strategic intervals that Colin must make all haste to gather a delegation to rescue Prince Leofwin from Trickle and bring the Everclear zombies under the dominion of certain responsible citizens of Little Darlingham.

Maggie was glad Colin had carefully omitted any mention of the unicorns in his account. The widow would probably want to know only if the unicorns involved were pedigreed or had any relations captured by kings. With that thought, Maggie left the table without excusing herself and, brushing aside the laundry, climbed the circular stairs, at last settling down for the night on a straw pallet that even her magic could not quite make comfortable.

"I'm afraid this situation is much worse than I'd feared," Pegeen said to the unicorns as the last puff from her smoke had flown away into the night. Eagledown, though still flattening his ears at her and swinging his horn her way once in a while to try to frighten her, had backed off, at Snowshadow's urging, and no longer seemed quite so actively menacing.

Snowshadow had grown calmer and, with the warmth of her body, exuded a protective serenity which Pegeen found greatly improved her own thinking processes. "I don't know what you both must think of Fearchar—and of me, for that matter," the princess said. "But I can assure you this whole thing isn't at all like him. He's usually such a charming man. Still, I'm afraid that the nymph person has cast an evil spell on him, and he can't be trusted to see reason. I don't think there's the least point at all in appealing to his sense of decency to let you go. He doesn't seem to have any left."

Eagledown brayed an ununicornly horse laugh. "You can say that again, sister."

"So I shall simply have to extricate you from this situation myself. It will take great courage and cunning on my part, but of course, I was brought up to do that sort of thing, as a princess of the realm and all."

"I don't see how any amount of rank will help us now, Lady," Snowshadow said doubtfully. "We are among knaves with no respect for your royal standing."

"Very true, my dear. I'm virtually a prisoner myself. However, there's always the usual way of escaping from a prison to be considered—which is not to let one's captors know what one intends. All I have to do, as I see it, is to sketch us a map of the maze, and simply open the door to this chamber and lead you safely through the maze and out the other side to freedom. It's as uncomplicated as that. I could have it done in a day or two and no one would be the wiser."

"Aren't you forgetting something?" Eagledown asked. "Don't you have to get out of here first? And what makes you think I'm going to let you? You may have Snowshadow fooled, but I'd just as soon skewer you as look at you."

"No, you wouldn't," Pegeen replied evenly, secretly pleased at how well she was keeping the terror out of her voice. "You'd be doing yourself a disservice if you did. Because I'm your only hope, actually. That hole you've been gouging with your horns doesn't lead anywhere in the least bit useful. As for escaping our present predicament, that's simply a matter of group cooperation and organizational management. You must allow me to stand on your back, so I may reach the edge of the wall and climb out the way I came in."

Wulfric concealed his grin beneath his outsized cap when he saw the minstrel stumble in through the rectangle of sunlight framed by the door of the dimly lit tavern, and grope among the tables and benches inside until his eyes adjusted to the darkness. The woman Belburga had done her work well, had she not, to drive Songsmith to him? For though early morning was a poor time for the minstrel to attempt to raise interest among the tavern's patrons in any activity more strenuous than staring into the bottom of a cup, had not Belburga, following Wulfric's hastily-concocted but clever plan, persuaded him to do so? And, oh, best of all, she had separated the minstrel and the witch and the unicorn one from the other, the better for him to dispose of them individually.

They could not plot to humiliate him again, as they had done before, appearing alive when he had reported them dead. How shamed he had been when Sally had learned from her latest one-horned conquest that those he had deemed devoured by the forest beasts were alive and united against them! He made haste to pick up their trail, though they were too far ahead for Sally's men to overtake. He could at least follow their movements and lay a plan, could he not? Surely he must try, or wear his tail between his legs forever after!

And had he not succeeded? For he had learned, from their speech, of the strange events at Everclear and had reported to Sally speedily to tell Her of the matter before returning to his tracking. And now, was not She, clever, crafty Sally, preparing Her snares not only for the unicorn but for their other enemies as well? Only this one man was left to Wulfric alone, and he knew how to deal with this man.

Songsmith cleared his throat. "I say, could anyone tell me who's the constable around here? One of your neighboring villages is having a bit of a problem and—"

"Constable, eh?" said a portly fellow with a bulbous nose. "Why, lad, constable was et by wild trolls must've been six months ago or so, ain't that right, Shearer?"

"Aye. Turrible thing it was too," answered a toothless ancient. "When they found 'im weren't naught left of 'im but 'is mustache and 'is gouty leg. I figgers the trolls thought gout'd give 'em sour stomachs."

"Naw," said the first man. "If they could stomach the rest ov 'im they could take anything."

The minstrel waxed perplexed at this rough teasing, reacting exactly as Wulfric desired. Soon Songsmith would find that none in this place save loyal, brave Wulfric would accompany him into the woods to lead forth the afflicted villagers.

"Oh, I *am* sorry to hear that," Songsmith was saying, and seated himself at the table opposite the bulbous-nosed man, the elder and two others. "He would have found my tale noteworthy, I'm sure, even if he didn't choose to take a look in the tavern himself."

"What tavern is that, lad?" the elder asked. "If this tale is so interestin', why don't you tell us? It be dull here, mostly."

Songsmith shook his head, sighed and ordered a round for the table. "It's not really worthy of your time, gentlemen, to tell. I only thought the constable would want to keep that poor addled innkeeper from giving away good ale while he didn't know what he was doing."

"Here, now!" said the tavern keeper who was setting the drinks before them. "What idiot is giving away good ale?"

"Not you, Brewer, that's for sure!" the elder wheezed.

"I'll thank the lot of you not to interrupt such a fascinatin' tale," said a third man, whose red face matched what was left of his hair. "Let the boy talk."

"There's not much to tell," Songsmith said. "But all the people of Everclear seem to have this peculiar illness—"

"Plague?" a fourth man asked.

"No, no. Nothing like that. They can walk around and eat and drink, they just don't know what they're doing. They've left all their possessions unguarded, and the innkeeper just keeps giving away pint after pint of ale. It's very sad. I thought—that is, Dame Belburga, at the tower where my companion and I are staying, thought the humane thing to do would be to take the townfolk of Everclear under the wing of Little Darlingham, so to speak, until they're mended." He swallowed a draught of ale, then studied it consideringly. "And I suppose it really would be a good idea to leave someone there in charge of that inn until the owner is well."

"Belburga said that?" asked the fourth man, a stocky young farmer whose face was like a baby's and whose muscles were like a blacksmith's. "Lily Pearl's ma? I suppose we'd have to take these folk over to Lily Pearl's place first off when we got back, so Dame Belburga could tell us what to do with 'em like, wouldn't we?"

"Oh, yes," Songsmith replied. "We'd certainly have to do that."

Wulfric had to intervene. This conversation was not going as he wished. "But have you not heard, good friends, that bandits prowl the forest near Everclear? And wild beasts, and yea, even the trolls of which you spoke? Is it not dangerous?"

But he had waited too long. The men were on their second round at Songsmith's expense. "Oh, aye, it's a bit risky all right," the man with the bulbous nose said. "But giving away ale, after all. That's a shame, all that waste."

"Aye, and I'd never have Lily Pearl thinkin' I was too afraid to help me neighbors," the young farmer added. "I'll go if you'll lead, stranger."

"And I," said bulbous nose.

"My aunt's first cousin's boy's daughter's nephew by marriage lives over to Everclear, or used to," the oldster mused. "Or was it her nephew's daughter's boy's first cousin by marriage? Anyway, I'd best go along too."

The innkeeper threw down his apron. "Well, if I'm going to lose half my trade, I may as well go along and see that a brother innkeeper doesn't go broke from giving away ale while he's ill. I could make sure he took in good coin for it."

"I have a bit of experience at inns m'self," the redhead said. "And bandits, too, if it comes to that. Until just lately I was in the border patrol, up at Castle Rowan."

"And could I do less than to offer to accompany you myself?"

Wulfric asked quickly, snatching his last opportunity to stay near his prey. "I know the woods well, and can guide you."

"I thought it was too dangerous for you," Songsmith said.

"I sought only to warn you, noble sir," Wulfric answered. "But in the company of such brave fellows, who am I to falter when my services could mean the difference between the success and failure of your mission?"

Maggie didn't care how noble his mission was or how much trouble he'd wished to spare her, it was bloody unfair of Colin Songsmith to run off back to Everclear without a word to her. Now she was stuck with the obnoxious widow and her three peerless progeny.

Belburga had been feeding her chickens when Maggie dragged herself down the stairs and out into the yard, snatching a hunk of bread left from the night before on the way. Though she'd said nothing, Belburga's smirk was eloquent. Evidently she'd suspected Maggie would be displeased to find Roundelay missing from the stable, and the minstrel gone.

Muttering to herself, Maggie ordered the night's accumulation of manure thrown out of the straw and onto the widow's compost heap, wishing she dared divert a few clods into the widow's face.

Moonshine watched her. He looked more confused and miserable and guiltier than a unicorn should have been able to look, but by now Maggie's own feelings were bandaged with a gauze of dullness which made it a little easier to disregard the impulse to stroke his neck and scratch his beard. Not that he'd want her to, anyway.

"I know it isn't pleasant here," she said. "But at least you don't have to listen to that widow. All she talked about all night were her gorgeous daughters. 'My Lily Pearl this, my Ruby-something that.' It was sickening."

"Daughters?" Moonshine's ears pricked up, Maggie's heart sank within her as she nodded. He really was going to pursue this idea of finding another maiden. In spite of everything, she still found it hard to believe. Hah. Where were all those brave sensible notions she'd lectured him with back at Aunt Sybil's now? That time seemed incredibly distant.

"I'm—not sure where they are," she said. "Let me have a bit of a look around. If I find one I'll come back for you."

But Moonshine rolled his eyes frantically. "Nay, nay. Lead me from this horse cage, I implore you. I would seek the maidens myself."

She laid her hand on his neck and let him follow her out into the morning. Although the sun was high and bright, a belt of cloud striped the foothills beneath the sharp, blue-veined whiteness of the peaks towering just beyond the forest, and from the stream and fresh-plowed meadows the dew steamed up in sharp contrast to the clarity of the day.

They first mistook the girl among the flowers of the mist-latticed garden for a wraith, for she seemed at a glance to be made of mist. Her skin was so pale as to make milk seem dingy, and her hair was fine and white as silk thread. She was small and slender, but seemed stately in a flowing white gown of shimmering fabric Maggie recognized from the clothesline the night before. Poor wench must do a lot of laundry, Maggie thought, living here and wearing that sort of get-up for everyday.

The girl took no notice of them, but busied herself plucking white roses with a pair of long silver shears. Her face reinforced the impression of wraithlike insubstantiality and overall pallor. Though it had the dark blue eyes and rosy cheeks and lips and flawless complexion requisite to the Argonian ideal of beauty, it bore absolutely no trace of ever having been flawed by the distortion of expression or emotion.

Moonshine didn't seem to notice. He was pacing and pawing like a warhorse before a battle. "NOW, please, friend, remove my disguise before she flees."

"Yes, I doubt she spends much time outdoors," Maggie said. "She'd be too afraid of getting dirty."

Before the disguise was back in her pocket, Moonshine was approaching the girl, who sat upon a stone bench and was arranging her flowers in a basket. When they were arranged to her liking, she began plucking off the petals.

Moonshine inhaled rapturously. The odor of chastity perfumed her presence more than the bruised rosepetals in her basket.

"Oh, maiden, look up," he sent his message to her, and presented his best profile while thinking high, pure thoughts until, lifting her lovely head from the basket over which she so daintily toiled, she would see him and love him.

She did look up, finally, and flicked at him a long, beautifully manicured hand with nails as opalescent as his own horn. The barest frown marred her perfect features as she said in a high, clear voice, "Excuse me, horse. Please stand aside. I'm keeping a vigil for a prince who's coming along any day now to fall in love with me. Mama will be furious if I miss him."

That was not the kind of reception Moonshine had hoped for,

but then, he supposed he had taken her by surprise. Perhaps instant rapport was too much to expect with one so exquisite. Ah well, there was always the classic gesture. Kneeling on the ground beside her, he started to lay his head in her lap, as duly prescribed in the Creed. "Not a horse, fairest maiden," he corrected her gently. "But a unicorn—behold!"

"Do you mind terribly taking your nap elsewhere?" she asked with the tiniest pretty hint of crossness. "You'll tear my gown with that sharp thing on your head and, oh dear, now look what you've done! You're getting me all wet. There's dew all over your skin. Besides, you're laying on the rose bushes."

He hastily stood. She brushed off her gown and extracted a silver looking glass from its pocket and inspected her hairdo. Part of her flaxen tresses was curled into an elaborate crown atop her head, while the rest frothed down her slender back.

"You are surpassing fair, maiden," Moonshine offered, somewhat shyly now.

"Naturally. I ought to be, with all the trouble I go to. One hundred strokes of the brush each and every day, morning and night, and three hours, mind you, to do my coiffure. Not to mention having to pluck all those rose petals for my rose petal and milk bath every day. For the complexion, mother says, although I daresay the scratches the thorns give my hands more than override the benefits. Still, it smells nice. The ideal thing, I suppose, is for one to have slavies to do these menial chores. But for now, one has to make the best of it until one's prince comes. But it isn't easy. Oh, no. I can dine only on robins' eggs and artichoke hearts except for once a week, when I'm allowed a little wild clover honey and a few white grapes—for the digestion, Mama says."

"But that's terrible! You poor dear maiden! They starve you!" Moonshine was genuinely upset. "Let me take you away from all this."

"Don't be an ass," she said, sounding very like Maggie. "If you take me away from all this now I shan't be here when my prince comes, and all my efforts would be wasted. I'd lose the chance to claim the heritage of my royal blood, and have to continue forever crushing my own rosepetals for my baths. I'm certainly not going to risk a cruel fate like that just for a unicorn." He hung his head and she added, consolingly, "Perhaps you might just walk along beside me though, while I wait. Just so long as you don't block my view of the road. You do look striking with my ensemble." She pressed the pleats in the front of her bodice between two slender fingers and tucked a lily

165

bloom against her bosom as she rose. "We might stroll a bit, but slowly, now. If one walks quickly one disarranges one's draperies."

Maggie sighed, and retreated a pace toward the stream when Moonshine approached the pristine Lily Pearl. She couldn't compete with that, she supposed. Dame Belburga's whey-faced daughter fairly reeked of maidenly purity. Well, then, let her have it. And Moonshine, too, if that was the way he wanted it. Maggie would just have to wait here by the stream until the two of them were well-acquainted enough that she could intrude to entrust the disguise to Moonshine's new companion—and warn her about the unicorn-nappers. Meanwhile, it wouldn't hurt to wash herself and keep an eye out for Dame Belburga, whom Maggie wasn't inclined to trust where unicorns were concerned any more than she was inclined to trust her where certain minstrels were concerned.

Keeping the garden within sight, Maggie found a spot near the water, blocked by trees from view of the road. As long as Moonshine and Lily Pearl didn't wander too far, she could keep an eye on them while she bathed.

She formed a washbowl of clay with some difficulty. Though her magic had worked well enough at shoveling manure, it was sluggish about obeying her commands now. At last she got the bowl shaped and baked, and dipped it into the stream to use for her bath. Since the townspeople of Little Darlingham no doubt used the water downstream, she wanted to be careful not to dirty the creek, lest Little Darlingham meet the same end as Everclear. Besides, using the basin meant she didn't have to actually get IN the stream and could keep her contact with the water minimal, considering the nature of her chore. Though she hadn't melted yet, one never knew.

And she didn't exactly relish being dirty, but on the other hand, to be perfectly fair about it, *she*, unlike other people she knew, was in the habit of using soaproot when she washed, which got her cleaner than mere water alone. The more-frequent-than-average application of soap ought to make up for the less frequent application of water. Too bad her preservative spells couldn't be used on her own washings-up, or that her magic didn't include a spell for cleaning oneself without getting wet.

Lathering herself a limb at a time with the piece of soaproot she carried in her medicine pouch, she thoroughly filthied four bowls of water, even before she washed her hair. But the end results were satisfying—she felt at least a stone's-weight lighter, and the crescents under her fingernails were white again instead

166

of black. Stripping to her coarse linen shift, she washed her woolen outer garments while her hair dried. Again, she needed more elbow grease than usual to do the job, as her magic seemed to respond only slowly. But the sun was warm, and between hearthcraft and sunlight her outer clothing dried swiftly enough that she could put it back on and wash her underclothing. She was relieved when that was dry; woolen shirt and shift were scratchy against bare skin.

Later, perhaps, she might dye the silk gown in which she'd escaped some pretty color, just to pass the time. And perhaps, in such competitive company as Lily Pearl and her mama, a drop or two of Gran's love potion behind the ears wouldn't do any harm. For now she occupied herself fingerplaiting her hair into a thick snood that reached halfway down her back.

On the whole she thought she washed up very well. Feeling much more self-respecting, she wandered farther up the grove to see if Moonshine and Lily Pearl might be ready for the disguise. She'd luckily remembered to tie it up in her still-grimy handkerchief before she'd washed out her skirt—one never knew how a good washing would affect delicate spells, and it would have been a bother to lose the cone in the grass.

Moonshine was kneeling before his new acquaintance. "Fairest maiden," he offered. "Perhaps you'd care to mount my back and ride like the wind?"

"I was afraid when I first saw you you would make indecent proposals like that!" Lily Pearl exclaimed, stamping her little foot in exasperation. "After I've spent simply HOURS washing and ironing my gown so that it drapes properly, you want me to spoil it with unseemly athletic adventures! You don't care a bit that we royally bred ladies have delicate skins. I should get nasty callouses on my legs if I followed your advice. Mama warned me about unicorns only last week. She *said* you were all alike— always wanting a girl to forget she's a lady and take her galloping off into the forest. I'm only letting you talk to me because we look so fine together . . ."

"Then—" Moonshine said incredulously, "then you feel *no* bond of love for me?"

"Well, of course not. I'd be a perfect ninny to feel a thing like that, wouldn't I? I mean, this is all so sudden—I hardly know you." As he backed away, she added more kindly, "But you *are* almost as beautiful as I am—only do stand over here to my left, won't you, and shield me from the sun? I burn rather easily."

But he leaped back through the garden and across the stream,

167

to plow through the grove of trees and into the forest to the west of the tower.

By the time Maggie found him, she was hot, panting, and annoyed. Her knees were skinned and dirty, and her nails once more begrimed, her carefully dressed hair snatched to a rat's nest by branches. Unreasonably, she blamed Lily Pearl for the ruin of her carefully-wrought toilette. The girl must have a monopoly on cleanliness around here. Thanks to her, Maggie couldn't seem to manage it.

Moonshine was standing on top of a hill within a grove of cedar. Like her dress and legs, he was coated with mud and scratches and wet leaves. His head was down and he didn't look up, though she knew he sensed her presence.

"There you are. What do you mean running around out here without your disguise? This is a very settled area, you know. And in case you haven't been paying attention, there are unicorn-nappers just waiting for an opportunity like this." Fumbling in her pocket, she felt the roll of invisible bark outlined in her hand. Moonshine made no protest as she lifted his head and slipped the cone over his horn, tying it at the base with her handkerchief. At least he didn't flinch from her touch. Perhaps, just to comfort him, she might stroke his nose. Something wet touched her hand and she saw that his amythest eyes glistened with—yes, those were tears.

She knelt on the ground before him and looked him in the face, "Moonshine, what's the matter? You can tell me. I'm still your friend, after all."

Like one of Wizard Raspberry's balloons with its air let out, the unicorn sank to the ground and laid his head in her lap, as he used to. She stroked his mane and neck and face until after a long time he answered.

"I am lost. That maiden must know I am a tainted unicorn unworthy of her purity—that I have dealt with men—she must sense that she is not my *first* maiden—I can tell, she loves me not. And oh, it wounds me more sorely than I can express, and I know not how to staunch the wound."

"I know the feeling," Maggie said. "Forget it. Don't try. I guess nobody can protect themselves against somebody they love—not even unicorns. And it isn't true, is it, that the first maiden always has to love you back?" She shook her head and answered her own question. "No, of course, it's not. It couldn't be, or unicorns wouldn't be betrayed so often."

Moonshine raised his head. "That's very true. Oh, Maggie, I

don't know how I am to ever find another maiden as clever as you."

She pulled a face. "I still don't see why *I* won't do. Then you wouldn't have to find another one." But that broke the ease between them and though he rested his chin on her knee again, the gesture was tentative and nervous.

"Lady Primrose says I am not a true unicorn if I consort with one who is not a true maiden," Moonshine insisted stubbornly. "Please, dear friend, you must try to understand. It is not my choice. Indeed, I know not what I am to do. The truest possible maiden loves me not and I do not know how to win her." He told Maggie then what had passed between himself and Lily Pearl.

"I wouldn't worry about it if I were you," Maggie answered. "From the sound of all that waiting for her prince business she doesn't seem to intend to remain a maiden long. Unless I miss my guess, if any male above the rank of page rides past her gate, Lily Pearl will be away and gone, and then where would you be? Back where you started from. If she follows her mother's advice and sets her cap for Leofwin you can bet your horn she'll be ineligible for unicorn companionship moments after His Highness claps eyes on her. Maybe you'd be better off trying one of her sisters instead." She made another face. "Their mother claims each is as wonderful as the other, but then, I suppose she would."

Moonshine considered this suggestion, at first enthusiastically, but finally rejected it. "Surely another maiden won't do. If Lady Primrose is correct and you aren't my first maiden as bespoken in the Creed, Lady Lily Pearl is. And truly—her face IS as fair as the full moon, and her voice *is* as sweet as honey, and her form is as graceful as the willow and all that—"

"Well, yes," Maggie agreed. "But she didn't like you very much, did she? Now, now, don't take on again. If you like I can have a word with her—perhaps if I arrange to do some of her grooming chores by magic for the next day or so she'll have more time to get acquainted with you. I'm sure once she's gotten to know you—"

"Nay, my friend. For her rejection of me, though it deeply troubles me, is made less irksome since you reminded me a first maiden may not always return the love of her unicorn. Nay, what troubles me is more that—I'm afraid that in spite of all of her beauty and grace and obvious fittingness as a unicorn maiden, I—I really don't like her very much."

"I—don't think I understand," Maggie said, carefully swallowing the note of hopefulness that tried to creep into her voice.

"Then we are well met, my good dear Maggie. For I am certain I do not."

The shadows were lengthening, and Maggie looked back down the hill towards the tower. Perhaps Colin would be back this evening, having sent his deputation on its way to Everclear. Knowing his aversion to danger, she was sure he would try to get someone else to brave the trip back through the woods if he could manage it, in spite of the widow's odd insistence that he personally should lead the rescue party.

She stood, and brushed the leaves from her skirt. "I'd best be getting back. It's rather a long walk, and I suppose I'll have to wash up again before the merry widow will feed me. Not that I couldn't show the old battleaxe a thing or two about cooking if I took the notion."

"Mount upon my back," he said. "You followed me in friendship, and I would ill reward your loyalty by causing you to miss your meal."

"Are you sure you won't feel less unicornish by associating with the likes of me?" she couldn't help asking sourly.

But he answered sadly, "Nay, my friend. My back is lonely for your weight. And besides, what's done is done." He seemed so resigned and weary that she was doubly ashamed of her sharpness.

The rescue party was seven in number; the elder, Shearer, bulbous-nosed Archie, Giles Thatcher, who was no farmer in spite of his appearance, Brewer the innkeeper, and the former guard, Griffin Hillman. Besides these and Colin, there was the stranger, who didn't give his name and seemed to have expended his full supply of words in the tavern, for he spoke to none of them once they entered the woods.

Not that anyone minded. The fellow was less than a brilliant conversationalist. The other fellows had a very good time among themselves without him, and Colin enjoyed their bawdy humor and attempts to bewilder him with stories like the one about the wild trolls (the cannibalistic ones hadn't existed in Argonia, to his knowledge, for at least one hundred fifty years).

These were the kind of men he grew up among, simple men, who took their names from their work, or from the work of their fathers. Colin's uncle, who raised him, had been a Farmer. Indeed, Colin had continued to think of himself as a farmer-turned-songsmith long after he had taken his new name at the minstrel academy, for the rustic life at East Headpenney was the only one he had ever known until then, and his aunt and uncle his only kinfolk. Because neither of them had ever confided to him any detail about his mother and father, he had always assumed shameful circumstances surrounded his birth, and that had always made him feel shy. Until he'd met the mermaid during his journey with Maggie to save Amberwine, he had always assumed his musical talent was born solely of his orphaned apartness from the other East Headpenncy children. Even before his ability to find his way around an octave won him a territorial appointment to the minstrel academy, he used it to make himself popular at dances and gatherings until, by the time he was granted journeyman status, he felt himself as good a man as any of his rank, and better than most, at his trade.

But of his lineage he had no idea until the meeting with the mermaid, who claimed to recognize him as a kinsman, and proved it to him by showing him how he could swim without harm or discomfort through the icy sea and suggested to him something of the power his songs held beyond that to entertain and inform. Knowing what he was explained so much else, too—his natural ability with sailing ships, and why he was always falling all over his own two feet—now that he knew not all of his ancestors even HAD feet, he felt much less ashamed of his awkwardness on land and had consequently become less awkward. Coupled with the knowledge that his musical talent held power beyond the ordinary, his position as companion to the King had lent him further confidence. Some of Rowan's gigantic self-assurance was communicable, no doubt because the King was fond of bragging that his musician was worth ten of any other lord's warriors. Rowan had a way of overstating things like that, but his loudly voiced pride in Colin did cause others in the King's retinue to treat the minstrel with respect, to his face at least.

He had all the rank and position he wanted, and the admiration of as many of the willowy blond ladies of high degree as he had ever dreamed of. But his position at court would mean nothing after his part in Maggie's private rebellion was known. Not that he cared, particularly. Rowan would surely forgive them both, once he understood the situation, and as for the others at court, their opinions meant far less to Colin than those of the plain workingmen who rode beside him now. As for the ladies, no one of them had magic as useful as Maggie's, and just lately he had found the prettiest of them faded into a colorless sameness. He could remember no detail of the appearance of a single one with the clarity he had been able to recall Maggie's bewildered brown eyes or the angry burgundy blush of her cheeks when she was made Princess. Now he found that his memories of his most ardent intimacies with his gently bred lady loves stirred him less than those of a red-nosed, tangle-haired witch weeping in his arms and returning his kiss with a warmth that was intensely personal. He'd have to watch himself from now on. It was all very well to ride off into the woods with the unclaimed bastard elder daughter of a minor nobleman when he'd thought her face plain and her magic minor. It was a different matter to stay with the same girl when he knew her for a princess destined for a royal marriage, a sorceress whose nurturing magic had subtly powerful applications, and a strong-willed, off-beat beauty whose divertingly original appeal for him caused him to ride into all manner of alarmingly chancy situations.

As soon as he got back to Little Darlingham, he would take her straight to Queenston, as he'd originally agreed, and she could marry some ally of the King's or bully Rowan into sending his army to fetch her every unicorn in the kingdom, for all Colin cared. He'd content himself with forgetting their almost accidental moment of dalliance and find himself some nice, frivolous nymph—someone with whom everything wouldn't be so complicated, though by comparison, it might be a little dull.

The others steered their horses single-file along a thickly overgrown rut, keeping under the trees as much as possible to avoid the worst of a soaking rain. The stranger, though on foot, seemed to have no trouble in this rough terrain keeping pace with them, and had disappeared again. No one complained. The smell of the fellow's badly tanned garment was not improved by wetting.

They stopped near a creek at noontime and sat on the banks to eat their lunches. The rain continued, though the sun came out and a rainbow arched above the treetops, and the Little Darlingham men delighted in the fineness of the day. With considerable gusto, they took turns telling Colin how miserable and dangerous their weather in these parts *usually* was.

They reached Everclear by nightfall. The town was much as it had been when Colin had first seen it: barren, deserted, and lifeless. Only the mud in the streets was well-tracked, and the smell had improved; otherwise no sign of the disturbing effects of Moonshine's rejuvenating magic were visible. The stream, though muddy, had remained clean enough, but rather than take a chance on being poisoned themselves, the men unanimously agreed to forego the water and fill their flasks with ale—purely for medicinal purposes, of course.

"It's not we don't believe you, lad, when you say the water's

172

been put right," Griffin Hillman said. "But I ain't clear yet in my mind how twas these folk come to be damaged like—and the lads and me, we're not that curious that we'd want to find out."

Colin was uneasy that the faery and Leofwin didn't appear at once with their work party, but decided that probably everyone was at the inn, eating and preparing to settle down for the night. Still, it seemed like someone should have heard the horsemen arrive and at least have come out to investigate.

But no sounds emerged from the inn, either, when the rescue party tied their horses up in front of it. The men of Little Darlingham were unimpressed by the silence and laughed and talked among themselves as they entered the inn, stomping the mud from their boots first, as they would at home.

Except for the torches they lit and their own conversations, however, the inn was dark and silent. With less boisterousness than before, the men filled flagons with what was left of the ale and sat watching one another's expressions by torchlight as they drank their draughts with long, determined swallows. Colin drank nothing. It made no sense to him that this place was empty. If the zombies were in their own beds and the faery by her stream, Leofwin, at least, should be here. But the only things he could see that had been busy were spiders, whose webs now curtained broader expanses of the ceiling and the spaces between table legs than before. Though the zombie stench was fainter, the smell of stale ale was much stronger and much staler than it had been.

The men of Little Darlingham were as ready to leave the tavern as they had been to reach it. They drank quickly, filled their skin flasks, and filed quietly out the door. They liked taverns very well, but not this one. Colin sat there after they'd left, staring into the heart of the flame burning atop the last torch. He was exhausted, and felt stupid and befuddled.

Maggie had said some fell magic was at work in this place and he thought now she was right. Something was amiss. He'd felt as if he were being covertly watched all day long. And what could have gotten into Leofwin and the faery and a town full of zombies to make them disappear like that, in only a day's time?

Suddenly, from the next table, there came a knocking, as of crockery on wood. He rose and approached the table cautiously. Mother, but he'd be glad to leave this spook-ridden hole! Not that he was afraid of ghosts—but neither was he particularly fond of them. The village witch at East Headpenney had specialized in raising spirits of the dead, and he could never understand why certainly no one ever paid her to do so, though he supposed some probably paid her to put the spirits back wherever they belonged. Anyway, he had never seen her magic to do any good for anyone. Mostly it was a nuisance, intruding on what little privacy country people had. You could never be sure when you were alone. There you'd be, bathing, or using the privy, or just making a little headway with the miller's daughter in the storeroom, and suddenly you would feel this eerie, chilling presence. In the privy, in mid-winter, nothing was less welcome than a chilling presence. Colin had always suspected the witch used the spirits to spy for her, but he never knew for sure.

But if he wasn't frightened of ghosts, neither was he entirely sure such entities here, where everyone was already half-dead, were as similar apparitions had been in East Headpenney. Possibly one of the locals hereabouts could have gone on to ghosthood and neglected to leave behind his mortal shell, in which case he might well pack quite a wallop.

Holding the torch higher, Colin saw that the noise emanated from an upside-down flagon, rocking back and forth on a far table as if to right itself. Well, that was the kind of sense this place seemed likely to make. The people had no personalities, so naturally the inanimate objects would have.

But Colin wasn't ready for dancing beer mugs yet. He slapped his palm over the upturned bottom and held the thing firmly to the table.

A thin, muffled voice screamed from within. "Hey! You! I felt that! Let go right now! If you don't get your big paw off this mug by the time I count to seven, so help me I'll—"

She needed to say no more. Colin recognized Trickle's voice and quickly upended the flagon.

"How did you get in there?" he asked the faery, who was preoccupied with kicking her former prison across the table with blows of her tiny bare foot. She turned to him, the rage dying only slowly in her face.

"So it's you, is it, big boy? Hi. Thanks. I was getting stinking drunk from the fumes in there. Of all the filthy tricks—" she kicked the flagon another one.

"But how—?" Colin repeated.

"Can't you guess? Prince Charming stuck me in there. He pretended to cooperate, then, when I wasn't looking, he picked me up and almost broke my wings cramming me under that thing." she spat.

"But what about the zom—the townspeople?" Colin asked.

"What about them? Aye—wait—what ABOUT them? I hope that overblown blackguard didn't leave without telling those poor

174

sods they could stop digging privy holes. Otherwise they'll be halfway to the other side of the world by now.''

"We didn't see any of them—or any privies," he told her.

She looked oddly guilt-stricken. "I haven't had a lot of experience with the living dead myself. I have no idea where they might be. You don't suppose they'd wander off in the forest to die alone, like dogs or something, do you, if left to their own devices?''

Colin half-shrugged, half-shuddered. "*If* left to their own devices—" he repeated significantly.

He was saved from having to explain his remark to her and to himself by Archie, who burst through the door.

"Hey, minstrel! This Prince chap. Is he a stocky fellow? Balding? Straight blondish hair?''

Colin nodded.

"We've found 'im then. But you'd best 'ave a look at 'im before you try to take 'im anywheres, 'e ain't in what you might call the best of shape.''

After walking barefoot through the forest for two days, Sir Cyril was never so glad to see anything in his life as he was the gaudy, broken-down wagons, nor was he ever so glad to hear anything as he was the gypsy woman's cry of recognition when she saw His Royal Highness.

"Hey, King! What you doing here? Why you not running kingdom?''

"Xenobia, me proud old black-hearted darlin','' Rowan roared back. "What brings you here? There are no purses to slit in this part of my realm, are there?''

"Hey, King, how's the wife?'' A handsome swarthy young man with flashing brown eyes, a blinding white smile, and a great quantity of cheap jewelry dangling from his neck, joined the woman. Close behind him, a doe-eyed pregnant gypsy girl peered around his back at them.

His Majesty ignored the man but pulled the girl to him by taking both her hands in one great paw. "Zorah, my little dearie, has your great brute of a husband been beating you? Shall I thrash him for you, my darlin'?''

"No, King,'' the girl replied, returning his smile. "My man's too busy beating his chest to beat me. See? I make him papa!''

"What's this?'' A very nongypsyish man in gypsy dress poked his head out of a wagon and when he saw the King leapt down and engulfed him in a bear hug. "Rowan, old chap!''

A bear hug? Of course, a bear hug. From their names, and the fact that the tribe was known to the King, Sir Cyril realized that these must be the Xenobian gypsies Colin Songsmith sang of in his epic ballad, "The Quest to Free Queen Amberwine." The nongypsy was none other than Prince H. David Worthyman, formerly an enchanted bear and presently consort to Xenobia, Queen of the Gypsies, the frumpy matron who had first greeted them.

Prince Worthyman, living with his paramour in voluntary exile from his own country, Ablemarle, was a sworn ally of King Rowan's and had been of great help to the national heroine, Maggie Brown (now the Princess Magdalene, though Cyril kept forgetting that; the girl in Songsmith's ballad scarcely sounded like a princess) in her daring rescue of the queen. The nice-looking young man was surely the Queen's original abductor, now pardoned, Xenobia's son by Prince Worthyman, popularly known as Gypsy Davey. The pretty pregnant girl, then, would be Zorah, who had led the King to the final rescue of Queen Amberwine, Maggie Brown, Songsmith, Prince Worthyman (then in bear form), and the by-then repentent Xenobia and son from the clutches of the at-that-time-unallied Royal Airforce, the Dragon Grimley. Perchingbird recalled these details with relief, for they explained to him the King's joy at seeing Zorah and Prince Worthyman and his coldness to Davey.

His Majesty the King was returning His Royal Highness the Prince's bear hug with a frost giant squeeze of his own. "Worthyman, what brrings you herre?" the king demanded, his thick hillman's brogue rolling broader with excitement and relief.

"Now, Rrrrowan, you don't want to know that. You already know it's something highly irregular," Prince Worthyman laughed. He still growled some of his R's, a speech impediment no doubt remaining from his years in captivity as a bear. "And you? Out for a stroll with yer boys, are you?"

"As a matter of fact, old friend," the King said with an eye to the knives at the gypsy's belts and the horses that pulled their wagons. "I'd like to talk wi' ye about that."

No further questions were asked. Rowan didn't demand to know how the gypsies, complete with caravan, came to be in the middle of the eastern coastal forests, whether for poaching or for smuggling, it did not matter. The King was wise enough to recognize that among his subjects, these gypsies were a law unto themselves. And the gypsies, having once been deceived into surrendering their autonomy to the sorcerer Fearchar and having been subsequently released by Maggie Brown and Colin Songsmith and pardoned by King Rowan, were glad enough to aid their overlord now.

"There's little enough we can do, lad," Prince Worthyman told him regretfully. "We stopped at Castle Rrowan on the way to—do our business here, y'know. None was about there. Place had an abandoned look."

"M'lads must be patrolling," the King said, looking anxious even while dismissing Worthyman's observation. "But I've changed m'mind about goin' there anyway. You folk have mounts, and arms of a sort. And this is no proper military mission, just a bit of policin' up I've got to do. How about showin' me along to Finbar's old retreat?" He held out his hand, and Sir Cyril placed in it the manuscript, which the navigator had saved from the wreck and returned to him for safe-keeping. "We was wrecked off t'coast by a snake two days ago, and we're a wee bit behind schedule. Can you muster the beasties, men and arms to take us along to this place?"

Xenobia peeked over Prince Worthyman's shoulder as he examined the map, and sprang back away again with a cat-like leap and a hiss to match. Perchingbird had heard it said that gypsy ladies had a tendency toward the dramatic in their deportment.

"Hear me, King! That place is no good!" she cried. "Ill luck will follow you there! If you don't heed my word, you'll rue the day you failed to listen to the gypsy woman!"

"Now, now, lovie," Prince Worthyman said, wrapping a burly arm around his mate's waist. "You're exaggeratin' a bit, now, aren't you? Be a real queen and have the men saddle mounts for these lads, eh?"

Xenobia stared at him for a moment with nostrils flaring and sparks flashing from her dark eyes, then said thickly, "Ah, love. I can deny you nothing. I am fool for you! But this time, I tell you. Be careful. I gotta feeling about that place. Death waits at Worm's Roost. Heed me."

The woman kissed him passionately, then broke away, flouncing off in a swirl of flamboyant dirty skirts. Worthyman smiled. "Rremarrkable lady, the queen, but has never made an honest prediction in her life. Shall we plan the logistics, old man?"

By the time Maggie finished giving Moonshine his rubdown and started back to the tower, the sun had set and the evening was growing chilly. If she was going to wash again before she faced Belburga, she figured she might as well do it before the night got any colder.

She didn't bother with the basin this time, but washed off the worst of the dirt and undid the plaits of her ruined hairdo, combing her hair to hang simply to her waist.

When she was presentable, she gathered her fortitude and started for the tower, but stopped. No light shone from the lower, kitchen level. Belburga evidently did not wait dinner, even on paying guests.

Maggie cursed fluently to herself, but was not too disappointed, though she was hungry. There was something rather repulsive about the widow, quite apart from her rudeness, which made Maggie's skin crawl and rendered her quite content to avoid the woman.

She thought she would sit on the banks of the stream for awhile and see if Colin might be returning late. Though he had seemed oblivious to Belburga's general odiousness, he had managed to leave at the first opportunity. And curse him for sneaking off alone like that, leaving her to deal with the widow.

She waited a long time, until it was quite dark, but he didn't appear. She hadn't really thought he would, but she wasn't exactly swamped with people begging for her company and she was lonely. She thought about going to talk to Moonshine, but she knew he needed more time to ponder, if he wasn't asleep already. She pulled a stick of jerked venison out of her pocket, looked at it, and stuck it back where it came from. It didn't seem worth it to eat alone. After traveling for most of a month with two close companions, she felt the need to talk to someone in the evening, but not someone like Dame Belburga. The idea of merely eating then going to bed in a dark, dismal tower was unappealing.

What would appeal to her, she thought, hugging herself for warmth, was to have this whole situation neatly dispatched, and herself blessedly divested of the crown with its attendant responsibilities and matrimonial obligations. But this time, when the questing was done, she would prefer that, instead of each of them going their separate ways, they would continue to travel together, resting at night by a series of magic campfires, with stars winking down at them while Colin made up silly songs about everything that had happened.

A salty tear trickled into the upturned corner of her mouth where a smile had begun to play in response to her pleasant thoughts. She brushed the tear aside. She was being a goose. Whatever else happened, in the end, they would not all be together. Moonshine would have to go do whatever it was unicorns had to do with some other girl—he'd made that abundantly clear. Colin was a busy man; she kept forgetting that. From his point of view, she supposed, he was biding his time, putting up with her until matters resolved themselves so he could go about his business with a clear conscience. Yet, he did like her. He really did. Hadn't he helped her overcome her fear of running water by singing her through it? Hadn't he saved her from all the nasty beasts at Wizard Raspberry's (though if they hadn't ganged up on her, she could have handled them herself) and hadn't he, after all, come back to free her from the tower to begin with? And in spite of all his scolding about her penchant for quests, he had been rather dear back there on the trail. She smiled to herself and brushed her lips with the tips of her fingers. Nobody was quite THAT dear out of mere kindness, was he?

The mist rose from the stream and obscured her view of the road leading from the woods, but she thought she would look just one more time before she gave up waiting and returned to the tower. She walked out to the middle of the little ornamental bridge spanning the stream, and scanned the treeline beyond the meadows.

Nothing was there, of course. If Colin had, indeed, gone to Everclear, and it seemed sure now that he had, it was no less than a day's journey from here and would require a day's journey back as well—and possibly more time than that, with the stricken villagers in tow. She wished again that he'd awakened her, so she might have gone with him. She worried that he hadn't found enough help, but reminded herself that nothing would have persuaded him back into those woods unless he had. He was not one for taking unnecessary chances. Not unless he was prodded, anyway. She grinned slyly to herself. Then he was capable of the most remarkable feats. She'd have to see about that, one last time, she thought with a trace of bitterness, after Moonshine had found his other maiden and just before she got carted off to marry some dismal duke or the other.

Maggie Brown, you are a truly *wicked* witch, she congratulated herself, and dropped her eyes from the treeline. Just as she did, a light blinked from within the forest. She searched the trees, looking for a trace of it. It rewarded her by blinking once more, and again, from the same place. Will-o'-the-wisp? But a will-o'-the-wisp should move and should keep reappearing. Providing will-o'-the-wisps did what they should, of course, and she wasn't exactly sure they did, since she'd never encountered one before, though she'd heard enough about them. Mostly they were supposed to confine themselves to swamps and lonely mountain roads, enticing travelers to become lost forever.

Which didn't fit. She was too far away to be its target, if it wanted to lure a traveler, and unless she was its target, she doubted it would have allowed her to see it. No accounting for some of the magic that happened in this country, as her father was fond of saying. She shook her head and started back for the tower—and barely caught the last glimmer of what seemed to be a companion light to the one in the forest shining from the tower's battlements. Abruptly, the light flicked out and the entire tower was dark, except for one arrowslit on the level above the one where her own room was. The narrow opening glowed faintly, casting a pale ray of light down the tower wall to melt impotently into the darkened yard.

Shivering, Maggie ran back into the old keep, relieved that the widow hadn't gone so far as to bar the door against her. The door thumped shut behind her, and she lit a wall torch after several tries—her magic was definitely not up to snuff—and climbed the spiral staircase.

She found the lighted room without difficulty, but hesitated, undecided whether to knock or catch the conspirator who was sending nocturnal signals in the act of carrying out some nefarious scheme, so she compromised. Rapping one loud, quick rap on the door, she shoved it open and barged in.

The foxiest-looking girl she had ever seen sprawled across a chair whose straight back and rigid arms had never been made for sprawling. The girl looked up, brushing back a bush of fiery red hair from eyes which were long and tilted and green as olives, and salted with fool's gold. Everything about her seemed pointed. She had a long, thin face, barely saved from horsiness by a dainty pointed chin. Her sharp nose pointed down and her ears pointed up every bit as much as Moonshine's. Seeing Maggie, the girl nearly choked on the apple she'd been munching, but caught herself and chewed the piece in her mouth deliberately and swallowed. In her lap, illuminated by a candle, was a heavy wood-bound tome.

Returning Maggie's stare levelly, she closed her book. Maggie barely caught a glimpse of what looked like gold leaf.

"Sight-seeing?" the redhead asked. From her coloring, she had to be the much-vaunted Ruby Rose. "Or maybe you'd like to claim you've got the wrong room? I know Mother told you you're not supposed to see us."

"I—" Maggie began, faltering, while she tried to think of a likely tale. Then it occurred to her that *she* was not the one who was up to no good and she might as well ask what she had to ask outright. "I saw a light in the forest and another one just above this room, in the battlements. And—"

"And you think I'm sending secret signals to my highwayman lover, is that it?" Ruby Rose asked. Maggie could see now that her eyes had adjusted to the light that the girl was barely old enough to qualify her for a lover of any sort—she couldn't be more than fourteen.

"You see these visions often, do you?" the girl inquired, goading.

"No, my aunt's the one who sees visions in our family," Maggie replied evenly. "But I DID see a light. And you know something about it, don't you?"

"Maybe I do," Ruby Rose admitted. "What day is this?"

"Saturday, I think. Why?"

"Not that, you ninny. I mean, what DATE?"

"I haven't the faintest idea. Sometime in late summer is all I know."

"Is it indeed?" the girl's voice sparked with interest, and she looked outside as if to verify the information—which she of course failed to do, since night had already fallen. "I really must make it a point to go out of doors from time to time. We scholars have little time for outings, and I find I quite lose track of whole seasons sometimes, and miss collecting valuable elements for my work. You're quite sure it's summer?"

"Well, yes. We held the christening at the solstice, as usual and—" she counted, as well as she could, the days and weeks since the christening, her incarceration in the tower, the time spent hiding in the forest, the day and night at Aunt Sybil's, the journey to Raspberry's and the trip to Everclear—then the night spent among the zombies, and the subsequent journey to Little Darlingham. She ran out of fingers to count on once, and had to start over, but since she did her counting aloud, Ruby Rose's sharp mind was way ahead of hers.

"About late August, then, isn't it?" the foxy girl asked.

"Yes, I should say so, from the nip in the air. Do you really never go out at all?"

"No more than I can help," the other answered. "It only makes my freckles worse." She pointed to her nose, on which the freckles swarmed, overflowing onto her cheeks and chin. "Mother says freckles are a blight. Besides, it's too rainy out most of the time. Rain would ruin my book."

"I see," Maggie answered, fidgeting. This young girl was every bit as weird as her mother.

"Oh, sit down, won't you? I have to think and you're making me nervous."

Maggie gingerly obeyed, pulling a footstool near Ruby Rose's uncomfortable looking chair and sitting down on the edge of it.

"You make me nervous too," she told the girl. "You're Ruby Rose, aren't you? Dame Belburga's middle daughter?"

The redhead grimaced. "Please! Ruby Rose is my mother's affected nomenclature, inflicted on me when I was yet too young to object. When I become a master alchemist, I shall change my name to Rusty. That's what my father calls me. How far away would you say he is, anyway?"

"Who?" Maggie looked around the room, but they were still alone.

"My father, of course. It must have been his signal you saw. He visits me about this time every year, and usually tries to send me some signal—a bird to my window, or something, so I'll come out and meet him and he doesn't have to face mother. I wonder how that old scold could have known he was coming in time to intercept his signal?"

Maggie shook her head. "Hold on. You're going too fast for me. I thought your father was dead."

"Then you shouldn't try to think at all," Ruby Rose Rusty said curtly. "Because he's not; he's alive. He just wears so many disguises when he travels—he always travels incognito—that nobody recognizes him when they see him, so everyone who doesn't know otherwise assumes he's dead, and mother lets them think it, so people will think her a widow instead of knowing the truth, which is that he just can't stand to live with her, so he doesn't. I don't blame him. I wouldn't either, if I had any choice."

Maggie tried to think of something sympathetic to say to comfort the fatherless waif, but the fatherless waif flashed a sudden voracious grin full of pearly pointed teeth.

"One day I'll get away from that ogress," the girl declared, making her voice theatrically deep and ominous and holding the candle that had served her as a study-light under her chin to cast sinister shadows across her face. "When I am an alchemist, I shall know the unknowable, and one day, while she is trying to scrub my freckles off with lye soap and is least suspecting it, I shall utter the unutterable and a simulacrum or a golem or something will come out of nowhere and haul her off to the netherworld. I plan that as only the first feat in my long and brilliant career, of course," she confided, setting the candle aside. "But won't it be a grand starting point?"

"It's pretty dreadful, actually," Maggie said, trying to suppress a smile. "Even for YOUR mother. But I know what you

182

mean. My granny is a witch, and sometimes when she's in top form I'd like to call in a demon or two for help, but I don't."

"Hmph," said Ruby Rose. "You probably couldn't call a demon if you wished, then, or else you're a complete fool, or if you can and you're not a fool, all I can say is that your granny must be a more agreeable witch than my mother is an ogress." She thought for a moment. "Perhaps I could have my minions just transport father here whenever I wished to see him, or, better yet, have a castle built for us where mother couldn't find us." Her face fell. "Though I suppose he could have done that himself, if he liked. I think he's afraid, with my ogress heritage, that I'll turn out like mother—though anyone can see I take more after his line," and she tugged at the lobe of one of her pointed ears. "I can't wait to tell him about the new variation I've invented on this ancient formula." She switched the topic deftly, tapping the book in front of her, obviously wanting to divert the conversation from the subject of her father.

"What does it do?" Maggie asked.

"Changes blueberry bushes into toadstools, at least theoretically. I haven't tested it yet."

"I can't see why you'd *want* to do a thing like that."

"That's because it's beyond your powers of understanding. You're not a genius who's destined to become an alchemist, like I am."

"Perhaps not, but I *am* a first-class witch," Maggie replied. She was annoyed and trying very hard not to show it. She felt she should be in control, and didn't like being made to feel small by a girl surely no more than two thirds her years. Ruby Rose's learning gave her the advantage, and her youth made Maggie feel long in the tooth, for if their reckoning of the days was correct, Maggie's twenty-first birthday, the three-times-seven so significant to witches, was either nigh or had already passed. She wished fervently for the first time that she had paid more attention to the tutor she and Winnie had shared as children, so that she might know other numbers than the magic ones, and other words than those in her own tongue. If only she hadn't spent those dreary hours shifting around the patterned woven borders on the hem of Winnie's gown instead of listening to her tutor, she might at least be able to show this superior little twit that Maggie Brown knew a thing or two, too. Since all she could recall were the colors of Winnie's gown and the whacking her knuckles had received from the tutor in payment for her inattention, she kept silent.

"If you're such a first-class witch," Ruby Rose challenged,

"do something magical. Don't try to trick me either. My father is a *really* first-class wizard, and I promise you, I'll know the difference."

Maggie sniffed haughtily. "I never accept childish dares."

"Hah! You can't! You're just a scullery maid who's run off with that minstrel, like my mother said. You can't stay here either, by the way, when he abandons you." She leaned back with a smug smile on her foxish face and propped her feet up next to Maggie on the stool.

"I'm not either a scullery maid, and it's not like that between Colin and me at all!" Maggie declared hotly. But was it? Never mind whether it was or not. It was no business of this wretched child's one way or the other. With considerable satisfaction, Maggie ordered the rafters to dump soot and splinters down around Ruby Rose's pointy little ears.

"You horrid witch!" the girl screamed, and jumped up, clawing the soot from her eyes so that she looked more like a racoon than a fox for a change. But it wasn't her face she was worried about. As soon as she could see, she began wiping at the blackened cover of her precious book. "You ruined it on purpose, just because you're too stupid to understand it!" the girl accused.

"You asked me to show you," Maggie reminded her mildly, and hoped her hearthcraft would be as prompt about cleaning the book as it had been about showering it with soot. That had been the liveliest her powers had been all day! They probably liked dealing with base matter like dirt and manure better than they liked dealing with soap and water, derived as they were from blood-kinship to her less-than-spotless wicked witch ancestresses. No wonder it was easier for her to perform spiteful magicks than useful ones. Suddenly, she wasn't very proud of herself, and realized she had indeed taken a childish dare to do the opposite of what her powers were supposed to do—to mess and soil and ruin instead of clean and mend and tidy. She concentrated very hard, much harder than she'd ever had to before, and executed a cleaning spell that left the book, if not the girl, as pristine and unmarred as before.

Mid-way through the spell, Ruby Rose stopped glowering at her, and by the time the book was clean, the girl was grinning again. "Very good, witch. I liked that one." She regarded her own grimy hands with interest. "Oh, that mother could see me now. Do you suppose I ought to go see if my big sister, Lily Pearl, would like me to do her hair for her?"

Maggie giggled and then they were both laughing. Finally,

Ruby Rose chortled to a stop and asked, "What else can you do?"

"Nothing that would impress you more than that, I'm afraid. My magic is useful in its way, but not very spectacular." It occurred to her then, however, that she had the perfect opportunity to advance Moonshine's cause. "The only other thing I can do that's very wonderful is talk to unicorns."

"To unicorns? Really?" Ruby Rose leaned forward, the gold in her eyes aglitter with—enthusiasm? At least she hardly seemed to share her mother's and sister's disparaging attitude towards Moonshine's kind. "Could *I* get one, do you suppose?"

Though Maggie didn't like the aquisitive gleam in the girl's eye, she admitted to herself that jealousy was probably making her over-suspicious. "I'll introduce you tomorrow," she promised.

"Can you make it early?" the girl asked, reassuming some of her former air of detached superiority. "After my father arrives I may not have the time." And she set her book carefully aside and strolled over to her little porcelain washbasin, and began delicately removing her coating of filth.

Knowing a dismissal when she saw one, Maggie left—and was careful to bang the door behind her.

When she awoke next morning she felt somewhat better. Colin should be back by evening, and then, with or without Moonshine, they would try to discover where the brigands had taken the unicorns and persuade King Roari to do something about it, as soon as he returned to Queenston. Or, if the brigands were really going to do anything despicable to the unicorns, perhaps she and Colin would find a way to take appropriate action themselves. Whatever he said about returning to Queenston, Colin certainly wouldn't want to return there without doing everything in his power to aid the King in the apprehension of the blackguards who were threatening the beasts. And hadn't Leofwin said something about a revolution as well? If they went to the King with that sort of information, he was much likelier to listen to her petition than if they went empty-handed. Surely Colin would see that.

And the signals—it hardly seemed reasonable that with the woods full of bandits and zombies, those stealthy beacons could only be from Ruby Rose's doting papa. Brilliant Belburga's middle daughter might be, but lacking in sense if she admitted no solution possible to that puzzle other than her own.

But who was right and who was wrong about that remained to be seen. Right now, Maggie needed her breakfast badly.

Belburga was still at the table, and ignored her, but she didn't protest when Maggie ladled gruel onto a plate from the kettle on the hearth. She might as well have. Just having to look at the woman was enough to spoil Maggie's appetite all over again. Maybe the widow really *was* an ogress, as her daughter claimed. Ogresses no more all had to be huge and hairy than witches all had to be wicked, or faeries small. Maggie decided to see for herself. Ruby Rose's pointed teeth didn't mean anything; though pointed teeth were commonly ascribed to ogresses, and would be a dead giveaway in the case of the otherwise normal looking widow, other beings also had them sometimes. Everything else about Ruby Rose was pointed, so why not her teeth? Her mama, however, was a different story.

So Maggie checked.

The rat wasn't strictly necessary, but she threw it in anyway. She felt she could do no less for a woman who had called her a wayward scullery maid behind her back, and who had given her the worst possible food and lodging in return for a very hefty fee.

She baited the rat out with a piece of bread while Belburga was mumbling to herself. It wasn't difficult. Belburga, for all her insistence on white dresses and clean hands among her daughters, was a slovenly housekeeper, and no self-respecting cat was likely to stay with such an odious woman.

The fat gray rodent was almost immediately forthcoming, scuttling out of its hole the minute she lowered the bread, bold as if it were a dog come for its rightful supper and, indeed, it was almost as big as a small dog. Maggie threw the bread across the widow's shoetops and the rat leaped after it.

The widow loosed an earsplitting shriek and flew after the rat, frightening the poor beast into a state of nervous prostration. The shriek revealed Belburga's throat, tonsils, and tongue in graphic detail, and also a set of teeth longer and far more sharply pointed than Ruby Rose's.

Having completed the ladylike amenities, Belburga picked up her broom and began chasing the hapless rat around the room. Maggie left abruptly, without touching the food on her plate. The impoverished gentlewoman was actually slavering as she chased the poor rat.

So Belburga *was* an ogress. No wonder she was so revolting. Ogresses, and even descendents of ogresses, were commonly known to eat PEOPLE. Oh, maybe not neighbors or relatives or friends, providing they had any. But visitors were certainly fair game. No wonder the good widow took in lodgers. Maggie wondered how many she ever sent on their way again. That thought sent her racing to the stable.

"You're panting, my friend," Moonshine said. "What ails you?" He was munching peacefully from a bucket of oats.

"Moonshine, this is *very* important," she said when she'd gotten her breath back. "WHO led Roundelay out of this stable? Was it Colin or someone else?"

"'Twas Colin himself, and none other. He gave me to understand that he was away to find help for the afflicted accomplices of the wicked captors of my kindred."

"Whew." Maggie sank with a sigh into the dirty straw inside the stall. She told Moonshine what she had learned about the widow and her daughters.

Moonshine was skeptical. "The fair Lily Pearl may be unpleasantly self-absorbed, but I cannot think she is an ogress. Mayhap Dame Belburga is but her stepmother, and perhaps her teeth are in somewise disfigured through hardship—"

"Like having to crunch through human bone to get the marrow out?" Maggie suggested.

"She has harmed neither Master Colin nor yourself, and lives at peace with the folk roundabout her," Moonshine pointed out. "Surely that is evidence contrary to your suspicions?"

"Ha!" Maggie said derisively. "Lives at peace with the folk roundabout her, indeed! Except for one very weird stranger, who have *we* met who even knows this woman, aside from her daughters, eh? As to why she hasn't devoured us yet, I don't know—maybe she's saving us for dessert. Or maybe she just likes princes best, and is waiting to sink her teeth into Leofwin." She smiled. "She'd bust a few fangs on *him*, wouldn't she though?"

"Goodwitch," Moonshine said kindly, "Methinks you are overtired from our wanderings."

"Is that so? Well, come along then, and I'll fetch Ruby or Rosie or Rusty or whatever she calls herself. She's a very odd girl, but she's smart enough to know who's an ogress and who's not. Not that it matters if the whole lot of them, Belburga, Lily, Ruby, and that other flowery brat, whatsername, are boiling up a kettle to cook me in right now. I'm not leaving this place until Colin returns. If you like this girl, though, I suggest, for safety's sake, you win her quickly. She's not crazy about living here, either. The instant Colin rides up, we should all flee together."

"Well spoken, my friend. Lead on. I am surpassing eager to meet this new maiden." He trotted cheerfully after her, into the concealment of the cedar grove which bordered the brook.

"Don't get too surpassing eager," Maggie cautioned. "I'll have to fetch her. She likes the indoors because she freckles and likes to study alchemy all the time. She's very set on being an alchemist, Moonshine. Won't that conflict with her being a unicorn maiden? If I remember correctly, my witchery was one of Primrose's objections to me."

"Ah, but if the maiden is not yet a sorceress, perhaps she may alter her ambition once we have met," the unicorn replied.

She gave him an exasperated look. "Are all unicorns so pigheadedly optimistic? Don't answer that. It *has* to be your own little idiosyncrasy. Primrose is a unicorn, and I don't think she has an optimistic bone in her head."

Moonshine rolled his eyes scoldingly, but Maggie noticed he didn't contradict her.

The ever-present mist swirled up from the stream to enclose them, isolating them from all but the dewy patch of ground directly before them. Maggie took advantage of the cover to remove Moonshine's disguise while he secreted himself among the hedges. When she was sure he was safe and Belburga was nowhere about, she ducked back into the tower and up the stairs to Ruby Rose's room.

The girl genius met her at the door. "You're a noisy sort of witch, aren't you?"

"I beg your pardon," Maggie said as civilly as possible. "But you said you wanted to meet my friend early. If you'll be so kind as to leave your musty old book, I think you'll find Moonshine worthy of even your exalted attention."

Swathing herself in a woolen shawl of the same olive as her eyes, Ruby Rose followed Maggie back down to the garden.

"Oh, I *say*," the girl cried in admiration when she beheld Moonshine. "What a *splendid* specimen he is!" She stretched out her pointed fingers and Moonshine nuzzled them, saying to Maggie, "I think you may leave us now."

"I guess I know when I'm not wanted," she replied, and retired to the cover of the streamside hedges, to keep an eye open for the ogress, who was conspicuously absent. Maybe ogresses liked to sleep during the day, like vampires, as soon as they'd breakfasted and fed the chickens. She'd never heard it said that they did, but one never knew. Whatever she was doing, Maggie thought grimly, Belburga'd be wise to continue doing it and not interfere with Moonshine. If she did, Maggie'd bash her one, and joyously, at that. Meanwhile, the best plan was to stay put. If she went looking for Colin, to try to meet him in the woods on his way back, she'd undoubtedly wind up missing him, and he would fall into the clutches of the man-eating (or at least, rat-eating) ogress. Besides, she couldn't very well pursue him on foot, and the only available mount was courting.

"Don't get me wrong, yer Grace," Eagledown said. "It's not that we don't appreciate the social call and the goodies, but when are you going to finish doodling around and loose us from this ice-bear's lair?"

"Please finish your tidbit," Pegeen implored. He'd only eaten half of his apple, though Snowshadow had daintily downed hers in one bite. "If the guards find anything they didn't bring you themselves, they'll know someone's been visiting you."

"Never fear, Lady," Eagledown lowered his head so that the jagged end of his horn's stump menaced the heavy doorway set into the thick blue ice. "They don't come in here—they're afraid they'll get what they've got coming to them if they do."

"Fine. Good. Keep them intimidated. With this beastly weather we've been having, you see, I'm only just getting started on our map tonight."

"TONIGHT?" they both cried together. Snowshadow spoke in a tone just short of a despairing wail. "But you said a week ago it would take you but two days to complete."

"I'm sorry. It really couldn't be helped. I can't work in the rain, in spite of my illuminating magic."

"What's the matter? Afraid to get your well-bred hide wet?" Eagledown asked.

"My well-bred hide dries. My inks do not. They run. While pen and ink wash is an excellent technique for achieving some effects, it is of no great use in cartography."

"He didn't mean it, Princess," Snowshadow said. "Only—time draws short. I feel it."

Pegeen felt it too. She had spent nights pacing her chambers, looking out at the low, roiling sky through sheets of driving rain and sleet, feeling useless as she listened to the drops pelt the castle walls. Everyone had worn boots of fish-gut all week, for the floors were awash with cold water, which seeped in under the doors. In spite of her heaviest shawl, Pegeen had felt the cold in her very marrow, as she wandered the corridors, too restless to draw or write or even to read, and listened to Fearchar consulting with his officers, making further plans for the ruin of King Roari's reign. The maze had been horribly slick this evening, for the rain had continued until sunset, when the sky miraculously lifted revealing the stars and moon. The unicorns stood in ankle-deep water that was rapidly crusting to ice, and their feed

189

was soaked. She was glad she had thought to bring them the apples, but sorry she was unable to bring better tidings about the escape plans.

"Very well, then. I have seen for myself that you are still safe, so I shall proceed as planned. But I must tell you, the map may take somewhat longer to do than I'd expected."

Both unicorns neighed with dismay.

"I simply can't see far enough to map the most distant reaches by night, and it's quite impossible to do it during the day. Fearchar wants me to do maps for his battle campaigns, and calligraphy for the proclamations he plans to issue once he has taken the throne. His suspicions will be less if I pretend to cooperate enthusiastically. To finish mapping the maze, I shall have to crawl farther out on the wall each night the weather is fine to draw more of the area—"

"Oh, Princess, do be careful. Don't risk your life!" Snowshadow said.

"My life won't be much longer than yours, I fear, if I cannot free you one way or the other. For on my word as the daughter of Finbar the Fireproof, and the last Ashburn heir, I shall not allow Fearchar and his lackeys to do you more harm than they have done already. But in the meantime, while you're waiting for me?"

"Yes?"

"Keep kicking at that hole of yours, why don't you."

When they reached the high, windswept plateaus where the snow and rain blew together in a continual swirling dance, Sir Cyril thought they must surely leave the gypsy wagons behind, or mire them in the man-high drifts. So he was surprised to see the women bend over the wheels of their wagons, three and four ladies to the wheel, and deftly remove them.

"My word, sir, whatever are your ladies doing?" he asked the man Davey, who lounged against one of the wagons waiting for the women's ministrations. The man had buttoned his shirt all the way to his chin for a change, covering his jewels, and wore a silken muffler around his neck, under a fleece-lined sheepskin coat covered with beautiful embroideries. He seemed to view the wretched weather as a fine excuse to display this new sartorial splendor, but of no particular interest otherwise. "Look around, King's man," he instructed Sir Cyril, flinging his fleece-mittened hands far out to the sides in an expansive gesture. "What you see ahead?"

"Snow? Or besides the snow?" Sir Cyril asked.

"Snow. That's *right*. Say, you pretty smart, King's man. Not like some of them, too stupid to let my wife read their hands. It's snow all around us. You know what happens to wagon wheels in snow?"

"They founder. I naturally assumed we would abandon the wagons."

"No—no such thing, King's man. These wagons our homes. Besides, who wants to walk to other side of mountains? Very tiring. Not the gypsy way."

Perchingbird agreed wholeheartedly that he didn't wish to walk to the other side of the mountains, and tried to go to the assistance of the group of women hoisting the wagon to his left. They peremptorily shoved him aside, paying no attention to the snow-laden wind whipping their skirts and hair around their lean brown bodies. Davey tugged at his elbow, pulling him back to the relative shelter of the wagon. The women seemed to take as much pride in holding up their wagons while hugging their heavy, fringed shawls around their shoulders as they did in their cooking or dancing.

"You can't mean to let them carry the wagons across the pass on their shoulders, though, can you?" Perchingbird demanded incredulously. Davey shook his head, grinning, and pointed. A couple of young girls ran around to the back of one of the wagons and began drawing out long wooden slats. As the other women held up the wagon bed, the girls slid the slats under it, in line with the hubs, which the other women then lashed to the slats.

"Skis?" Perchingbird asked.

Davey, greatly diverted by his amazement, grinned. "Of course, skis! It's old gypsy trick. This pass is easy pass. We take nice sleigh ride to where is level or goes up, nice sled ride where goes down. Smart, no? Horses ride in wagons where is too deep to walk—men ski. Come, pick skis."

The King was already selecting his, a pair of long pieces broken off from wagon slides. The King's face was grim. Perchingbird knew his Majesty fretted because his men from Castle Rowan had not yet replied to the message sent with Grimley. Gypsy sleighs and belt knives were all very well, but what was required before one met with evil sorcerers was reinforcements.

Leofwin's inert body bloodied up a thicket near the smithy. Fortunately for the Prince, the spear in his chest, which had

191

originally drained such a considerable quantity of his vital fluids, served as a plug to keep the rest from draining. He still breathed.

Also fortunately for the Prince, Colin had been so lost in thought at the tavern he had failed to empty the unicorn-blessed water he still carried in his own water skin, and had therefore not replaced the healing liquid with brew from the Everclear tavern.

Before he could wet the prince down with the flask's contents, however, Colin felt a hand on his arm. The gray-bearded stranger placed himself between the flask and Leofwin, saying, "Did you not tell us, o minstrel, that this is an *evil* man? A man who would have raped your female companion save for your brave intervention? A man connected with the captors of the very beasts whose water you would use to heal him? A rake, in short, and a loathsome bully. I say unto you, o minstrel, this man is not fit to live. Let him die. Will such a one be missed by any?"

Colin blinked at him, then shook loose the hand. "You make a persuasive argument—er—um, stranger. But Dame Belburga, for one, wants his royal carcass delivered to her lodgings. And I doubt there's a man here intrepid enough to say that lady nay." Collectively and individually, each of the companions affirmed his own lack of the required intrepidity. At Colin's signal, Giles jerked the sword from Leofwin's wound, and Colin sluiced unicorn water over it, diluting the dark red which welled up from the puncture to pale pink.

"Do as you will," the stranger said, and since no one was paying him any attention, left. Colin had the feeling he hadn't exactly won the man over, but he was too preoccupied to care, between pouring the unicorn water over Leofwin and physically divesting himself of his own distaste for the task. He wished Maggie had come. She was much better at this sort of thing than he was. Healing, of course, not throwing up. It would have been nice to have had her there if for no other reason than to hold HIS head, though she would have made some scathing comment while she was at it.

Leofwin sputtered to consciousness. "Drat it all, Sally," he grumbled deliriously. "You've spitted me already. Must you drown me as well?"

Colin stopped pouring and smacked the wounded man's cheeks instead. "Upsy-daisy, old man. You've a lot of explaining to do, and I insist you survive long enough to do it."

"Gently, lad," cautioned old Shearer. "Would you save him and slay him all in the same hour? There's time enough for his tale on the morrow."

General sentiment and the prince's pallor were with the

oldster, and the rescue party bedded down in the abandoned smithy for the night. All save the stranger, who was evidently still offended enough by Colin's rejection of his suggestion to prefer solitude.

The next morning dawned as gray and feeble as their patient.

Weakly, Leofwin peeled back an eyelid, and peered at them through an orb russet and vein-lined as an oak leaf in the fall. "Eh? So it's you, is it?" he groaned on seeing Colin.

"It's me. The question is, what happened to you, and even more important, what happened to the zom—er—good folk of this town?"

The Prince struggled to gain his elbows, but sank back. Colin supposed that though the wound had closed within moments after being touched by the water from his flask, even unicorn magic would take some time to regenerate all the ale-saturated royal gore decorating the landscape.

"It's all your fault!" the prince gasped accusingly. "If you hadn't stolen my sword like the sneaky little thief you are, you and your great horny horse and your dark-haired demoness, they'd never have gotten the best of me!"

"Who's that, yer 'ighness?" Giles asked.

"Sally Forth and Wulfric and their gang of cutthroats, that's who. They came back for your precious zombies, and put paid to me while they were in the neighborhood. I reckon they think the good folk of Everclear will make excellent slaves—bandits are good enough at fighting, but not much at work. I overheard one of them to say their master would be happy to have women servants for 'the lady' again. Whoever that is. They can't have meant the nymph." And he proceded with increasing vigor to describe in colorful, imaginative, and often sadistic, but erotic, detail why the term 'lady' could not have been used in reference to Sally Forth. His rescuers were impressed. It was quite a performance for a mortally wounded man.

"Master?" Colin echoed. "Come now, you mustn't have heard properly. Bandits don't have masters. That's why they become outlaws—to stay outside the law and not have to put up with masters. Or that's the way I've always heard it."

But the prince lapsed back into unconsciousness and snored loudly, unmoved by Colin's arguments.

"Now what?" Archie asked, rubbing the side of his nose with the side of his calloused hand. "I'm in no hurry to make the acquaintanceship of no bandits. And we'll 'ave to be gettin' 'is Lor'ship 'ere back to Belburga—if he don't croak first."

"He wouldn't dare," Colin said. "Belburga's expecting him."

193

Though he couldn't have said when the stranger rejoined them, Colin was suddenly facing the man, who seized his arm and hissed to him in a low voice. "I found tracks, o minstrel, of many persons. You would not be so neglectful of your duty as to fail to pursue them?"

Colin gulped. "Well, naturally I wouldn't, but you see there's the wounded man to consider, and—"

Griffin Hillman spoke up quickly. "Don't worry about the prince, lad. Me and the boys can rig a litter and carry him to Belburga, safe as a babe in arms. You, now, you're the hero. YOU go after the bandits."

"Not to smite them ourselves, o minstrel," the stranger soothingly reassured him. "That would be folly. But may we not spy to see where the bad ones lurk, holding the poor townspeople and the unicorns? Then would not great honor fall upon your shoulders as one who could lead King's men back to the lair of the evildoers, and so cleanse our fair land of their foulness?"

Colin thought the man was overstating his case somewhat, but Archie said, "Good idea," and lashed the prince to the upturned work table from the smithy, tying the other end to his horse and to Hillman's.

"Aye, sounds fine," Giles agreed. "Much as I'd love to help you and see a real bandit hideout, I'm sure too many folk at the trackin' would spoil the secretness of it all. And Lily Pearl's ma *is* countin' on us bringin' this prince fella back."

"Oh, I really don't think having an extra man would hurt," Colin began, but by then Giles and Brewer had mounted and were waving goodbye, while Shearer claimed that he couldn't hardly stand not to help with the tracking, but his rheumatism was bothering him so fiercely he wasn't sure but what he wouldn't have to climb aboard the stretcher with the prince before the ride was over.

"But you tell us all about it, son, when you get back tomorrow—" the old man finished.

"But I'm a terrible tracker!" Colin cried after them. "I can hardly find my way to the privy and back without a map!" He turned to the stranger, who was the only one left in earshot. "I'm sure you have a splendid plan, but it's bound to be a waste of time. We can't possibly follow such an old trail through all these woods—"

The stranger shook his head, and the sneer Colin had just noticed playing about his mouth deepened. "Not an old trail. Fresh tracks, o hero. Fragrant with sweat smell and droppings."

"They would be," Colin sighed, resigned. "Very well. I

suppose we'd better see where they lead. The King *will* want to know. But mind you, we don't want to attract their attention."

He didn't like the peculiar fellow, and didn't trust him either. What he WOULD have liked was to get on his horse and follow the others down the road. But every time he turned his back on it, this business with the bandits became increasingly more complicated. First unicorns, then a rebellious plot, then an injured prince and two dozen or so captured townspeople. Could he really afford to pass up the opportunity to have at least some idea of where the rascals were going to strike next? Besides, if he went back without the townfolk, Maggie was likely to insist on coming back and slaying the bandits all by themselves. If he could already assure her he'd taken charge of the situation and had helpful information which had to be passed on immediately to the King, he was much more likely to persuade her to follow him out of danger, rather than having to follow her back into it. Besides, the stranger had no weapon, and Colin had Leofwin's sword. And the Little Darlingham men were rapidly disappearing down the road and into the woods. So there seemed no hope for it. Summoning his iron-reinforced courage, Colin waded into the woods after the stranger.

And promptly found himself alone and disoriented. Had the man actually been trying to lose him, he certainly couldn't have done a better job, Colin thought. In the thicket just around a small hill in his path he heard a loud rustling and snapping, and took that to be the stranger. He called out, and a voice seemed to answer, though it sounded a good way off.

Following the sound and looking around for other signs to follow, he thought he had badly estimated the man in one area of endeavor; the man must be a superb tracker. Though Colin was far from being an adept woodsman, any boy growing up in East Headpenney at least learned how to track rabbits and deer through the meadows. So he wasn't altogether ignorant of tracking techniques. Yet he could see no track, no broken twig or bent bush, no bruised leaves nor peeled bark, nor nary so much as a drooping blade of grass to mark the trail they were supposed to be following. For all he could tell, not only had the bandits not passed this way, but neither had the stranger.

As a matter of fact, this wasn't a path he was on, merely a clear border of grass and moss winding among the trees. In order to stay out of thick clumps of bushes, he had to take countless turns and uphill and downhill circumnavigations until he began to empathize with mountain goats. The footing was no great joy, either—it was humpy and spongey with moss, rugged with fallen limbs and extremely rocky about the hillsides, a soggy quagmire in the hollows.

Now and then, the stranger's dirty sheepskin would be visible in an ephemeral sort of way, but the man always seemed to melt back immediately into the forest. The difficult terrain apparently gave him no problem.

Soon Colin, who could hold the high notes longer than any man in his academy class, began to feel winded. His chest heaved, his eyes watered, his throat rasped with each breath, his mouth felt parched, his calves and sides were leaden and throbbed painfully. The iron sword weighed more than he did. He had to rest, if only for a moment.

But as he plumped himself down, he looked up through blurring eyes to see how far he had yet to go. The gray-haired stranger backtracked for a moment, seemingly just to make sure Colin didn't become permanently lost. When he saw Colin sitting, the stranger laughed one short, barking laugh, and loped on.

A minstrel with no measure of bravado is a poor minstrel, unworthy of the title. Cursing under what breath he had remaining, Colin struggled to his aching feet and set them one in front of the other a few more times. Now his throat felt as if it intended to close for repair, and his legs were numb and stumbling, but he could see the stranger, just ahead, trotting merrily along.

At last the man bounded up one hill too many—the worst of it was that ALL the hills had begun to look alike by now; rocky, slippery, muddy, moldering-leaf-encrusted pinnacles of torture—and Colin gave into his good sense as his legs gave out.

"H—h—halt," he gasped. He had to face it. Some people were just naturally more agile than others. Though there ought to be a law against anything mortal being THAT agile.

He'd almost begun to think the stranger COULDN'T stop, that the hills were pulling him into them on some sort of cord or by some enchantment. But to his surprised relief, the man stopped almost immediately, smirking at him. "Winded, are we, eh?"

Colin nodded, ignoring the smirk, and sank to the ground, elbows drooping across each knee with his lead lolling between them.

"I thought you could not endure much longer," the man said, his voice changing and growing huskier. "The four-legged, even when running on two legs, can outrun those who are always deficient by two."

"Wha—whatever you say," Colin panted agreeably.

"Grr," the stranger said, whatever that meant. The voice was

196

changing before Colin could place it—and he knew now he'd heard it before, in surroundings similar to these, with Maggie and Moonshine and—

"S—say there, good man. I don't suppose you have any relatives in high places? There's a Count Jivemgood who sounds—no." He looked up as he finished his question. The creature who had been his guide grew a long bristly snout, changed his sheepskin into a wolfskin, and suddenly sprouted a bushy tail. Then, without further ado, he dropped to all fours. "No, no, I beg your pardon," Colin apologized quickly. "Couldn't have been you after all. I must have mistaken you for some other chap."

The wolf growled low in his throat and crouched, slobbering through yellow fangs like a cavern full of dripping stalactites and stalagmites. The growl and the glittering green eyes promised a messy death, but Colin, too weary even to be frightened, much less do anything about it, was mainly baffled.

"It seems to me you're not going about this fairly," he pointed out in an injured tone that was quite detached from himself. "I have it from very good sources that werewolves have to have a full moon to turn into their—er—baser selves."

"Just like a lackey for the royal tyrant to bandy about ignorant superstition!"

Colin felt a delightful cool breeze as the whirlwind containing the voice addressing him spun itself—herself, as he could see now—between him and the ravening wolf. With a final dainty pirouette the wind swept away and an extremely lovely golden-haired woman in skimpy huntress garb stood in front of him, a cross look causing her soft pink mouth to pout provocatively.

"Mortals *do* have such anachronistic notions about we magical folk," she complained. "Any dumb dryad knows that it's only were*wolves* who have to have a full moon to turn, whereas were*people*, poor dears, can naturally assume their true animal forms at any time, but must become human for at least a few hours of each day, when their magic takes its dire form and they are vicious and dangerous to all around them. Once they've given vent to their profane human nature, they're free to resume their normal bestial form, and are just as nice as anybody you'd want to know. Wulfric comes from a long line of hereditary weres, poor thing. He was resigned to a destiny of meaningless brutality, and had cast his lot with cruel ruffians until I delivered unto him the saving message of the cause and our Dark Pilgrim. He and all his men are now my brothers-in-arms, dedicated to the salvation of Argonia and the overthrow of tyranny. Though

197

he still must change to man form, he now utilizes his ferocious human wiles to further our cause, don't you, Wulfie?"

Wulfric wagged his brushy tail and whined, happily groveling.

And no wonder. Colin thought he had never seen a more beautiful woman. Her movements reminded him of rippling water flowing to an inner song, her voice of music, her hair of honey into which new-minted gold coins had been melted, her eyes of spring grass. The peachy pink of her lips and cheeks made him feel the traditional rose color maiden's cheeks were always supposed to be was garish. Under—just barely under—her diaphanous one-shouldered dress, her body was slim and white as a birch, and warm and vibrant-looking as a bird's breast. Colin's head began to spin. He was growing more bewildered by the moment. Though he thought he'd done well with Wulfric, and had pretty much managed to take it in stride when the sinister stranger had metamorphosed into a wolf, perhaps the shock was starting to catch up with him. The whirlwind turning into a beautiful woman kept him from absorbing the significance of the were's quick-change artistry. She was a distracting event, merely standing still. And she looked so pure and innocent and childlike—well, an older sort of childlike—and sweet. Yet her speech indicated otherwise. Could this possibly be the infamous nymph he'd been hearing entirely too much about lately? He had to know, particularly since her appearance inclined him to fall madly in love with her, which, if his guess was correct, he'd rather not do.

"I beg your pardon, Miss. Are you by any chance the legendary lady revolutionary leader, Sally Forth?" Minstrels were always supposed to be courtly, even when addressing the criminal element, particularly when the criminal element was armed, protected by a wolf, and looked like the beautiful bandit/whirlwind.

A smile blossomed on her face. "Why, yes, I am. Why do you ask?"

"I simply—hadn't expected anyone so comely. I'd always thought of revolutionary leaders as older, and more dour, somehow."

"How sweet. But I hope you won't take me any less seriously because of my appearance. That," she said with a meaningful frown, "would be a great mistake on your part."

"I couldn't agree with you more," he said. "Why, I have this friend, for instance, a witch, and to look at her, anyone would take her for a kitchen drudge or a gooseherd, but she does the most amazing—" he broke off as Sally's fair brow darkened. "Yes, well, she's nowhere near as pretty and interesting as you

198

are, of course." He watched her closely as he babbled, trying to think of something else diverting to say to her. He had the distinct feeling that when he stopped talking this time he was going to stop for good.

Wulfric growled impatiently, and Colin scrunched backwards. As he did so, his flute fell from his pocket. He retrieved it. "Yes, ma'am, Mistress Forth, I have followed your career with great interest—long before I knew you were so fair of face. You see, I've always had a secret hankering to be a revolutionary myself, but I could never seem to get the hang of it—heh, heh. But I composed this little tune in your honor. Had I some instrument on which I could accompany myself, I'd sing you the words, but as it is, I can play the melody on my flute for you—"

"A song? In my honor?" Sally clearly was intrigued and batted Wulfric behind her with an impatient gesture. "What kind of song?"

"Oh—a nice one. A very nice one indeed," said Colin, who had no idea what he could play on his flute that would placate her, and only hoped his siren gift of song would lead him to play for her what she would most want to hear. Ideas began coming to him. "A—it's a stirring martial ballad, of course, in a subtly stealthy minor key with a delicate overlay of ornamentation—rather like yourself, ma'am, if I may make so bold as to say so?"

Wulfric had changed back to man form behind Sally's back, and now demanded her attention. "O Sally, this sly one dallies to save his miserable life. Shall I not spare you his noises by biting his gullet in twain here and now?"

Sally was otherwise inclined. "Wulfric, this man has written a hymn to our cause, inspired by my example. The least I can do is listen. If it's good, the Dark Pilgrim will want to hear it. You are an excellent spy, but you know little of maintaining the morale of our men. Go now in wolf form, and tell my steed I require her. We have yet unfinished business at the tower. You," she said, returning her attention to Colin, "Play."

He did, with all his heart.

To his surprise, he managed to tootle out a number very like the one he had described. If he could have held his breath and played the flute at the same time, he would have done so in anticipation of the tune soaring from his instrument. But his apprehension was unnecessary. Almost without any help from him, his flute produced a tune with the required marching lilt, minor insinuations and fluid ornamentations. He knew it was going well, but he didn't realize how well until he opened his eyes. He'd closed them both to concentrate and because he didn't really want to see what would happen to him if his song failed. He needn't have worried. Sally Forth was swaying her lovely body to the music, almost dancing, with Prince Leofwin's great iron sword held aloft between her slender hands for a partner.

"Ah," she said, when she saw him watching. "That was very moving. I have little doubt that the Dark Pilgrim will proclaim it our national anthem when he hears it. You must have been greatly impressed by my example to write such a song."

"Oh, yes. Yes, indeed, I was. *Greatly* impressed," he averred.

"Well, then, per*haps* I can arrange for you to live a bit longer. If you're very good and very cooperative and don't make me slit your throat, which would be a shame, since then the Dark Pilgrim would never hear your song. MY song. Could you manage that, do you think?"

Colin agreed that he could, which was all he had time to do before a great many men began popping out of bushes like flowers in the spring, tra la. But that was not the greatest surprise. That was the sight of Primrose, walking daintily through the bushes of her own accord to nuzzle Sally Forth's ear.

CHAPTER 10

Maggie sat crosslegged beside the stream, watching the sun sparkle on the water and feeling thoroughly sorry for herself. She'd tried to listen to the conversation between Moonshine and Ruby Rose, but without success. They were too far away. Or deliberately shutting her out, more likely. It wasn't fair. Witches weren't a bit less pure than quasi-ogress alchemists, and it was cruel of Moonshine not to see that. Even if Ruby Rose was more learned and brilliant than she was, what did Moonshine care about that? Unicorns didn't read and he had never shown the slightest interest in alchemy.

Fine way to treat her on what might very well, from her calculations of the time of year the night before, be her birthday. There weren't even any rocks to skip across the water. The bank was smooth and grassy, with nothing harder to throw than flowers, which would not make a satisfactory thunk. She almost wished Belburga would appear and try to eat them up here and now. Battling an ogress would at least give her something to do. She hated waiting.

She looked up as a duck squawked a panic-stricken squawk. A large mallard, wings flapping furiously, dove toward the stream in front of her. He wasn't making a very good job of it, and Maggie thought his eyes almost seemed to roll in terror. His squawk sounded like, "Watchit! Watchit!" Whatever it meant, she did as it seemed to suggest, and wriggled backwards a few feet as the duck landed, belly first, then beak, then tail pointed to the sky as, to her amazement, the so-called waterfowl sank in a sputtering splashing mass of confusion to the bottom of the brook.

Before she had time to remember how much she disliked direct personal contact with bodies of water, or perhaps because her own horror of the stuff triggered her sympathy for the drowning duck, she waded in after him. The water was surprisingly deep, covering her to mid-thigh, and very cold. Marking where the duck fell, she plunged her arm and shoulder into the cold, rippling water, turning her head sideways to keep the water out of her mouth and nose, soaking one of her braids in the process. Stretching her arm as low as it would go, she groped for feathers, but found none.

Instead, a hand reached up and grasped her elbow.

She squealed an unwitchly squeal. A nix! She'd been grabbed by a nix! She should have considered the possibility before wading around in strange streams. River men, or nixen, like their female counterparts, the nixies, were very fond of seducing mortal members of the opposite sex into the water, where they could be drowned. And Maggie hadn't even had the fun of being seduced first! Well, what could you expect from a river man who operated out of a creek? She fought wildly, slapping and slithering in the muddy stream bed. She couldn't see the creature who had hold of her, but she struggled with all her might to free herself. Then, all at once, her foot slipped out from under her.

Gargling, she fell to her knees, the water closing frigidly around the top of her scalp. Strong hands grabbed her hair and—pulled her to the surface again!

"My dear girl," said the dripping countenance of Wizard Raspberry. "I thought you were trying to help me. You very nearly finished me off. Are you all right?"

Maggie spat water from her mouth and clouted water from her ears by striking the heel of her hand against either temple. Then, together, she and the wizard sloshed back to shore.

"How did you get in there?" she asked.

"I flew in. Didn't you see me? I tried to warn you. I'm afraid I'm not very good at three-point landings yet. One gets to concentrating on flying and forgets the finer points of being a duck—like gliding on top of the water. I seem to have washed away my costume," he said regretfully, leaning over the water and scanning it for some sign of mallard feathers. He was clad in his own dripping, badly embroidered tunic and bare legs again. "I only used a duck disguise because it's the fastest. It's a difficult one, because I have to contain my mass in such a small form—which is why I tend to sink instead of swim, though I'd have gotten the hang of it sooner or later. Luckily, I happen to have brought along my second-fastest disguise." He hauled from his tunic a very wet rabbit skin.

"Fascinating," Maggie said as dryly as possible under the circumstances. "But don't try to tell me you were in the neighborhood and thought you'd just drop in. What brings you here, and why were you in such a hurry? And if you don't mind my asking, why a duck?"

"I'm very sorry," he said, pulling the rabbit skin over his left foot. "But I keep getting the feeling I'm very late and I don't really think I have the time to explain right now." As he spoke, his nose, which was neither small nor cute, began to wrinkle in the middle and, like his pointed ears, to twitch from side to side. "I have to get into costume and be off again!"

"Wait just a moment," Maggie said, watching his twitching ears with enlightened eyes. "Pointed ears! Of course! You're Ruby Rose's father!"

"Guilty," he admitted, pulling off the rabbit skin again and casting furtive glances in all directions. "I really must apologize. That costume always makes me feel as though I'm in the most dreadful hurry—and there's someone here I don't wish to meet. But I can hardly leave without telling you why I came, since I mostly came to see you, and naturally, I have to say hello to Rusty as long as I'm here. One of the difficulties of disguising oneself well is that one begins to FEEL the part." Most of his timidity vanished as he laid the rabbit skin aside but his ears continued to twitch for several moments before they calmed down. "Belburga's not about, is she?" he asked at last, with what seemed only a very sensible human wish to avoid the ogress.

"I don't know where she is, but your daughter's talking to Moonshine." Maggie found she didn't especially care to talk about that so she changed the subject. "That is an amazing disguise. How do you do it? How did you make the costume?"

"I didn't make it, not the rabbit one. It's special. The skin belonged to a rabbit friend of mine who died. He specifically willed it to me for the purpose. I suppose he felt that becoming a disguise was much more interesting than becoming a coat or a rug or some sort of stuffed trophy."

Maggie had never heard of anyone stuffing a trophy rabbit, but the wizard had obviously been touched by his friend's gesture and she didn't wish to denigrate it, so she agreed with him.

"The spell is very simple, if you're born to this type of magic," he elaborated. Now that he'd started talking, he seemed happy to continue. Probably needed a rest from all that flying. "I just put as much of me as possible into the skin, and then I say a temporary spell of invisibility over the rest of me—oh, nothing so dire as the one on Moonshine's cone. This is a spell that only works on me, because I'm the wizard, you see—or rather, you *don't* see once I've started it, or at least I can't see myself—at any rate, I sort of—well, what actually happens is—uh—then I—well, I seem to BECOME the animal. Of course, I have to work out the proper behavior ahead of time to do it well," he indicated his occasionally twitching ears. "But the time I spend with my friends in the woods is spent almost entirely in observation, so I'm able to imitate most of them satisfactorily. Except ducks."

"That sounds much more interesting than hearthcrafting," Maggie said. "Could you teach me to be something?"

"I'm afraid not," he said regretfully. "I can teach you the things I've had to learn from the start myself—like balloon-making—but disguise is something that comes so naturally to me I'm afraid I wouldn't even know where to start *teaching* it. I have no idea of what you don't know, if you know what I mean. I can't even seem to teach Rusty. I wish I could. I don't like this alchemy study she's taken up, though I gave her an old crucible I had laying around for her last birthday. I really don't feel it's a suitable occupation for a young lady. Too artificial. And the Mother only knows she gets enough artificiality from Belburga."

"Perhaps you needn't worry. Moonshine is going to try to persuade her to give all that up and become his maiden. Which reminds me, you'd better let her know you're here. I told her about your signal last night."

"My signal? What signal? I sent no signal. It was your aunt who sent the signal, by her budgie bird. I was just on my way to Castle Rowan to try to speak to the Dragon Grimley about it. But then I saw you sitting here and thought you ought to know, though I don't normally like to come here without letting Rusty know to meet me somewhere first."

"Let me know about WHAT?" If the rabbit disguise made

him chatter so anxiously all the time, the wizard was far easier to take in his moat monster manifestation, Maggie thought.

"The King. He's in dire peril. He's been shipwrecked with only a handful of men, and has sent Dragon Grimley for reinforcements from Castle Rowan. But Sybil was scanning the country the other night, and saw smoke coming from the old summer castle at Worm's Roost Glacier, and turned her power there. There was a shield over most of the place, but she did see the troops all around the glacier, armed ruffians, the Princess Pegeen and two unicorns being held in some sort of an ice enclosure. She saw a spontaneous vision of the King and his shipwrecked party then, and of Dragon Grimley. She's afraid, and I quite agree, that the situation at Worm's Roost looks very much like a trap. I thought I might go along to Grimley and help him gather the reinforcements—I speak dragonese, at least the central and coastal dialects. With the dragon's help, we could all hop or fly or march or ride to the King's aid." He looked sadly into the water which had claimed his duck skin. "Now I shall have to hop the rest of the way, and trust Grimley to fly ahead and warn the King's party. It will be much slower. But I must try, or it's Rowan and his men will be dead ducks." He stopped and looked momentarily chagrined, running his hand over mouth and beard. "I'm sorry to have put it to you that way, lass. I know you're fond of the King."

"It's not as if it were our only problem," she told him. "Bandits who kidnap kings and unicorns both don't strike me as having the welfare of Argonia at heart."

"My connections among the woodland creatures say the bandit chieftain is a woman."

"Prince Leofwin mentioned as much," she said. "It doesn't make any sense. I suppose some women might want to be bandits for the novelty of the thing, but most bandits are in banditry for fat purses instead of kings and unicorns, from what I know of them." She thought awhile longer, and hoisted her shoulders to disavow ability to figure the situation out. "Perhaps they mean to hold the King for ransom and sell the unicorns to the highest bidders. At any rate, while you're gathering reinforcements, Colin and I shall go spy out the bandit stronghold and make sure they don't harm the unicorns or the Princess Pegeen. Colin and the rescue party will be returning soon now." She searched the woods with her eyes again, though it was still too early in the day.

"You can't go by yourselves," Raspberry said firmly. "That's much too dangerous."

"No more dangerous than flying around like a duck," she pointed out. "And we'll just go for a look."

"Well, I suppose that's true enough," Raspberry admitted. "And you'll be alright with Colin and Moonshine to look after you."

At that Maggie couldn't help crying again. Raspberry tut-tutted and patted her shoulder in a rabbity fashion until she'd stopped, and she explained to him about Primrose and Moonshine's current campaign to find another maiden.

"That's not sporting at all," Raspberry said indignantly. "A first maiden is a first maiden if you ask me, and that's the end of it. I'm surprised you bother to continue to interest yourself in the unicorn problem at all, what with Moonshine galivanting about after other girls and Primrose's general mean-mindedness."

But Maggie shrugged. "There's the King, too. And Princess Pegeen, from what you say. And while I'm sure you and the King's troops will manage to protect THEM from the bandits, I'm afraid the unicorns may be injured or sacrificed in the process. And they're VERY valuable creatures—something happened at a town Colin and I came through that makes me think they're more valuable than anyone has ever realized. They must be protected." She paused, choosing her words carefully, stumbling along as she spoke, hoping she didn't sound insipid or arrogant. "Besides, there's this matter of me being a princess. Prince Leofwin, the one I told you about meeting in Everclear, had some strange attitudes about how royalty is supposed to act. But I don't think Rowan feels that way—and I don't think he put a crown on my head just because he thought it looked well on my bonny brown hair. I think—I think even if he wanted me to be a princess so I could marry someone suitable, he wanted *me* to be princess because he felt he could trust me to—oh, I don't know, look after the peasants and make sure whoever I married did the right thing for the realm. I don't know much about politics, but I know what's right and wrong and one of the things that's right is that royalty are supposed to protect their subjects—all of their subjects, and here that means witches, giants, elves, unicorns, wee folk, mortals and everyone. In Everclear, thanks to Moonshine's magic, we were able to more or less save a whole village from disease that would never have struck the place except that their unicorn had been stolen. Unicorns are vital to the well-being of this country, mighty wizard. They keep the water clean and the animals and people from poisoning themselves. So if Moonshine chooses to stay with Rusty or Lily Pearl, or Belburga for that matter, it's up to him. As for me, I've come too far already. I'm not going to turn my back on Rowan or the most valuable creatures in this realm simply because I no longer happen to have a personal stake in one particular unicorn. Besides," she said with a small wry smile, "You *will* be bringing the soldiers, won't you?"

"As soon as I can. But what if I'm too late? Then what will you do?"

She shrugged again. "I don't know. I'll have to think about that when I get to it."

Suddenly they heard a hard thudding and looked up to see Moonshine galloping straight at them. Flecks of froth flew from his mouth and his eyes were rolled so far back that only the whites showed. His razor-sharp hooves bore down on them until the very last minute when, gathering all four feet beneath him, he leaped the stream.

"Not again!" Maggie cried. "Moonshine, wait! I do NOT have the time to beat the bushes for you again! We have bigger problems now. Stop and tell me what's wrong."

To her surprise, at the sound of her voice he did stop. His sides heaved deeply, and his legs trembled, but when she had crossed the bridge to stroke and pet him for awhile he was able to form a coherent thought. "Don't let that awful girl come any closer, *please*, Maggie dearest. She's a disgusting person."

Behind them, Wizard Raspberry, who had waded the stream to join them, sighed. "I suppose that's my fault for marrying an ogress."

Ruby Rose peeked around a tree on the far shore and Moonshine tried to hide behind Maggie.

Wizard Raspberry said severely, "Rusty, what have you been up to now?"

"Father!" she cried, and splashed across the water, launching herself at him, wrapping his soggy form in her long, thin arms. "Oh, father, you DID come!"

"I came. I always come to see you this time of year, don't I? But right now, I want to know how you've managed to frighten this creature, who is an old friend of mine, by the way."

"It was nothing very much," she said with a light scornfulness directed towards Moonshine. "He said I could ask anything of him and all I asked for was the tiniest little portion of his horn." She pouted. "He did. He said he'd do anything for me. He SAID so. And then he took it back, and ran and told on me, the horrid beast. I only wanted to use the horn for my alchemy."

Raspberry sighed again and lifted his eyes to the heavens. "I *know* it's because she's a neglected middle child with a mostly absent father and an ogress for a mother," he pleaded to some nameless deity. "But she's a very smart girl. A good girl, basically. She really is. WHY in the name of seven sacred rituals and the thirteen sacred names of the Mother can't she see that it is a deplorable, despicable thing to maim a kindly magical creature in order to turn her mother into a toad?"

"Oh, *Daddy*," the girl groaned. "You're always exaggerating. I wasn't going to turn mother into a toad—not exactly." Then she wheedled, "But *could* you show me how, without unicorn horn, I mean, just in case?"

Maggie didn't wait to hear the wizard's answer, but led Moonshine to his stall, and brushed him and talked to him until he fell into an exhausted sleep. Gently, she slipped his disguise back over his horn. When she rejoined the wizard and his daughter, they were sitting by the stream again, but had moved to a point which was better concealed from the tower by a thick stand of trees.

"How COULD you?" she demanded of the girl, who looked up at her in surprise. "You've shaken him so badly I don't know if he'll ever recover. Unicorns are sensitive and high-strung and they don't offer their friendship to many. He wanted to love you, to be your protector and companion and all you could think of was vivisecting him for your so-called studies! If that's what learning does to a person, I want none of it! I think staying indoors poring over your stupid old book has caused your brain to mold!"

Ruby Rose was unimpressed. "I don't see what all the fuss is about. I didn't mean to hurt the stupid animal's feelings. I only thought I could take a little of that horn and enhance my power." She turned angrily on her father. "If being an ogress is so awful, and I'm not supposed to behave like one, why did you marry mother in the first place? And why do I have to live with her? All I did was try to satisfy my normal magical curiosity, which you know very well I get from you. You can't blame that on her. The only thing she's ever curious about is how much money and power Lily Pearl's beaux have."

"Please," Raspberry said with a pained expression. "Don't call your mother an ogress."

"Well, you do. And she is," replied the girl, her thin little mouth drawing into a bitter line.

Raspberry fell silent for a moment, staring out across the stream, into the horizon beyond the trees. The sky was fuzzy and gray, with distant detail so blurred that the nearby glacier-riddled mountains appeared insubstantial as a tall bank of clouds. "I wish I had a disguise that would make me turn into a father," he said to Maggie, who had seated herself beside him.

"She does have a point," Maggie agreed.

"Eh?" He looked at her blankly, then slowly the twinkle poured back into his troubled elfin eyes. "Oh, she does, indeed. Several of them. Not counting the extra one she almost chopped off your friend."

"No, truly," Maggie insisted. "She's right. If you marry an ogress, how can you expect her to beget anything but little ogresses?"

"Belburga isn't *that* much of an ogress," Raspberry replied. "Not until you get to know her, that is. There's a good deal of nymph in her family line, and a bit of witch, and some faery, too, I believe—though they must have been odd nymphs, witches, and faeries to intermarry with ogres. But like a lot of folk these days, her powers are only vestigial—diluted and weakened by the intermarriages."

"I still don't see how if ogresses are so awful, you got involved with mother to begin with." Ruby Rose's face was the picture of childish innocence, but her voice mocked him. "After all, you're not a stupid man."

"Little girl," he said, "You have a lot to learn. When a man meets a woman as attractive as your mother was, brains have no part in it. And then, too, one gets wiser as one grows older—something you'd do well to remember, my little genius. I met Belburga, as a matter of fact, when I was on the rebound from a certain pretty young witch—your Aunt Sybil, Maggie." He smiled at the amazement on Maggie's face. "Oh, yes, we were—very close—but she finally broke it off, though we've remained friends. She never said why, but I suppose it was because I was an awkward, untried stripling at the time, and so lacking in judgment that I immediately fell in love with the next lady who smiled in my direction. I was still doing false mustaches, and wigs, and noses made of river clay in those days, and didn't have much to offer a girl. But I took Sybil's refusal hard, and fancied myself broken-hearted, having no notion at the time how flexible that organ really is. I went about singing dreary love songs, composing bad poetry, and wearing woebegone clown faces until at last my father could stand me no longer and sent me off to study with an elfin second cousin of high degree. My cousin Maisie held a position of trust in King Finbar's court.

"She was very worldly, Maisie, a city elf born and bred. She knew a love-sick calf when she saw one, and took care that I met all of her prettiest friends, and I suspect gave them to understand

208

that they were to make themselves agreeable to me. As I said, she had considerable influence. But somehow most of them made me feel more of a bumpkin than I already knew I was.

"Then one day I overheard Maisie complaining to a friend of the roughness of her hairdresser. Elfin damsels have very sensitive scalps, as you probably know." He ruffled the sullen Rusty's brilliant tight-curled mop. "Also, the pure elves have fine, thin hair that doesn't curl fashionably. That's one of MY less desirable traits you escaped, my girl. In the woods, they wear leaf caps to keep the branches from snagging their hair, but in the city, when the fashion isn't running to hats, a good hairdresser is invaluable to someone like my cousin. Her friend told her of a new lady-in-waiting, the widow of a prince from some obscure little island kingdom. The woman was supposed to do marvels with hair.

"A week or so later one of Maisie's admirers begged me, backing his pleas with a new silver coin, to take my cousin a bouquet of moonflowers he'd picked for her just before dawn. You know how delicate those are. They would have been wilted had I waited until Maisie had finished her toilette, so I interrupted.

"The new hairdresser answered my knock. Oh, my cynical little love, you should have seen your mother then. She was graceful as a lynx, pretty as a vixen, and as dainty. Her eyes were black as slocs and, had I but known it, were better at disguise than I. For under a cloak of sweetness as demure as a baby hare's, she had the disposition of a hungry wolverine. But I didn't know that then.

"I thought I saw in her smile an echo of Sybil's, so I wooed her. A stripling clown was not your mother's idea of a new husband, so she kept me at a distance with her coquetry for a time. But the more elusive she was, the more ardent I became. I dreamed up new, fantastic costumes to amuse her, always striving for the novel, the surprising. I would steal up on her in the garden, disguised as one of the peacocks, and present her with a feather. Once I pretended to be a little dog who yearned to sit on her knee, but she wasn't fooled for a moment; animals have never cared for your mother, you know. But whether she was impressed or not, my skills grew to an astonishing degree. Thereby I gained King Finbar's attention and was in time made Chief Concealment Officer for the palace guard. I concocted costumes, and made suggestions for camouflage, that sort of thing. Then, as we saw each other more often, the King took a liking to me and promoted me to Intracourt Espionage Officer. I could, in those days, look like any person I chose, as well as imitating dogs and peacocks.

"I grew full of self-importance as I tittled on this one and tattled on someone else. I no longer had time to moon over Sybil or Belburga. That, naturally, proved your mother's undoing, and subsequently my own, for if there's anything your mother cannot stand, it's to be ignored. As my prominence rose, so did her ardor, and she began to follow me about. Probably I would have stayed free of her connivings then if I hadn't, at that time, uncovered a plot to do away with the young princes and substitute changelings. Belburga knew of the plot, and pretended to reveal it to me, though I think she knew I was already aware of it. But she stunned me when she told me who the perpetrator was. I knew at once I had to conceal what she'd told me forever, for she laid the blame at the feet of my sponsor, Cousin Maisie.

"I had only two options—one was to destroy my cousin, and the other to silence Belburga. I told Maisie what I knew, and though she denied it, at my insistence she retired from court life. I thought marrying your mother, since I was already half in love with her, an attractive alternative to silencing her in a more permanent way, so I asked the King's permission and we were wed. I took her far from the capital, but as you may well guess, by giving up my position in court, I also gave up any claim I had to Belburga's affection.

"She did not take kindly to my bringing her home to my father's house with twenty elfin brothers and sisters. And though I built for us a dwelling apart shortly after you were born, she left me. By then I had seen—and felt—her pointed teeth often enough that I had no desire to pursue her."

He smiled at Maggie. "Make no mistake. My former wife is a man-eater well enough, but only in the figurative sense. Her grandmother, I understand, was a great deal more literal."

Ruby Rose, no longer distressed or indignant, was instead as enchanted as any child by a story, and snuggled close in the shelter of her father's arm. Raspberry gave her the same dreamy smile he had given Maggie. "No, little one, your mother is no more apt to rend a man's flesh with her teeth than any other woman. It is only by her wiles, which can make him eat out his own heart, that she has the power of her ancestors. She demands much, and gives nothing." His eyes held his daughter's for a long moment, and the girl hunched her shoulders and shrank a little, but closer to him. "The trait is at the base of ogre nature, Rusty. I am pleased with your elfin side, your curiosity, your accomplishments. But a certain—balance—is necessary to truly achieve mastery of any art. You have to learn from all things, nature and other people as well as books, and in giving yourself to what can teach you, you give yourself to your magic. Otherwise, you'll become its victim, devoured by your lust for it even as your mother's people devoured themselves and others in years past.''

Ruby Rose smiled with adolescent cynicism, which she tried to conceal, but her father saw it.

"Neither a fair face nor a good brain is protection from the ill your mother's heritage can cause you to do to yourself, child, and to others. Your mother was once as fair as you, if not so clever. She is fair still, for her age, so I'm told, though you may not think her so. I cannot look upon her again, having once been in her power, for fear I'll fall prey to her all over again. That's one reason my visits to you are so infrequent.''

"All right, all right. I'm not stupid. I take your meaning all too well.'' She sighed a put-upon sigh and turned to Maggie. ''You may tell your unicorn he may pay me court if he wishes, and I won't trouble him further about his silly horn.'' Looking back at her father's face, which was strangely atwitch at the corners of his eyes and mouth, she said, ''Better. Right?''

"Er—it's a start,'' he replied, adding quickly, ''It isn't easy to think of others. It takes patience and practice. But an adept with your brilliance should be able to handle it.''

"I'll take your word for it,'' his daughter replied. ''But I want to know something, Daddy. If you came with so much secrecy—'' her eyes dropped to his slowly drying tunic, ''What did you come as, anyway, a fish? But if you did come secretly,'' she continued, not waiting for a reply, ''why didn't you signal me in a way I could respond to?'' She nodded toward Maggie. ''SHE thinks mother got the signal, and returned it.''

"Not to me,'' he said. ''I didn't signal. This was a surprise visit.''

"If you didn't signal,'' Maggie asked, ''Who did?''

"Probably it was no more than an innocent woodcutter's fire,'' he said, his voice lacking all conviction.

"There was a return signal,'' Maggie reminded him.

"You couldn't have been mistaken?''

"I'd stake Granny Brown's secret ale recipe on it.''

"Belburga's unlikely to align herself with bandits—she'd be bound to consider them too uncouth.'' The wizard lifted his pinky in parody of his former wife and Rusty giggled.

"I wouldn't be too sure of that,'' Maggie said, remembering the rat.

"*I* overheard mother talking to a funny-looking man only last week," Rusty volunteered self-importantly. "She was talking about the man's people owing her something, and marrying us off properly. She's ALWAYS talking about that."

"It's not a man who leads these bandits, sweet," her father said. "It's a woman. A nymph, the beasts say."

"Like Daisy's father? The one who turned himself into a tree to get away from mother? He was a man nymph, but he had a sister who was in charge of her own stream. I remember seeing her when I was little, when she came to see Daisy after she was born. *She* was beautiful—she made Lily Pearl look washed out. But sort of serious and unhappy looking. I remember because I couldn't imagine how anyone so pretty could possibly have anything to be unhappy about."

"What do you think?" Maggie asked. "Sounds like our bandit leader to me."

"If it's as serious as that, I think you should put on your bunny suit, father, and go tell somebody."

"I fully intend to put on my bunny suit, dear," the wizard replied, and gallantly tugged the rabbit skin over one bare foot again, and rose to his feet, towering with a certain eccentric authority above Maggie, who remained seated. "But first I want Princess Magdalene's oath that she will do nothing at all until Master Songsmith returns, and then will only follow at a distance and keep watch on the bandits' movements. We can't risk losing two members of the royal house at once."

"I must say, I consider this very stuffy of you, mighty wizard," Maggie said indignantly.

"Nevertheless, I insist. Your pledge?"

"Oh, very well. I so pledge," she promised, but crossed her fingers inside her skirt pocket.

Raspberry was satisfied. With a last kiss for his daughter and increasingly feverish twitches of his ears and nose, he muttered a spell under his breath. As he grew thinner and paler and more transparent, the rabbit skin on his foot grew plumper and more lifelike. At last, the wraith-like wizard winked out completely, an invisible hand ruffled Ruby-Rose's hair, and with a final warning thump of its hind foot for Maggie's benefit, the rabbit hopped off into the forest.

Leofwin bounced and rattled against the table-cum-stretcher on which he was being borne, until he thought every bone in his body would break. There was no question whatsoever of resting and recuperating aboard such a contraption, and the men sponsoring his torture disregarded his yelps and moans, laughing and talking loudly among themselves, jesting about the cocky young minstrel's face when they left him behind with the smelly stranger.

Leofwin knew what minstrel, but he didn't know what stranger and he didn't care. He was too busy wishing he'd been left for dead.

The heartless peasants splashed his makeshift litter through a stream, soaking him to the skin, drat and damn the lot of them! Had they no idea how to treat an injured man? He'd sooner be drawn and quartered than endure this much longer!

The string of curses he was inventing solely for the benefit of his bearers was interrupted by a titter near his left ear.

"Eh?" he tried to look in that direction, but couldn't move his head sufficiently.

The titter escalated to a giggle and finally became a deep chuckle.

"Who the dwarf drool is laughing at me?" the Prince demanded. "Tell me what's so funny or so help me, I'll pulverize you the instant I'm loose from this oversized infant swaddling."

"You heroes arc *so* ferocious," his tormenter laughed, and landed none too gently on the tip of his nose. Trickle, the little wasp. He should have known. "The mighty minstrel is singing love songs to that good-for-nothing nymph while your hearty comrades pollute my stream by dragging your stinking behind through it. And you all wrapped up like a baby for its nappie-poo!" She laughed again, a bitter laugh, and her tiny face was bitter.

"I don't see what you're angry with me about," complained Leofwin, worried about having the insect-sized faery so close to his eyes. "I'm hardly in a position to hurt you. Oh, well, the ale flagon—I suppose you might still be a little miffed about that. But it was a jest; can't you take a jest?"

"I can take a jest all right, big boy," she replied, baring her tiny glistening teeth. "I'm going to die laughing, as a matter of fact, when your fellow unicorn thieves pop out of the bushes up ahead and slice all of you to noodles."

"Fellow unicor—WHA-AT?! Hey, you! Bumpkins! Stop! Turn this thing around immediately! Let me out! Give me a sword!" His volume was sufficient to blow the faery off his nose. She was still laughing as she somersaulted through the air and out of sight.

It never occurred to Leofwin to wonder why she had mentioned the ambush to him if she was so eager, as she claimed, to see him and the men from Little Darlingham minced. He inwardly

213

cursed her the whole time it took Giles and Archie to unstrap him and the lot of them to dismount and lead their horses in a great arc swinging wide of the path where the bandits were said to be waiting.

Wulfric's startled thought flew to his adored leader as she alighted from Primrose's back and began to twirl, her preparation for becoming a whirlwind. "O Sally, will you leave your steed and me alone in this forest while you blow away? Were we not all to travel together?"

"Surely my most able lieutenant can take independent initiative and carry out a simple little execution by himself. Can't you, Wulfie? Well, can't you?" she asked sternly. He whined and covered his nose with his paws. "Belburga has answered my signal. She will let you into the witch's chamber, so you may slay her in her sleep. The lecher Leofwin and the townsmen you so stupidly involved should be dead by now. Primrose knows what to do about the unicorn. I must go thither and see to the preparations to make welcome our new recruit."

"Then you will not enchant this other creature, this new unicorn, with your beauty as you have the others, O Sally?"

"Why, Wulfie," she said, with a meaningful glance toward Primrose, whose back was towards them, "What others can you mean? Primrose is my faithful steed. I could not possibly take another. Anyway, no unicorn who has already befriended an ordinary girl would be susceptible to my word alone. He will need the example of his own kind to dispel the woman's common influence and lead him down the true path."

"If I were not a stupid beast, wise and gracious leader, I would have thought of that myself. Forgive me for impeding your progress. I shall do all that you have commanded."

The unicorn stamped and gave him a scornful look as Sally cycloned away from them, but Wulfric laughed to himself a crafty laugh. Oh, no. He would not betray his beloved leader, but there was a certain lamb at Little Darlingham belonging to a certain odiferous ogress, and that lamb would make him a charming hors d'oeuvre before he devoured the undoubtedly tough and stringy witch.

He practically tripped over his dripping tongue, thinking of the feast ahead, until the unicorn, who could tolerate him only in wolf form, reminded him that SHE knew not the way to Little Darlingham, and he must hurry and lead them forth.

* * *

214

"You haven't touched your food," Maggie remarked when she ducked into Moonshine's stall to tell him Wizard Raspberry's bad tidings about the King, and also to convey Rusty's grudging apologies.

The unicorn huddled in a corner of his stall, and though he no longer trembled, his head hung as if the weight of his horn was too great for him to bear. His horn seemed dimmer, too, and had lost some of its opalescent beauty.

"Where's your disguise?" she asked, kneeling in the straw and patting her palms against it, searching for the outline of the missing cone.

He didn't answer, and merely lifted his head briefly and lowered it again, failing to meet her eyes.

"Look, Moonshine," she said firmly, crawling on hands and knees across the stall, still patting, "This maiden business is depressing both of us, but we really have more urgent matters to attend to. An ogress's tower doesn't strike me as a fruitful place to look for virgins, anyway. Why don't you postpone this venture for awhile? As soon as Colin returns, we've got to see about rescuing those other unicorns. We'll need your help seeking them out, and I do think you owe it to your fellows to help us. Won't you forget all this nonsense and join us? Surely associating with me a day or so longer isn't going to taint you any worse than you've been tainted already."

"I would go with you willingly, my friend," he told her after a long pause. "But how could I face my fellows? You must free them alone, for the sight of me would offend them. Obviously I am unfit to be a unicorn—the second as well as the first maiden has rejected me, and the second would have maimed me as well."

Maggie rose to her knees and patted her way through the food in his trough. "I meant to tell you. She's sorry about that. She's a bright child, but not the sensitive type. She was so busy thinking about her private projects she didn't stop to consider your feelings. But I don't think she's all bad. She IS Wizard Raspberry's daughter, as well as Belburga's. You could give her another chance. She must have some redeeming qualities."

"SHE is perfect," Moonshine's sigh was bleak as winter wind. "It is I who have failed."

"Oh, toad feathers!" Maggie said impatiently, then looked at the food trough again, and sniffed suspiciously at its contents. He was disproportionately maudlin about this situation—perhaps his barley had fermented and he was drunk.

No, the barley smelled good enough. Nevertheless, she said briskly, "You are simply not getting enough fresh air and

215

exercise since we've come here, and it's muddling your thinking. Why don't we go for a jog, and maybe we'll find Belburga's last daughter. If you want to bother. She, at least, is supposed to be kind to animals, and spends all her time outdoors, which should suit you. Of them all, she sounds like the nicest to me." She shifted her left knee, and something crackled beneath it. "Ah, here we are," she said, picking up the bent but still invisible disguise. "Slip this on now and let's go. I'm sick of seeing you pine away over these fickle girls. The sooner we're out of here, the better."

She patted his nose when she had disguised him, and he nuzzled her hand as he had used to. "I would we had never started this quest, friend Maggie, and that I had never met Lady Primrose. For though I know it is not meet that I should love you, still—is it possible there might be an error, do you think? Might not Primrose have been misled by a false hearing of our Creed?"

"I'd like to think so but I don't suppose you'd ever get her to admit it," Maggie said.

When they were beyond view of the tower, she mounted him and they rode up into the little glade that joined the forest to the west. Moonshine ran for all he was worth, driving his hooves into the ground, his tail furled behind him, his mane bannering in the wind.

Maggie rode with an exhilaration that was bittersweet. At this moment she was as close to her friend as she had ever been, yet knew he'd be gone from her in an instant if he found someone more suitable. Not a better friend, or one who loved him more, simply someone more suitable. She had almost stopped resenting it, and had stopped blaming Moonshine altogether. She was getting used to being rejected after all this time, she thought. All through her life, someone or other had decided she wasn't suitable for one reason or the other, and all of the reasons beyond her control. In the village she was not one of them because her father was noble, though among the nobles her common origins were suspect. Her father would have preferred she was a boy, and her grandmother would have liked for her magic to have been more witch-worthy than simple hearthcrafting. Colin liked tall, sweet elegant blonds instead of brown girls like her, and even Winnie had always told her she should try to be less overwhelming, less opinionated, less vocal, and more tactful, and she couldn't seem to manage any of that any better than she could changing her magic or her hair color. Moonshine was pushing her away, she saw now, not because she was homelier than Lily Pearl or stupider than Rusty or less ladylike than Primrose, but because he was seeking something *he* didn't know how to look for. She was a little disappointed to realize that their perfect understanding had not been perfect after all, and inside herself drew apart from him a hair's breadth. Though she would help him however she could, she no longer felt responsible for failing to be his ideal. She would have liked to make him see that, by the same token, not even a unicorn could possibly be the entire dream of a young girl like Lily Pearl or Ruby Rose—or even of herself. He had no more chance of winning any of them totally to him than she had of winning him back to the boundless love of their first days together. But somehow, though their thoughts still ran freely between them, her caution and reassurance did not reach him, and he continued to blame himself.

The ride helped. She could feel his relief at escaping the dark, smelly stall. When he danced up to a cliff, where the stream cascaded from ten times his height into a jade waterfall frothing into liquid lace at its bottom, she knew when he thought of diving, of ending his guilt and of freeing her. But she clung to his mane, and refused to be freed, and let him know in no uncertain terms that she would kill him if he ever thought anything like that again, and the moment passed.

The sky was bruised with dusk, throwing purple shadows onto the not-so-distant mountains by the time they trotted back down the hill leading to the grove surrounding the tower. There it was that Moonshine saw the animals assembled by the stream, and the flower-like girl in their midst, and it was also there that Maggie saw a very small group of horsemen descending the upper road from the forest, crossing the meadows to the tower. Among them, the horsemen dragged an overturned table with a man's body strapped to it.

"Colin!" Maggie cried. "That's the rescue party, but where's Colin?"

But Moonshine was wandering dreamily toward the crowd of animals and the girl among them. Maggie slid from his back and ran along the stream, through the ogress's glade and across the bridge, into the meadow to meet the approaching riders.

The creatures gathered around the charming child were more numerous and varied than any collection Moonshine had beheld since the throng at Wizard Raspberry's. One of them, a wolf, even looked familiar, much like the one who had skulked on the edge of that other gathering. But that a wolf would travel so far from his own territory was improbable.

More improbable, however, was the sweet beauty of the gentle girl who sat serenely among her admirers, stroking first one and then another of the great herd of bears, rabbits, deer, moose, fox, the wolf, a wild boar, lynx, and a family of weasels—not to mention various domestic dogs and cats, probably from the town, and horses, lambs, cattle, goats, geese, chicken and ducks.

Though she yet bore about her the roundness of a human child, the young maid was full of womanly loveliness as well. Beneath daisy-yellow curls, merry moss-green eyes twinkled from within a perfect little heart-shaped face. Her lips smiled encouragement to each of the animals clustered around her, and her cheeks glowed pink with the pleasure of their company. A striped, tawny cat sat on one of her knees, while a gray bird fluttered at her finger and she made playful pecking moues at it. Her other hand stroked the nape of a bear cub whose mother, amazingly, looked on in a doting fashion, with no sign of hostility.

Moonshine watched from the edge of the crowd, enchanted, feeling with growing certainty that here at last was the perfect maiden companion for a unicorn; beautiful, gentle, wise, and sweet-natured, loving to the beasts of the field and woodland, whose languages she seemed to know. Surely this girl met the highest requirements of even the most discriminating unicorns?

Her voice was as dulcet as dew dripping from pansy petals as she addressed the animals closest to her, each in his turn. "*Dear* little birdie, *sweet* little pussycat, how I love you both! And my brave boy bear—aren't you just looking more and more like your darling fuzzy wuzzy mummy every day?"

The other animals immediately crowded closer and began chattering and chirping comments which Moonshine made little effort to understand. Most of them followed a similar theme, crying, "Me! Me! I was first! Remember me? You called me your favorite little pet, Daisy Esmeralda! Oh me, please!" As they called out to her they would drop little presents at her dainty feet—flowers, pretty pebbles, bits of old ribbon and nesting materials—even a dead mouse, for which the cat received a fond scolding. "See what I've brought you!" they cried. "See my gift! Isn't it fine? It's all for you. Aren't I your very *nicest* friend, Daisy Esmeralda?"

And she, for her part, would say to each of them that he was, indeed, her nicest friend.

All of this business took considerable time. A great many of the girl's admirers had contrived to have thorns in their paws, arthritis in their tails, or burrs in their fur—plus one absolutely legitimate broken wing—and all of these required strokings and pickings and bindings and cooings from their gentle darling.

Moonshine shifted from one hoof to the other—he was not really very good at standing still—and waited to draw a bead on her lap so he could rest his head in it and tell her about how unicorns and first maidens—well, maidens anyway—were supposed to be inseparable companions, etc. He knew what he was going to say by now, having had considerable recent practice. But he advanced only very slowly towards the fore, afraid of stepping on somebody if he tried to use his size to edge forward even slightly.

The wolf he had spotted from the edge of the wood had no such scruples. Slyly, the wolf insinuated himself between a cow with a front-running position and the mother bear, which might have been a dangerous move except that the bear was temporarily preoccupied in disciplining her overstimulated cub. The bristly gray lupine then used an almost inaudible snarl to intimidate a baby bunny, bowled over a beaver with one swipe of a powerful front paw, and nipped the striped cat's tail so that she flew from the girl's lap. Slinking forward, the wolf calmly nuzzled his head into the lap in which Moonshine had begun to take a proprietory interest. The nasty bully then wriggled forward, heedless that his claws scratched the girl's tender flesh as he pawed his way up her chest to cover her face with slobbering kisses.

"What an adorable—yecch—wolf!" she exclaimed, but her heart clearly wasn't in it. He was ruining her pretty green and yellow sprigged dress, ripping and rending it with his feet, and leaving muddy spots. Moonshine could tell from the way she averted her face that the carnivore's breath was not sweet.

Mother bear waddled forward, bawling a complaint, but the wolf turned and snarled at her so fiercely that she backed off and with her cubs rolled away into the trees.

"You—uck—are such an enthus—ak—tic creature!" said the girl, trying both to pet the wolf and push him off her lap at the same time. "What big eyes you have!"

"Are they not the better to see you with, my dear little sister to the forest denizens?" asked the wolf in wolvish in a tone Moonshine clearly understood. "And is it not my tail's duty to wag in your presence and my nose's duty to savor your essence and my tongue's duty to lick your taste?" He looked, wagged, sniffed, and licked in demonstration, clearly warming to the subject as he opened even more tears in the girl's gown. "And are these teeth not to—"

"Hold, lupine lecher! That's quite enough of that," Moonshine commanded. He knew exactly what wolf teeth were for. Before the wicked creature had a chance to demonstrate them, the unicorn stepped past a cow and over a squirrel and planted the tip of his horn beneath the wagging wolf tail, giving a sharp upward jab. The wolf jerked up, cartwheeled three times in mid-air, and careened, howling, back into the woods.

Moonshine turned shyly to the girl, ready to assume his place as her staunch defender and savior and true friend. But though she reached out and stroked his nose in a manner he liked very much, her words were not all he had wished for.

"Aren't you a pretty creature?" she asked. "And you must be new here, too—or you'd know that all of my friends behave courteously to one another. That wasn't a very nice thing to do, what you did to Mr. Wolf. And the dear little squirrel was ahead of you, too. I think, to show you're sorry, you ought to wait behind the others until we can have a serious talk about this problem of rash behavior you seem to have."

"But MAIDEN!" he protested, "I sought only to—" he was going to say "defend you" but she fixed him with a sweet, sad, but very stern stare, and pointed to a position behind three foxes, a duck, a horse and a weasel with a limp. Humiliation heated Moonshine's hide as he slowly moved to obey her. The others returned their attention to Daisy Esmeralda, and she resumed chatting with them.

Moonshine moped. He hated standing in line, and he disliked crowds. Unicorns were not, after all, herd animals. As the only one of his species in his part of the woods, he had always been alone until he met Maggie. And *she* had always been considerate of his privacy. Or was it only that he'd never felt the need for privacy when she was near?

For a long time he studied the same veins in the same leaves, admired the waving colors of the sunset, watched the wildflowers behind Daisy Esmeralda fade to gray shadows. He memorized her dress, the rents in her dress, the curve of her arm and throat and each curl of her hair, until the dying light robbed her appearance of detail. But still the crowd grew no smaller, the din no less clamorous. At last, to see something other than what he had been watching for what seemed hours, he turned to the woods—just as another unicorn stepped forth.

"Lady Primrose!" he cried, and trotted several steps towards her, before looking back over his shoulder. No one noticed he'd gone, except the animals who'd come in behind him, and who now crowded forward, filling the gap created by his absence.

Giving his mane a decisive shake, he followed the beckoning Primrose into the forest. "How did you come here?" he asked eagerly. "And why? You *did* recall a section of the Creed that changed what you said about Maid Maggie, didn't you? You came to tell me that she—"

"Don't speak to me of that hussy!" Primrose huffed, switching her tail. "Do you never learn, foolish youngster? Coming here so close to a TOWN! Have you let her make a horse of you in spite of my warnings? Now, hear me, unicorn lad. I've come to take you back to the woods to meet a truly PERFECT maiden."

"The one you spoke of, Lady Primrose?" Moonshine felt uneasy, remembering Maggie's speculation that Primrose's long-lost maiden was the bandit nymph, but even clever Maggie could be wrong. Certainly Primrose seemed to have suffered no harm.

"Yes. She's even more pure and more highly principled than I had dreamed. She has a wondrous exalted mission for which— but I'll let her tell you of that. Quickly now, across the meadow with us before we're seen!"

"But—" he started to protest that Maggie would worry, but thought he would be returning soon anyway, as soon as he'd satisfied his curiosity, and would have interesting news to tell her then, when she came to tell him of Master Colin's mission. He was so weary of the stable and of the gloomy shadow of the tower and of the widow's lovely but peculiar daughters. Now Primrose, instead of merely explaining, would show him an example of a proper unicorn maiden. Then, at least, he would know what manner of girl he sought. With their horns held high and proud as standards, and their manes and tails silver and golden against the night-darkened glade, the two of them thudded past a startled Daisy Esmeralda and company, leapt the stream, and galloped across the open meadow into the woods beyond.

Maggie was not relieved by the Little Darlingham men's explanation that Colin had "Gone a-trappin' with the smelly one, mum," nor was she particularly moved by the injured Leofwin's plight. She wasn't very happy about it, either, though. Neither was she pleased when they mentioned to her the warning Leofwin had received from Trickle, and she was further unsettled when they told her that the zombified townsmen of Everclear had been abducted by bandits.

"What a queer lot of bandits!" she said, half to herself. "I never in my life heard of bandits who went around abducting unicorns, kings, and zombies."

221

"Well, mum," said the ancient who bore up the right-hand forepart of Leofwin's stretcher, "When you gets to be my age, you finds it takes all kinds."

With that bit of venerable wisdom duly noted, Maggie decided to return to Moonshine, for running toward them she saw Belburga, Lily Pearl, and Rusty, and she had no desire to be as disgusted as she was alarmed.

But she couldn't make her getaway immediately. Belburga lashed out and clasped her arm in an iron grasp as Maggie attempted to brush past her. In a tone that would have done credit to a dragoon, the ogress informed her that she was to begin tearing her petticoats into bandages for the wounded prince.

"He don't need no bandages, mum," said the cherubic-faced young man the others called Giles, addressing Belburga without removing his eyes from Lily Pearl. "His wound's 'most healed."

"We ALL must tear bandages," Belburga insisted. "It's the womanly thing to do."

"Oh, very well," Maggie said. "I'll tear bandages till we get him back to the tower. You may want them to restrain his wandering hands once he's himself again. But you'll have to give up your own petticoats—I've only the one, and I'll be blasted if I'll give it up for Leofwin."

So there was no help for it but that she had to help the ogress and her daughters make the prince comfortable while she heard a full account from the so-called rescue party of what had befallen them on their journey. The more she heard, the more worried she became, and at last, while Belburga was preparing what she termed a nourishing brew, while Rusty was asking excited questions of the rescuers about how much blood there'd been lying about, while Lily Pearl was holding Leofwin's hand, stroking his fevered brow and gazing soulfully into his eyes, and while Leofwin's hand crept beneath Lily Pearl's skirt, Maggie prepared to slip away.

To her amazement, as she started to slide out the door, the ogress turned to her and said in the syrupy voice Maggie'd presumed she reserved only for princes, "My dear girl, you needn't wash at the stream before you go to bed, you know. We have lots and lots of hot water here in the kettle for you. Why don't you just tidy up and go to your room and get some sleep? You must be exhausted after this long harrowing day, and you'll want to be your freshest, won't you, when your handsome minstrel returns?"

Of all of the alarming events of the afternoon, none alarmed and shocked Maggie more than this: Belburga actually being civil to her and considerate of her comfort! Inconceivable! She raced out the door like a loosed arrow.

Moonshine was not where she had left him, nor where she expected him to be, and her agitation grew by leaps and bounds.

"But he was here only a moment ago," protested Daisy Esmeralda, when Maggie had scattered her admirers and confronted her with Moonshine's disappearance.

"He's not here now," she said grimly, and shooed a few more cows, geese, and foxes. "Git! Go tend your own business, you!" She addressed the last to a particularly stubborn crane who'd been waiting all afternoon. "Don't you have eggs to hatch or something?" she demanded impatiently of the creature, then turned back to Daisy Esmeralda. "The question is, where did he go, and how long ago did he leave? Come on, girl, out with it. I've no more time to waste with you. Moonshine and my friend Colin may be in grave danger."

"I don't know. I honestly don't! I was just discussing with Mr. Squirrel here the winter nut market, and Mr. Unicorn was standing right over there when—" the girl stopped, flustered. She was shy with people, and had no idea how to deal with this wild-eyed witch. Tears and confusion made pools of her green eyes.

"Right *where*?" Maggie insisted.

"Why—right about there, where Goody Cow is standing—"

Maggie shoved Goody Cow aside, and found óne of Moonshine's footprints intact—enough of it visible, at least, that she could tell its direction and from it find the next one. Then she paused, puzzled. Other similar but smaller prints appeared from the opposite direction, blended with Moonshine's for a few paces, and then both sets stopped at the stream.

Daisy Esmeralda gathered her sprigged skirts in one hand and came to join her mother's gypsyish lodger where she hunkered close to the earth, tracing something with a blunt brown finger. The animals had all fled, anyway. They didn't like strangers, especially rude ones like this woman.

"When did the other unicorn come?" Maggie asked her. "Was she white, by any chance, with gold mane and tail?"

"Why, now that you mention it, there *was* another unicorn and she and your friend DID gallop off together! I remember now! I was just telling Goody Duck that her eggs were showing a marked improvement, and I happened to look up as the unicorns ran past. But really, you frightened me so, you completely drove it out of my mind. You're wilder than ANY of my woodland friends, Goody Witch.''

But Maggie was paying her no attention. Instead, the witch hitched up her skirts and started across the stream, leaping from stone to stone, missing once and splashing to her knees within arm's reach of the opposite bank.

Daisy Esmeralda shook her bright curls as the wet witch swore and sloshed ashore and continued across the meadow, moving slowly but with urgent intensity as she bent close to the earth so that she could see in the moonlight where the tall grass was furrowed by the recent press of unicorn feet.

CHAPTER 11

Once Moonshine and Primrose reached the forest's protective cover, Primrose sped ahead of him, her hooves spewing water, mud and leaves back at him as he galloped behind her. She set a slalom course, in and out of trees, around corners, over belly-up deadwood, dodging dense thickets. For what seemed half the night, until the moon studded the sky's very center, she raced and he followed. They stopped only for streams and ponds, and then for no longer than it took to skim their horn tips across the surface. Finally, he paused long enough to drink. When he looked up, he could no longer see Primrose.

Leaping the stream, he charged through the trees in the direction still holding her scent and the echo of her thudding hooves.

Something jumped, like an out-thrust branch of the spreading cedar beside him snapping into his face, but it wasn't a branch. He found himself suddenly straining against a barrier. Before he could rear or thrust or slash out with his hooves, a roughness jerked down over his ears, abraded his nose, and cut off his wind.

He reared and plunged, trumpeting, sure that Primrose would hear him and come to his aid. But he saw the men then, and before he could stab at one, they tangled his hooves with another rope, and threw many more over his head, tightening around his neck so that he could no longer breathe.

His nostrils flared and the suddenly inhabited moonlight forest around him blurred as his eyes rolled in terror. He tried to rear again, to grind his attackers beneath his hooves, but the ropes would not let him move. He tried to gouge at them, but could pull his head no more than a horn-tip's length one way or the other without the rope jerking him back.

Evil-smelling men swarmed all around him now, and more ropes, binding and choking him in a net. He reared one last desperate time, cringing from their cruel hands, but the ropes were too many and too tight, and he fell heavily. A sharp pain sprang into his side as he fell and his insides jarred upward and tried to come out his strangling throat.

When his eyes finally stopped rolling and he could focus again, though he could do nothing else, he saw her. Primrose's perfect maiden stood over him, a sweet smug smile curving her perfect lips.

Maggie realized before she was halfway across the meadow that tracking unicorns at night was not going to be easy. She'd need a light. She pulled a green branch from a nearby tree and used her sewing shears to strip it of its leaves, then wrapped around its top the hem of her shift, the garment she'd refused to sacrifice for Leofwin's bandages. She thought of using the pretty silk dress balled up in her pocket, but, remembering the hours needed to spin the silk even magically, she decided to save it. She could make her shift last most of the night by expanding the threads and spinning them out further, if she needed to. She hoped she wouldn't need to. Such tricks took time.

As it happened, the one strip she had was going to last all night. Her magic would not produce its basic, customary flame, no matter how she mumbled, pointed, cursed or invoked the name of the Mother.

It was as much of a shock as if she'd suddenly looked down to find her hands missing, and a damned nuisance, but that it could be more than a nuisance she refused to consider. The loss was temporary, she was sure, though due to what she couldn't say. Time enough to think about that when she'd found Moonshine and, with his help, located Colin. Inconvenient and ill-timed as her inexplicable loss was, for she could have used the light, she was still a strong, healthy, competent witch, magic or no. That a witch without magic was no better off than an ordinary girl alone and unarmed in a hostile woods was not a view she chose to consider.

To keep from considering it, in fact, she concentrated on the hoofprints, finding that since the unicorns had been traveling very fast over ground that was apparently permanently damp from this country's daily rains, the tracks were deep enough that she could feel them through the soles of her soft-bottomed leather boots. Indeed, very often she could see the whole trail where the trees parted overhead, allowing the moonlight to illuminate her surroundings.

Except for the slight chill and dampness, and an occasional shower when she happened into a rain-webbed branch, she was not too uncomfortable. Despite the way the wheezing wind sent the shadows lumbering about in the moonlight, there was certainly nothing to be frightened of in the night that hadn't been there during the day. Poor Colin was the one who had reason to be frightened, tracking bandits all alone except for "the smelly one," whom she judged from Griffin Hillman's description to be the same unsavory character she and Colin and Moonshine had met on the road from Everclear to Little Darlingham. And Moonshine— what could have made him run off like that without a word to her when he had promised to help her find the other unicorns? And why had Primrose come to fetch him? Had she learned something about the bandits?

The shadowy trail in front of her suddenly smeared, and overlaying it a picture rose in her mind every bit as clear as the ones in Aunt Sybil's crystal of Moonshine earnestly dipping his horn into a stream. That picture was snatched away, and replaced by one of her unicorn lying injured and bloodied, silently crying out to her to come and help him. Once having fallen victim to this morbid train of thought, she continued—though she remembered Colin at first not so much with her mind's eye as with her inner ear—hearing again all of the silly songs he'd sung to amuse her. Then she did see him, singing, acting out stories with his face and hands, and abruptly, before she could block the image, staring at her with blank eyes, his expressive body cold and still and immobile, no longer able to argue with her or tease her or scold her or kiss her or simply hold her on the bloody horse when she no longer had the will to continue. She shut her eyes hard, and when she opened them again, the woods was there where it ought to be. She stalked forward, feeling the mud squish up around her soles. If anyone had harmed Moonshine, or Colin, who for all his perverse balkiness was the only fellow she'd ever met she could genuinely profess herself to be fond of, she would categorically dismember the culprit with her own hands. IF she ever found her way out of this horrid wood, and the probability looked more remote all the time. Her tears kept blinding her to what little the moon permitted her to see.

She didn't need the moon at all, though, the next time she looked up after kneeling to inspect a hoofprint. She could see

226

perfectly clearly the feral yellow eyes gleaming down at her, and heard with equal clarity the low threatening growl. Before she could stand, the beast sprang.

Colin tried to learn the bandits' intentions and destination, but soon found that was no easy task to accomplish from within their camp. The main problem was that all of his fellow prisoners were zombies, and were no more communicative now than when he'd first met them, though they smelled better. The guards were not overly friendly, and their vocabularies seemed limited to physical threats with occasional verbal punctuation which sounded like "arragh now."

They camped at the mouth of a cave east of Everclear, within the foothills of the ice-encrusted mountains looming above the forest.

Colin and the others were linked together with ropes loosely tied around their necks. Colin's hands were also bound, and his ankles as well, though none of the zombies were similarly shackled. Since they were totally compliant to everything they were told to do, there was no need to restrain them. The ropes around their necks served mainly, he guessed, to keep them from straying and getting lost.

The bandits left to guard them, a group of about five men, lounged inside the entrance to a cave, around a fire they'd built at the cave's mouth. Colin and his companions were left outside, near enough to feel the fire's warmth, but with no protection from the rain which had been pelting them for the last hour.

Most of the zombies appeared to be sleeping, and the guards looked none too alert. With a little encouragement from a nice lullabye, Colin thought his captors might succumb to slumber too. He searched his repertoire, and decided the lullabye containing the Revised Judicial Code of the Kingdom of Argonia would be just the thing to woo them off to dreamland. He cleared his throat and opened his mouth.

And promptly shut it again. An arrow whizzed past his nose and embedded itself in a half-dead tree leaning against the cave's entrance.

The most alert of the guards opened one eye and stretched out one hand to pluck the arrow from the tree. "Arragh now," he growled, scratching his head and yawning. "Whassis?" He held the feather end of the shaft over the fire, which cast a reddish glow upon it.

"Reddisit?" asked another guard, sleepily, squinting down at the missile.

"Aye," the first one replied, and planted two filthy fingers in either side of his pit-like mouth, emitting a piercing whistle. "Coomonin and ootwizit," he grumbled as his whistle died out to be replaced by scrabbling sounds from the shadows beyond their hideout. "A body can't rest nowise here 'boots wizzoot sommun wantin' ter jabber at 'im."

The arrow's apparent author crashed out of the woods and into the circle of firelight. He led a sweating horse and was himself wet and exhausted looking. "Where's 'erself?" he asked. "Gotta message frum 'is worship."

"She's oot baggin' nuthern," replied the first guard. "Whassee want?"

"Wants ya backita castle is whut. Gotta bite or a drap for a poor soul?"

"Got nawt. 'ave to feed THEM, 'erself says," and he jerked a thumb at the Everclear folk and Colin.

The messenger peered at them across the fire. "Who're they?"

"Slavies. 'll do what they're told. Best kinda civilians to 'ave aboot. Though they eats o're much."

"Dead-lookin', kinda, ain't they? 'Cept that one." He nodded at Colin, who courteously nodded back.

"He'll be deader'n they are, soon's she tires of 'im, I reckon," said the first guard, then stiffened as if listening for something. Colin heard it at once. A great agitation in the forest, borne forward on a rising wind.

"She's coomin'," the guard said.

Immediately all the others began poking the fire, packing supplies, sharpening bows, bullying prisoners, and performing other brigandly activities, as if trying to appear busy and purposeful.

It was a good thing for them they did, for Sally Forth had whipped herself into a veritable tornado, and was driving several hapless highwaymen before her, hurtling tree limbs and gusty abuses upon them as they staggered into camp and cringed beside their fellows.

Her stormy wind whipped the fire into an inferno that threatened to engulf them all, then it and Sally's fury seemed to spend themselves and the wind died away, leaving the nymph spinning in its center.

"If you'd but let me explain, mum," the bravest of the new arrivals begged.

"Explain failure? That you let down the side? Betrayed the Cause with your carelessness?" Sally's blossom-like mouth was square with anger, but she paused, foot tapping, long enough to give the guard a chance to offer his explanation.

"The swine never showed, mum. We waited for 'em right where you said, at the second fork where the hill and trees 'id us good, but nawt did we see t'whole time but a little nightbird and an old hooty owl."

With suspicious rapidity, the storm in Sally's lovely eyes blew itself out and her voice was as smooth as oiled water as she said, "Why didn't you tell me that in the first place? Obviously, someone must have warned them. I'd never have blown up at you lads if you'd told me that before. Who could have known you were there? The witch?" Her gaze slid to Colin. "You didn't lie to me, did you, my dear, about the witch? Did she come with you?"

Colin's throat tightened as her eyes burned into him, and he shrank back against the uncomforting bulk of the nearest zombie. But she smiled at him with the same mercurial shift of expression she'd displayed to her men. "No. It couldn't have been her," she said. "Wulfie would have known. He was with you. Who was it then, who betrayed us? I think you know." Almost tenderly, she lifted a burning stick from the fire and, skirting the flames, advanced on him.

The soft light of the flaming brand was as flattering as candleglow to her skin tones, giving them a warm, honeyed gloss. Her movements were supple, her body graceful as she swayed toward him, extending the end of the brand like a gift. He felt the heat against his cheek as she smiled kindly, saying, "You must tell the truth, you know. If you protect this spy, our work could be seriously hampered. We'll have to take time away from important tasks now to arrange for the demise of Prince Leofwin and your friends. You understand how inconvenient that is going to be, for us *all*, don't you?"

The brand dipped closer to his eye, barely leaving him room to lift and lower his head. The flame danced, filling his vision. His muscles strained, bulging against the ropes at his ankles and wrists, and he pressed far back against the unyielding mass of the other captives, but the fire still jigged within singeing distance of his nose. She meant to torture him, and he had no doubt it would hurt a great deal. Erratic pounding filled his ears, and he thought it was the wild pumping of his own heart. Then the pounding was drowned out by a roaring sensation in his ears, the flame blurred into a sheet of light, and a blessed coolness bathed his face as darkness overtook him.

The rain on his face and the tension of the rope half-strangling

229

him revived him more quickly than he would have liked. Voices surged around him, some of them not in his ears, but within the interior of his mind, with his own chaotic thoughts.

"Where d'ye want these 'ere 'corns, Sal?" a gruff voice asked. "Yer old nag is 'most as mean as t'new 'un."

"Maiden, you said you meant only to *recruit* my kinsman," one of the mind-voices protested.

"Oh, foolish, foolish me!" another mind-voice, Moonshine, sobbed, "To think I left my dear Maid Maggie to mourn me while I followed Primrose's wicked path!"

Colin tried to peek without seeming to, but he could see little in the darkness beyond the fire, so he lay still against the lap of one of the Everclear ladies and listened.

Sally Forth's voice throbbed with compassion as she said, "Now, now, Primrose, my love, don't take on so. The ropes are only to hold him until we have a chance to persuade him to join us. He's been under the dreadful influence of that witch, and we can't hope he'll be amenable to our persuasions until Wulfric's dealt with the woman once and for all."

Primrose's next thought was less outraged, more subdued, "I suppose you know best, Maiden. Once your wolf-pet has devoured that awful person, perhaps Moonshine will see the merit in your plan."

"Devoured?" Moonshine whinnied hoarsely and Colin heard heavy cudgels thunk as the bandits clouted the straining unicorn back to his knees. The wave of despair that swept over Colin only partially emanated from Moonshine. The rest was his own fear that these ridiculous and vastly mad people could somehow slaughter his bright, brave Maggie as she risked herself in her own bullheaded way to save them, as he had no doubt she was already doing unless, perish the thought, she was instead providing nourishment for the loathsome wolf-man.

"Steady on, Moonshine," he tried to convey encouragement and a positiveness he didn't possess, "Maggie wouldn't care for hysterics, you know."

"Master Colin?" He could almost feel the unicorn's ears prick up.

"I'm afraid so. Try not to provoke them into hurting you, will you, and keep your wits about you. We won't be able to fight our way out of this, just the two of us, but—" he started to add something about tricking their way out, but Primrose's obnoxious bray entered his mind just at that time.

"Very sound advice, for such a lowlife as yourself, Man. If you have any influence over my kinsman at all, you'll convince

230

him to follow my maiden's lead. She's wise beyond your piddling understanding. Moonshine will soon be free of that wicked witch's spell, and eager to join us. I myself saw the wolf stalking your paramour, and he is a very hungry animal, that wolf.''

"Truly?" Colin mentally snapped back. "I shouldn't count my dog bones before they were chewed if I were Sally. Maggie has a way with animals, present company excepted, as Moonshine and certain dragons will be glad to tell you." But it was all bravado. He knew Wulfric was no ordinary animal but a ferocious, magical monster against whom even a witch would have a difficult time alone. And what could a hearthcrafter do to a wolf? There was always that fire trick of hers, of course. He reminded Moonshine of that, quietly, hoping Primrose would occupy herself in adoring Sally Forth and forget about eavesdropping for a moment.

Unfortunately, the misanthropic mare was not only adoring Sally, she was also confiding in her her knowledge of Colin's recovery and his communication with Moonshine.

Colin groaned as the nymph turned back to him with what could have passed on any other nymph's face for an engaging curiosity, a sweet sort of "tell me all about yourself" look. But she didn't fool him this time.

"No matter what they do to me, Moonshine," he cautioned silently, "Don't do anything that will get you hurt—unless, that is, you think it might work."

Sally knelt beside him, but didn't pick up the firebrand again. "I'm afraid I was hasty toward you before, dear minstrel," she apologized. "And I regret that, for you are a very useful person. Not only do you write stirring songs, but you also seem to have a calming influence on my new recruit. I realize now that I can hardly hold you responsible for every bit of magic adverse to our cause that occurs in these woods. The enemies of our Cause are legion, but we shall, you understand, smite them all down in time. It's a great pity your witch friend, being of such fine stock, has chosen to oppose us, but I'm sure you understand that, like any royal lackey, she must either be converted or disposed of. As for you, why, until you meet the Dark Pilgrim yourself, and pledge yourself personally to his service, you must practice your song and help transport this new beast peacefully to the stronghold. Then I won't have to slay you. All right?"

Colin was flabbergasted by the reprieve, and almost as much by the fickle shifting of the lady's moods, but he hastened to agree. He couldn't have proposed a better device for gaining time until Maggie could rescue them himself. He cheerfully sent Moonshine an image of Maggie stopping long enough for a toasted wolf sandwich to bolster her strength before she led a small army to save them.

"It ain't easy bein' a messenger on the best of days," the arrow-bearing emissary complained in a whining voice. "But with women in command, a man can't get a word in to save 'is soul." He muttered his complaint to the burly bandit to whom he had first spoken, out of earshot of the nymph.

The other man shoved the arrow back into his hand and growled, " 'erself don't read minds, ya knows. Tell 'er."

The messenger rose and went to Sally, presenting her with the arrow as a gentleman would present a calling card. " 'is Worship needs you 'n' t'lads back ter t'stronghold, mum. Now. 'E says t' tell you that t' king's forces've landed, an' 'e needs you ter wipe 'em out, like."

Sally's face brightened and softened at once as if she'd received a pretty compliment. "Why, certainly. At once," she agreed, and put her silver hunting horn to her lips and blew a blast worthy of a woman whose alter ego was a wind storm.

Maggie rolled to one side of the charging wolf, leaping to her feet as he flew past her and landed on the ground.

"Shoo, you stupid animal!" she said. "I haven't the patience to put up with your nastiness right now. Get on with you, and I'll forget it happened."

Unimpressed by her magnanimity, the wolf sprang again, but she ducked around a tree and began to try to shinny up it. Fangs snapped shut on her skirt tail, and she felt a tug and heard a rip. She tried to conjure up a fire, just a little hotfoot for the beast, but no flame appeared, and the animal's feet remained busily engaged in propelling him past her skirt, toward her fleshier outcroppings.

Of all the times for her magic to fail! If she lived to think about it, she decided, she'd have to try to discover why it had chosen this particular time, but right now she was preoccupied with losing her grip. She clutched desperately at a fungus growth near her fingertips, trying to use it to pull herself up. It broke, and she fell.

She landed squarely in the middle of a furry, squirming, snarling mass of wolf, her knee in his midsection, his claws raking her arm. She rolled to the side, but this time he rolled with her, and then they both rolled over and over down a slight incline at the base of which was a stream.

Just before they rolled into the water, they stopped. She was on top, and grabbed his muzzle in one hand to keep him from biting her nose off. With her other hand she sought his throat, determined to throttle him if she could. His hind legs pedaled at her middle, trying to disembowel her, and almost succeeded when she leaned in to try to make her stranglehold more secure. She leapt aside and scrambled to her feet and ran, heedless of what the sensible thing to do when faced with wild animals was supposed to be.

He was on her again before she knew it, slamming against her back and knocking her to the ground again. One arm was pinned under her. The other she braced against his neck, keeping his teeth at bay and also getting a much closer look than she really wanted at the inside of a wolf's mouth.

Then the mouth started to change, and the entire face with it, dissolving into something neither wolf nor man, and horrible in its indecision. In a moment, the paws on her shoulders became long-nailed, bristle-covered hands and the face before her melted into a man's. Someone she'd met, as a matter of fact.

"Jivemgood!" she exclaimed. "Aren't you Count Jivemgood?"

"Yeeess," he said, slobbering, mocking her, "And aren't you delicious?"

But he shifted his weight slightly when he said it, and she shifted hers enough to free her hand. She grabbed for her medicine pouch, dangling out of her skirt pocket, and pulled forth its contents, whatever it was. "Not without seasoning," she replied, and flung assorted herbs and powders straight into his face.

They parted, sneezing, but he got the worst of it, and hacked and choked, and in the process changed back into a wolf, who hacked and choked even more violently.

Now that she knew what he was and that he had no intention of running off into the woods like a decent, sane wild animal, and also realized that no retreat of hers would be fast enough to save her, she had no scruples about slaying him. Closing her hand over the sewing shears she had dropped into her pocket after using them to make her useless torch, she opened them, clutching them like a dagger in her fist, and attacked while the monster was incapacitated.

He was not, however, as incapacitated as she'd thought, and he rounded on her again just as she leaped, snatching at the first piece of fur her hand met and trying to stab at it with the open shears. With his body rolling beneath her, her grip loosened and shifted on the shears and she didn't quite make a stab—she made a thumb-straining snip instead.

The wolf emitted an unearthly howl and leapt up, spouting gore, and sprinted into the shadows.

Maggie sat on the ground and tried to catch her breath. She couldn't believe the monster was gone and she was still alive. She couldn't believe her magic had failed her so completely and—she couldn't believe she was holding a sickeningly severed wolf tail in her scratched and bloodied hand.

Mechanically, she rose and went to the stream to wash herself off. Her knees kept buckling, refusing to support her, and finally she had to sit and splash water up on herself. It was chilly, but revived her.

She didn't hear the flutter of wings until the faery was hovering right in front of her, looking at her curiously. "Hey, you look terrible. What happened? Why're you bloodying up my stream?"

"This—beast—attacked me," Maggie explained, indicating the tail.

Trickle flew to it and landed in the middle of the strip of fur, wriggling her toes in it and petting it. "This is good stuff. Reminds me of someone, too. Say, what would you take for this?"

"Take for it?" Maggie failed for a moment to grasp the question. "But it's—the beast, I mean, was human, sometimes anyway. Maybe that thing'll change into something—else?"

"Like what? People don't have tails. Hey, wait, you mean a WEREWOLF attacked you?"

"I suppose it must have been."

"Well, well, well. How interesting. Look, what if I give you something for this? I know the beast in question, and believe me, he may change into something that looks human, but he's all wolf underneath. It would make a great carpet for my place, lots better than the bird's nest I'm using now."

But Maggie wasn't listening. "He was going to eat me," she muttered as much to herself as to the faery. "He was actually going to eat me. I was polite enough. I never harmed him. I've never in my whole life made a slighting remark about were-wolves. The forest is full of edible game, and that son of a wolf bitch was going to eat ME." An indignant scowl crawled across the shock overlaying her face. "But he didn't. I got this instead." She picked up the tail and slowly the shock and the scowl turned into a grin—the same kind of wicked witch grin that must have petrified victims of her distant ancestresses. Even

Trickle backflapped away from her a little. "You want it?" Maggie asked. "What'll you give me for it? Haven't you got some kind of faery magic you can spare me? My own seems to have run out of power."

"We-ell, I could probably manage to let go of a spell of bewilderment for you to cover your path," Trickle offered.

"No, that wouldn't work. Except for werewolves, no one is looking for me. I'm the one who's trying to find everyone else."

"Everyone wouldn't refer to a certain minstrel and a certain unicorn, would it?" the faery asked slyly. "Because if so, I'm afraid you're a little late. They've sort of fallen in with evil companions, so to speak."

"Well, I must say you're a lot of help," Maggie said. "Why didn't you try to save them?"

Trickle shrugged. "They seemed to know what they were doing till they got there and then, well, I don't care for werewolves or nasty nymphs or brigands any more than the next faery. Besides, I have my stream to look after, you know."

"I thought you LIKED unicorns. Moonshine purified your stream for you, didn't he?"

"Well, yes, but then his friends are always mucking it up again." But shame was beginning to invade the belligerency of her voice, and she said defensively, "I did warn that lummox of a prince about the ambush, but I was too late to save your boyfriend or Moonshine."

"Couldn't your magic help them?"

"Not used by somebody my size."

"How about by somebody my size? I won't give this to you if you don't help me. In fact, if you don't help me somehow . . ." She snipped the bloody shears menacingly.

"Very scarey," Trickle replied scornfully, deflecting them with one tiny hand. "Come on, witch. I'm wise to you. You're like me. You talk mean, but it takes somebody really getting to you for you to let them have it. Why, if I'd had any idea the spell I cast on those poor slobs at Everclear was going to keep them from noticing when the water spoiled I—"

"I THOUGHT there was some strange magic afoot there," Maggie said. "Go on. I'm finding this confession very interesting."

Suddenly the forest was filled with a single, silvery blast. Both Trickle and Maggie listened, and when the note died away, they exchanged a long, penetrating stare.

"Time's a-wasting, witch," Trickle said. "Whatever I've done or haven't done is none of your business. If you want to help your friends, you'd better get moving. I'll tell you what. I can't go along with you, and my magic doesn't amount to much at long range, mostly, but if you give me that thing, I'll give you something that will put you in contact with certain people I know who might be able to help you later on."

"Oh, very well," Maggie said. "Take it."

Trickle did, and flew away with it, returning a few minutes later with a stalk of small blue flowers in her hand. "Faery bells," she explained. "Just ring them if you get in a bind, and I have friends who'll help you out."

Maggie looked skeptical, but accepted the flowers. "Is that all?" she asked.

Trickle sighed. "No. Look, witch, I have my job to do here at the stream, or I'd come with you, I really would. But you know how it is. Look, I'll tell you what. I'm putting your feet on the right path now, and I promise you they'll keep you on it as long as you're in these woods. Just follow your toes, and if you hustle and Sally doesn't, you'll catch up with her. But—uh—"

"But what?"

"But you'd better hurry. That was her hunting horn we heard just now, and she uses it to call her flunkeys. Sounds to me like they're getting ready to move."

Maggie was more than ready to leave the faery's company. She was afraid she had more in common with the waspish little being than she cared to admit. If she seemed as hard and vengeful and jealous of her own powers as all that, no wonder Winnie and her father had been after her for years about her bad temper. Trickle was very much like what Maggie imagined her Grandma Oonaugh must have been—ready to throw evil spells indiscriminately about and never mind where they landed.

Of course, Trickle *was* a Little Person, and everybody knew they were touchy and tricky and as ready to do a human in as to help one. Unlike the larger varieties of faery folk, the general category of whom Trickle's smaller sort were a sub-tribe, Little People could not mingle or intermarry with larger folk, and apparently the size difference made them more likely to be antagonistic than conciliatory—most of them Maggie had met were at least grouchy, if not downright malicious, and they all seemed to have chips on their shoulders.

Still, she had to admit, she was a fine one to talk about malice. Hadn't she just maimed another creature? She was glad Trickle had wanted the tail—just thinking about it made Maggie feel vaguely unclean. Not dirty. She didn't particularly mind dirty, but, as Winnie used to say, felt as if she'd "lowered herself" by doing to the wolf what he obviously intended to do to her, though not quite the same, of course, since she didn't have a tail.

Perhaps *that* kind of thing, that uncleanliness, was what made Primrose think a witch was unfit to befriend a unicorn. And maybe she was right. But just now, Moonshine seemed to be in need of friends who weren't worried about dirtying themselves, so she didn't intend to worry about it. At least she, unlike some small faeries she could name, wasn't so blindly devoted to her own magical pursuits that she refused to leave them even for a short time to help someone else.

As a matter of fact, it had happened quite the other way around with her, she thought ruefully. She hadn't had to leave her magical pursuits—her magic had left her, instead. But it was a temporary loss, surely. No Brown witch Maggie'd ever heard of had ever permanently lost her powers, unless you counted Maggie's mother, who Granny Brown claimed had never developed her sorcerous potential because she'd been wooed and won, if not wed, at such an early age that all of her magic poured itself into dealing with her lover and her daughter.

Which wasn't at all Maggie's case. She had never mated, which was part of her dilemma, but even by witchly standards, she was definitely old enough to take a mate if she wished. Granny Brown had stressed it in fact, and had frequently reminded her of her impending twenty-first birthday, a day of some significance in ancient lore, associated with the ebb and flow of forces vital to all life and power. Well, whatever that meant, here she was now, her feet on an invisible trail by alien magic while her own failed to keep the rain from soaking through her torn dress, and would no longer provide her with light, food or fire. At least in this rainy climate she was unlikely to get thirsty, she thought, as she tongued water droplets out of the air. And dawn was coming, and with it, with any luck at all, the sun and warmth, though in this miserable country one could never be sure. She wondered if she shouldn't ring the flowery bells and ask one of Trickle's colleagues if she mightn't borrow a cloak, but a faery cloak would be too small for her, anyway. Possibly she was just passing through an area ruled by another witch or wizard powerful enough to negate her own magic, and when she'd gone far enough her powers would return. She'd heard of things like that happening. But if that were true, why hadn't it happened when she and Colin passed through this same territory before?

Maybe Granny had been right. Maybe taking up with a unicorn at this stage in her life, when most witches mated, was depleting her power. She had expended quite a lot of it trying to help Moonshine, but no more than she would during a similar length of time in her father's castle, and it had always replenished itself before. Of course, back at the castle, she used her powers in the way they were intended to be used, and didn't have to distort them to meet demands for her own protection and that of her companions. And why should mating have so much to do with it, anyway? Aunt Sybil hadn't mated, or at least she'd as much as said she hadn't, but then Sybil was a seer, not a hearthcrafter. People didn't have to live with her to benefit from her powers—in fact, she lived alone because most people were uncomfortable living with someone who could see their intimate lives with so little effort, though, actually, Sybil was never one to pry.

What could Granny have meant by that, then? The implication had been that Maggie's own power could not sustain itself and her indefinitely unless she reinforced it by—what? Forsaking one sort of love—the unicorn's—for another—a man's? But why? Unless it was because Moonshine didn't really need her magic. He had plenty of magic of his own. Were men any different? Colin had his magic, after all, though it wasn't nearly as powerful or useful as hers or Moonshine's, and he didn't use it usually, except for show. Perhaps it all came down to what Wizard Raspberry had tried to tell Rusty about strengthening one's power through sharing it. Well, for the time being hers would have to sulk wherever it was hiding. She hadn't time to go satisfying its caprices.

But she wished the faery's spell setting her feet on the proper path had included an anti-blister clause. Trying to sit and rest did no good; her feet kept marching even while her bottom was sitting, and the soles of her boots were quite worn through. Her calves ached and her back was beginning to pain her as well, but her bleeding feet marched relentlessly on their appointed course, all that night, and into the next day and following evening.

She ought to have known better than to have accepted a spell from a faery without learning all the complications first! Her aching muscles and feet, the cold, hunger and weariness began to bother her less than a new fear. Unless Trickle had thought this stupid spell out better than it appeared she had, the silly thing was quite likely to march Maggie right into the bandit camp too footsore and exhausted even to put up a good fight.

That fear took complete possession of her for a time, as she strode past a cabin late in the afternoon. Coals lay inside a ring of stones at the cave's entrance, and human and unicorn droppings marred the trampled moss in front of the cave. Still, the fire was dead and she had heard the hunting horn long before dawn. The quarry must yet be far ahead of her, but she was really too tired to think about it. All she could think of was rest.

Sometime in the middle of the night she heard the wind rise to a howl, and realized that she heard more the wind itself now than the leaves rustling or the brushing of the branches against each other. The moon stayed hidden, and often she tripped or blundered into things she couldn't see, but before long she missed the impediments. The foliage in her path had dwindled, and so had her protection from the wind.

It turned her clothing and hair into flails against her cold-chaffed skin. The only positive benefit from it all was that her feet were more or less numb, though for some time they kept moving. But finally, when the wind was fiercest and the shadows of the night were reduced to two outlines, a serrated blackness rearing like the single blackened tooth of some monstrous giant against the paler black of the sky, her feet stopped moving. Without further ado, her legs folded under her. She never knew where she landed; she was fast asleep before she hit the ground.

Colin couldn't laugh openly when the tailless Wulfric limped out of the woods to join the ranks of marching bandits and zombies. So he contented himself with a smothered snicker, containing not so much mirth as relief. Maggie, it seemed, struck again.

Primrose sniffed and said to Sally Forth, "I think your minions are made of inferior matter, O Maiden, to turn tail on such a lowborn one as that witch, and run."

"That's very unfair," Colin told her with a straight face. "He couldn't very well turn tail when he'd been relieved of it, could he?" The nymph examined her second-in-command's wound. Her lips were pressed tightly together, and she seemed both awed and incredulous that anyone could have inflicted such damage on the up-till-now invincible Wulfric. Colin decided to press the point. "O Sally, in the interest of a successful revolution, I beg to give you some advice. If I were you, I'd release all of the captives and beasts, and not become involved with the witch. I've known her for some time now, and her powers are the mightiest I've ever encountered—judging from the condition of our poor comrade, I'd say if anything she just seems to be getting stronger all the time. I hardly think it will do the cause any good to have a force such as hers aligned against you."

Sally chose to ignore him. Wulfric whimpered, and looked up

at her with large, sad wolf eyes. She petted him absently and asked with what Colin felt this time was real gentleness, "Wouldn't it hurt less if you changed back into man form?"

The wolf blinked, as if he'd never thought of that, and proceeded to follow her suggestion.

"There, isn't that better?" she asked. Wulfric rose to his feet, rubbing his lower back as he did so. His human face wore a pained grimace.

"Oh, Sally, though my man-form wears no tail, my back remembers it from wolf form, and mourns its loss. I fear I can do no more than limp, and will sorely slow you. Leave me, if you must."

"I can't, Wulfie. You know you'll never be able to cross the glacier alone. I'm the only one who can guide us safely across. And besides, the Dark Pilgrim has ordered us to return to the stronghold."

"Ah, Sally, then I must perish, a martyr to the Cause." The last ended on a note that sounded suspiciously like a howl.

"I've always known you were a true believer," Sally cried, throwing her arms around his neck in a gesture that temporarily brightened his woebegone expression. "Any worthwhile cause can always use a martyr, but I shall be so sorry to lose you. Tell me, is there any last request you have of us before we leave you here to die?"

Wulfric's eyes lit with greed. He obviously didn't want to waste the opportunity for one last outstanding favor. Colin shifted uneasily as the wolf's eyes lit first on himself, then Moonshine, then returned to Colin. Though his face bore only a shadow of its former wolfish grin, that shadow was enough to make Colin quake. The wolf-man answered Sally's question. "Yon beast would have taken my tail long before the wily witch, and though I know you treasure the man for now, he was for a time the evil female's companion. Let me slay them both, O Sally, and I shall endure my martyrdom with great joy."

"Now, Wulfie, let's be reasonable. You know you can't slay the unicorn. The Dark Pilgrim needs all the unicorns we can bring him, and we have so far caught only four. Besides," she jerked her head with a meaningful look in Primrose's direction. "However," she continued, "The Dark Pilgrim would undoubtedly see that a tail for a tail was a fair trade, and allow you to take the unicorn's tail as vengeance for your own loss. You could leave it with the minstrel's body, so the witch could find it and see to her sorrow what happens to those who thwart our Cause."

Wulfric seemed satisfied by this compromise. He withdrew his knife from the smelly sheepskin cloak which clothed his man-form, and walked up behind Moonshine, grabbing his tail.

Moonshine screamed, aloud to the bandits and silently to Colin, but he was so tightly bound that he could not without help withdraw his tail from the were-man's grasp.

"Hold on a moment, ma'am," Colin said, "You can't let him do that to a helpless prisoner. How would it look for the Cause?" He had no idea what he could do or say to save Moonshine and himself and spoke only to gain time. Help came from an unexpected source.

"Maiden, you promised me no harm would come to him!" Primrose protested, trotting up to stare Sally Forth in the face. "You said he would find glory with our cause. How can you let that filthy pet of yours TOUCH one of us? Why, that nasty wolf can do nothing but turn into an even nastier man! Moonshine and I can purify water, prevent poisoning, cure illness—"

"Heal wounds!" Colin added with sudden inspiration. "Why, ma'am, you'd be wasting three of your most valuable supporters, and maybe losing the loyalty of the lady unicorn there, if you let your friend have his way."

Sally was unimpressed. "You don't seem to understand, minstrel. I've given my word. Your unicorn injured a brave captain of the Cause, and your witch mutilated him. It is only just that you suffer in your turn, and your beast forfeit his tail. If I'm not just, my men will cease to have any respect for me. Besides, you've cost me my most devoted assistant."

Colin mustered all of his balladry play-acting skills to seem casual. "I don't see how you can call him devoted when he'd rather slink off into the bushes after murdering us than continue to serve the Cause. Moonshine didn't know who your wolf was when he attacked him, did you, Moonshine?"

"Naaayyy, Minstrel!" Moonshine cried. "Had I known, I would have run him through!"

"See there," Colin said, translating the audible neigh and tactfully neglecting to mention the latter part of the unicorn's reply. "He didn't know he was tickling a comrade-in-arms. As for Maggie, that was a fair fight, and after all, she's just a *girl*, and he's a big bad werewolf."

"*I* am a girl," Sally reminded him, drawing herself up.

"Yes, ma'am, you certainly are, which proves my point exactly. You NEED your assistant to help you. So why don't you make him take the cure and come along to the stronghold with the rest of us instead of letting him butcher us and slink around licking his wounds while your people honor him as a martyr?"

241

"Take the cure?" Wulfric asked. "What nonsense is this? Cure?"

"Come off it now, Wulfie, old boy. You can't tell *me* you didn't know all along that Moonshine's magic could cure you. You SAW it heal Leofwin's stab wound. Why, I'll wager Moonshine can grow you back another tail just like—" But Colin's fingers refused to snap. "Or at least heal over the wound so you can walk again. You can do that, can't you, Moonshine?"

"Never!" Moonshine said.

'See there, of course he can," Colin said aloud, and to Moonshine added privately, "If you ever want us to get out of this alive, you'd better show a little unicornly charity, and heal this beastie with all your heart."

"But I've never grown a tail back." Moonshine said. "I wouldn't know where to begin."

"Just let your magic do its work."

"Very well. If you can make Wulfie well enough to accompany us, you both may live," Sally said.

"*I want my tail,*" Wulfric insisted, growling.

"Oh, all right. If he can't grow yours back you may still take his," she agreed. "But this is all taking an enormous amount of time and we should be making all speed to the stronghold. Have the beast do his magic at once, minstrel."

Trying to make it look as mysterious and complicated as possible, Colin obtained another flask of water from one of the guards, and with extreme ceremony held the flask in place while Moonshine threaded the tip of his horn through the narrow opening at the top.

Mumbling the nonsense syllables which served in some songs as euphemisms for indelicate bodily parts and functions, the minstrel then sprinkled the water over Wulfric's re-enwolfed rump. And held his breath.

He needn't have worried. The wound began to heal nicely at once, and within a few minutes a growth sprouted from the end of Wulfric's spine. It was thin and hairless and pale, and rather resembled an anemic carrot, but it wagged properly, when Wulfric saw it and realized what it was. In fact, the were was so relieved to have his tail back that he chased it like a puppy before Sally could calm him.

"It doesn't look like a proper tail," she said critically.

"I don't *do* fur," Moonshine, still miffed at having been forced to perform his magic for an enemy, told Colin haughtily.

"He says fur takes time to grow back, ma'am, but grow back it will. Why, I understand some magical cures for baldness even

242

include shaving off all the hair ahead of time to make it grow back thicker and more luxurious.''

"Is that so?''

"Yes, indeed.'' He nodded vigorously. "But, excuse me, ma'am, now that we've solved this minor difficulty, don't you think we should get on to your stronghold right away? I mean, your Dark Pilgrm might need us.''

Sally's blue eyes regarded him with almost coquettish interest. "I wish I could be sure of your loyalty, minstrel. But yes, you're right. We must proceed at once.''

They wrapped a bandage of cloth around Wulfric's new tail to keep it from the cold. Colin was still bound, but loosely, and Moonshine's bonds were also loosened. Colin was permitted to lead the unicorn on the restated condition that he keep him quiet and cooperative.

He sang as they traveled through the woods, and out and up into the sparsely covered country that was the skirt of the great jagged mountain in whose shadow they shivered. He made up a song about Wulfric's tail called, fittingly enough, The Ballad of Wulfric's Tail, in which he made Moonshine out to be a great and misunderstood hero for Sally's cause, making up wildly flattering words as he went along to describe both Sally and Moonshine, and emphasizing the marching beat, which made it easier for him to walk and also put the guards in a good humor, so they didn't clout him and the other prisoners so often, but stomped and growled along in a kind of brutish contentment.

Sally allowed Wulfric to range ahead, and, with Primrose, she dropped back to walk beside Colin. They were climbing up a wide, treeless meadow now, and though there was plenty of room all around, Sally walked very close to him, cocking her head attentively as if she only wished to hear his songs more closely. But he knew the signs. The ravishing rebel leader made it as plain as had any of the court ladies that she fancied Colin himself as well as his music. One had to put up with that sort of thing when one was possessed of such an abundance of talent and charm as he, but in this particular case the attention made him more than a little uneasy. His charm for this lady, if mishandled, could very well prove fatal, and not in the figurative sense.

Not that it was particularly difficult to be charming to someone as fetching as Sally Forth. However spurious his interest in her political philosophy, and however dubious the logic behind that philosophy, her physical attractions were absolutely, irrefutably genuine and beyond question. Still, entertaining her reminded him a bit of a tale the chief archivist, Sir Cyril Perchingbird, had once told him about Finbar the Fireproof's great-grandfather's performing magic. The Ashburn ancestor, Selwyn the Serpent Slayer, was possessed, like all Ashburns, of a love and talent for the flashy, entertaining sort of magic which was shown to best advantage when done before an audience. In his later years, Selwyn, who had ignored his gifts for the dour business of serpent slaying, a necessity during his day, when Argonia's coast was plagued with the snakes, decided that slaying the sea serpents was a boring and unchallenging occupation. He had taken to whistling tunes calling them up to the shores near Queenston, giving them such a good show that the monsters came happily to the harpoons of Selwyn's more belligerent friends, who took advantage of the situation to slay as many snakes as possible. Still, Selwyn's wondrous feat impressed as many of the populace as it did sea serpents, and from that day forward Argonians ceased to call their king Selwyn the Serpent Slayer and began to call him instead Selwyn the Snake Charmer. Colin thought that singing for Sally Forth was a little like that.

He had to stop singing by midday, for they had climbed high enough that footing was steep and difficult, and even the unicorns were less sure-footed than before. They were able to travel only an hour or two longer after that, and made camp, high up on the side of the mountain, in the shadow of the glacier's edge, which cupped around them on three sides. Colin was grateful for the rest, for he was unused to heights, and even more unused to long marches, particularly during performances.

Besides, he was beginning to fear for the health of the Everclear folk, among whom he was once again shackled. They looked, if possible, even deader than usual, most of them having turned an unattractive dusky blue which matched the haze veiling the pinnacle rising at their backs. Their noses ran, and of course they didn't wipe them, so that froze, adding to the general unsavoriness of their collective overall appearance.

Most of the bandits had equipped themselves with winter clothing, which they drew from packsacks and donned, but, oddly enough, their leader still shivered in her thin, translucent garment, and hugged herself near the fire. Either she believed in traveling light, Colin thought, or else she felt her attire was good for morale. In either case, her patronage was too important to his own survival for him to allow her to risk catching even a slight cold.

"See here, guard," he said to no one in particular. "If I weren't trussed up like this, *I'd* offer *my* jacket to our beautiful leader, if I had a jacket, that is. What kind of fellows are you, anyway?''

His gallantry paid unexpected dividends. Sally was swamped with so many warm wraps she even shared one with him. "You know how to treat your leader with respect, don't you, minstrel? I like that in a man."

Colin did the safe thing, and pretended to fall asleep.

Maggie eyed the impossible heights of the glacier, and felt like crying. The wretched thing looked straight up and down, with deep crevasses tinged a cold and forbidding blue, and gusts of snow skimming its lower slopes. The upper slopes she couldn't even see. They were blanketed with the pearl gray clouds muffling most of the landscape around her.

She'd awakened that morning stiff and cold, her hair and back covered with a powdering of new snow, the impression of the faery bells engraved on her cheek were she'd crushed them under her when she fell.

At least her feet had stopped marching, but for a long time she had no idea why, nor did she know why they'd deposited her in this unpromising place. But then the wind had blown away a patch of cloud and had revealed for a moment a line of dark dots on the upper portion of the glacier.

Maggie tried to convince herself that the dots were black mountain sheep, or rock-climbing gnomes, but she knew they weren't. Her feet had brought her, as the faery's spell specified, on the correct path through the forest. Only now, here on this barren mountainside, she was no longer IN the forest. Nor were Moonshine and Colin. That was them, up there, in all that fog and snow and wind. And the wind, cold and snow right here where she was were no laughing matters either. Even if her feet could be persuaded to move, she had no idea how she would survive the cold without her magic.

Her magic still wasn't working. She tried it, and wasted precious moments weeping when she failed. Toads, but she was turning into a crybaby. Lots of people couldn't build a magic fire whenever they wanted, and they didn't cry about it. What did they do to keep warm while climbing glaciers, then? She studied the low-lying moss hugging the chilly earth under her feet, the tiny, cold-looking flowers, the springy hummocks of damp earth covered with a carpet of plants, none of which offered a stem or twig larger than Trickle's little finger. People without magic for fires would never come to places like this to look for fuel, that was for certain. And, undoubtedly, they would have had the sense to wear coats and mittens and boots with the soles still in them if they were to do any ice climbing. But what was *she* to do?

Listen to yourself, she thought angrily, moaning and wringing your hands like a milkmaid with a dry cow. You'll do the best you can, of course, and if that's not good enough you'll simply have to deal with it when you find that out.

So she slipped the silk dress from her pocket on over her woolen one, which kept some of the wind out, and sewed shut the holes in her boot soles with thread pulled from her skirt and a bone needle from her medicine pouch. She padded the insoles of each boot with moss before she slipped them back on, which would make them considerably warmer when her body heat warmed the damp, chilly moss enough that it could act as insulation, the way trappers she knew always claimed it did. Now she wished she hadn't given Trickle the tail. It might have served as a hat, or a muff, or even to warm her neck. She used the material she had torn from her shift for a head wrap, and stuffed her hands into her pockets, along with everything else that wasn't immediately useful, including Trickle's flower. If faery help was no more practical than Trickle's had been so far, she'd manage on her own, thank you just the same.

None of her precautions was very affective, though she was a little warmer than she had been. She labored up the side of the mountain all that day, hearing nothing but the rasp of her own breath and feeling the pounding of her heart in her throat. All she could think of, apart from her own misery, was Granny Brown saying, when she found out as she undoubtedly would, that Maggie had frozen to death, "If I told that girl once I told her a thousand times always to wear her cloak when she goes outdoors."

Still, though her legs were so sore they could hardly carry her and her tongue was soon too dry to wet her lips, she could no more stop now than she could the night before. Though she had no hope of being able to scale the entire glacier dressed as she was, she thought she might at least be able to see from higher on the mountain where her friends were being taken, so that later on she might return with help, if she were still able. Which she doubted, actually. But Colin and Moonshine were up there somewhere, and needed her, and she couldn't stand not doing something, anything, to try to help them.

Every time she almost succeeded in convincing herself that she was being foolish and that the correct course of action would be to return to Little Darlingham and wait for Wizard Raspberry, the wind would die down for a moment, or she'd think she spotted the specks high atop the glacier's tip again, and she'd go on a little farther. The morning snow, which had never melted, but merely sank into a kind of icy crust over the mossy growth on the mountainside, was reinforced in midafternoon by another flurry.

Maggie trudged on a few more paces, but soon the snow was flying faster, and the wind began to swirl it in front of her eyes so that she could no longer see where she was. She sank to her heels, thinking she would wait it out. The edge of the glacier had looked so close, just a moment ago, and she couldn't go much further, anyway, but perhaps when the storm had blown over she'd be able to see something.

It rapidly became evident, however, that the storm had no intention of clearing. Instead, it became steadily worse, until the wind penetrated everything she wore, and the snow piled in drifts all around her.

However clearly she had imagined freezing to death, she hadn't really thought she would. And she couldn't say she fancied it. But before long, she could no longer feel her toes or nose or eyes or fingers and her lips and cheeks stung with each flake that hit them.

Since it didn't seem that the situation could possibly deteriorate any further, she decided to see if any of Trickle's little friends cared for high altitudes. Her left hand had to be persuaded to drift across the front of her body to join her right hand in her skirt pocket on that side, and she had to hold up the silk dress with her teeth while her hands juggled the withered flower stalk between them. The wind threatened to blow the flowers away as soon as she pulled them from her pocket, so she pressed her face against her lap, and thus shielded her hands until she could take the flowers in her teeth. Then she shook the flowers, as a dog would shake an old slipper. If she expected to hear bells, she was disappointed, for she heard nothing but the wind, though she tasted the bitter plant taste of the faery bell stalk where she'd bitten it.

So that was a wasted effort. No faery appeared to stop the snowstorm, or to drop a magic necklace around her neck that would transport her with a wish where ever she wished to go. The faery bells seemed to have been Trickle's demented idea of a joke. It seemed a bad way to die, spending one's last thoughts heaping curses on the head of a wretched little sawed-off water sprite. But, bad way to die or not, Maggie's anger heated her up enough that she remained alive until help came.

Though she didn't see it at first, and when she did, she almost fled from it, failing to recognize it as such.

It could have been a tall drift of snow blowing towards her, except that it was blowing the wrong way. It should have been blowing to the side and down off the mountain with the rest of the snow, but instead it circled her from above, and blew up at her. That was when she saw that it wasn't made of flakes but of shaggy white fur which separated into arms and legs extending from a vast trunk, and topped with a face so broad and brushy with beard and hair it appeared to be an animal. Its gait as it closed in on her was strange and tottering, and its face rose far, far above her. It was taller than any man she'd ever seen, except perhaps the King, though it was smaller than the average giant. She crouched down into herself, and decided her best bet might be to roll up into a ball and snowball down the hill. Even if she broke her neck, it might be better than what the thing had in store for her.

But the thing stood squarely in front of her now, blocking any chance she would have to roll. It opened its yawning maw, and through the raging wind she could make out its words quite plainly.

"You the young party what rang for assistance?"

She nodded dazedly, and the bells wobbled in her teeth again. She spat the flowers out, and jammed them back into her pocket with her frozen fingers. That was all she had time to do before the thing scooped her up from the center of the drift that had been building around her. Being held like that by the creature wasn't at all unpleasant—it was rather like being wrapped in a warm, pulsing fur coat.

"We'll just thaw you out a bit, Miss," it said. "And you can tell me just who you are, how you come to be on my mountain, and how you happen to have the bells on yer person."

She could detect nothing really sinister about his tone, and nothing even disrespectful about the grip in which he held and warmed her, enveloping at once her frozen face and hands and feet, which were already beginning to tingle again with life. Still, there was something very stiff and guarded about his tone which made her uncomfortable.

"At least you know WHAT I am," she said. "Which is more than I can say for you."

He sauntered up the mountain with her in his big fuzzy arms, his tone conversational, now, as if he were out for his constitutional on a warm, sunny day instead of in the middle of a blizzard which made Maggie feel as if they were being stirred into the middle of a rice pudding. "Now, Miss, we mustn't ask personal questions, must we, now? Goodness knows I've already put myself out for you quite enough. I'd just about run down a grizzly for me supper when I heard you tinklin' them little bells, and I ask you, did *I* hesitate to answer *you*?"

"But why DID you answer me?" she asked, mumbling into his fur and having to spit some out before she could clarify her questions. "I mean, why did YOU answer me? You're not a faery—are you?"

Instead of answering immediately, he paused. By twisting slightly, Maggie could peek out over the crook of one of his furry elbows. She immediately wished she hadn't. All around, the snow still swirled as madly as ever, so that she could see nothing in front of her or on either side.

But directly in front of them, where her captor/rescuer's toes should have been, the snow fell, and fell, and kept on falling, straight past them, feathering its way eternally down into a deep, gaping, blue-walled crevasse slicing halfway into the mountain's core.

She was trying to judge how far that might be, and to think why the creature had paused just here, above all this incredibly sharp blue ice, when he shifted his weight, tightened his grip on her, and jumped.

And landed, lightly as a bird. When she was quite sure she was alive, Maggie risked another peek, and saw that they had landed on the crevasse floor. Surrounding them, tiers of ice rose in sheer walls, fissured now and then with long deep cracks. In front of them, one such crack split the wall, broad enough for a man to walk through at the base, narrowing to an infinitesimal crack as far above their heads as she could see. In two strides, the creature bundled her into this fissure and deposited her on a pile of furs.

The cave was oddly cozy; with its sapphire walls protecting them from the blanketing snow and surging winds whining outside, it practically invited her to give in to her weariness and nap among the thickly strewn multicolored furs. But the creature bustled around at the back of the cave, and interrupted her just as she was enjoying a nice drowsy reverie, trying to count the waves of snow as they rippled down in front of the den's entrance.

"Here, Miss. Have a spot of herb tea," the monster said, holding a goblet of faceted ice to her mouth, and bracing her head with one paw as if he meant to force the stuff down her throat.

"Wait. What is this?" she asked, rousing.

"Just as I said. Herb tea. Gathered down below by me friends. Be a nice lass, now, and drink it down quickly, won't you, before it melts me goblet?"

Though she was still suspicious, she noted that the goblet was indeed melting, diluting and cooling the tangy-smelling drink it contained. Oh well, if he was going to do away with her, she supposed the creature could have done it in other ways besides poisoning her long before now. She'd have frozen without his help. She drank—and gagged, sure that she had after all been poisoned. The stuff tasted sulfurous.

"Wh-what kind of herbs did you say those were?" she asked.

"Just the usual kind," he said. "The secret ingredient is the water. There's a hot spring seeping up in back of this fissure. Gives it that special taste—supposed to be very healthful, I'm told. Seems to have had a good effect on you, anyway. You're much redder now. That's a good sign on you furless ones, ain't it? Even faeries gets redder when they drink me tea. I keeps it special for 'em. They supply the herbs, and I supplies the water."

"Aha," she said, eager to change the subject so she wouldn't be tempted to tell him what she really thought of his tea. "So you don't claim to be a faery then, even though you answered the bells?"

"Maybe I do and maybe I don't," he said, sinking down onto the furs across from her and rubbing his palms against his knees. She could see now that he did have hands—very furry ones, but hands, nevertheless, not paws. "I'm who you get if you go ringing for supernatural assistance in these parts, at any rate. Actually, I suppose you might say I am a sort of faery. You smooth folk seem to have the idea that ALL faeries are simple sorts with nothing to do but dance about in dear little circles all the time. Or else be like the big 'uns who mix with YOUR people. But some of us are a bit different, and we have our responsibilities too, which we take very seriously, I can tell you. Like little Trickle, for instance, fine little thing, does a first-class job of guardin' a MOST strategic bit of moisture. From the tone of your bell, I'd say it was she who sent you t'me. Am I right?"

Maggie nodded, continuing to stare in fascination at him. His fur masked most of his outline, but she kept feeling as if there were something vaguely out of kilter with the way he looked.

He stared at her in almost the same way, but continued to talk. His voice was deep and soothing and drowned out the wind. "Trickle's just one example of a faery doin' a fine job looking after her bit of country. There's them as guards the trees, too, yer

250

nymphs and dryads and such, but they're not overly dependable. There's a couple of them down yonder on the lower slopes, watchin' over the foothills. Then there's dwarves. Generally it's dwarves for the high country, where there's likely to be mines, and gnomes in the fields and woods and such. I'm what you gets in the glaciers.''

Maggie shook her head, wonderingly. "I've never seen the like of you before, or heard of anyone like you."

"Pardon me for being blunt, Miss," he replied. "But unless you're a young lady of rather broad experience, you can see how unlikely it might be that you would have. It's my job to keep your sort of person from frequenting glaciers, you might say.''

"Are you some kind of talking bear?" she asked. Talking bears *were* within her experience. One of her close friends was a former enchanted bear.

"I should say not." He held out his hands for inspection. Each contained ten fingers, the undersides soft and padded like feet, though smoother. Each digit was six-jointed, except the thumb, which had only four joints. Sharp claws curved from each fingertip. He next raised a meat-platter-sized foot, and she saw what had bothered her about him. It was on backwards. His toes pointed behind, and his heel pointed forward. It looked painful.

He grinned through a mouthful of what looked like icicles. "Clever way to throw you people off one's track, eh? Inherited me drift-hoppers from me great-great-great-great-gran, who was a snow faery, come to these lands as an immigrant durin' the great Purges in Chai-yong. Aristocrat, she was, my gran. Guarded the royal sacred mountain. But that didn't stop them smoothies from tryin' t' purge 'er.''

"Chai-yong?" Maggie was puzzled. She'd heard the name only in connection with certain luxury items, and hadn't heard it at all recently. "I didn't know they even HAD faeries in Chai-yong.''

"Don't suppose they did after them purges," he said. "Say, do you want to hear this or don't you?"

She nodded, chastened.

"It was me grandam's job to keep the snows free of you pesky smoothies by luring any man foolish enough to intrude on 'er mountain to 'is death. She'd appear to him all pale and pretty, and smile at him friendly-like, you know, then throw him off the track with her backward feet trick. Poor devil would freeze to death chasin' around in circles. Work every time, these drift-hoppers do.'' He slapped his knee with a fur muted plop, and laughed a volcanic laugh. "You should see 'em tryin' to figure out if I'm watching 'em or not. Drives 'em mad, it does."

"Who? Drives who mad?"

"The blokes comes up with the nymph. Mind you, I don't dally with 'em while she's about—she's a bit queer in the head, takin' up with mortals and the like, but the big 'uns are like that, and she *is* one of us, after all. But they knows I watch, and just let one of 'em get out of hand, and try to find the treasure they thinks I'm hiding."

"Are you?"

He grinned another icicle grin and asked, "Is that why you called me, Miss? To find me treasure?"

"No, sir," she said emphatically. "The last thing I want or need is a treasure. But if you have a horse—or better yet, some wings, perhaps?"

He laughed again and a shower of snow shook loose from an overhead ledge and slid to the floor, making a shining pile on the gray fur covering her feet.

"If I had me a horse, I'd eat it, and you can see I haven't got wings. But that little posey you tinkled entitles you to any reasonable help I can give you, compliments of Trickle. Unless I want to be in her bad graces, which I can tell you, I'm no coward, but I do not!" And he laughed again, this time crashing half the roof of his cave down around their ears. He remained unperturbed, however, and simply tented his furry form over Maggie until all the ice which had been shaken loose shattered onto the floor. He was a good host that way, at least.

"Has to watch me sense of humor around here," he confided. "Don't get company too often, and I gets carried away. Get it from me dad's folk, I suppose."

Maggie could tell by the pride in his voice that she wasn't going to get any help out of him, Trickle or no Trickle, until he'd told her all about it. "Who," she asked obligingly, "Were your dad's folk?"

"Frost giants, Miss, frost giants, of course! Can't you tell?" He shook his furry arms and twinkled at her with blue eyes which were, now that she looked at them, very like the King's. "One of the blokes got lost up here one time, chasin' after little grandam, just like they always did. Only she'd never seen the like of 'im before, and took a shine to 'im. He wasn't as furry as me, of course. That all come later. But he was used to the snow and cold, and didn't freeze, just got baffled-like. Once she unbaffled 'im, they sort of got together and started my kind."

"And what, if it's not too rude to ask, *is* your kind?"

"The faeries as knew grandam calls me Yeti, though of course, that was 'er name, not mine. Some calls me the snowman."

"Ah, then I HAVE heard of you," she said, her interest genuinely piqued now. "Trappers tell tales in my father's tavern, sometimes, of abominable snowmen."

"Poo," said the Yeti. "They don't know nothing. There's only me and my two brothers in this whole country, and we does our job and keeps ourselves to ourselves. We think your trappers are pretty abominable too, scarin' away what little game comes up to this high country. The smoothies we have dealings with mostly know us by our tracks, and the ones of 'em that gets away've got no need to call us abominable. Mostly, I hear, they calls us Bigfoot." He looked down again proudly at his upturned heels, then, as if remembering his manners, added, "Me personal name is Sebastian."

"Er—I'm Maggie. Maggie Brown, daughter of Bronwyn, daughter of Maud, daughter of Oonaugh, daughter of Elspat," she added, since Sebastian liked talking about relatives.

"Oh, you're a witch then," he said, impressed by her long matrilineage. "Well, now, why didn't you say so? No wonder little Trickle thinks you're all right. What can I do for you?"

"I thought you'd never ask," she said, and told him about Sally's unicorn-napping activities.

"That's her game, is it? Unicorns, is it? I should have known 'corns wouldn't be around roughnecks like the ones Nasturtium's been keeping company with." He glowered at Maggie and his glower was so fierce that if she were the trembling sort she would have trembled to see it. "You should have told me this sooner, Miss. We're a good day and a half behind 'em now. The only way we can possibly make it up is by taking you through the Needle's Eye."

"Needle's Eye?" It sounded painful to her.

"Aye," he nodded vigorously. "The Eye. It's what we Wee Folk call our secret way through the mountains. She'll have used it, too, and will've taken 'er filthy unicorn baiters with her, she should only turn mortal for it! But she's no descendant of Grandam Yeti for all that, and she doesn't know this old glacier like I does. Come along, girl." And without further discussion, he swept her once more into his high-pile embrace and carried her out of the cave, back out into the whistling wind and blowing snow. With a leap that cost him no more effort than the jump down had, he sprang upwards, landing as softly as a falling leaf on the lip of the crevasse. "Not bad for a bloke with backward feet, eh, Missy?" he asked.

Now that Maggie knew she was literally in good hands, she wasn't afraid to twist her head so that she could see where they were going, though she kept her nose buried in the fur of his forearm, ticklish as it was.

He used a sliding step where the new snow covered the ground, thrusting his heel forward like a skate. Once beyond the level snowfield, he used the small blue cracks in the glacier as stair steps, climbing easily with his feet practically at right angles to each other. He never needed to resort to handholds. On one side, Maggie found herself pressed against hard blue ice, while on the other side she cuddled against Sebastian. The Bigfoot romped up the mountainside more easily than Granny Brown's cat climbed trees. Maggie's weight didn't seem to encumber him. Listening to the deep bass beat of his great heart, she began to feel like a baby being rocked to sleep. In fact, she had to jerk herself awake when he spoke to her again.

"Here we are, Missy. You'll want to remember this to tell your grandchildren, I expect. It's not many smoothies come this way."

Maggie looked. The Needle's Eye was a verticle slit in the glacier, a fissure much like the one in which Sebastian camped. Only this one was perhaps a furlong thick from their side of the peak to the other. Looking around and down, she saw that where they had scaled the steepest, most direct access to the opening, a narrow trail wound up the mountain, a longer, tortuous path which Sally Forth and her men must have used.

The snowstorm raged on below them, and the wind moaned through the Eye, though no snow fell near them. The sun looked like a snowball frozen fast to the sky, and cast a deep plum shadow where the pinnacle shaded them.

Sebastian set her down and gave her a gentle shove. "You're on your own here, Missy. I can barely make it through with my skin intact as it is, much less carrying you."

She slid carefully ahead of him, bracing herself against the walls to keep her feet from sliding out from under her. She skated through as quickly as she could go, for it was very cold inside the tunnel. Once they were outside again, Sebastian hugged her back up into his dense fur.

The glacier was largest on this side of the mountain, and it took him hours to carry her down it. By the time he was halfway down, and her nose and fingers had again thawed, the sun was dying in the sky. All around them, a vast panorama of mountains and valleys layered itself dark purple in the chasms, then indigo, violet, and pale pink on the mountain's snowy peaks, finally turning pale yellow where the range met the last of the sunlit sky, then deepening again as the light died above into another range of pinks and purples, in bands as straight and striped as the threads on Maggie's loom.

All of this changed and darkened as Sebastian loped easily down the icy slopes. When he had reached the edge of the ice, where it was dirty and dark and butted against the mountain's soil, he let her down. At the foot of the peak a broad silver ribbon of river ran, and two ranges distant from them she saw the sea. Glinting randomly among the distant ridges, other glaciers shone like pink jewels, flirting back the dying light from their surfaces.

A babbling rose to meet them, and Maggie started, straining her eyes to see where it came from. A fairly large band of people moved around the single bright point of a campfire, like insects around a candle. "They don't seem to mind who hears them, do they?" she remarked to Sebastian.

"Oh, that ain't them, Missy. You're new to Blabbermouth country, I see. That's the river you're hearing. Enchanted, you know. Used to be a mighty witch lived here in the old days. She was born in a little village you can't see from here, but it sits over underneath the ledge of Worm's Roost Maze—that scarred-looking bit of ice just opposite us. You see it?"

Maggie followed his fuzzy finger to the glacier scored with a maze of curlicues and zigzags on the peak directly opposite them. Aha! Now they were getting someplace. That had to be the cliff castle the wizard had mentioned, there, carved into the ice just beneath the maze formation. She could barely make out the towers.

"The witch was a wretched sort of woman," Sebastian continued his story. "Drove all the people away from their village. They left just to be rid of 'er. I can tell you, she didn't care for that at all. One of the worst things about her was that she liked to talk all the time, but she didn't like to talk to herself. So she spelled the river so it would babble all the time, and never say anything, just like the village women she was lonesome for. Her spell worked so good not even she could stand it, and pretty soon she threw herself into the river and drowned, which ought to have shut the Blabbermouth up, if it had been a normal river and a normal spell, but it wasn't, you see, so it didn't. Some faeries claim the old girl's in there yet, and will tell you anything in the world if you want to wait that long, but I sometimes think them little 'uns gets muddled from all that thick mucky air they breathe down yonder. Anyway, Missy, this is as far as I can take you. I don't care for that dirty sort of ground, you know. Burns my feet.''

Maggie nodded and mumbled and started striding down the mountain, for she had already spotted the unicorns and was impatient to be off.

"Softly, Missy," the snowman cautioned. "Softly."

She turned, flushed. "I beg your pardon. I haven't even thanked you, and you've been very kind." Her hands scrabbled restlessly in her pockets as she sought the words to show her appreciation, and her right hand found the faery bells, which it drew forth. She looked at it as she would look at a broken pot, though for all the abuse the flowers had taken, the blooms were still bright and their petals intact, no doubt due to the influence of the magic. "I don't suppose these would signal one of your brothers over on that other glacier, should I happen to get into a tight spot over there?"

Sebastian shook his head until the fur flew. "Oh, no, Missy. No indeed, no. Don't you go getting stuck over there on any account. None of my kind needs to guard that place. There's a worm, you know. Big fellow, steamy breath that'll melt you in a puff, and all that. And definitely not a faery. No, Missy, don't you go tanglin' with no worm. None of our sort hereabouts—the neighborhood's much too noisy, what with the river and all. I'm afraid your flowers won't do you much good from now on. Trickle probably only meant you to get as far as me with them anyway—it's our signal, like, when she comes to call, she always brings a spray along to tinkle and to brighten up me lair. They're the only thing I like about down below I can't get up on me glacier.''

Knowing a hint when she heard one, Maggie held the flower stalk out to him. "In that case, I'd be pleased if you'd accept these. They're a bit bedraggled, but still colorful. Take them, please, and thank you."

Sebastian accepted them tenderly, twining them in the fur above his ear, lending himself a rakish and rather tropical air.

"You're very welcome, Missy, I'm sure," he said, and in three giant upward steps blended with the ice so well that she could no longer see him.

CHAPTER 12

Rusty crouched under the bridge, where they'd never look for her, and leafed through the heavy alchemy tome balanced on her knees. The spell she needed to combat her mother had to be in there somewhere.

Any spell would do, really, as long as it incapacitated the old harpy. The ogress had gone too far this time. Entirely too far. Bad enough that Rusty had had to fetch and carry all night long two nights in a row for that ignoble Prince, who was only faking, anyway, while Lily Pearl and he drooled over each other and Mother and Leofwin discussed family lines. Daisy Esmeralda had shown unusually good sense, for her, and had fled back into the woods the moment she saw their tower filled with strange men.

The rescue party had left soon after they arrived, which was a pity, since their stories were much more interesting than the Prince's. Rusty was absolutely sure Leofwin had made up all the tales he told about slaying several bandits before they got him and defeating two or three evil wizards in the bargain.

The water slipped through the bridge's shadow, swaying the cattails near the bank. Rusty concentrated on the soothing gurgle to block out the sound of her mother and sister calling her. They wanted her to leave with them. It had taken Mother and Lily Pearl only a single day and night to break down the Prince, who didn't seem to mind being broken down at all. He'd readily believed Mother's usual braggadocio about Lily Pearl being a princess, especially after the old ogress had had Lily dig out her father's signet ring. Her Imperial Pale and Wanness always wore that silly thing on a ribbon around her neck. Leofwin had appeared almost as interested in the ring as he was in the show she gave him digging the ring out of her bodice.

"Ruby Rooooo-oo-sse!" Belburga's flat, nasal voice, immediately overhead, startled Rusty out of her reverie. Footsteps prowled across the bridge, then back again; each thump echoed in the pulse pounding in Rusty's ears. Her palms sweated so that she had to wipe them off to keep from smearing the ink in her book. She would NOT go live in some other country with them, where her father would never find her. She would NOT leave without telling him. It wasn't fair of them to expect her to, and

257

she wasn't about to do it. Besides, Leofwin had bragged that magic wasn't allowed in *his* country, and how could she ever get to be an alchemist if she went somewhere as backward as that?

"Come along, Ruby Rose, dear," her mother chirped overhead again, in her falsest sweet voice. "You must hurry now. Your sisters and I are all packed. We wouldn't like to leave you behind."

Hah! There was nothing the old bag would like better. She knew very well how her second daughter felt about her and privately, Rusty was sure, felt the same, though she always kept up the illusion of being the doting mother for anyone who came within shouting distance. Rusty thought she probably kept up the act because she couldn't be sure which of the girls would bag the richest husband. Mother was too clever not to have learned from the examples of certain legendary mothers who had thrown out their least-liked offspring, only to have the girls immediately snatched up by eagerly waiting kings and princes.

They called her for a few hours longer, never thinking to look under the bridge. This was the first time she had stirred from her room for any longer than necessary in months, and they had no idea where to look. Besides, neither of them was likely to soil herself crawling about on hands and knees and peering under bridges. Only Daisy Esmeralda might think of doing that, and she was probably saying farewell to the chickens or something.

So Rusty stayed there all afternoon while they called, tuning them out, searching her book for a spell to convince them to change their minds, and not finding one. Perhaps by the time she had to come out for dinner, the Prince would decide he didn't like Lily after all, or Mother would decide she didn't like the Prince.

But then she heard her mother's voice again, and her footsteps on the bridge, as if she were calling out into the woods. "Come along now, dear. We're leaving! It'll be dusk soon and you know Mother always travels best after dark! Ruby Rose? You hear me now? Come at once. We'll leave you, you wretched imp! I swear we will! I won't let you spoil my ch—your sister's chance for a good marriage!"

Even for a good marriage, Mama was in an uncommon hurry to leave. Why so sudden, and in the middle of the night? Even if Mother was nocturnal, neither Lily nor Daisy were, and the prince didn't seem to be either. Could all this haste have to do with that strange-looking visitor Mother had entertained, the one Father and the witch said had something to do with unicorns and bandits? Rusty suspected strongly that her mother had gotten involved in something really dirty this time and was trying to climb out of it on Lily Pearl's snow white back, and Rusty had no intention of helping her do it.

Still, she was surprised to hear the horses, evidently ordered from the village, clatter across the bridge overhead just before dusk, spattering dirt and rock into the pages of her book and sprinkling little piles of dirt onto her hair and dress.

But she was totally unprepared for the shock she felt when the horses clattered, now heavily laden, back across the bridge. Her mother's voice shrilly called out directions and admonitions, but did not call for her again, and all of Lily Pearl's remarks were addressed to the Prince.

Rusty tried to scramble out from under the bridge without tearing her dress or losing her book, but she couldn't move quickly enough to pop out of her hiding place before her family and the prince had crossed the meadow at an angle and were headed into the woods to the southwest. She ran onto the bridge and stood, staring into the woods as the last horse's tail disappeared and the small voice of her little sister floated tearfully back on the wind, "Fare thee well, Goody Chicken. Farewell, Goody Cow. Farewell, sweet little birdies. . . . 'bye, Ruby."

After a three-day hop, Wizard Raspberry changed back into a wizard, folded his bunny costume into his trick pocket, and knocked on Castle Rowan's great outer gate. And waited. And waited.

He hooted and halloed, but no guards challenged him and no servants greeted him. And even in his rabbit guise he couldn't hop high enough to leap the walls. Weary and worried, he sat down in front of the gate and watched the moor grass wave and the birds sail over the denuded plains surrounding the castle while he tried to think what to do and waited for his ears and nose to stop twitching. The only problem with the rabbit guise was that it tended to make him too flighty to think properly, so he purposely tried not to think, concentrating instead on relaxing from his journey, and letting his eyes and mind wander.

The plains around the castle were surrounded by the famed forest of rowan trees, which grew in profusion only in this spot, the ancestral home of King Roari Rowan, hereditary Border Lord. Beyond the trees, to the north and east, the ice-studded, cave-riddled mountains thrust into the sky, walling off Argonia from invasion from the north and east. These were the mountains Rowan had patroled, and which the men who should have been in this castle should have been patroling.

But they weren't here, and he doubted they were patroling either. His knocks on the great gate rang hollow, echoing deep and lonely around the circular keep before returning emptily to him. He supposed he'd have to go looking for someone when he was rested, but right now he was too tired for even another tiny hop.

So he watched the birds dipping over the moors awhile longer, enjoying, as he always did, their carefree diving as they glided, soaring above the treetops to return to the distant crags. Riding the wind, catching the currents, swooping, sailing, calling, breathing bright vermilion flames. Breathing *what*?

Raspberry got clumsily to his feet, which had fallen asleep, and scanned the mountains and the woods again. The day was gray and dreary, pregnant with unshed rain, and he had been watching only general movements of the fauna in the surrounding countryside. But that was definitely a flash he'd seen, definitely coming from a flying form.

And . . . yes. The form was red. Grimley the dragon, out hunting, no doubt, flaming up to have a better look at the topography on this hazy day. Raspberry waved both hands. Though the dragon didn't seem to see him, the creature nevertheless swooped out of the forest and made a great circle around the castle.

Raspberry hollered, in the elfin pan-tongue, the one all beasts could understand, and Grimley stopped, almost falling out of the sky, backflapped hurriedly, and flew over to investigate, landing on tippy-claw atop the crenelations of the round stone gate tower.

"Dragon Grimley," the wizard panted, exhausted from his leaping and shouting, not to mention all the hopping he'd done earlier, "Am I glad to see you!"

"What's cookin', hot shot?" the dragon asked, amiably enough. "Say, you haven't seen any game down here, have you? There's s'posed to be a herd of cattle for me and the missus, but I haven't found 'em. The missus is due to hatch any time now, and she can't keep her mind on it proper-like when she's hungry, now can she?"

Raspberry said he supposed not, and tried to tell Grimley of the King's plight, but to his chagrin the dragon was unsympathetic.

"He'll keep till my son's hatched, hot shot. The agreement was he kept us a herd, and we provide him with a dragon's-eye view of the country. *I* don't see a herd, do you?"

Raspberry had to admit he didn't.

"Well then, just cool your heels here for awhile, while I hunt up some meat before Grizel takes a bite out of me."

Raspberry did the only sensible thing to do when such a large, determined dragon suggested that he cool his heels. He waited.

"We're almost there!" Sally shouted to the men when they had eaten. She shouted not because the men were making any more noise than usual, and certainly not because of the zombies or the unicorns, but because of the river.

True to its name, the sluggish, mud-brown Blabbermouth babbled loudly and unceasingly, allowing no one to be heard above it without effort. "Now that can't be true, says I, oh no, that will never do at all and then he says to me, he goes, lookit here, if you didn't take on so about every little thing but I can tell you I was having none of that, and *I* goes . . ." The raucous river sounded rather like the chatter of the King's courtiers, Colin thought, allowing for certain lapses in diction.

Sally valiantly raised her voice several decibels higher than the river, and most of her men strained with unbanditlike courtesy to hear her. "Always at times like this," she screamed, "I feel it lightens our loads—"

"WHAT?!" demanded a few on the outer fringes, reluctant to miss the message.

"LIGHTENS. OUR. LOADS." Sally obligingly screamed louder. "LIGHTENS OUR LOADS AND QUICKENS OUR STEP TO RECALL THE HISTORY OF OUR GALLANT—"

"COME AGAIN?"

"OUR GALLANT MOVEMENT. THEREFORE I WOULD HAVE YOU DRAW ASIDE WITH ME, AT THIS TIME, SO I MAY SPEAK WITH YOU, MY BROTHERS-IN-ARMS, OF OUR GOALS IN OUR GLORIOUS REVOLUTION."

"WHAT WAS THAT?"

"OUR GLORIOUS REV—COME ON." And with a graceful sweeping arc of her shapely arm, the nymph led them as far back up the mountain and away from the river's babbling as she could go. Primrose and Wulfric, still in wolf form, bounded after her, each claiming one of the nymph's knees for a chin rest when she had seated herself.

Colin saw her point imperiously, and one of the bandits loosened the noose binding him to the zombies and shoved him forward. "She wants you to come too, songbird," the bandit snarled, and grabbing the ropes binding Colin's wrists dragged him up the hill.

Sally smiled a polite, social smile to the assembled ruffians.

"I know you are all impatient to be at our stronghold, as am I, and I regret the necessity of pitching our camp beside this noisy river. But unlike myself, our brother, Wulfric, and the unicorns, you men, and certainly our Master's new servants, would endanger yourselves if you tried to cross the river at night—"

"We know that, Sal," said Colin's escort.

Sally's voice was filled with emotion as she began speaking. In the deep shadows from the distant campfire beyond and the soft wash of moonlight from above, the planes and hollows of her face took on mysterious significance. Her voice was all the more effective because they had to listen carefully to hear her when it dropped into its lowest registers, though when she spoke excitedly it fairly sang across the night, cutting through the riverine rattling as if the Blabbermouth were an ordinary stream.

Pent-up tears glittered in her eyes, all the more starlike because there were no stars in this cloud-shrouded night to compete. Her hands flew like nightbirds illustrating her points, which were, as far as Colin could tell, excellently dramatized illogical poppycock. The men around him didn't share his views, however. Watching their faces as they lapped up her oratory was enough to make his skin crawl in three different directions.

"Is she like this often?" he whispered to the bandit beside him.

"Oh, no. Better most times. We generally does this every night, when we're all together and Sal ain't out on patrol or chasin' 'round after 'corns. Gives a man a wonderful lift, don't it?"

They were shushed angrily by the men closest to them, but Sally seemed not to notice. Her bosom was heaving with pride as she told how the Dark Pilgrim had come to her stream, recognizing her at once as no mere nymph but as a being of intelligence and resource as well as charm and beauty.

The bandits nodded, listening open-mouthed and rapt, though Colin thought at times one or more of them looked rather puzzled, as if he was trying to remember something. Wulfric whimpered now and then to punctuate the narrative. He looked very much as if he'd like to howl.

"Our great leader explained to me," Sally continued, "that it was my duty, and even my holy destiny, to gather you together and lead you in gathering together the tools with which we will purge this land of our oppressors. I was chosen, I, who had been favored above you poor mortals with an inborn knowledge of our land, important friends among faery and mortal, were and even ogre-kind, since my brother husbanded the quasi-ogress, our sister-in-the-cause, Belburga.''

"Tell us again how that ogress was so hot your brother had to turn into a tree to get some rest, Sal," the ruffian next to Colin shouted.

Sally continued with a sweet smile, "My brother will recover in time to take his rightful place in our new regime, I'm sure, for it will be a wonder and a glory, with health, youth and beauty for the righteous, and punishment for the wicked. Our magnificent hand-picked army, of which you, my beloved comrades, are the vanguard, shall be the backbone of a reign whose like has never been seen in the world."

"I beg your pardon, ma'am," Colin said, trying to sound like an eager acolyte. "But what exactly *is* our mission and—please excuse my ignorance, but why do we need a new order?"

Sally regarded him as kindly as if he was a child who had just asked why larks sing and she was his mother. "To replace the OLD order, of course. Because this land is now ruled by a magically endowed few who control the hard working, deserving masses—folk who gain what little they have by personal merit alone." She said it word for word, he was sure, just as she had learned it from her so-called "Dark Pilgrim."

Naturally it didn't take into account that she herself, and the pilgrim too, no doubt, were magic, as were the unicorns, but Colin thought he had best not go into that. It would sound too much as if he were arguing with her, and he was really not in any position to debate anything. Clearly she and all her men were thoroughly convinced by something beyond good sense of the truth of the twaddle she was feeding them.

He looked away, disgusted. For someone who claimed to disdain magic, the Dark Pilgrim was certainly using a lot of it to his advantage. No wonder Sally and the helpless villagers could travel with this bunch of cutthroats unmolested, and no wonder the ruffians cooperated with a scheme that had no visible profit in store for them except the distant promises of "health, youth, and beauty." They were as ensorcelled as the poor villagers. He hated to think what lay in store for the Everclear folk at the bandit stronghold. And for himself, as far as that went. But at least he knew what he was doing, unlike those poor unseeing clods. Look at them. They didn't even close their eyes to sleep, and their breath smelled terrible from their lower jaws hanging slack all the time. Why, only the tricks of the firelight gave them any expression at all—like that one just at the edge, toward the back, the woman in the kerchief who seemed to wink at him.

263

Sally droned on, "Do you, my comrades, remember all that I have told you?"

"Aye," the bandits chorused in a voice as solemn as one of the classes at the minstrel academy being asked to recite all seventy-eight verses of some obscure dirge. "And the Dark Pilgrim met her at the stream and . . ."

Colin, for his part, nodded and smiled as if he understood, and shuddered, and looked back at the zombies. He preferred the honestly idiotic faces of those who were at least visibly bewitched to those of the bandits, who were under the illusion they were thinking for themselves.

He rubbed his eyes, tired, and looked back at the zombies again. Then repeated the process. It actually looked as if one of those will-less beings, the woman he had noticed before, had moved forward, to the edge of the group, just beyond the burly smith. She now occupied the place he was sure had formerly contained the cobbler's wife. Then, very slowly, she raised her head and looked straight at him, and winked.

Moonshine's voice touched his mind, whispering. "Softly, minstrel, if you would not betray her to our enemy's nag. I felt her near even as *you* sat enthralled by that nymph person."

That nymph person was giving the bandits a good-night speech after hearing their lesson, presumably before she tucked each of them in.

"Sing them a lullabye," Maggie's thought came to him through Moonshine. "They'll never doze off by themselves with this stupid river carrying on all night."

"I know just the one!" Colin answered, relieved both that she was still in one piece and that she had arrived to rescue them. "I'll sing it as soon as Sally's done talking. Then you can have your troops spring out of where ever it is that you've concealed them and capture this whole verminous lot, right?"

"Not exactly," she said. "Something like that."

"You mean you're going to try to get us out of here using your magic alone?"

Maggie hedged for a moment. "Well, YOUR magic, actually. Mine seems to be—er—malfunctioning. If you'll just do as I say and sing them to sleep, instead of asking so many questions, I'll get you loose and we can escape."

"What do you mean, 'malfunctioning'?" he asked, so upset by the implications that he failed to notice Wulfric, rising from Sally's lap and shaking himself, wandering off to sniff out some rock or tree upon which he could leave his lupine calling card. "Are you mad? Without magic you're nothing but a regular girl, and this is no place, I can tell you, for regular girls. Don't you consider it troublesome enough that Sally and her little band have Moonshine and me? Did you get so awfully lonesome, or feel so terribly left out that you had to fling yourself into the fray just for company? It's that rescuing business of yours again, isn't it, Maggie? Well, let me tell you, darling Maggie, you bloody well can't rescue anybody if you haven't got anything to do it with and nowhere to go once you've done it. They could catch us easily. How did you intend that we outrun a whirlwind and a werewolf?''

"They'd be asleep," she said. "And there's Moonshine—"

"Maybe one of them is hard of hearing and wouldn't FALL asleep. Did that ever occur to you? I suppose not. And for your information, *they* have a unicorn too. And *she* knows perfectly well you're no zombie."

"If you'll just kindly shut up and sing your friends to sleep, she'll never even know I'm here," Maggie retorted.

":Master Colin, do as she asked," Moonshine pleaded. "For though she is clever and wise, you alone can help us. I can outrun Primrose, for she is old and more sullied than she ever claimed I was, and I know right is on our side."

"Is it really?" Colin replied. "How comforting."

"Well, really, Colin," Maggie's thoughts interrupted before his own was completed. "I know you think we haven't got a chance, but even if you're angry about it, that's no reason to growl at Moonshine."

"I only said 'how comforting,'" Colin protested. "I didn't growl."

He'd been facing back towards Sally Forth in order to avoid any suspicion in the direction of the zombies, but now he looked back down the hill automatically, puzzled.

On the far side of the dwarf, between Maggie and the mountain, a long, dark, bristling form crouched, the fire reflecting light from the bandages at one end and the fangs at the other. Maggie's memory was indelibly engraved on both ends, the wolf's nose as well as his backside, as Colin very well knew.

Launching himself to his hobbled feet, Colin fumbled in his pocket for his flute and feverishly tried to think of a wolvish lullabye.

It didn't work. He tripped on his hobbles and fell, bowling down the hill and into the wolf, zombies, Maggie and all.

"That's certainly one way to stop a werewolf," Maggie's grim thought came to him as he attempted to disentangle himself. His legs were scissored across the dwarf's chest, his arms outflung, pushing Maggie into the oblivious baker's ample lap. Beneath him, panting heavily, lay the wolf, knocked breathless when Colin's head had driven into his belly.

"How very rude!" exclaimed Sally Forth, who had dumped Primrose to the ground and whirlwinded herself down the slope to investigate the disturbance. "I gave this whole talk this evening, under these adverse conditions, particularly for your benefit, minstrel, and this is how—"

"Uppity, are we," babbled the river, "I'll have that out of you soon enough says I, and she says..."

"Oooowwwoooo!" Wulfric howled.

"Why, lookit, Sal," said the ruffian who'd been punctuating Sally's speech with his own enthusiastic remarks all evening. He grabbed Maggie's chin in his hand and jerked her face toward the firelight. "Our Wulfric's caught 'imself a live one."

Maggie slapped the man's hands smartly, but, entangled as she was in the baker, she couldn't get enough balance to do him any real harm. He dragged her to her feet, pinioning her arms behind her.

Sally stepped in front of him and studied Maggie's face for a moment, then snatched the kerchief from the tangled brown hair and examined her even more closely. "This is your witch?" the bandit leader asked Colin.

Primrose, who had trotted down the hill behind her, said, "That's the witch, O Maiden. Ugly hussy, isn't she?"

But Sally's face was filled with a kind of pleased surprise. "Why, no, Primrose. How can you say such a thing? She's beautiful. The very image of the Dark Pilgrim."

Wizard Raspberry was glad to see the dragon, Grimley, return. What he was not so pleased to see was the predatory gleam in the eye of the large, dangerous, and very hungry-looking beast. "Any luck?" the wizard asked solicitously.

Grimley settled down on the path in front of the wizard this time, instead of on the castle's ramparts, a position which would block Raspberry's escape, should escape become necessary. "Not so's you could notice it, hot-shot. You seen any likely looking game?"

"Nothing at all," the wizard replied with authentic regret, made even more sincere by the manner in which the dragon eyed him, as if visibly dividing him into steaks, ribs, chops, and loins. "But you have my complete sympathy. I'm hungry myself— so hungry I can quite feel my bones poking through my skin," he emphasized, rubbing his bony knees to illustrate the point.

"Say," he added, changing the subject. "Do you know what I think happened to your cattle?"

"No," the dragon said. "But looks like you're going to tell me. Fire away."

"I've been thinking about it, and I'll wager those brigands the King is going after dispersed his men and took all of your cattle for themselves. Doesn't that make you want to help the King?"

"Makes me hungry, is what it does," Grimley said, being a single-minded creature who never allowed himself to be distracted by emotionally laden side issues. "Never fear, if you're right, I'll remember them blokes for stealing from me. But meanwhile, my missus needs her nourishment, and I can't go too far afield to fetch it, neither."

"If only I knew where there was a pleasant stream, I'd be glad to catch us some fish for supper, but I don't suppose—"

"Fish!" The dragon puffed a small sooty cloud of gray smoke to show what he thought of the idea. "Fish is no kind of food for a dragon. Do you suppose I'd be flying my wings off looking for real game if the missus would eat fish? The south fork of the Blabbermouth runs just north of here, and it's packed with the puny-scaled things, but a hatching dragon deserves nothing but the best—"

"Oh, I quite agree!" said Raspberry quickly. Grimley was putting on a head of steam now, his scales glowing deeper red than usual with an inner light and the smoke he was involuntarily belching into the wizard's face caused Raspberry to cough. Haste was definitely in order. "What if the fish don't look or taste like fish? It's very nourishing food, you know, makes the er—scales shiny, I'm told. Do you suppose if Madame Grimley didn't know, since there's no other food about, I mean—"

"Didn't know? Fish not taste like fish? What kinda smoke-screen you tryin' to throw up on me, hotshot?"

"It's no smokescreen, noble dragon. It's a little something I just happen to be able to do as a little fringe benefit to being a master of disguise. If you'll show me to this river, I'll be happy to give you a free demonstration."

Grimley bared his flagon-sized conical teeth in a draconian grin. "Sure thing, hot shot. Climb aboard. I'm game if you are, heh heh."

"It's Uncle Fearchar," Maggie said. "The Dark Pilgrim she keeps talking about is Uncle Fearchar."

Morning had come, and the bandits were breaking camp. Between the river's incessant yammering and the torrential rains

267

which had started around midnight, everyone had had the worst possible night. Colin and Maggie were tied close together, in front of the zombies, but Sally, greatly impressed by Maggie's resemblance to the leader of the Cause, had ordered that neither witch nor minstrel were to be molested. The Dark Pilgrim would decide their fate.

Maggie shivered in her sodden clothing. Her wet hair was plastered to her skull. She leaned against Colin, and they squished together from shoulder to hip. "I don't suppose we can hope Uncle remembers me with affection, can we?" she asked wearily.

"N-n-na-naCHOO! No," he replied, fighting down another sneeze. "I don't suppose we can." The wretched weather and lack of sleep were finally catching up with him. He'd been coughing and sneezing most of the night.

"*I* shall save us, never fear," Moonshine said. "Primrose tells me this uncle of Maggie's wishes me to perform a unicornly task for him. Well, then, I shall simply refuse to do it, no matter what, until he frees you both."

"Somehow, darling, I don't think you get to choose," Maggie said. "But thanks for the thought."

"If we get far enough from the river today, I'll sing them to sleep if I have to ya-ya-yaCH—" Colin's nose twitched and he said "yodel" quickly, and finished the sneeze.

But even if Sally had not decided to follow the banks of the Blabbermouth without deviation, Colin couldn't have carried out his plan. The night of coughing left his throat dry and sore and his chest aching from the constant racking. His boots got wet when they forded the river, adding to his discomfort. None of them got any chance to dry out. Streaks of cold gray rain flogged them all the way across the valley.

Maggie looked anxiously for the ice-bound castle she had seen from the top of the glacier, but with the sky so low and the foothills swelling up in the distance, she could see no trace of it. No one spoke all that day, and as the dim daylight faded into a deeper gray, many of the zombies and one or two of the bandits were coughing and sneezing too.

At the next bend in the river they forded again, and she saw the town. At first she thought that it, and not the castle, must be their destination, but then she saw that rain poured inside several of the buildings, which were without roofs, washing gutted interiors. This must be the town Sebastian had mentioned, the one everybody left because of the witch. As they passed through, brigands swarmed out of the walls like roaches, falling in beside and around them.

"Puny-lookin' lot you 'ave there, mum," said one of these newcomers to Sally Forth. "And women? What's this revolution comin' to?"

"You forget yourself, Sergeant," she said, and puffed out her chest in what Maggie thought was a very obvious way to remind him she was a woman.

They passed through the town, and climbed a path leading up and over a tall, brush-covered slope. Rounding this hill, Maggie looked up. She was not too surprised to see the icy underpinnings of the cliff castle.

"All right then, men," Sally said briskly. "Attend to the unicorns." She turned to Primrose, who had been following her like a lap dog, and suddenly flung the strap of her hunting horn around the unicorn's neck. The new arrivals quickly added their ropes to the strap.

Primrose, firmly bound in no time, was too amazed to buck. "Maiden, what is this?"

"It's for your own good, my love. You've got to be hauled up—there," she pointed. "And the ropes are necessary."

"But I don't WANT to go up there," the unicorn whinnied. "I loathe high places! Can't I wait for you here? Surely if your leader requires a boon from me, he can have the common decency to come down here to get it!"

"She's going to be a problem," Sally told the men coldly. "Take her first, then the other, and pen them in the usual place. As for these," she indicated the villagers, "I saw a house with part of a roof on it, just this side of the river. Keep them there until I've spoken with the Dark Pilgrim about his plans for them. Just now," she said, turning in a quick circle, "I think I shall blow up and apprise the Dark Pilgrim of the arrival of his visiting relative. He may wish to prepare a special reception for her."

Business was just picking up for the evening at the Inn of the Scalded Cat. The lamps were lit, sending a cozy glow through the smokey haze emanating from the customers' pipes. Giles Thatcher and old Shearer nodded and commented from time to time, as Hillman regaled their friends with tales of their recent adventures. The innkeeper, Brewer, smiled and slid full flagons back across the bar to his wife, who delivered them to his customers. Even though his little jaunt to Everclear had cost him a day's business, he was making up for it now. Every herder, farmer, and hunter with a spare moment's time came to the inn for a drop, and to hear the story of the deserted village and the injured Prince first hand.

The inn was so bustling and noisy, in fact, that it was some time before anyone noticed the forlorn figure standing in the doorway, clutching what looked like a bowl and a book. It was Goodwife Brewer who spotted her. "Shoo, child. Go 'way. This is no place for little girls," she admonished, flapping her hands at the girl as she would at one of her own children.

"I beg your pardon, my good woman," the girl said, "You cannot talk to me in that fashion. I am the daughter of the ogress Belburga and the mighty Wizard Raspberry, and am a powerful alchemist in my own right. I wish to purchase a meal from you, and a horse, so that I may seek my father at Castle Rowan."

"Well, my word," Goody Brewer said, squinting at her. "I believe—why, yes, you ARE the Dame's—middle child, isn't it? The red one? What was the name?"

"Rusty," the girl said promptly.

"Ah, yes. Rusty it was. Though that doesn't sound quite right, but never mind. Now then, Rusty, you just run along home to your own mama before she gets peeved at the likes of me, and have her feed you your supper and put you to bed like a good girl. This isn't a nice place for a young lady like you, a tavern."

"My mother and sisters have left to marry my eldest sister to a prince, and have left no food in MY tower," Rusty informed her coldly, but with a slight trembling of her chin. "I need to purchase food and a horse so that I may join my father. I can pay you handsomely—I'll be happy to barter my magic favors in exchange—"

"Belburga's gone? Are you sure?" But before the girl could answer, the woman called back over her shoulder. "Hey there, lads, what do you think? The child here says Belburga and her girls run off with that Prince fella. Thought you boys said 'e was laid up?"

"Only tired-like, Molly," her husband corrected, calling back to her. "Unicorn water had 'im mostly healed before we ever got back here."

"YOU-nee-corn water?" Goody Brewer asked scornfully, as if she'd never heard of such a thing.

"Aye. Of course, unicorn water, woman! Are you so ignorant you don't know about THAT?"

"Of course, I know, but—"

"Bring the lass indoors, Molly," Hillman hollered. He was

270

anxious for his host and hostess to stop bellowing back and forth at each other so he could continue his story.

"I'd best, at that," Molly Brewer agreed, and looped her arm around Rusty's shoulders. Not particularly to Molly's surprise, the girl was shaking. "We'd best get some bread and cheese into you, dearie, and a wee bit of ale, what?"

"Yes, ma'am," Rusty agreed, eagerness replacing her hauteur. "And then I'll pay you."

"Pooh? A child like you? If the constable hadn't died of gout, he'd close us down for selling to children! I wouldn't hear of it. You sit over there next to Giles and—"

"Why, it's Ruby Rose, Lily Pearl's little sister!" Giles Thatcher exclaimed. "How's your lovely sister, Miss? And the prince?"

"Gone is how," Rusty informed him bitterly, and to her dismay, began to cry, contradicting the image she had been trying to present as an independent but brilliant young alchemist setting out on her own. Sniffling, she told them of her suspicions of her mother's part in a plot against the King, and of her father's journey in rabbit form to Castle Rowan to find help for his Highness, and her mother's subsequent departure at Leofwin's side, with both her sisters. "I didn't want to go," she explained, "So I hid. But she took everything. The only things I have left are this," she held up her book, "and my crucible," she indicated the bronze bowl. "If it hadn't fallen half through a mousehole in the bottom of my cupboard, she would have taken that, too. I'm glad she didn't. I do all my best magic in it, and besides, Daddy gave it to me for my birthday. He said he got it in payment for some magic he did for an important Eastern potentate."

Hillman leaned forward, chest pressing against his big beefy arms.

"You say your dad's at Rowan Castle? 'e'll get no 'elp there, little girl. I served there till six months ago, but me and the other blokes was all discharged. Messenger said 'is 'ighness wanted us to go back to our 'ome towns and keep watch from there."

"Nevertheless, that's where my father's gone. He says the King is in dire peril over at some glacier, and he's going to try to get the King's dragon friend to help him. That's why I need a horse, so I can go to my father's aid," she sniffed, and said very seriously, "If what you say is true, all the more reason why he'll need all the arcane forces at my disposal to help the King."

"I'll go on up there and talk to your father about this meself," Hillman told her. "But arcane forces or none, you're not going along. War's no place for children."

"I'm *not* a child," Rusty said with great dignity, the effect of which was spoiled by the aggressive thrust of her pointed chin. "I'll help whether you like it or not, churl."

"Is that so?" Hillman asked easily. "Then you'd better do some magic, ducks, because that's the only way you're going along."

Rusty set her book down and turned decisively to a random page. Though she had yet to make one single formula come out the way she wanted it to, she wasn't about to let these louts know it. She'd let on that this time was a special case, that usually her magic worked smoothly. As it would, some day— only why not now? She had studied very hard, though the writing and pictures in the book were cramped and faded and sometimes ran off the pages, she knew roughly half of the formulae. They *should* work for her—only they never did. Nevertheless, she moved the crucible from her lap to the table, keeping her eyes tight to the book's page and not watching what she was doing.

The crucible clanged against a flagon, which tipped over into it, spilling brew inside the bronze bowl. Rusty snatched up her precious book before the ale could smear the pages. "Clumsy!" she accused everyone in general.

"I'll say, 'clumsy,'" complained Shearer. "That was good ale."

"Lookit there!" Giles exclaimed. "If that ain't slick! Her bowl's smokin'-like. And her not even touchin' a fire!"

"Humph," said Shearer, still mourning the ale, "Cheap trick. No proper magic in a small thing like that."

Rusty watched gleefully as the smoke dribbled down from the crucible and across the floor. It was not dense smoke, nor particularly impressive, no more interesting in itself than the mist that had covered the stream outside her window every morning of her life. Gradually, it solidified and took on color, and from within it came a deep chuckle.

"'Ere now, what're you laughin' at, Bub?" asked Shearer, addressing the smoke. Everyone else had fallen silent by now, and the chuckling was very obviously not coming from the sort of place one was accustomed to hear emitting chuckling.

"That was SO good!" the voice replied. "And I was dry as a grass fire. Haven't had a proper drink in two hundred years or better! Now then, to settle the tab. To whom do I owe this edifyin' lubrication?"

"Me," Rusty exclaimed, jumping off her bench. "I conjured you forth. You *are* a simulacrum, aren't you?"

The thing in the smoke was still not visibly anything other than a vaguely manlike blob of pastel protoplasm. Abruptly, it rose and leaned towards her. "A simu-what?" it asked, and suddenly gelled into a pirate.

Anyone could see he was a pirate. Though he remained a little misty at the bottom, the red bandana on his head was clear enough, and the peg leg which started at his right knee, and the black patch on his right eye, and the knowing leer on his weather-beaten face.

"A simulacrum," Rusty repeated firmly. One had to be firm with riffraff. Her mother had at least taught her that. "I ordered a simulacrum, not a pirate. If you're not a simulacrum, you'll simply have to leave and send one out."

"Why, blow me down, little lassie, yer tongue's as sharp as me last skipper's and makes as little sense!" He hovered at knee height in the air and beamed down at her as if he'd just given her an enormous vote of approval. "Only thing twas in there," he nodded to the crucible, "was me, and I was dried 'most to dust. Nothin' but yer timely infusion of spirits—tee hee, ain't that somethin'? Spirits for the spirit—nothin' but them spirits coulda revived me. I say, you wouldn't have another wee drop, would you?"

"No!" said Molly Brewer. "She would not. I said the girl's food was free, but I'll not extend free service to ever' guzzlin' golem she dirties up me floor with!"

"Ah, a fine-spirited buxom wench if ever I saw one—twould be revivin' enough to see the likes o' you, me beauty, after all these long lonesome years, if it hadn't been that that wily wazir dried me out in the desert before passin' me pot along. And me a sea-goin' man! Didn't agree with me, all that hot air and sand, I can tell you that, darlin'. Dry as powder I got, dry as bone. But I can see yer a woman of principle and—"

"Oh, well, maybe just one more," Molly relented.

"If you aren't a simulacrum, who are you?" Rusty interrupted impatiently.

"Aye, and what's yer business 'ere, I might ask?" Hillman added. "We has a national 'mergency goin' on at t' present time, and if you're of no use, I'll thank ye t' be on yer way. Don't like vagrants and vagabonds in Little Darlingham, we don't."

"Well now," the pirate said after due consideration enhanced by swallowing in one long gulp the free drink from Molly Brewer. "What I USED to be was a simple sea-farin' man, workin' for an independent import-export merchant whose offices, you might say, were on the high seas."

"Ha!" Rusty said. "You look like a pirate to me." She'd heard pirates described often and in great detail by the bards and minstrels among Lily's suitors.

"Now, now, lassie. I do declare I never saw such a youngster for name callin' as you be. But very well, pirate, if you prefer. I was known as Jehan the Fleet till I lost one of me pins in a—er—dispute me employer 'ad with a business rival over a merger. Same kinda thing as got me inta me pot. THAT happened when me employer went out of business—permanent-like, at the end of a Kaboolian warship. Me mates was killed to a man, but I was tossed into the briny, and fished out by them as put me there in the first place. Ship's master was a mean bastard, a wily wicked wizard—"

"My father is a wizard," Rusty informed him coldly.

"Ah, but is he a Kaboolian wizard? I think not, and oh, they're a different breed of fish altogether, lassie, I can tell you. It was him put me in this 'ere pot and run me all over this country, bringin' me out long enough to tell 'is mates how 'e sunk us, then clappin' me back in again. Got tired of it eventually, 'e did, and sold the pot, which is how I come to end up in yer good company."

"Worthless," Hillman said. "I thought as much. This girl's no more magic than I am. I'm leavin' now, boys, to serve the King. Anyone comin'?"

"Hold on there, soldier," Jehan the formerly Fleet snarled, "Just 'oo is callin' 'oo worthless? So happens as this lass 'ere is me present employer, and under the terms of me contract she gets the standard three wishes. What'll it be, darlin'?"

"Take me—us—to my father at Castle Rowan," she commanded, sweeping her hand to include all of the tavern's patrons. She was sure her father would know what to do with a crowd of people who could help the King, even if she wasn't sure how. And he would think very well of her indeed for being thoughtful enough to bring them along.

"Here now, lass, don't be so 'asty!" Shearer cried. "Some of us mayn't be up to the journey." He hated the idea of parting with his ale, not to mention his bed, with which he had been anticipating a restful reunion after the fruitless two-day trek to Little Darlingham.

Rusty turned her determined little pointy face back to Jehan the Genie. "MAKE them want to," she commanded, "THEN take us."

"That's two wishes," Jehan told her. "But no sooner said than done."

*   *   *

"There's your glacier, King," Gypsy Davey said, pointing out to King Rowan and his party what may or may not have been a solid bit of white among all of the gray and white mist, rain, cloud, snow and ice blanketing both the horizon and the more immediate atmosphere that day.

"Amazing," Sir Cyril Perchingbird said, shaking his head, still unsure of what he saw. "You must have very good eyes. I'd never have spotted it myself."

"Naw, King's man," Davey replied modestly. "Not so good eyes. My mother, she knows this place. When she was little girl, our people come here summers to dance for King Finbar. She knows this valley."

"Ah, I see. That explains it." Perchingbird nodded and looked back through the rain toward where the castle allegedly lurked. He was taking careful mental notes, to enter in the archives when he returned. No minstrel had traveled here that he knew, and the gypsies shared little of their lore with the archives. Princess Pegeen, naturally, knew this place well, but she did not often see fit to mention her physical surroundings in her letters. She had mentioned, however, a magic river. He believed she had said that it talked. And last night, when the gypsies had at last ceased chattering and all were settled out of the rain, inside the wagons, hadn't he heard a sort of low murmuring in the distance, to the north and slightly west?

King Rowan strode back and forth in the rain as if it wasn't there. "Verry well, lads. It looks as if we're to do this thing alone. Our gypsy comrades here will accompany us, with their weapons and horses. The ladies will remain with the wagons at a safe distance."

"We're going in without the dragons, sire?" a general asked.

"We're takin' all the dragons you see round about us now, Warfield. Does that answer your question?"

Sir Cyril thought King Roari cared as little for the decision as his men did, judging from the surliness of his Highness's answer. Sarcasm was not one of Rowan's usual modes of expression. He didn't do it particularly well.

But, of course, the King had good reason to worry. To risk himself with a small party of hand-picked fighting men (and one scholarly observer) armed to the teeth, with war horses and two dragons in attendance, was one thing. To risk himself with what was left of those men after a shipwreck, with twenty-odd footsore, half-drowned sailors and a handful of gypsies who understood fighting over women or gold but did not understand fighting over matters of policy, was quite another. Particularly when there was only one horse for every five men, and a few gypsy daggers among them for weapons.

Their only other assets were the King's sword, Old Gutbuster, and the swords retained through the shipwreck by two other generals. Sir Cyril had placed in his own belt a handy little pen knife, a gift from a smolderingly pretty gypsy girl who had been pleased to tell him all she knew of palm reading, and of his future, which she saw as including a dark, beautiful and mysterious woman—herself.

Xenobia emerged from one of the wagons and stalked across the sodden valley floor to join the group of men. Flinging the fringed edge of her black shawl across her chest so that it covered her as completely as a cloak, she glared at them all defiantly, finally turning to Prince Worthyman.

"You are responsible for my men who die with your King," she said. "They will die. You, you will die also."

"Now, now, Zenobia, old gurrl," the Prince said, giving her a brief sideways bear hug with one strong arm. "I appreciate you worrying about me, but you mustn't carry on so. Bad for morale."

The gypsy whipped herself from his grasp and threw her arms around his neck, kissing him passionately. "Xenobia will not worry, love. They will kill you, then we will kill them. Right?"

Worthyman beamed fondly down at her. "Rrright."

"Now that we've established our rear guard," the King said, nodding to Xenobia's retreating back, "Shall we move out smartly?"

THINGS ARE ALREADY BAD ENOUGH FOR COLIN, MAGGIE, AND MOONSHINE WITHOUT MAKING THIS CHAPTER 13.

CHAPTER 14

Sally Forth threw a rope ladder down from a hole in the narrow ledge running along the castle's eastern side. A guard clanked down it and at the foot of the cliff turned to salute the sergeant, ignoring Wulfric, who was still in wolf form.

"Pilgrim says to send four men up with t' witch and the minstrel, and the rest of you quarter down here for tonight."

Despite the castle's sinister appearance, Maggie was glad she and Colin were going there instead of staying with the bandits in the mostly roofless hovels in the village. Colin's cough was so bad by now that he had difficulty hanging onto the rope ladder. She tried to help him, but the guard ahead of her on the ladder reached down to yank her hair. From below she heard Moonshine's terrified screams as Sally's henchmen, having passed a sling under his belly, prepared to draw him up. Then the feet of the guard above her disappeared through the hole, to be replaced by his hands snatching her off the ladder and dragging her onto the icy ledge.

He waited until Colin and the other guards had joined them, then thrust her before him into a long, dank corridor lit only by smoking, sizzling torches.

"Mother!" she complained, dodging drips from the ceiling and struggling for her balance on the slick surface underfoot. "I think the weather was better outside." Colin coughed and managed a ghost of his wry grin before a guard shoved her forward, growling, "Arragh, now!"

She slid to the end of the corridor, skidding against a wall which opened onto a large chamber. At first she could see little, the darkness made only more profoundly confusing by cobwebs of smoky light emanating from the torches lining the walls. Gradually, she made out the pike-armed guards flanking the doorway in which she stood, and others like them on either side of four other arched doorways opposite her and to her left and right. The room sloped downward from the center, a slope subtle enough to permit walking but steep enough to allow drips from the ceiling to run out of the room and into the outer corridors. A fine layer of ashes spread on the floor allowed the guards in the chamber to walk without falling. From the ceiling hung several water-ruined and tattered banners whose crests and colors were familiar to Maggie as those of the great houses of Argonia. Above the room's center, a canopy was suspended to keep the constant overhead drip from wetting the heads of those on or near the throne dominating the entire chamber.

The throne was of grandiose size and design, carved in some dark substance and draped with fur. On it sat her uncle, Fearchar Brown, looking very pleased with himself indeed, and as though he thought he looked so grand sitting there he couldn't bring himself to rise. On a soggy rug at his feet knelt Sally Forth.

Maggie stumbled forward again as Colin was shoved into her back. Their guards drove them to the center of the room, and threw them to their knees in the ashes.

"Fine catch we have today, m'lord," Sally said, smiling up at Maggie's uncle.

Fearchar regarded them with elaborately casual interest. He had changed little from when Maggie last saw him, still tall, dark, and dangerous-looking, the lively complexion and strong features of her Brown forebears gone cruel and treacherous in his face. The rich clothing he had worn at his castle on Evil Island had been replaced by a dark, cowled robe whose hood protected his head, but did not shadow his face. It wouldn't. He was much too vain for that, she thought. His eyes glittered like poisoned spear points.

"Dear niece. How kind of you to seek me out," he said finally.

"Do you wear that thing on your head, Uncle, because these barbarians of yours have plucked you bald-headed, as this one tried to do me?" she asked, for want of anything better to say. Her uncle raised his hand and then dropped it as if it were too heavy. The guard who seemed so fond of tugging Maggie around by the hair released his grip on it.

"Ah, sweet child, you're as quick and lovely as ever. And you brought your fishy friend along too, I see. Good. Our Sally tells me he's made us up a little air to lighten our revolutionary load." He turned his venomous stare on Colin. "Play."

But Colin couldn't play. He was coughing again.

Fearchar laughed. "These royal lackeys lack stamina!" To the guard at Colin's right he said lazily, "He's quite useless. Kill him."

"No!" Maggie cried, throwing herself over Colin, who was still coughing too hard to ward off the guard's spear. Maggie thrust out a leg and tripped, more than kicked, the man as he lunged, and he slid sprawling across both of them. The other three guards jumped forward, but Fearchar held up his hand.

"Wait," he said. "Now then, Maggie, my dear, am I correct in assuming your undignified display is intended to persuade me to spare a useless royal parasite who can't even do his job properly?"

Rising to her knees, but still hovering protectively above her friend, Maggie said, "I want you to spare Colin, if that's what you mean. Yes."

"You know I would do almost anything for you, dear niece, but you young girls are ignorant of military matters, and are far too apt to place emotional concerns over sound judgment. This man is a spy—as are you, my dear, though I'm sorry to have to say it of one of my own dear kinswomen."

"If that's not the pot calling the kettle black, I don't know what is!" she snapped, losing her temper. "We're not spies, and we're certainly not traitors, like some people I could mention. If you want to be angry at someone, be angry at me. Colin only came along because I—"

Fearchar, who had looked as if he might explode for a moment, settled back into his chair and with some effort resumed his indolent, cat-and-mouse tone. "That's all immaterial. I'm afraid he'll have to die. You see, you're too dangerous, even alone, to allow me to grant you any allies or concessions. You call me names and spite me, even when I tried to make you a queen. You used that scrub-drudge magic of yours to defy me and—"

"But I won't now! You don't have to worry about that!" she said. "I can't use it against you any more. My magic is gone. I can't do you any harm, and neither can Colin, and we're leagues away from anyone who can. So why don't you just let us go?"

Not that she had expected him to, but the suggestion popped out before she had time to think how silly it sounded. At least it seemed to put him in a better mood. He was laughing himself sick.

"Oh, you cunning little witch, you. Let you go? No magic? Do you really expect me to believe that?" He flashed his teeth at her, looking very like Wulfric, though meaner and hungrier. "And at any rate, what good is a witch without her powers? Unless, perhaps as a serving wench, and to warm and decorate the barracks of my loyal guards."

Colin bolted upright, knocking down the guard who had just gotten to his feet again, and grabbing his spear away from him in the process. The long end of the weapon swung behind him, making a clean sweep of the stomachs of the other three guards, as Colin pressed the point into Sally's neck. Maggie, who had also been flung aside when her friend made his move, watched Sally drop her weapon and the guards, at a gesture from Fearchar, take another step backwards. Colin, panting heavily, rasped to Fearchar, "She's your own niece, you filthy bast—" and abruptly broke into another spell of coughing that left him so weak Sally had only to pluck the spear from his grasp and turn it against him.

Maggie got to her knees in time to haul him back from the nymph's forward thrust, and the guards closed in again around them. With an amused smile which tried to give lie to the earlier panic on his face, her uncle flicked his fingers at the guards, saying, "Halt. Let him live, for now. I'm terribly moved by his sense of gallantry. What say you now, niece? If I don't kill your little lap dog, will you do my bidding? ALL of my bidding?"

"You have a sick idea of how to make a girl popular, Uncle, but yes. Spare Colin, and I'll do as you say."

"Good, good. Let's adjourn, then, to the guest chambers, and you can help us make him comfortable."

It took a lot of effort for Maggie to stand again. Her knees were a lot weaker than she would allow her tongue to reveal. She tried to help Colin, but the guards had closed around him and were pushing him forward. He was still coughing as if he would turn wrong side out. Fearchar descended from his throne and grasped her elbow in iron fingers.

He led them to the farthest arch, which entered into the barracks, a long double row of dismal pallets at which Maggie carefully avoided looking. At the end of the room was another arch, and a pair of heavy cedar doors which two of the guards swung ponderously open. Cold wind and hail swept into the room, blasting them all back for a moment.

Then another guard trudged out against the storm and opened another door, this one leading to an open, empty, ice-walled chamber. The others dragged Colin forward and threw him into it.

Maggie pulled away from her uncle's bruising fingers, and went for his eyes. The guards skated out of Colin's cell and jumped for her, pulling her away. "You said you wouldn't kill him!" she shrieked against the pelting hail. "He's ill! He'll be dead before morning!"

Fearchar withdrew from the path of the storm, clucking. "You're such an excitable girl. Did I not say I had a task for you? You see, I don't quite trust you, niece. I want to see for myself if you spoke the truth about your wretched domestic magic tricks. If you can still perform them, you may provide whatever amenities your friend needs to keep him comfortable in the accommodations I have so graciously provided for him. Go on, my dear, make his clothing warmer and dry. Build him one of your delightful little fires, provide him with a light, and perhaps a bit of a tent to keep him from the elements. It's all up to you, you see. As you say, you got him into this. I certainly can't afford to have my revolution bogged down by supporting a lot of camp followers, just to please my relatives. If you want him to stay alive, you'll have to provide for him yourself. Otherwise . . ." he shrugged.

Maggie glared at him, pushed the guards aside, gritted her teeth and tried, but it was as if she had never had the power. Nothing happened. Nothing entered Colin's cell or changed there except that the hail accumulated and the wind whisked the pellets around the floor. Colin was leaning in a corner, doubled over, coughing, when they closed the door and bolted it.

She didn't have to see her uncle's gloating smile, blinded as she was by her own scalding, angry, frustrated tears. Her nails shredded her palms as the guards took her in tow again.

"You're a truthful girl," Fearchar said. "But with a little training, we shall break you of that."

He had the guards haul her back into the throne room, and himself resumed the throne. "Now then, what to do with you. You're as bad as your friend, really. What a burden leadership is! All these useless people on my doorstep! A minstrel who can't play, and a witch who can't do the simplest magic! And you *are* a Brown, of course, so I truly would rather not have you consorting with my guards if there's any other useful function you can perform—"

He paused and looked past her as a lady wandered into the chamber, looking to her right and left and back again as if lost. Her plump body fairly quivered with agitation, but an aura of pinkish light surrounded her, particularly bright at her head, which was covered with a nest of wildly disorganized gray curls with a goose quill stuck in their midst, just above her ear. "Fearchar—oh, excuse me, dear, I mean, Dark Pilgrim, dear. I didn't realize you were holding court. Do pardon me for interrupting, but I was just finishing that chart you asked me to do and I seem to have mislaid my favorite stylus. I do hope it hasn't fallen on the floor in here somewhere and washed overboard or gotten its feathers all nasty in the ashes." She had Fearchar shift from one hip to the other as she poked under the fur drape and cushions of the throne, then stood up, scratching her head, and turned to the rug, pulling one dripping end of it and sending Sally Forth sprawling backwards. "Pardon," the former Princess of Argonia said not at all contritely. Then, mumbling to herself, she made first Maggie's guards, then Maggie, lift their feet as she looked underneath for the missing implement. Looking up again, she seemed for the first time to notice Maggie. "Why, how do you do, my dear. Have we met?" she asked, extending her hand. One of Maggie's guards shoved her back to her knees and pushed her face toward the outstretched, ink-stained fingers, indicating that she should kiss them. Before she could do so, Pegeen snatched the hand back to her mouth. "Oh! I know. You must be the new serving girl Fearchar's been promising me!"

Fearchar's smile faded for the first time since his guards had brought Maggie and Colin to him at spearpoint. "She is no serving wench, my dear. Do you not note the family resemblance? This is my niece, Magdalene, who has lately been raised by the usurper of your father's throne to a rank equal to, if not greater than, your own. Princess Magdalene of Argonia, may I present Princess Pegeen Ashburn, legitimate heiress to the throne of Argonia, who shall rule beside me when our revolution bears its glorious fruit."

Sally Forth's mouth flew open. "But, Dark Pilgrim, you promised ME—"

"Ah, yes. I've promised Captain Forth that her men shall be given food and drink, and that I will now go and review the other prisoners. Pegeen, dear, if you'll be so good as to take Maggie with you to your chambers, and see to it that she's kept away from sharp implements and salt. Guards, will you be so good as to see that neither Princess leaves her Highness's quarters without my express invitation?" He smiled apologetically to Pegeen. "Our agents have spotted Rowan's party a day's march from the Blabbermouth, my dear. I want to insure your safety, and must from now on keep you under the protection of my guard."

Pegeen raised on tiptoe and planted a kiss in the hollow of Fearchar's sharp-boned cheek. "Of course, darling. You're so thoughtful. Come along, dear Magdalene." She seemed not to feel there was anything irregular about the guard escorting Maggie poising his spear at his leader's niece's neck.

Moonshine quietly allowed his captors to remove their sling and ropes, thinking to bite them as soon as he was free, but Primrose shrieked and bucked and gouged and whinnied. "Where is this VILE place?" she demanded, though naturally none of the guards possessed the gift of unicorn understanding. "There has been an error here! My maiden surely did not intend for you to abuse me in this hideous fashion!"

But the guards, who had profited from previous experiences, flicked their ropes quickly from her and from Moonshine, and backed off immediately, to be replaced by others who goaded the unicorns at spearpoint into an icy cell at the rear of the castle.

The cell was barren, and open to the hail-spitting sky, but at least, Moonshine thought, he would be able to do what he had set out to do, and meet other unicorns. Two more of them were crowded in one corner, heads down and ears flicking the hail stones aside. The stallion looked up at them, deflecting stones with his broken horn. "Huh. Here comes two more fools. You two ready to do your bit for the revolution, too?"

"I WAS," Primrose said, kicking at the door with her back

hooves. "But I most certainly don't intend to now. Not until I've had a full explanation and a complete apology for this despicable treatment!"

The stallion emitted the longest horselaugh Moonshine had ever heard. "Oh, say, you're a corker, aren't you?" he chortled when he'd finally regained control of himself. "That's the best one yet. Apology! Explanation!"

"Those men will sorely regret the way they've mishandled me when my maiden finds out how they've bungled her commands," Primrose said primly.

"Your maiden?" the strange stallion asked with mock innocence. "Blond woman, sports a silver hunting horn and wears practically nothing?"

"That is an accurate if unseemly description of her," Primrose admitted.

"Hold onto your horn, honey, but that trollop is fixing to watch them cut off your horn and grind it into powder and flay you alive to make a belt for herself from your hide."

"LIAR!" screamed Primrose, and charged him.

The stallion was on his feet, neatly parrying her thrust with a deft movement of his own broken horn before she knew what was happening. "Oh, no. I couldn't lie," he said. "I'm a unicorn like you, remember?

> "And it is the Unicorn Creed
>   That a unicorn may not mislead
>   But always say sooth
>   Without mercy or ruth
>   Though sooth may in truth make you bleed."

Moonshine was more confused by that than by any of the more catastrophic events that had taken place that day. "You just made that up, didn't you?" he asked the stallion. "I never heard that part of the Creed before."

The stallion studied him warily for a moment, then trotted over, circling him. "You calling me a liar too, sonny?"

"No—I just—"

"Eagledown, have you no shame!" scolded the other unicorn, getting to her feet. She was a pretty snow-white filly with eyes the soft green of moss. "These are captives, like ourselves, hurt and confused. And instead of offering solace, you mock them!"

"Whatever has become of your horn, young lady!" Primrose

demanded of the filly, whose horn was in as sad a state of repair as the stallion's.

"It broke," she said. "While we were digging."

"Digging? Are you a unicorn or a gopher?"

"Leave her alone, Primrose," Moonshine warned. "After the way you betrayed me, you can hardly hold yourself up, still, as a model of unicorn behavior and knowledge."

The filly walked over to him and sniffed, seeming to like what she smelled. "Don't be too hard on her," she said softly, gazing at him with those lovely green eyes.

> "For it is the Unicorn Creed
>   To follow wherever love leads..."

"And the primary lesson," Primrose finished for her,

> "Is when your love beckons
>   Tis a priv'lege to die at her knee."

The older unicorn seemed momentarily buoyed by the nobility of the verse's sentiment, then added, plaintively, "Except that my love has taken her knee away. How can I die at her knee if she's not here?"

"If she were here," Eagledown promised, "I'd see to it that she died with you. And you both have that verse wrong. Once the maiden betrays you, it's every 'corn for himself, as the Creed clearly states in THIS verse:

> "For it is the Unicorn Creed
>   To fight till you've no blood to bleed
>   To run like the wind
>   From the whole race of men
>   And kill them if they force the need."

He sighed. "Too bad I had to meet up with someone like that outlaw filly. I'd always looked forward to the kind of love a unicorn is supposed to have with his girl, you know, like in the verse about unicorns and maidens, the one you botched up:

> "For it is the Unicorn Creed
>   To follow wherever love leads.
>   If she's light-haired or ruddy
>   She's your bosomy buddy
>   Your friend both in need and indeed."

"Wait," Moonshine said, more puzzled than ever. "That's NOT the way it goes. I know that's not the Creed my dam taught me. It doesn't go like that at all. It's the first maiden and it's, let's see, 'wherever love leads—' "

"You gainsaying me, greenhorn?" the stallion challenged. "'Cause if you are, don't let the fact that my horn's damaged stop you. I don't need a horn to kick your tail all around this stall."

"For shame, Eagledown!" Snowshadow interjected, putting herself between the feisty stallion and Moonshine. "Forgive him," she said to Moonshine. "He feels keenly the pain of betrayal, as do we all, and only wants to fight in order to lash out at something. But we must not fight among ourselves."

"You are so wise," Moonshine agreed, looking into her eyes and smelling her sweet though soiled scent, feeling oddly happy and benevolent, despite his captive state. "Your pardon, noble Eagledown," he said to the stallion, without looking away from Snowshadow. "I'm sure you speak the Creed as you know it. It is only that I, an ignorant youngster, do not know as much of the Creed as I would, and was on a quest to learn it all. Never had it occured to me that the Creed as given me by my dam might have other variations."

Snowshadow laughed and replied in rhyme:

> "How else could the Unicorn Creed
>   Begin to meet unicorn need?
>   We aren't beasts of the herd
>   To use others' words
>   To govern our thoughts and our deeds."

"Of course not," Moonshine agreed. "But—but there IS a Creed—isn't there?"

"Certainly there's a Creed," Eagledown snorted. "We all follow one—it just seems to vary slightly from 'corn to 'corn, from what the filly here and I have found."

"Are you—?" Moonshine began, but didn't know quite how to finish his thought. He needn't have bothereed. Snowshadow read him very well.

"No, I do not belong to Eagledown. He was captured before me, and both of us by the same maiden, if maiden she is indeed. Therefore, neither of us, none of us here, have anyone. She has betrayed us all."

"I have someone," Moonshine said.

"Do you misunderstand me?" Snowshadow asked sadly. "The bandit girl is false, I tell you."

"But she is *not* MY maiden," Moonshine insisted. "My maiden is a beautiful witch, and very fierce. She's temporarily without her power, but I'm sure once she gets it back she'll force her uncle to free us all."

"Her UNCLE?" Snowshadow asked.

"The evil sorcerer who commands the bandit girl is a distant relative of my maiden," Moonshine explained as casually as possible. "But she's not a bit like him, and she hates him and loves me, so I know she'll set us free—"

"She won't free me," Primrose said in a voice suddenly changed and quiet. "Not after what I've done to you, and said about her. She won't free me."

The older mare's head hung desolately between her forelegs. She seemed finally to have accepted the truth of her situation and what the others told her, and in the absence of Sally Forth's spellbinding charm perceived the dismal truth of her plight.

Snowshadow nudged her neck gently. "Don't despair, elder sister. We shall all be freed together. If Moonshine's maiden is as good and wonderful as he says, she will save you for his sake if for no other. And if not, why, *I* shall insist on it."

Eagledown snorted again. "Haven't you all got it through your pointy heads yet that no mortal maiden is going to bother saving a bunch of corralled 'corns? I almost believed that pudgy princess, but I think we'd stand a better chance getting Moonshine and Primrose to help enlarge our bolt hole than we would waiting on human help."

"Well, perhaps it wouldn't hurt to do what we can," Snowshadow agreed.

"What hole?" Moonshine asked.

"Our escape route," Snowshadow said. "Come see. It's almost big enough."

Pegeen waited until the door had slammed behind them to take Maggie's hands in her own and pull her over to the wall farthest from the door. "Oh, my dear girl, I saw it all and I'm so terribly sorry. You must believe that your uncle hasn't always been like this. He's very fond of you in his way, you know."

"He has an odd way of showing it," Maggie said. "His overwhelming affection is going to be the death of me probably, and of my friend absolutely." She laughed with a bitterness just short of hysteria. "Oh, no, milady. You're dead wrong. My uncle hates me all right. He's threatened to—well, never mind."

"Never mind indeed," sniffed Pegeen, patting Maggie's knee with brisk sympathy. "You needn't worry about that. Fearchar does not hate you, I tell you. He could never dislike anyone who reminds him so of himself. Nevertheless, he has quite taken leave of his senses in regard to this so-called revolution, and it is up to us to do something about it.''

Maggie started, so taken aback by the Princess's unexpected sympathy that she momentarily stopped looking around the room for something with which to hit the other woman over the head. ''You mean you came in when you did on purpose?''

''Yes. I must apologize for not being able to save your young man from the maze, but I'm not really very brave, you see, and I could tell Fearchar meant to do something awful to him, no matter what you or I could do. Though he is fond of you, Fearchar's quite vexed at you still over his first attempt to gain the throne. I'm afraid he's punishing you through your friend. He might have done something nasty to you, too, but he's much too proud to degrade a member of his own family in front of me. He's almost come to believe his blood is as noble as mine. Not that it makes any difference, you understand, but he could hardly shame you publicly and keep his own face, could he?''

''Then you mean to help me?'' Maggie asked. ''You're not on his side?''

''Well, naturally I'm on his side,'' the princess replied. ''But it's all rather complicated, you see, because though *I* am, he's *not* any longer. What I mean is, I love Fearchar. But that horrid woman has completely corrupted him, and I must protect him from doing perfectly dreadful things he couldn't really mean to do. He'll be glad of it and thank me when he comes to his senses—I hope.''

Maggie looked at the princess suspiciously. ''Excuse me, milady, but has your food been tasting rather flat and bland the past few months?''

''You mean because of salt being the antidote to Fearchar's magic charm? No, my dear, my diet is quite sufficient, thank you. I'm afraid neither salt nor magic have anything to do with Fearchar's charm for me. Even if one is a Princess, and quite used to the idea of being no great beauty, approaching middle age without so much as a once-upon-a-time, not to mention a happily-ever-after, is not a pleasant prospect. Fearchar suffers from a certain ruthless ambition which he's allowed to get out of hand, but I can't help but hope that with the proper guidance, he'll . . .'' She stopped, seeing Maggie's skeptical look, and finished lamely. ''He's provided me with a great many rather beautiful dreams, you see.''

''Nightmares would be easier to believe,'' Maggie said. ''Colin

287

is freezing in his wretched prison, and Mother only knows what's happened to the unicorns.''

"They're safe," Pegeen told her in a tone whose self-satisfaction was not unmixed with anxiety. "For now, at least."

"He'll murder King Rowan, too, unless—"

"Murder him? But surely m'lord Rowan is bringing sufficient men and arms to deal with this ragtag bunch of ruffians Fearchar has gathered?''

"They had an accident," Maggie informed her glumly. "Now they're to be slaughtered, and so, I suspect, are we."

"Umm," Pegeen said noncommittally. "Fearchar *has* grown distant lately—and he's promised that wretched nymph something besides quarters for her men, unless I miss my guess." She smiled sadly, "I—don't like to think what that promise might be, you see." She was quiet for a moment, and when she looked up her eyes were unnaturally bright. Stretching out ink-stained fingers that trembled slightly, she traced Maggie's cheek and jawline. "You're so very like him, you know. So very *much* like him. You could be his daughter, instead of his niece, you're so alike. And yet, from all I've heard said of you, you're a kind, honest, forthright girl, as good as—as he is—"

"Yes," Maggie said gently. "I am, and he is. Quite. But the point is, what are we going to do about it? Colin is ill. That fever will kill him before the night's out, if he doesn't freeze to death first. And somehow we must keep the King from being slaughtered, and I still don't know *what* Fearchar intends doing with the unicorns—"

"I do," Pegeen said grimly, worrying her lower lip with her teeth.

"Then do you intend to lure the guard in and let me knock him senseless or shall I lure him in and let you do the honors?''

"Neither," Pegeen said. "There's another way. But we must wait until it's quite dark."

Colin's main consolation, as he lay on the floor of his icy prison being scourged by wind and hailstones, was thinking of how grand he must have looked, defying Sally Forth and her bandits and the wicked sorcerer for Maggie's sake. Just like in the ballads, he thought. In fact, certainly an act worthy of a ballad in itself. And it wasn't just play-acting this time, either, as it had been in the tavern at Everclear when he'd known very well that Leofwin was covered not only by himself but by Maggie's magic and Moonshine's horn. This time he had really braved actual danger for the love of his lady, though, in all likelihood, it not only would do neither of them a bit of good but would also go unsung, due to the untimely demise of all parties sympathetic enough to record his deed.

Ah, well, if he'd wanted everything to go smoothly, he ought to have stuck with minstrel halls and never have taken up with witches. But he knew Maggie appreciated his gesture, as he loved her for trying to save him. Perhaps, at least, he had delayed her end until Fearchar could torment her with the sight of his frozen, lifeless body. What a cheering thought. Shouldn't take too long, at this rate. Already he had no feeling in his arms or legs, nor could he feel his nose, mouth or chin, which was a blessing, considering the hail. But within, he felt as he'd always imagined dragons must, plagued as they were with a continual case of heartburn; unbearably, overwhelmingly hot. The coughing and sneezing forced his stiffened body to double over painfully, whether he felt otherwise able to do so or not.

Perhaps, if he took long enough about this dismal business of dying, he might buy Maggie enough time so that King Rowan could arrive and rescue her. If anyone had ever deserved rescuing, it was Maggie. She certainly went out of her way to rescue everyone else, and now she'd got him doing it, too. Very well, then. He felt so hot inside he was pretty sure he could stretch the freezing process out over quite a long time. But the coughing hurt, sending searing pains through his chest, waggling numbed and useless limbs helplessly about with each spasmodic, throat-rasping explosion. His head, too, felt as if it were on fire—a blacksmith's fire, with blacksmith and hammer and anvil in attendance.

Between coughs, he tried to distract himself by concentrating on the castanet clickings of his teeth, and finally gave that up. At last, though he fought it, he slept. He dreamed of softly tangled brown hair, brown eyes melting with love and admiration for him, the voluptuous embrace of a warm, cinnamon-colored body enfolding his own, and best of all, a sweet, generous mouth too busy returning his kisses to say a single word.

After a long hour of pacing and nail-biting, Pegeen cracked open the door of her room and spoke to the guard. "The Princess Magdalene and I are retiring now. Please see to it that we aren't disturbed."

The guard smirked insolently. Pegeen took that for acquiescence, and closed the door again, throwing the bolt vengefully from the inside. Gathering up the woolen cloaks and mittens she'd dug from her traveling trunk, she beckoned Maggie to the wall screen and slid it aside, revealing the entrance to her secret tunnel.

"Fancy that!" Maggie whispered. "You'd think there'd be a draft."

"Quickly," Pegeen said. "We'll have just enough time before the castle's quiet and it's safe to venture out onto the maze."

"Enough time for what?" Maggie asked, hunkering down slightly to keep from bumping her head on the tunnel's ceiling and slipping in her haste to stay within the wake of Pegeen's pink aura.

Pegeen knelt and shoved aside the oversized snowball she used to barricade her tunnel, and sat down, scooting on her bottom along the top of the high maze wall until there was room for Maggie beside her.

The hail storm had cleared now, and the wind had died down. The maze wall was littered with small white pellets, tinted rose by Pegeen's aura.

"Put the snowball back, will you, Maggie? There's a dear. It makes a lovely plug, but I do have to replace it every time there's a warm spell." She spoke quickly, rummaging in her dress pocket as she chattered. "Ah, there it is."

Pulling forth a torch the length of her forearm and a tinderbox, she lit the torch, and smiled at it as if it were her dearest friend. "It's been days since I've had a smoke," she told Maggie. "The weather has been beastly."

"Yes," Maggie agreed. "But it seems to be clearing up now." A faint gray light was visible along the upper edge of the horizon, above the glacier behind the castle, but all else extending beyond the Princess's aura was black as pitch. That aura was a handy sort of power to have. Thoughtful as it was of the Princess to bring along a torch, Maggie thought she really wouldn't need it as long as she stayed close to Pegeen.

She was about to say so when Pegeen leaned luxuriously back, arching her neck pleasurably, and lowered the lighted end of the upended torch into her eagerly waiting mouth, plunging it half-way down to her stomach, it seemed to Maggie, who was too stunned to comment. After a long moment during which the princess actually seemed to be sucking on the torch, she pulled it forth, extinguished, and emitted a blissful sigh. She sat for a time, serenely blowing irridescent curls of smoke from her nostrils, which glowed a faint shell pink. She reminded Maggie of the dragon Grizel in a happy frame of mind.

With a small cough and a clearer eye and steadier voice than she'd had before, Pegeen said, "Pity you can't have a nice smoke, too, before we set out. It's wonderfully warming, besides having such a calming effect on the nerves."

"Oh, yes, I can see where it would be warming," Maggie agreed. "Speaking of that, do you suppose we could see to Colin now?"

The hail had left their precarious pathway even slicker than usual, and at times they had to abandon crawling for sliding along astride the wall's top. Pegeen grew worried that she might become confused or lose her way. Never before had it been so dark when she visited the unicorn enclosure. Each time one of the worm's convolutions led them back to the rear castle wall, she breathed a sigh of relief.

Maggie's legs were bare beneath her skirt, and numb from direct contact with the ice. She tried to arrange the folds of material to protect her skin, but only succeeded in hampering her movements and slowing her progress. Even with the cloak and mittens borrowed from Pegeen, she was frozen by the wind and wet ice. Soon she began slipping more often, because her hands and knees were numb from crawling, and her muscles tired and jellied from supporting her weight. They had been crawling for an impossibly long time when Pegeen stopped and leaned forward, casting her aura into the depths on the left side of their wall.

Before the princess had time to explain, Maggie felt Moonshine touch her mind.

"Maiden? Oh, Maiden, I told them you'd come!"

Forgetting her weariness and the cold, Maggie scuttled forward and peered over the edge, to see her beloved Moonshine and three other unicorns staring up at them.

"Have they hurt you?" she asked.

"Nay, Maiden. They have not. And you?"

"No. I'm fine."

"Hey, Highness," another unicorn challenged. "Have you come to get us out of here?"

"Oh, dear, how thoughtless of me!" Pegeen cried, her thumbnail flying to her teeth. "I should have brought the map, shouldn't I, so we could all escape together? I was so upset about Maggie's young man that I quite forgot."

"Just like a human," the stallion snorted. "Your own kind first, eh?"

"Master Colin is imperiled?" Moonshine asked, and Maggie showed him the image of Colin as she had seen him last, coughing and freezing in a cell like the one containing the

291

unicorns. "Free him at once!" Moonshine said. "I, for one, shall not flee at his expense!"

"Nor I!" trumpeted the filly at his side. Her snowy coat so blended with the ice that only her eyes were clearly defined. She began to recite:

> "For it is the Unicorn Creed
> To abandon unseemly stampede
> If a friend of a friend
> Has an end round the bend
> The unicorn must intercede!"

"I wish you wouldn't do that, Snowshadow," Moonshine complained. "It confuses me when you keep reciting stanzas of the Creed I've never heard before."

"Your pardon," the filly said to him, then to the princess and Maggie, "Onward, valiant maidens, and deliver your friend from his fell fate!"

"But—Moonshine's maiden?" Primrose's voice was subdued.

"Yes?" Maggie asked, the chill in her voice not entirely due to the weather.

"You—you will come back, won't you?"

Pegeen answered. "I'm just going to take her to her friend, and lead them back here, then I'll go fetch the map, and we'll all crawl out through your hole and escape through the maze at first light. You have my word as a royal Ashburn and the daughter of my father, Finbar."

"That's more like it!" the stallion Eagledown trumpeted. "Rally round me, friends, and let's apply our hind hooves to that hole again!"

Maggie and Pegeen crawled around the unicorns' prison, and up and over the long loop at the castle's rear entrance, before finally reaching the chamber into which Fearchar had cast Colin.

Maggie swore under her breath when she saw him, lying on his side with his knees wrapped close to his chest, frost winking back into the princess's aura from his beard, hair and lashes. At first she thought he was dead already, and they had arrived too late, but a weak cough which stirred his rigid body soon told her differently.

"Gracious!" Pegeen said. "He doesn't look as if he'll be able to stand. I had hoped the two of us could grab hold of him and pull him up, but—"

"Of course, he can't stand!" Maggie snapped. "He's sick and

nearly frozen to death. We should never have waited so long to come! Give me a hand down."

"But—what are you going to DO?" Pegeen asked. "You can't get out of there by yourself, and I can't help you both. I'm simply not strong enough. The barracks is only a wall away. Oh, my dear, if they should catch you."

"I'll make them wish they hadn't," Maggie said grimly. Even a hollow threat bolstered her courage a little. Pegeen lay down on her stomach across the ice wall and Maggie eased herself down the Princess's outstretched legs to an easy drop into the chamber below.

Colin was as cold to her touch as the ice itself, but when she felt the points Granny had once showed her, through which a person's spirit passes closest to the skin, she could feel his, slow and weak, but present, and could hear his breath trying to force its way through his frozen nostrils.

"Throw me down your tinderbox and the torch!" Maggie called up to Pegeen. "I'll try to warm him while you fetch your map. Perhaps by the time you return, he'll be thawed enough so we can move him between us to the unicorn pen. Moonshine can cure his ailments and injuries, and carry him through the maze, if need be."

Pegeen nodded with nervous eagerness. "Perhaps I can bring something to help bring him up—and some ashes from my fire to make the footing less risky."

The tinderbox and torch clattered as they hit the ice and rolled against Maggie's feet. She lit the torch, and scraped together fresh snow and hailstones into a mound, where she planted the light.

"I'll hurry," Pegeen promised, and then, with depressing speed, her voice and light were absorbed by the bitter night.

Maggie mourned her magic sorely when she saw how puny the warmth and faint flickering light of the torch were, and thought of the cozy blaze she had once been able to command at will. But there was no use crying over doused fires, she supposed. Anyone at Fort Iceworm knew other techniques for thawing frostbite victims, and she'd use those to warm Colin until he could walk or crawl to the unicorn pen, where they could melt ice with the torch and have Moonshine dip his horn in the water and cure their friend.

Whatever happened after that would just have to be faced when the time came.

Her hands and knees were almost as cold as Colin's, so it was with great difficulty that she passed Pegeen's cloak beneath his stiff body, at an angle that left the rest of the cloth free to pass around them both when she lay down beside him. Prying his hands away from his own flesh, she awkwardly wrestled them beneath her tunic, to nestle chillingly in each of her armpits, two of the warmest areas on a person's body, according to Granny. Then she had to prise his boots from his feet, no mean task in such a clumsy position, and one made possible only by the fact that his boots, like her own, were falling apart at the seams already and could be disassembled rather than pulled off whole. Once his feet were bare, she stuck them inside her skirt and clasped them between her thighs. Having begun warming his limbs, the parts most endangered by the cold, she wriggled upward slightly again, and drew his face down so that her nose and eyes could be warmed by her breath, thrusting her own numbed hands into his shirt at the top of his trousers, to warm between his belly and legs.

For what seemed eons, she felt and heard only the slow thump of his pulses and the pounding of her own. Gradually, the chill in his body blended with her warmth until he was no longer so cold as he had been, nor she so warm. Maybe she'd freeze to death with him, if Pegeen failed to return. Wouldn't that entertain the guards though, trying to pry apart the braided bodies? If only the torch weren't so small and inadequate! She cuddled Colin closer, and he seemed much warmer.

So did she suddenly, and with her head shrouded by the cloak, she imagined she felt a warmth at her back as well as that coming from Colin, but soon she forgot about it, distracted by a trickle of cold wetness trailing down the hollow of her throat to seep between her breasts. Raising her head, she brushed her face against Colin's beard. It had thawed, and was dripping wet.

Encouraged, she snuggled closer. His face moved against her neck, burrowing into her shoulder and she felt his eyelashes flutter, tickling her collarbone. She shifted to make it easier for him, and with her free hand stroked the back of his neck to warm it, knowing that area for one particularly sensitive to cold.

"Mmm, Maggie?" He moved quite freely then, sliding his feet down until they rested between her knees, at the hem of the cloak.

She held him closer. "About time you woke," she murmured, and his hands shifted a bit, warm now, and obviously no longer unfeeling, as they cupped the sides of her breasts.

"Mmmm," he replied, burrowing his face lower, until his still-chilly nose rested in the cleavage created by her tunic's gaping neckline. The movement caused the hand she still armed against his skin to move too, until it found a very strong pulse indeed, which it gently investigated.

"Bloody uncomfortable position," he said hoarsely, and they rearranged themselves into one that was not only more comfortable but seemed to apply a great deal more warming pressure in a far more satisfying fashion to areas previously left vacant and drafty.

"Your ear," she complained softly, "feels like an icecube."

"Your breast," he replied, sighing, "feels wonderful. May I warm my nose just a bit more? It hurts now that the feeling's returning." His voice was weak yet, and trembling, and she still felt him shake with a slight cough now and then. In reply, she pressed his head more firmly against her bosom and kissed his dripping hair. She was no longer aware of the cold, and stroked the bristling hairs at his nape with her free hand until they lay down in submission to her touch.

"Ah," he said. "Your hands feel so good. But here, you're in the cold," and he shifted again so that now he lay on top of her, sheltering her from the night sky.

She thought it the wrong time to mention that not only was she not cold, she felt deliciously steamy.

"We aren't doing this properly, you know," he breathed into her ear.

"We're not?"

"No. I have it on the best authority that for maximum effectiveness, there should be no clothing between skin surfaces."

"Well then, if that's what the best authority says," she concurred, and together they managed to remedy the error.

"What are we waiting for?" he asked.

"Princess Pegeen. She's coming back with a—ahh, a map or something."

"I know the most wonderful way to pass the time."

Pegeen heard the pounding on her chamber door while she was still in the tunnel. Shedding her cloak and mittens behind the screen, she ducked around it and pushed it back in place before strolling to the door, and throwing the bolt. Fearchar poked his head in.

"Shhh," she said, putting a fingertip to her lips. "Your niece is sleeping."

"Excellent. Then you're quite free to lend me your assistance in my study. We must finish deciphering the exact formulas for concocting the unicorn medicines and charms before daybreak. My men will gain great confidence when they see, in this first

295

battle, how my foresight in capturing the unicorns will protect them. Once they realize they cannot be permanently injured, my army will be invincible."

"You aren't going to sacrifice the beasts tonight?" Pegeen asked, trying to display less alarm than she felt.

"Not sacrifice, my dear. They are far too valuable to sacrifice. But we shall excise the parts we need from two of them, at least, as soon as we have the formulas transcribed. I trust you will not dawdle?"

"I'll be right along. Only let me fetch my cloak first. The halls are so drafty, particularly at night. I'll only be a moment."

"One of the guards will escort you. I'll await you in my study," and he stepped back from the door.

Pegeen bolted the door behind him, and rummaged in the oiled leather case that held her drawing things until she found the map. It was woefully incomplete, but that couldn't be helped. It was all they had now.

Slipping back into the tunnel, she retrieved her cloak and slid out onto the maze again, crawling forward until she was upwind of the chamber adjacent to the unicorn pen. Shaping her map into the form of a bird, she called upon a minor spell her father had taught her, one known to all performing magicians, of making birds, temporarily, of inanimate objects such as paper and handkerchiefs. With a flip of her wrist and a mumbled incantation she had learned as other children learned nursery songs, she sent the precious map sailing towards the cell containing Maggie and the minstrel. As soon as it left her hand, the map became a glowing pink dove, which flew straight to its target, and dropped, a map once more. Perhaps later in the night, when Fearchar was concentrating on his battle preparations, she'd be able to break away again and warn them, but for now the map was the best help she had to offer.

"We shouldn't have done that," Maggie said, when they had finished.

"I know," Colin replied. "Now you can't be Moonshine's maiden anymore, can y-y-ya-CHOO!"

"I don't mean that, silly. I mean we shouldn't have done that because it's made your cough worse. And you must have a fever. Feel how wet it is beneath us." Indeed, the cloak under her was soaked and Colin's face was crimson.

"Nonsense. I feel much better thanks to you and this great fire you've built. That's what's making everything so wet. It's melted a hole in the wall.''

Maggie peeked out from the folds of the cloak. Flames roared to the top of the wall, an enormous fuelless bonfire blazing where the feeble torch had formerly burned. She got to her knees and began pulling her clothing on. Colin pulled his clothes on, too, except for his dismantled boots, which he regarded sadly until Maggie, with an almost automatic wink of her eye, stitched them instantly back together again. Her magic, like a freshly healed minor physical injury to a hand or foot, suddenly functioned again, as naturally if it had never been impaired.

Colin smiled fondly at his boots as he tugged them on, then at Maggie, who doused the fire and already had one leg through the hole melted in the ice wall. "I see you've got it back again," he said, indicating the hole heralding the return of her powers. "I—thank you for taking care of me, I mean."

She pulled her leg back out of the hole and returned to stand beside him, touching his shoulder. "I'm not sure who cured whom. It didn't come back until we—at any rate, stay close. Who knows what magic is apt to do? It may decide to desert us again and we'd need to take—similar measures." She grinned at him and he rose, clasped her in his arms, and kissed her soundly, but briefly, before another fit of coughing disrupted their embrace.

"We'd better melt our way through to Moonshine right away," she said. "That cough is sounding worse all the time."

He was going to tell her that it didn't feel any better than it looked when his eye was caught by a strange, faintly glowing, shape against the ice wall. Stooping, he picked up a bit of parchment, folded into a triangular shape. The tip of it was wet. "Here now, what's this?" he asked, smoothing it against his thigh.

Maggie peered down at it. Three quarters of one side was covered in glowing wiggling lines, through which a heavier, black line snaked from an arrow at the lower edge of the drawing, dribbling off into the unfinished and slightly soggy nothingness at the top.

"It's a map—this must be the map Pegeen went for," she said.

"Why would she send it this way? Do you think she may have come back while we were—you know—and was too courteous to interrupt?"

Maggie shook her head and headed back through the hole. "No. Something's happened, and she can't meet us after all. This must mean we're to take the map and go without her. Hurry."

On the other side of the hole was the chamber adjoining the castle's back doors. Maggie started her fire well back from the doors, sending flames shooting up the wall the chamber shared with the unicorn pen.

"We could have used the door," Colin said.

"This is quieter," she assured him. "Besides, I didn't think of it. And it won't take but a moment, anyway. Look at that fire!" He heard an artisan's pride in her voice as she watched her robust orange and blue flames eat ice.

"Your magic certainly returned with a vengeance," he agreed. "You'll have to watch building campfires in the woods with me around, or you might start forest fires!"

The unicorns were waiting for them with ready horns and rolling, terrified eyes when they broke through the second wall.

"Whoa!" Colin said, holding up his hands to fend off an attack. "It's only us!"

"We took you for an iceworm," Snowshadow explained.

"N—n—no," Colin answered, and sneezed, which started another round of coughing.

Maggie pointed to the pool of melted ice at their feet, and pleaded. "Moonshine, quickly, please, purify this water so he can drink it and get well. He's still very ill."

"Wait up, now," Eagledown said, edging forward, his nostrils flaring high, sniffing in Maggie's direction. "I thought you said she was a maiden, sonny. There's no odor of chastity here. If she's a maiden, then I'm a phalarope."

Moonshine paused with his horn in the puddle. "Of course, she's a mai—Maid Maggie?! What have you done?"

Maggie looked guiltily to Colin, who looked sheepishly back at her before both turned to Moonshine with a tandem shrug.

"Minstrel Colin, I TRUSTED you!" Moonshine wailed. "And look what you've done!"

"They seem to know very well what they've done," Primrose remarked, with a return to her old vinegar.

"Of course, they do," Snowshadow said. "And I, for one, think it's rather sweet. And exciting. I've never met lovers before. And just think, they actually seem to have retained the gift of unicorn understanding! How peculiar. And how grand!"

She sidled up to Maggie, keeping herself between Maggie and Colin and the other unicorns. "Tell me, between you and me, was it very wonderful?"

"Er—Colin, if you'll drink some of that now, perhaps we'd best be on our way," Maggie suggested.

He knelt and cupped some of the water in his hands, lapped it up, and wiped his mouth. "In the dark?" he asked.

Before she could answer, they heard the sound of something heavy dragging across ice and a loud creaking, accompanied by voices and footsteps. Princess Pegeen's voice shrilled above the rest, protesting loudly, "But, Fearchar, I told you already that that translation is faulty! We mustn't rush this thing!"

"Rush is exactly what we must do, my dear," the wizard answered in a lower voice, which grew louder as the footsteps approached. "You needn't maintain your pretense any longer, Pegeen. I know very well how squeamish you are. You would delay me from using the beasts indefinitely, if possible. I have no more time to humor you."

Maggie climbed through the unicorn's bolt hole in the back of the cell and began melting another hole in the wall to the chamber adjoining theirs.

"You could at least wait until morning!" Pegeen was almost screaming now. Eagledown bolted through the hole after Maggie.

The bolt to the cell door rasped on its hooks and thunked to the ground.

"Now why should you want to wait until morning, my *lady*?" Sally Forth's voice asked with barely concealed contempt. Primrose, hearing her, paused halfway through the hole. With a none-too-gentle jab of his horn, Moonshine sent her sailing through the rest of the way.

"I only meant that the beasts might be difficult to control, that one of our men could be hurt or slain trying to subdue them in the darkness," Pegeen said.

First Snowshadow, then Moonshine, disappeared through the hole, and Colin followed them.

Maggie's fire had melted a hole half large enough for the unicorns in the next wall by now.

Fearchar sounded menacing as he said, "It strikes me, Pegeen, that yours is a very peculiar concern for a woman who has just spent half the night translating texts which readily testify that by use of one part or another of these beasts, any man slain by one of them could be revived."

"My prisoners are ample evidence of that," Sally Forth said.

"If you truly have the welfare of the Cause at heart. Or have you other concerns, Princess?"

Maggie turned from a hole now melted to the proper size, and brushed past the unicorns to climb back into the pen from which they'd just escaped.

Colin snatched at her arm. "What are you doing?"

"We can't leave Pegeen behind," she said, just as the door to the cell opened and Pegeen was pushed forward, followed by Sally Forth, Fearchar, and several armed soldiers.

Maggie grabbed the Princess and thrust her through the opening to Colin, then leaped back through the hole herself and started a roaring blaze, spanning the width of the cell in front of the bolt hole.

"That should hold them," she said, rejoining the others, and smiling slightly at the screams and curses that followed her.

The segment of maze into which Maggie had melted an entrance was one of the main channels rather than another cul-de-sac like those nearer the rear of the castle. Eagledown reluctantly allowed Pegeen to mount him, and with Maggie on Moonshine and Colin on Snowshadow, they galloped into the heart of the maze.

CHAPTER 15

Wizard Raspberry paced the rocky prominence jutting from the mouth of the dragon's cave. He had to hop once in a while to avoid the anxious lashing of Grimley's tail. The rest of the dragon blocked the cave's entrance, where Grimley watched over his mate and their hatching egg.

For the last two days the dragon had moved from his current position only long enough to pick up the wizard, fly him to the river to catch more fish, which he disguised as deer meat, and return with him and the meat to the ledge. Grimley had been considerate enough to spare a fish or two for Raspberry from each trip, it was true, but the wizard chafed under even such hospitable captivity when he thought of the King's plight.

He grew tired of pacing and sat down against the rocky wall into which Grimley's cave bored. The sun was pleasant and warm for a change, the rain having stopped an hour or so before. A double rainbow streaked overhead, close enough to touch.

Rock lichens softened the seat beneath him, a seat well out of the way of the lashing spiked tail of his host.

In the face of so much pleasantness, he found it increasingly difficult to concern himself with the King. After all, the man was a warrior, the veteran of many battles; surely he'd think of something to do to help himself. And one could hardly blame the dragon Grimley for retiring from the Royal Air Force so abruptly. He had his family to look after, and for whatever reason, the cattle Rowan had promised the scaly pair as payment for their services had disappeared. Dragons weren't exactly known for their selfless sense of patriotism.

Finally, the wizard fell asleep reflecting that if one had to be the involuntary guest of dragons, it was fortunate to be captured by beasts whose cave had such a nice southern exposure.

He was shaken awake by the earth rumbling beneath him, and by thunderous roars. A singed smell invaded his nostrils, and he sat up, rubbing his eyes. In mid-air, just beyond the ledge, above a scenic ragged purple plunge into oblivion hundreds of leagues below, Dragon Grimley flew cartwheels, wing-springs, and aerial acrobatics of amazing agility and variety. Both the roaring and the singed smell emanated from the excited dragon, who bellowed at the top of his lungs while belching forth a furnace full of flame, charring anything in the direction in which the dragon's snout happened to be pointing at the time.

"AAAAROOOGAH! AAAROOGAH!" the dragon cheered.

Raspberry tiptoed to the cave's entrance, keeping close to the wall to avoid being broiled by Grimley.

Grizel sat in the midst of a lot of broken eggshell, her blue and green tail curled around a small gold and green miniature of herself. She was brushing the little dragon's scales with her tongue, and looking exceptionally pleased with herself.

A breath of foul hot air at his back and a sudden thud, and Raspberry looked up to see Grimley, who had landed on the ledge behind him.

"It's a girl," the dragon told him, and reached into the cave, extracting something glittering, which he pressed into the wizard's hands with his great clawed foot. "Here, have a diamond. Have two. I'm a father! Isn't she beautiful? Going to be as pretty as 'er mother, I'll wager. Hot dog!"

But before Raspberry could compliment the dragons on their new offspring, the ledge was suddenly invaded by a large party of people who abruptly materialized out of thin air. They carried with them the fragrance of spirits, but not the kind that walked

301

through walls. Several of them still held flagons clenched in their fists. Among them, amazingly, was his own pointy-eared child.

"Hello, father," she said. "We've come to help."

"Oh, Grimley! How thoughtful!" Grizel cried from within the cave. "Your meat-bringer's brought us a baby present! How did he know it would be just the thing? Our poor little Grippeldice is famished!"

All through the night the unicorns galloped, bearing their riders and themselves higher and deeper into the maze. Though they stumbled and slid and sometimes fell on the steep, glassy surface of the maze floor, they pressed on, driven by fear of pursuit, struggling against the keening wind. Pegeen's aura was their beacon, but the black cracks in the glittering crystal had a way of not appearing until Eagledown was almost upon them.

By first light they were still deep inside the maze, in front of the mouth of a tunnel. Colin twisted on Snowshadow's back and listened carefully. Several times during the night he'd heard the shouts of men, and once had seen torchlight far back down the maze. But now, except for the banshee wind, he heard nothing.

"Seems we've lost them," he yawned, stretching. Though the unicorn water had cleansed even the stiffness of being frozen in one position from his body along with his illness, and he felt better than he could ever remember having felt, physically, he was nevertheless weary from lack of sleep, and sore again from riding bareback all night long. Maggie arched her back and pointed her toes and stretched, too. Pegeen dismounted and walked over to inspect the tunnel.

"Very little wonder I could never get a clear picture of the maze from the castle," she said, returning to them after satisfying her curiosity. "If I had a brain in my head, I would have realized that an iceworm boring through a glacier isn't going to make the same sort of maze a rich lord has his gardener plot to amuse the houseguests. We must be now in a part of the glacier where the ice is so thick the worm couldn't melt all of that on top. See? He's simply drilled through it."

"I hope he didn't go underground instead of back up," Maggie said. "I could probably melt our way out, but it would take time."

"No. There's light at the other end," Pegeen assured her. "That's what I wanted to check. But I think we should walk through. Carefully. The worm's breath and the pressure of his passing seem to have fused most of the glacier's natural fissures, but perhaps we won't find it so inside the tunnel. I'll take it slowly."

They passed through three more of the tunnels without mishap. Fortunately, the darker it got inside, the brighter the princess's aura grew. By the time they had negotiated the last tunnel, morning had broken.

A short, steep climb led them above the tunnels, to a high plateau whose rock was so thinly coated with ice that the maze walls were less than thigh-high in places, allowing the fugitives to gaze out over acres of channeled ice.

On all sides of the plateau, deeper ice contained high walls and tunnels similar to those through which they had just passed. Far down to the right, the castle fused with the glacier. The unusual angle of their vantage point to the valley allowed them also to see the ruined village, teeming with the active black spots which were Fearchar's troops. The Blabbermouth River still wore its morning cloak of mist so heavily upon its surface that it masked the water completely.

"Under other circumstances, I'd enjoy a day like this," Pegeen told them. "It's not often so clear in the valley. It's amazing the detail one can see." She shaded her eyes with her hand as she looked across the ice and into the valley. "Why, most days you can't even see where the river is, much less—oh, dear." She pointed. "Look, there to the south. Do you see them?"

Colin and Maggie shaded their eyes and squinted in the direction of her finger. A double handful of specks probably twenty furlongs from the river moved slowly toward its banks. At the head of the specks was a speck twice as large as the others, and from the top of it the sun glinted molten copper.

"Your royal brother-in-law has arrived," Colin told Maggie. She nodded slowly. Pegeen's face bore a stricken, guilty look. "This is all my fault," she said. "I meant to help. I never intended to lure him into a trap. But you see, when I coded that message telling him where we were, I simply meant to let him know what he might do to lift Fearchar's wretched curse from that poor little baby. Now all of those good men will be slain!"

"And we won't be able to do anything but watch," Colin said bitterly.

Primrose looked down her long muzzle at the scene in the valley. "Yes, your friends will surely perish. For my mai—Sally is very brave. She cannot but triumph."

Eagledown snorted. "I thought you'd caught on, but I guess
303

you're a little slow, aren't you, nag? Your precious Sally isn't down *there*. She's up here prowling this worm-eaten glacier, looking for us with a big flaying knife."

Primrose stared at him for a moment, her watery gray eyes watering even more, then wheeled and galloped down the far side of the plateau and out of sight into a tunnel.

"Wait!" Snowshadow called after her. "Wait! We must all stay together!"

"Let the bird-brain go," Eagledown said. "She'll just be in our way anyhow, the silly, flighty creature."

"I wouldn't mind being flighty right now," Colin said. "Remember, Maggie, when your Granny changed me into a mockingbird and sicced Ching on me? I thought I'd never want to see another bird."

Maggie's eyes were still glued to Rowan's party, moving slowly but surely towards death. "I remember," she said absently.

"What I wouldn't give if she could make me fly again right now!" he mused. "I could warn Rowan, and when the deed was sung of later, he would say 'and then a little bird told me...'"

Maggie whirled to face him, light dawning in her eyes. "Say that again."

"I merely said that he would say 'and then a little bird told me' when—"

"No. I mean the part about flying. Never mind. You brilliant man! You've given me an idea and—yes, I think we have all we need to do it."

"I did? We do? Well, always happy to be of service." Then he stopped beaming and scratched his head, puzzled. "What?"

"We *can* fly to warn the King," she told them. "Remember Wizard Raspberry's little toys?"

"The 'belows' you mean?" Colin asked. "Or were they called 'bellows'? Perhaps it was 'ballasts.'"

"Surely you don't mean he's still working on those balloon things," Pegeen laughed. "Why, he was trying to make those work while he was still an agent in my father's court. I don't see how those can help us, Maggie. Even if you could build one in time, you'd never be able to get it to land in the right place with a message, unless, of course, you control wind as well as fire."

"I don't. Not from such a great distance, anyway, but I can sometimes do a thing or two with air currents if I can stretch my magic by making it simulate doing certain household chores. I had in mind something different." She pulled the silk gown out of her pocket, where she'd stuck it when she disguised herself as an Everclear peasant before joining Sally Forth's band at the foot

304

of the glacier. From her medicine pouch, she took her bone needle, sewing shears, and pocket spindle. "Now then." She closed her eyes and concentrated, seeing in her mind enlarged versions of the shapes she had cut for the wizard from silk handkerchiefs.

Pegeen nodded with the appreciation of a fellow craftswoman as Maggie's shears cut balloon pieces from the dress skirt, raveled the bodice for silk thread, and turned the operation over to the spindle, which spun the thread out long and fine. The thread snaked through the slim eye of the bone needle, which whipped together the pieces of balloon in less time than it would have taken Pegeen to sew ten stitches. The unicorns shied away from the snapping shears and flying needle, and jumped over the low wall to the next path over, where they watched with rolling eyes.

Colin simply sat atop the ice wall and tootled softly on his flute. He was getting used to this sort of thing.

"Now then," Maggie said, when the completed sack lay at her feet. "There's not a moment to lose. Colin, Primrose, please help me find any straw still sticking to the unicorns' coats."

"Not another basket, surely?" Colin asked, looking up and tucking his flute back into his pocket at the same time.

"Absolutely another basket. I'll need something to ride in if I'm to fly down and warn Rowan, won't I?"

"*You're* going to fly down? In this? Don't be ridiculous. It won't even work. It has to be—you know," he cupped his hands in semi-circles, "*rounder*, or something, doesn't it?" But he nevertheless jumped the wall and began brushing Snowshadow's coat free of straw from the pen.

The Princess did likewise to Eagledown and Moonshine. "Naturally, it will need inflation," she told Colin, "But there is quite a lot of wind up here."

"Don't look at me when you say that," he laughed. "I may be able to sing an eighty-verse chantey without stopping, but I'm not windy enough to blow up that thing!"

"No, but if we stretch it across the mouth of a tunnel, you see?"

"Good idea, Princess," Maggie said. "I hadn't thought of using the tunnels."

They gathered the pieces of straw into a pile, and Maggie sat down beside it and began pulling the short pieces until they lengthened, stretching into long fibers that, with minimal assistance from her, began twining themselves around each other, writhing like a nest of snakes. "There, that should do it," she

305

said, when the basket had grown as high as her head. Abruptly, the straws tucked themselves into their last completed row and were quiet. Maggie stood, dusting her hands off on her skirt. "To the tunnel!" she said.

It took all three of them to control the bag when the wind gusted through the tunnel and filled it with cold air. They had less problem holding onto the bag than they did keeping the air inside while they closed the sack and Maggie tied it shut.

Finally, they had managed to haul the half-filled balloon back up to the plateau when Primrose galloped, wild-eyed and dripping foam, up from the path she had taken into the maze a short time before.

"Flee!" she cried. "Flee at once or be steamed alive as I nearly was! The worm has turned!" She would have slid back down the other path except that Colin and the princess caught her, and calmed her until she'd stopped her terrified rearing.

"You mean the worm is awake?" Pegeen asked. "But he's never *been* awake."

"Maybe all the recent activity has disturbed him," Colin suggested. "And us coming into the glacier. Worms aren't supposed to be overly bright, but they are guardians, of a sort."

"Stop talking and FLEE!" the lathered unicorn advised shrilly.

"Where?" Pegeen demanded. "We could get trapped into one of the deep channels, or a tunnel, and have the thing on top of us. Here, it's shallow and we can side-step the monster if need be. It seems to me we're in the safest possible place for dealing with ice worms right where we are."

Maggie looked down at the half-inflated balloon and down across the glacier again, to where the specks were stopped now, close to the banks of the river. "We'll never be able to warn Rowan now."

"We certainly won't be able to if we're steamed alive," Pegeen told her.

"Steamed?" Maggie asked. "Don't you mean burned?"

"You're thinking of dragons, dear. Iceworms steam. That's how these passages were created."

"It was dreadful!" cried Primrose. "Billows and billows of hot putrid stuff boiling out at me through that tunnel! I ran as I have never run before, and when I looked back down, I saw it! It was larger than ten of the tallest cedars lashed together, and it was covered all over with nasty blue fur."

"Not scales?" Pegeen asked.

"No. No, fur! And—and it RIPPLED, and slid behind all that steam and oh, it was dis*gust*ing!"

"Steam, hum?" Maggie said.

306

"And ripples," shivered Primrose. "Great, nasty, undulating ones."

"How much steam?"

"Quite enough for me, thank you. It must have gone on thrice the length of the worm, at least. Horrible! And it hissed!"

"Hissed, you say?" Colin asked. "Like that, maybe?"

A low, leaking sound filled the air, accompanied by a sibilant slithering and thumping noise.

"Over the wall!" Pegeen cried.

"No. Help me." Maggie wrestled the silk sack to the farthest edge of the plateau, across the path Primrose had used to escape the worm. "We can use the worm's steam to inflate the balloon, don't you see? Then all we have to do is pull it out of the worm's way, step over the wall, and while the worm slides merrily on his way, we attach the basket and I fly down to warn Rowan!"

Colin didn't think much of the idea. He didn't like the thought of the worm being awake with them on its glacier, and felt that if only he could sing an appropriate lullabye loud enough, he'd be able to lull the thing back to sleep. But since he was less loathe to brave a little advance steam to fill Maggie's balloon than he was to getting himself steamed while trying to serenade the worm back into slumber, he kept quiet.

Unfortunately, others on the glacier did not. As the first breath of steam shot up from the tunnel to the left of their plateau, they heard, along with the slumping, slithering sound of the worm's approach, clanging swords and cursing and Sally Forth's voice, ringing high and girlish, crying, "Onward, men!"

But by then the balloon was filling with rushing steam, blossoming like some mushroom-shaped flower, and it took all of their strength to hold it while Maggie tied the precious steam inside. They had a hot, uncomfortable time of it, dragging the balloon out of the way before the steam could totally engulf them.

No sooner had they boosted the balloon over the wall than the beast was upon them. Maggie looked up from tying the basket to the balloon just in time to see the monster pour into view behind its steamy veil. The sight of it so unnerved her that she forgot balloon, King, bandits, and all, hypnotized by the slither and slump of a column of blue fur long enough to fill the great hall at Fort Iceworm twice over.

Pegeen couldn't stand to look at the beast. It was too fearsome. She averted her eyes just in time to see their last hope rise, bobbling in the air just above the unicorns' backs.

She leaped, and landed on the basket's rim, head, chest, arms and shoulders inside the basket, legs and feet flailing the sky as the balloon rose, drifting gently above the worm, above the maze, and beyond, to glide above the soon-to-be-embattled valley.

Difficult as it was to think rationally with one's head in a basket and one's bottom keeping company with the clouds, Pegeen endeavored to do so. It wouldn't do to panic, or even to scream. The others couldn't help her even if they could hear her, which she doubted. But if she wasn't screaming, someone certainly was. Awful cries of agony screeched up to her from somewhere near the point of her unanticipated launching. She hoped it wasn't her friends screaming, but she really had quite enough problems of her own to worry about just then, without troubling herself with theirs.

Like how to have her rear half join the front INside the basket. By the time she accomplished that, calling on gymnastic skill she would have sworn she did not possess, she was unfit for any activity more strenuous than panting in the bottom of the basket.

As she began to recover, her eye was caught by the fluttering of the little thread holding the balloon together at its bottom. It seemed perilously slender for something so vital to keeping her aloft. And though staying aloft was definitely preferable to crashing into the valley, it would have been nice if Maggie had been thoughtful enough to explain how one was supposed to get this cursed thing DOWN, slowly, and in an orderly fashion that would permit one to place oneself somewhere in close proximity to Roari Rowan so that one might warn him. That was supposed to be the purpose of all of this strenuous exercise, after all.

A gruesome thought occured to her. Perhaps, since Maggie had meant to fly the balloon herself, the control of the thing was intricately bound up with the hearth witch's magic powers. She brushed the thought resolutely from her mind. After all, Maggie was not the only one with talent. Hadn't Pegeen's people always said of her, during her father's reign, that Pegeen the Illuminator could put a silver lining in any cloud? She ought to have a go at these clouds, if that were true, she thought. As she was in a very good position to see, all of them had distinctly dismal GRAY linings. She was practically close enough now to count the raindrops in them.

But surely she wasn't THAT high. Clouds tended to hang low over the valley, as a rule. Oh, don't be such a coward, she told herself. You can at least have a peek to get your bearings.

Raising herself to her knees, she gazed down across the vast expanses of empty gray air to a rapidly flattening field with a tiny town on one side of it and a thin gray yarn, the fog-shrouded Blabbermouth, running through it.

She sank quickly to the bottom of the basket, shaking. Curiosity was no great virtue either, she decided.

She regretted looking down, regretted catching the balloon, regretted sending the message to Rowan, and bitterly regretted ever setting eyes on Fearchar Brown. But she most regretted neglecting to bring along another torch and tinderbox. She would give absolutely *anything* for a smoke.

"Oh, no!"

Colin tore himself away from the sight of the worm's retreating tail to see what had prompted Maggie's cry.

She pointed. Far beyond the glacier, out over the edge of the valley, their balloon wafted through the clouds. "The princess took it," Maggie said. "I would never have thought her to betray us."

Colin patted her shoulder and watched helplessly as their last hope floated nonchalantly away. All of their time and effort was wasted. The bandits would be upon Rowan before he knew it, while Colin and Maggie were stuck up here on the glacier with the unicorns. It wasn't even much good thinking about escaping. What would Argonia be like under Fearchar's rule? Colin was too discouraged to think about that, so instead he helped Maggie to her feet. "Come along, now. We'd best get moving. I heard Sally's men just before the worm—"

Screams began filling the air, masculine screams, high-pitched, terrified, gargling, dying screams. Sizzling screams.

Eagledown chuckled. "Sounds like all the worms just got together."

"Oh, those poor men!" Snowshadow said quietly.

"Maiden!" Primrose sobbed.

"Don't waste any sympathy on her," Maggie snapped. "She's probably turned into another whirlwind and blown clean away before the thing touched her. I only wish we could do the same."

"Why can't we?" Colin asked, with sudden inspiration. "The worm doesn't steam from its back end, does it? And it's blind, you know. I noticed that as it passed. It won't be able to see us, and it's too ungainly to double back on itself. It seems to me all we have to do is follow it back down to the castle, and let it take care of Fearchar's henchmen for us."

"Not bad thinking for a mortal!" Eagledown applauded.

"Yes," Primrose said, leaping onto the ice. "I'll see for

309

myself if Sally got awaaaaayyyy—'' and slid spraddle-legged down the worm's path, newly slicked with fresh-melted ice. Her frightened neighing echoed back to them as she shot through the first tunnel, and out of sight.

Colin had lunged for the terrified unicorn as she slid past him, and tried to grab her. But no sooner had he set foot over the wall than he, too, slipped and slid swooshing down the tunnel.

"Now what?" Maggie asked, blinking rapidly, baffled by the speed with which Colin had followed his own suggestion.

Moonshine touched a hoof to the path, and retracted it again. "Tis too slick for the likes of us, friend Maggie. We cannot follow."

"Nonsense!" said Eagledown. "Looks like fun to me!" He stepped out onto the path too, but was perhaps unwittingly more cautious than Colin or the mare had been, having seen their fate. He neither slipped nor fell. "Huh," he said, and looked down the long slope where the others had traveled before him. "Maybe— maybe if I laid on my side, and you gave me a little push, I wouldn't be so likely to break a leg," he suggested to Maggie.

"What about the cracks in the ice?" Moonshine asked. "We could fall in."

"True," Maggie said, "But we'll just have to hope the iceworm melted them all back together again. Besides, by the time we get past the first tunnel, we should be traveling so fast we'll fly right over the cracks. It's either that or stay up here."

"Aw, quit dallying around and push, will you?" Eagledown said, lying down on his side and tucking his legs under him. Maggie pushed and he shot down into the tunnel.

The other two unicorns followed him, with varying degrees of reluctance, and by the time she had shoved them, she was grateful she wouldn't have to walk down. She was far too tired.

She took three skating-running steps and dove onto the ice, head first. But just before she did, she looked up again. She could no longer see the balloon.

Roari Rowan was an old infantryman of long standing, and he never tired of marching, or of skiing through snowfields beside gypsy sleighs, for that matter. That was the sort of thing a good soldier took in his stride, and Rowan was King by virtue of being the best soldier in Argonia.

So when he saw the vision, he put it down not to weariness, but rather to some residue of ill effect that perhaps lingered from his near-drowning.

Otherwise, he thought it damned unfair that a man should be

310

seeing a thing like that when he hadn't had a good stout drink in weeks.

Whatever its origin, the vision did not go away, but continued hovering before him, just within the mist covering the river.

His men were finishing their morning meal. He'd finished his quickly, having little stomach for it. His usual voracious appetite was spoiled by an uneasy feeling gnawing at his vitals. Part of it was simply due to the mist. He liked to see where he was going. He'd wait for it to clear before he took his men anywhere. They were getting too near their goal to go blundering about blindly. He'd been pacing the bank, listening to the river prattle to itself, hoping it might drop a clue as to what lay beyond it, when the vision descended.

Cyril Perchingbird approached the river, and Rowan stretched out a hamlike hand and collared the man, pointing before him at what he thought he saw through the drifting mist. The river was no match for Rowan's booming voice, even discreetly lowered as it was, in case enemy ears were listening.

"There now, Perchingbird, what's that look to you to be, just there, beyond yon fog?"

Sir Cyril looked, and stood on tiptoe to shout up to his lord's ear. "'Tis a lady, Sire. Wouldn't you say so?"

"I would that, Perchingbird. I would indeed, if you could just tell me which lady, and why a lady who so resembles Her Highness the Princess Pegeen the Illuminator at that, and what she is doing floating about up there, making me think I've had one too many."

"Well, Sire," Perchingbird said, shouting his reply through cupped hands, "I've never met the lady face to face. But since we're near the castle in her chart, and since the lady resembles her so closely, as you say, I wonder if we might consider the possibility that the lady might BE the Princess Pegeen?"

"Nonsense!" the King bellowed, casting discretion momentarily to the wind. "What would Milady Pegeen be doing riding round in a flower basket blowing that great silly bubble from her mouth?"

The basket chose that moment to set itself and its cargo softly down on the riverbank. The lady turned toward them startled eyes and cheeks puffed out like a chipmunk's. Then, slowly, her cheeks deflated and steam curled exuberantly from her nostrils. Her expression was normal and even serene by the time the steam cleared, and slowly, the bubble to which she'd been orally connected collapsed into a mantle which settled on her shoulders like a garment of state.

311

Holding forth her hand for their assistance, she smiled a smile that was both regal and proud. Now Rowan was quite certain she was indeed the Princess Pegeen, and he strode forward to assist her, lifting her from the basket as easily as if she was a child.

Smoothing her tattered skirts with great aplomb, she looked from one of them to the other. "I never again wish to hear anyone say that smoking is a nasty, useless habit," she told them.

"Yes, m'lady," Sir Cyril replied, kneeling.

By then, Pegeen was kneeling before Rowan. "My Liege. I am Pegeen Ashburn of the royal house of Finbar, called the Fireproof, and I have come to warn you that you are in immediate and deadly peril."

Before she had finished speaking, a fresh wind blew the mist from the river.

Colin shot down the glacial slide, ricocheting off the high maze walls like a confused arrow. Sunlight flashed in his eyes, blinding him one moment and vanishing the next as he rocketed into a tunnel. His teeth rattled loose in his head, the seat of his pants burned, and everything else was numb with cold. Once he closed his eyes and slammed head-first into a wall; after that he kept his eyes open and his hands out to shove away from such obstacles.

The sight of the steamrollered bandits would have no doubt made him ill had be been able to stick around long enough to indulge his sensitivities. Fortunately the bandits' bodies, like all other landmarks save the brilliant spots flashing before his eyes as the sun hit the ice, blurred past him too quickly for him to see them clearly.

But suddenly he was looking straight down the chute and ahead to the humping blue behind of the great worm, and over the worm into the cliff castle, directly in the monster's path. Surely the worm wouldn't risk invading the castle, would it? It was a dumb, blind thing, true, but it had avoided the place when it made the maze, after all. Or had it? Had the castle been built before or after the maze? No matter. The question was rhetorical now. Steam geysered into the air high enough to obscure the sun as the worm slump-slithered through the castle's back wall.

The worm's tail jumped out to meet Colin. He threw his arm up over his face as he plumped into it. Then he uncovered his eyes again. He hadn't dared hope for such a soft landing.

Primrose was there, coasting along in the worm's wake. The two of them and the tail were yet well outside the castle, but they slid quickly forward with each giant hump of the worm's body. Within moments the worm would have penetrated the castle, and would then plunge out the front and down the cliff and they would plummet behind him. Primrose seemed unaware of their predicament. Her pupils had disappeared into quivering whites, her mouth foamed and her body shook with more than the great worm's movement. While Colin thought he might manage to stop himself by grasping some stationary object in the castle and clinging to it, Primrose hadn't the same option, even if she had had her senses about her.

From behind him came a high, frightened whinny, and looking up, he saw the other three unicorns, tail over horn, spinning down the maze. Collision seemed imminent.

He climbed the worm's tail as if it were a staircase and clung, clutching handsful of fur. He had barely cleared the ice before Moonshine, Eagledown, and Snowshadow thumped into the worm. Wonderful! Now he had four unicorns to worry about, besides his own hide.

When the worm humped again, Colin did too, and dragged himself along the creature's back hand-over-hand, twining his fingers in the pale blue fur. He crawled very fast and prayed the worm wasn't deaf as well as blind. Since it had seemingly responded to the disturbance on its glacier, it at least must be sensitive to vibrations, if not sounds.

Ah well. No time like the present to find out, he supposed. He crawled up the worm's middle, most of which occupied the throne room and barracks, shifting his weight with the humping and straightening until he reached the head. Steam rose hot and acrid in front of him, and dissipated into the empty air. Less than a cartlength away from the monster's head, the castle's outer ledge puddled and ran down the cliff, cascading into the valley below.

Colin pressed the magic flute to his lips and prayed for a worm lullabye.

A long, thin ululation warbled from the flute. The worm reared its head and Colin felt a rise at his feet as the beast began to hump its middle up for the last forward push, the one that would plunge them all into the valley. Then the blind befurred snout began to weave back and forth, swaying to the eerie melody. The steam dribbled to nothing and the long body relaxed, and stayed that way.

"Some people will go to any lengths to get an audience," Maggie said in a shaking voice. She waded toward him from behind, sinking knee-deep in worm fur with each step. The beast

313

dozed heedlessly on, apparently good for another half century or so of napping.

Colin grabbed her up and held her until *he'd* stopped shaking.

By then it was time for them both to start all over again. Maggie gripped his arm and turned him to face the valley. "Look," she whispered.

Though the streets of the village appeared as empty as the ruined buildings suggested they would be, their gutted interiors swarmed with armed men. The nymph was there too, concealed within the old inn, the were Wulfric braced and bristling beside her. From where they stood, she looked none the worse for wear. She poised her silver hunting horn near her mouth, and her body leaned toward the river. It glittered and gossiped along, no longer bearing any taint of mist, oblivious to the ragged party fording it, led by a red-haired giant and a woman whose hair was of a faintly dimmer hue. The woman's arm swung to gesture to each of the buildings, and the King's men clustered cautiously about him, stopping near the first building to form a defensive ring around him.

"Pegeen's warned him!" Maggie said, almost cheering. "But why don't they stop?"

As if in answer, Rowan's voice rang out across the valley, drowning out the river and all other sounds, so commanding and thunderous that Colin was concerned lest the worm waken again. "'Tis no use hidin' like wee little weasles!" the King bellowed. "I know yer back there, and I know what manner of churls ye be, and I tell you straight out, I can slay the lot of you. But I've no quarrel with you men, whoever you are, if you'll come forth and pledge me fealty here and now. My quarrel is with the black-hearted villain who's laid a curse on my wee daughter. Send him out now and 't will go the gentler with you."

His answer was a blast from Sally's horn and a volley of arrows from the rooftops. Pegeen fell at once. So did three of Rowan's men.

"Bastards!" Colin said, his voice thickened. He cast about for a way off the cliff and found it almost immediately. The revolutionaries had left their rope ladder looped over its iron moorings on the ledge; fortunately, on the part of the ledge unmelted by the worm. He reached for the ladder, but Maggie pulled him back.

"Wait. What about the unicorns? They'll never get down alone and they could help us—"

"Afterwards, Maggie. Only afterwards. They're no match for that army of Sally's, and she'd love to recapture them. Stay here with them. If we fail, don't let them fall into Fearchar's hands again.''

Before she could protest, he swung out and down onto the ladder. By the time she'd collected her wits and started to follow, he was at the foot of the cliff where, with a guilty, defiant look up at her, he jerked the ladder up and out, snatching it from its hooks. It fell beside him, and he turned and sprinted into the village.

"Blast him!" she swore, furious at his underhanded, over-protective gesture. "Show a man a little affection and he gets uppity every time!"

She walked tiredly back down to the worm's tail, where the unicorns were waiting, and slid down the furry back to join them. Primrose seemed somewhat quieter than she had been and the others looked at her expectantly.

"Don't blame me!" she snapped. "Everything's falling apart down there and that blundering bard has stranded us here. Any ideas?"

Eagledown blew and stamped for a moment before saying, "The truth is, witch, we unicorns could use a break from all the hubbub you people are causing around here."

"You WHAT?" she asked.

Moonshine stepped forward, but kept his eyes lowered as he said, "We have decided we have the need for a brief council among ourselves, and would request that you grant us a moment of privacy."

"A brief moment only," Snowshadow pleaded gently. "There are matters we must decide among us."

Maggie stared at them with injured incredulity, then shrugged as if their rejection of her didn't hurt, and walked off, saying, "I can use the time to look for a weapon, I suppose. Or another way out of here. Never let it be said that Maggie Brown stays where she's not wanted."

Sally Forth, and she alone, had kept her men to the task at hand. Not even the great worm had kept her from this battle, though it had slain the valiant comrades who accompanied her into the maze. In her whirlwind, she had escaped. And now, by sheer force of will, she had bent her men's minds from the worm's attack on their stronghold, directing them with all her skillful charms to watch the mist, and wait, and never mind the slither and slump and steam above.

She was unsurprised when the monster stopped and did not venture into the valley. Ice monsters stayed on ice and if they

315

strayed from ice, they died. Surely even the dumb brute who had slain her men knew as much. And then too, right was on her side, and justice, and the good will of the Dark Pilgrim, who looked to her to win this, the definitive battle in support of their great Cause. She would not let him down, even if she had to fight this battle single-handedly.

At her side, Wulfric growled and whined, anxious for blood. She wished almost that he was in man form, to consult with her, but she had not seen him in that guise since they arrived at the castle and, indeed, his fighting skill and ferocity were greater in his present form.

But he was no more ferocious than she. She was patient as a spinning spider when the usurping giant strode arrogantly into her web, but the moment he stopped, she had blown her signal, and had loosed her first arrow into the breast of the Pilgrim's traitorous woman, the elitist "Princess," Pegeen.

With the woman many others had fallen, and the usurper could not spare many. As her men nocked more arrows and retrieved spears fallen short of their mark, the enemy collected their dead and wounded and retreated to the cover of the house containing the half-dead servants from the village near the stream she'd once guarded.

Her men were ready now, and the enemy would not withstand them again. Stepping into the street, she showed herself, and putting her horn to lip, blew the charge. Then, with a wave of her arm, she led her men to battle.

Maggie seethed and stormed through the castle's rooms, wishing she could lay hands on her uncle, or Sally Forth, or even Colin, to let them know the danger of crossing a witch. She felt like destroying everything she passed, but the castle was sparsely furnished, and if she was truly trapped up here she might have need of the bedding and clothing and food remaining within the castle. No weapons were left behind, nor armor of any kind.

She slammed the door of the storage room. Empty. The slamming reverberated through the wall, and it must have been the strange acoustics in the cavernous corridor which made the sound seem to repeat itself with equal force at the end of the passage.

Or did that other door really still vibrate with the force of its closing, as it seemed to her when she approached it?

She paused for a moment, listening again, but heard only the splatter of water dropping from the ceiling. Cautiously, she opened the door, and smiled. Here at last was something useless

316

she could tear apart without a twinge of conscience. Lining the walls and long tables were the paraphernalia of her uncle's largely bogus magic practice: animal skeletons, scrolls, tomes, flasks and beakers, lamps and crucibles and jars of this and that. All the makings of a good bonfire.

But as she looked around the room, she noticed that the water dripping from above didn't pool on the floor, but ran off somewhere in the middle. Investigating, she saw the rucked-back rug, and the outline of the trap door beneath it.

She pushed the rug aside and pulled the door up by the iron ring set into it. Under it was a stone staircase, broad enough for two people abreast and surprisingly dry for being in such a drippy location.

She whooped with joy and hurried back to the unicorns. Here was a way to get them all off the cliff.

"But the point is, we don't think we ought to get involved in men's battles," Snowshadow told her. "It's bad enough when you people hurt each other, much less involving unicorns. Our power is a healing one."

"Hold on there, filly, and let this witch tell us again where the staircase is," Eagledown interrupted. "I don't know about this healing business, though I'm as quick to dip my horn in a puddle to protect the local wildlife as any 'corn. But what I'm anxious to dip it in NOW is the scum who've caused me to break it off. If people think we 'corns are a lot of silly foals, they aren't going to let us live long enough to heal anything. I say, spit the lot of 'em!"

"But the Creed!" Snowshadow protested.

"That IS the Creed, you ignorant filly," Eagledown said, and repeated his stanza about making men bleed.

"And I say why horn in where we aren't concerned?" Primrose said. "At least when the horrid two-legged monsters are bashing each other, they aren't deceiving, imprisoning and mutilating us."

"*I* didn't deceive any of you, and it just may interest you to know that Princess Pegeen has intercepted an arrow in your behalf," Maggie said hotly. "That's right. She died trying to help you. And I'm trying to help you too if you'll only stop bickering long enough to pay attention. As long as you remain up here you'd damn well *better* care who wins down below—you could end up stewing in the same broth we just got you out of."

"For my fodder, we'd be best off letting you destroy each other," Primrose snorted back. "But very well, I'll come. The

317

forest beasts can only make do so long without a noble unicorn to minister to their wounds and purify their water."

"But we must NOT slay, save in defense of our lives," Snowshadow insisted. "Is that not true, Moonshine?"

He shook his mane impatiently. "I must see for myself what betides my friends, and whether by horning or healing I will do what I'm able to aid them, for if it be ununicornly or no, I love them well."

"I'm glad to see someone has kept his senses around here," Maggie said, lighting a torch with a snap of her fingers. "This is a fine time, if you ask me, for the lot of you to turn balky. Come along."

She led them down the staircase slowly, for the steps were worn and in places heavily coated with ice.

"I'd sooner have walked down the glacier!" Primrose complained.

"I only wish you'd walk on your own feet instead of mine," Maggie retorted.

"Watch that torch, witch, or you'll blind me!" Eagledown commanded.

The battle centered on one small building, farthest of all the village dwellings from the castle and closest to the river. From the doorway, Rowan and his men defended themselves. The building was ringed ten deep in bandits. Arrows and spears rained against it, for the most part futilely. Ankle-deep mud mired the attackers, and the pungent smell of carnage and sweat seethed through the sunlit morning.

Rowan chopped his way through his attackers with the every-day ease of a woodcutter plying his trade. He was the only one of his band visible above the heads of Fearchar's pack, and for a moment she feared he stood alone. But now and then, when his attention and the solid wooden cartwheel he used for a shield were turned to the left or to the right, he would suddenly grow another set of arms on his blind side.

Still, he essentially defended the place by himself.

Maggie made her way toward the battle, keeping close to the houses and out of the way of the rooftop archers, looking in all directions before she dared to dart from one sanctuary to another.

Not that she had the faintest idea what she was going to do once she got there. Get herself killed by the King's enemies, or entrapped as his allies were? Neither situation held much promise.

Then she saw the wolf.

He crouched on the roof top, a little behind Rowan's head.

The King was taller than the doorway he defended, and while he had friends at his back, none guarded his head.

Maggie ran forward, shouting her spell so that as soon as she was within range, it would take effect. She was still well back from the enemy's rear, when the roof disintegrated into a shower of toothpicks. The wolf leaped at the same moment. He yelped once and pawed air and splintering ceiling before falling into the house, where she hoped the rest of Rowan's supporters would dispose of him.

A horn sounded, and the attackers surged forward more urgently than before. Rowan hefted his cartwheel, and pressed the front lines back, whacking and gouging at them. He grinned ferociously all the while, teeth bared and eyes deceptively merry.

The horn sounded again, and a flight of arrows sprang by overhead, peppering the newly roofless building. Some of the grunting and screaming now seemed to be coming from inside. Maggie took cover behind the corner of the house opposite the one defended by the King just before the horn blasted once more.

She squinted, tracking the sound. Sally Forth stood in the front line of her troops, but was standing on something near a corner of the house, well away from the King's sword, protectively walled off by her followers. The last flight of arrows had been scantier than the one before, and the nymph raised her horn again.

At least Maggie knew how to put a stop to that. "Make that noisy instrument into a drinking horn," she commanded. The horn met the nymph's mouth, but no sound interrupted the bangings, clangings, moanings and cryings of battle, and no flight of arrows followed.

Even a giant like the King couldn't help but weary under such an onslaught. Bards might sing of him killing hundreds single-handed, but Maggie for one was ill-prepared to wager her life and the lives of her friends that the bards weren't exaggerating, as usual, on that score.

The more Rowan hacked down to be trampled under their comrades' feet, the more comrades clamored forward to be hacked down in their turn. How could mere hearthcraft aid an impossible situation like that? She couldn't risk fire. To do so would be to burn friends and foes alike.

Arrows came singly and in small bunches now, but there were far fewer than before. Tracing their pattern, she saw that only the three houses closest to the King's stronghold were now involved in the attack. A boon, truly, but not one she could spare time to consider.

But she did consider the laced leggings worn by most of the bandits, binding their britches into their boots. Such laces would weave well, and once woven, would make effective hobbles.

She had to show herself enough to come in range again of her subjects, and to be close enough to the materials she meant to use. At least her brown dress and dark coloring blended well with mud so she was fairly inconspicuous. Extending her arms low and toward her enemies' feet, she pantomined with her fingers the unlacing, the twining and interweaving of the laces, repeating and interlocking the movements for as many times as she could count heads, until sweat rolled into her eyes and her fingers and forearms cramped. Each time her fingers signed, leggings unlaced and laces tangled in a mating dance.

The enemy stopped fighting Rowan and began fighting each other, tugging, cursing, falling, hopping and sometimes stabbing and sawing as they tried to free themselves.

Maggie ducked for cover again, as more arrows rained down. This time only two houses were involved.

Eagledown and Moonshine galloped forward and began harrying the jumbled brigands from the perimeters, darting forward to slash with their hooves and gouge with their horns, inflicting injury and adding to the general pandemonium. Eagledown's broken horn had shorter striking range but inflicted worse damage than Moonshine's.

Their efforts, combined with Maggie's, provided the King with the respite he needed to clear the doorway, mowing a path in front of and around him. From inside the house behind him poured Neddy Pinchpurse, Maggie's old friend, Prince H. David Worthyman, his son, Davey, and other gypsies, nobles, and sailors, armed with daggers and an occasional sword, and shielded by pot lids, planks, and plates, and any other portable solid item which might afford them some small measure of protection. As they advanced, they captured better weapons from their fallen foes.

Now the doorway was guarded by only two men, and from her hiding place Maggie could see something of the inside, which was still heavily peopled with the refugees from Everclear and a few prone bodies, Rowan's dead and wounded.

A very pale pink glow lit one shadowy corner, where a portly gentleman cradled the body of a woman to him. He looked down at her with a look that was both grieving and beseeching, his face bathed in the glow that came from her body. As Maggie watched, the glow faded and died, and both figures were lost in shadow.

One last house sent up a feeble volley of arrows, and close by a familiar voice sang the text of Argonia's Royal Penal Code. Maggie smiled and looked around, but couldn't see him.

Then she heard more hooves, and Snowshadow pounded forward. "My people!" she trumpeted, "My people are in there! My villagers! They'll be slain!"

But now the brigands were hacking their bootlaces apart, and striking back at Rowan's band with more vigor. And from the formerly quiet houses in the rear of the village, more bandits swarmed, drowsy and yawning but well-armed with short swords and shields.

Then they were pouring from the house next to hers, and the one behind which she hid, and close by she heard a strangled cry, in the direction opposite from the battle.

Close to the western wall of the house to the right of hers, Colin lay face down in the mud, a dagger in his back, his eyes already starting to glaze. Blood trickled in a thin string from the corner of his mouth. Maggie fell to her knees beside him, but knew even before she touched him that he was dead. His cheek was still warm, and the breeze rippled his hair and billowed the bloodied back of his tunic. She gathered him in her arms and stroked his face and hair, rocking back and forth. "Colin, you ass," she lectured his limp form, "If you hadn't tried to leave me behind, I could have watched your silly back for you."

CHAPTER 16

"Your pardon, gentle mother," Raspberry shouted into Grizel's cave, "But my daughter's not for eating."

"You think not? Well, I can tell *you*, master meat-maker, MY daughter is hungry and I will feed her NOW."

Rusty smiled expectantly at her father, waiting for his approval. She didn't speak dragonese, nor pan-elfin for that matter. The men from the tavern shrank against the cliff wall, their improvised weapons and flagons clattering to their feet. They didn't speak dragonese either, but they had a sound theoretical grasp of dragon nature.

"Aw, com'on, hot shot, don't be that way," Grimley said.

"She's just a baby. She won't eat much. Just one or two of them."

"What's the problem, father?" Rusty asked. "Do the dragons require magical help? Perhaps I can be of assistance."

"No!" Raspberry said. "Didn't your mother ever teach you anything? A hungry dragon's den is no place for little girls!"

"I'm NOT a little girl," Rusty replied. "I have magic, too."

Grizel poked her head out of the cave and surveyed the people crowding her ledge as a housewife would study produce at the market. "The red-topped female is the proper size for a nice appetizer," she told her mate, "but spikey looking. How about that nice fat one over there, and the young one? You can let the old one go. He'll be far too tough."

"Dragon Grimley, you can't do this!" the wizard cried, blocking Grimley's claws as he reached for his mate's selections.

The dragon was fortunately still in a mellow mood. "No need to get hot under the collar there, fella. Look, I pre-cook everything for the baby. Just a little blast and it's over. They never feel a thing."

"That's NOT the point, noble dragon," the wizard told him. "These are loyal subjects like yourself, and this is my only daughter. How would you like it if I were to try to cook *your* daughter?"

"Let's go easy on the inflammatory remarks, eh, hot stuff?" the dragon suggested in a menace-edged tone.

Rusty laid her hand on her father's shoulder. "Really, father, if these beasts are hungry and you're unable to aid them, I'm sure I can with my magic. Just tell me what you need and I'll have my genie, Jehan, fetch it."

A peg-legged pirate whom Raspberry had taken to be just another of the men from the tavern spirited to the ledge by the uncorrigible Rusty drifted forward, neither foot nor peg quite meeting the lichen-covered rock. "You're wishin' you had a feast fit for dragons, lassie?" he asked.

"I do," she replied grandly, as she imagined all powerful mages answered their minions.

"Done," the pirate said. "But it's your last wish, and I'm free."

"My last wish?" Rusty wailed. "But it wasn't for *me*, it was for Daddy."

Jehan was not listening. Instead, he dissolved. When he reappeared, he had in tow ten cattle, six deer, and a grunting boar. "Tell your dragons to fire away," he said to the wizard. "I've brought 'em a spot of supper."

Grimley roasted the boar on the spot, and soon from the interior of the cave they heard satisfied smackings and slurpings, followed by a soft burp.

Grizel poked her head out again. "Little Grippeldice may have my eyes, m'love, but she has your appetite. Roast her just one more teensy little cow, won't you, my flame, and then I think she should nap. I'm rather burned out myself. Perhaps while we're resting, you would be a love and clear this ledge? It's getting so dreadfully cluttered!"

When she'd popped her snout back inside the cave, Grimley, the scales of his head puffed to right angles with pride, turned to Raspberry. "Don't that just warm up your insides, hot shot? Ah, fatherhood! Why, I feel hot enough to slay a dozen knights in shining armor."

"In that case, noble dragon, perhaps now that you're a family beast and will want to consider providing your mate and child with comfort and security, you'd consider re-entering the King's service? My daughter, as his Majesty's agent, has just provided you with your back pay, and his Majesty does need your help badly. I daresay that if we tarry much longer, it may well be that our liege will no longer be alive to require your services."

"Aw, blazes, hot shot, I'd like to help you out, but you heard my little spitfire. I have to clean this flamin' ledge off."

"May I suggest, noble dragon, that if you carry us instead of push us from the ledge, and transport us to the Worm's Maze Glacier, we might all accomplish our goals. Namely, we would stay alive, you would clean your ledge and provide yourself with exercise and recreation while re-establishing your service to the King, and we could all help preserve our sovereign land of Argonia."

"You mean to say, you want these creatures to ride on my back and then we'll ALL go slay knights together?" the dragon asked, regarding Rusty's band skeptically.

"Yes, noble dragon."

"Well, then," Grimley snaked a claw inside the mouth of his cave and snared a talon-full of sparkling gems, tossing them amid the townsmen. "As long as we're stokin' the same fire, so to speak, have some diamonds, boys, in honor of my new little spark."

A unicorn shrilled a long high scream. Maggie straightened, wincing as she pulled the knife from Colin's back, though she knew he felt nothing. She wanted a more direct weapon than her magic now. Unicorn healing had reclaimed the bodies of the

Everclear villagers and mended the wounds of Leofwin and Wulfric. Perhaps it would also save Colin and Pegeen, if it were used quickly. But she'd never know, if Fearchar's men won this battle.

Scattered groups of fighters clashed all over the road now.

Moonshine and Eagledown fought back to back, surrounded by packs of brigands. Cloven hooves and horns took a goodly toll, but new enemies quickly replaced the fallen ones.

Rowan stood alone in the middle of the road, spinning like a dervish while his sword scythed its grisly harvest.

Gypsies fought dagger-to-shortsword, but neither Prince Worthyman nor Davey still stood.

Neddy Pinchpurse and a few of his mates skirmished near the riverbank, neither they nor their attackers seeming ever to get the upper hand.

And always, for each of Fearchar's men who fell, ten more waited to engage the slayer.

The unicorn screamed again, from the building the King had defended.

Maggie zigzagged across the muddy road, avoiding engagement, running for the house.

Snowshadow reared, screaming, in the doorway. Her coat was blood-striped. Sally Forth brandished a sword, smaller and lighter than the men's, but just as effectively carving the unicorn.

"Go *away*!" Snowshadow shrilled. "I won't let you kill my people! I won't! They can't defend themselves! Go! They can't hurt you! Go! Go!"

The nymph struck and struck again, but Snowshadow would neither move from the doorway nor strike back. A blow fell across the unicorn's neck, deep and hard, and Snowshadow fell to her knees. Sally raised the sword again.

Maggie rushed the house, but tripped and fell sprawling across a bandit's body.

She heard one hoofbeat before a shadow leaped over her, and Primrose dived, horn first, into Sally Forth's back.

Then it was as if a high wind blew, and smoke and fire and screaming men were everywhere. A bandit grappled with a sailor, but a farmer, one she had never seen before, brained him from behind with a timber.

Other new bodies scrambled into the melee, while overhead the sun was blotted out by wild, looping shadows and belching flame.

She raised her head. From the doorway of the building, the Everclear villagers stepped carefully over their fallen unicorn, and wandered into the field of battle. At first she feared they'd be slain, but then she saw that the faces were no longer blank and the eyes held purpose. Some retrieved the weapons of the fallen and others simply launched themselves onto the back of the nearest enemy.

Crawling to Snowshadow, she stroked the blood-soaked mane, and the unicorn whickered softly, blowing pink bubbles. "They were frightened people, with no understanding of my magic." Her thought was thin and weak. "But they have good hearts. I could not let the false maiden slay them."

"Shh," Maggie kissed her forelock. "You've released them from their spell. They're helping us now. Rest."

She spent what was left of the battle fighting brigands away from the wounded unicorn. She had unexpected help from a one-legged pirate who was an excellent hand with a cutlass.

The dragon was the decisive factor, of course. No one cared to be charred alive. But the brigands also grew disheartened by having their weapons snatched from their hands by no corporeal force they could see.

Those who were able began to flee, keeping close to the rocks to save themselves from the dragon.

All three unicorns gathered at the doorway, over their fallen kinswoman. "She lives?" Moonshine asked Maggie.

"Aye, but not for long, without help. And Moonshine, Colin— you must try to help Colin. He's been slain but—"

Primrose interrupted, and her voice was not so harsh with censure this time as with grief. "Have your friends bear our sister to the river, and we will do for her what we can. Then we'll discuss your casualties."

"But Colin—"

Moonshine nuzzled her with a bloody muzzle. "Many are wounded and slain, friend Maggie. We'll save your love if we have the power, but we must put order to our tasks, and also there must be words passing between us and your King. Will you see to it?"

She wiped her tears on her bloody arm and nodded.

Rowan still stood in the middle of the road, directing the separation of dead from wounded, friend from foe. One of the men who had flown in on the dragon knelt before him. "Hillman, here, my Liege, of the Castle Rowan garrison. Request permission to return to active duty."

"Permission granted, as is bloody well obvious, I should think," the King replied. "Arm four men, Hillman, and scour this village. I want none of these rascals escaping."

"Yes, my Liege."

"Well, Maggie? And what are you doin' here, may I ask?" the King said, turning to her. "You're supposed to be back at your father's hall bein' courted and cosseted." But he gave her a grim smile and held out his hand. She knelt and kissed it. It was covered with blood, like the rest of him. Only his eyes still shone blue and white through the gore, some of it his own, some of it that of his enemies.

"I need men to carry the injured unicorn to the water," she said. "The unicorns can heal our casualties and bring the dead back to life only—"

"Bring the dead back to life? My poor little sister, you're too gentle for battle after all, I think. The sight of it's addled yer brain. But very well." Striding to Snowshadow, he pushed the other unicorns aside and lifted the injured one in his corded, bloodied arms as if she was a lamb. He bore her to the river, setting her down among the reeds poking up from the shallows.

"Well, I never in all my days!" the Blabbermouth blabbered, "A pure disgrace is what I call it, and that's the truth and no lie . . ."

Moonshine, Primrose, and Eagledown joined Snowshadow in the river, each dipping his horn or what remained of it into the chattering water.

The water instantly cleared, and its raucous voice lowered to a pleasant, well-modulated conversational tone. "Oooh, that feels very good indeed," it said gratefully. "It's been soooooo looooooong since I've felt anything as purely edifying as this. Why, look at how I sparkle now, and how deep into me you can see. I'm rather like an emerald, aren't I?"

Maggie had no patience for admiring the water, for now another wonder was taking place. Eagledown lifted his head, and his horn came out long, glittering, diamond-bright, boldly scrolled, and best of all, entirely whole. The wounds on his body, as on the bodies of the others, washed away in the sparkling river as easily as the blood and grime. Snowshadow's coat gleamed white again, and her horn grew and mended, spiraling into whole opalescent beauty even as they watched.

"Oh, I feel so much *better*," she sighed, splashing to her feet.

"Then we must set to work," Moonshine said, also rising. "Maggie, have your King convey *all* the dead and wounded here, into these waters, and they shall be healed."

"All?" she asked.

"Of course, all," Primrose said. "You don't suppose we discriminate between good injured bears and bad injured bears when we're practicing our art in the greenwood, do you? Though

326

there's been some discussion about it, we ultimately decided to put your kind in the injured bear category. We will heal *all*. What you decide to do with them later is up to you.''

The scene that followed reminded her a bit of a summer washday with her father's servants pounding laundry against the rocks—a practice she limited as much as possible by use of her magic, since the process tended to be rough on fabric. Only instead of sheets and towels and skirts and veils and waistcoats, people were being doused, dunked and half-drowned in the enchanted waters.

Moonshine went with her to Colin, and carried the minstrel to the river across his back.

Maggie knelt in the river and held Colin's head aloft while the water lapped his body. Next to her, the portly, kind-faced gentleman she had seen in the ruined house was performing the same service for Pegeen.

"You mustn't worry, my dear," he told her, comfortingly. "Why, her Highness has been here barely a moment, and already I vow her cheeks are pinking and her lashes flutter." Maggie looked. It was true. Pegeen did indeed live again, and her aura, though imperceptible in the sunlight, cast its rosy glow into the emerald waters beneath her.

Colin's color seemed improved too, though perhaps it was just the absence of mud and blood which made him look better. She stroked away the last vestiges of that with her fingers. Wet though her fingers were, when she bathed his face, she thought it felt warm again.

"I must say, though," the gentleman remarked, waving his arms at the soldiers who regrew limbs, the sailors revitalized after suffering mortal wounds, the gypsies whose skin deepened from pallor to its natural swarthiness, the bandits whose burns and gouges disappeared, all of the welter of wet humanity boiling around them. "I find this sort of thing disturbing. What do you suppose the consequences will be?"

"What consequences?" Maggie asked, not really paying attention for now Colin's eyelids were moving and his chest rose and fell with a motion quite separate from the lapping wavelets. "Oh, I suppose the bandits will be imprisoned or hanged, eventually, but everyone else . . .''

"I wasn't referring to them, actually," the man said. "It's the consequences for the unicorns which concern me. Once these people leave here and the news is heralded throughout the land that unicorns possess this sort of power, they'll never be free beasts again. Anyone of any means at all will try to round them

327

up and breed them like cattle or pigs, for the profit to be gained from selling their healing magic."

"That would never work," Maggie said. "I don't think unicorns could live in captivity that long. Snowshadow and Eagledown would surely have died if it hadn't been for the princess."

"Yes? Was someone addressing me?" Pegeen tried to sit erect and succeeded instead in dunking both herself and the gentleman. He surfaced, dog-paddling, and guided the sputtering Princess to the surface.

"Your pardon, madam," he said. "Sir Cyril Perchingbird, Royal Archivist, at your service. Allow me to escort your Highness back to shore."

Colin wandered the former battlefield, filled with a disturbing sense of unreality. He knew very little about battles. Only what he'd learned in songs and stories, and that didn't go into the emotional side of things much, aside from swellings of patriotism and bloodlust and so forth. But he was almost certain it couldn't be usual that everyone would look so refreshed afterwards as the people around him did.

The newly cleaned and revitalized bandits had cooperatively, almost cheerfully, allowed themselves to be bound with strips of their own clothing. The King roared happily about, barking orders, while Princess Pegeen and Cyril Perchingbird tried futilely to catch up with him. Wizard Raspberry and the dragon were fishing upstream, catching the evening meal which would feed this horde. He was aided by his daughter Rusty, whose piratical companion hunkered down with Neddy Pinchpurse and his mates, reminiscing, apparently, about the high seas.

Maggie presided over a large fire and a boiling crock from which she ladled cups of herb tea for all and sundry. The tea was more than mere refreshment—into it she had poured a quantity of salt from her medicine pouch sufficient to counter her uncle's magic. Sally Forth sat against the house which had been the major scene of battle, and the wolf lay at her feet. She appeared to be chatting with the river, which continued to speak quietly and rationally.

Only the unicorns seemed ill at ease, and clustered together, stamping and shaking their manes.

Weird was what it was. Surely there had never been a less bloody aftermath? No one even appeared to harbor any hostile feelings toward his co-belligerants of the previous hours.

Colin was almost relieved to see Griffin Hillman and his

friends herding a group of sweating, bloodied escaped brigands and carrying a thrashing, moaning, brown-garbed figure among them.

Pegeen's cheeks lost their new bloom. "Fearchar!" she said.

"My goodness, sir," said a bandit who was standing near the newcomers to Hillman, "Whatever 'as become of our Dark Pilgrim? 'E looks the worse for wear, sommat, 'e does."

The rowdy brigand who had seemed, when Maggie was first captured, so much less subdued by Sally's magic than the others was among Hillman's prisoners and it was he who snarled back. "'E'd be worse off yet if King's man 'ere hadn't saved 'em. There we was sweatin' like swine, bleedin' and dyin' and we sees 'im sneakin' off into that fancy swan car of 'is. All of a sudden I swallowed me own sweat and blood once too often, and I says to the boys, 'Get 'im.' All that fancy talk about savin' our skins with the beasts' magic was a lot of rot! 'E was gonter fly off 'n' leave us to 'ang alone. So we was givin' 'im a personal demonstration of what it felt like to be real broken up."

"Both arms and legs are broke, Majesty," Hillman said. "And several ribs as well, I think." The farmer-soldiers unceremoniously dumped their cargo into a howling heap at the King's feet.

Wizard Raspberry and his daughter heard the noise and came running. The dragon flew off, dangling a writhing silvery bundle from one claw.

The King drew his sword. "Now, knave, my inclination is t'cut ye into wee little pieces t' feed tae the birdies. But free my child from your wicked spell and I'll make it quick, and easier than you deserve."

Fearchar whimpered, and Rowan raised the blade. Suddenly, Pegeen leaped between them, shielding her former lover. "Majesty, I claim a boon for warning you twice of threats against your house," she said boldly.

Rowan lowered the sword, and the cold fire in his blue eyes banked somewhat. "Gracious lady, there's much I will grant ye, but nivver the life of this crawlin' crafty craven coward. He has nae the decency tae fight wi' me like a man, but wages wizardy wars against m' wife and bairn. But speak yer piece."

"I would converse with you privily, m'lord," Pegeen said, and when the King seemed about to refuse, Sir Cyril Perchingbird whispered something to him and the three of them stepped into the nearest hovel.

Maggie glared at her hated relative's quivering form for a moment, then strode over and knelt beside him, pushing aside the cowl which had flopped over his face and giving him a sip of tea. "Uncle," she said, "For the Mother's sake, spare yourself pain and undo the spell against the baby. It can do you no good now, and the King may decide to spare you if you do as he bids."

Fearchar spat feebly and said in an even feebler voice, "Bah! He'll squash me like an ant, and you, too, if you ever cross him. Know, niece, that the nobles are our enemies. They'll use us up entirely and—and discard us—if—if—"

"Save your breath, Uncle. I've had my dose of salt today."

Raspberry came and knelt at the wizard's other elbow. Hillman looked as if he'd like to restrain him, but hesitated to challenge anyone on such friendly terms with the royal dragon as the kindly wizard was. "You're one of the strongest magicians in the realm, Brown," Raspberry told him. "Your magic is, in its own way, the equal of either of your sisters'. Listen, I've been high up in court circles, and I can tell you, running a country is no enviable task. Release the spell on the baby, and I'll add my plea for your life to the Princess's."

"Bah," Fearchar said again. "He'll never—ach!—spare me. You pretend to sympathize with me only to glory in my agony!"

But then Maggie and the Wizard were joined by Snowshadow and Moonshine.

"Friend Maggie," Colin felt the touch of the unicorn's mind stronger than ever. "Remind your King he agreed we would heal *all* of the injured."

"Moonshine, you realize this is my uncle, the wizard who would have destroyed you and the others?"

"We know, but the creed must be heeded, and:

"It is the Unicorn Creed
 On which we are all now agreed
 To make no exception,
 Heal all to perfection
 To exceptions we will not accede."

"I see," she said, "Though you certainly switch that around a lot these days. But I'll tell him."

The King returned and Colin noticed his sword was sheathed. "What is this?" he asked. "A new plot against m' crown?"

Maggie told him quickly what the unicorns had said.

"Humph," Rowan replied. "Might as well, I suppose. He'll be less trouble on the journey back tae Queenston if he's of a piece. If m' horned subjects insist on curin' every ache and pain, it'll do me no good tae behead t'bastard here and now. They'll

330

only dump 'im in t'river and grow 'im another one. And I'll not waste m'good steel that way. Only first, he's got t'lift the curse."

Fearchar seemed finally to be encouraged enough by the intervention on his behalf to cough out a civil reply. "I cannot."

Rowan's sword was half out of its sheath before Sally Forth cried, "It's true! He didn't curse your child, King!"

"If he didn't, who did? Did you, ye faithless trollop?"

"Nay, King. Not I. But I confess I arranged for it through a relative of mine."

"Mother's done it again," Rusty Raspberry sighed.

"What d'ye mean, child?" the King demanded.

"My mother's always boasting about her international circle of sorceress friends, Sire," the girl replied. "They used to meet at our tower once in awhile, flying in with magic rings and carpets and such. Stupid old crones. A curse on a baby would be just their idea of high-class magic. It WAS Mother you got that curse from, wasn't it?" she asked Sally.

"She obtained the box for us, yes, and the basic spell that accompanied it," the nymph admitted.

"And the release?" Rowan roared. "What of the release, woman?"

Sally prostrated herself. "Sire, we didn't expect to need a release. None was obtained that I know of. But you could question the ogress, Belburga."

"No, you can't," Rusty said, shaking her head. When the King glared at her, she shrugged. "Sorry, your Majesty, but my dear mama's taken my sisters and moved to Greater Frostingdung. Prince Leofwin's going to make Lily Pearl his queen."

Instead of roaring again, Rowan sighed and all the iron seemed to leave his spine. "I cannot save my Bronwyn from it then, this curse? She's only a wee little baby."

Cyril Perchingbird laid his hand on his sovereign's shoulder, and said encouragingly. "Exactly, your Majesty. She's only a baby. She can't even talk yet. What harm can the curse do her now? By the time it can have any possible effect on her, you can send emissaries to Greater Frostingdung and demand the name of the sorceress who devised the curse from Dame Belburga. Are not the other issues of which we spoke of greater urgency to the security of your realm?"

"Aye, you're right as usual, Cyril. Dunk this smelling heap of offal in t' river first, and we'll speak our royal mind t' our subjects here."

Fearchar went screaming into the river, and came smiling out of it, straight for the King's feet, where his smile faded as he knelt. "Majesty, whatever you do to me is no more than I deserve. I would I could obtain for you the lifting of the curse I have so heinously placed upon your child, and will do so personally if you command it. I only beg you and my beloved niece and my gracious lady and these wondrous beasts whose magic I would have defiled, to blame none but this greedy and vicious man before you for the harm he has done. And if you cannot forgive me, it will be no more than my just punishment to go to my death tormented by your hatred."

"Oh, Fearchar," Pegeen said in a sad, soft voice.

"But I implore you, Majesty, to blame me solely, and to pardon and take back as your devoted subjects these, my dupes in this plot; the nymph Sally, the were Wulfric, and all of these men who fled their own countries to find a living in your own as brothers of the greenwood. For I did pervert them by my magicks to my treasonous cause."

"Aw, don't be so hard on tourself, Dark Pilgrim," a bandit cried. "They'll 'ang us no 'igher for bein' traitors than for bein' brigands, though I do confess I don't know 'ow I could 'ave wronged such a goodly King as ours."

"Aye," several others echoed, and, "I'm with ye there, brother."

Rowan regarded the entire group with slit-eyed suspicion. "Ye'd hae all saved yerselves much grief if ye'd coom tae that conclusion before this mornin'," he told them.

Sally Forth, who had remained kneeling, now raised her head. Her right hand rested between Wulfric's pointed ears and she said, "Highness, do with me what you will, but I would beg you to spare the were Wulfric, who was my accomplice, but now seems to be no more than another dumb beast, and a were no longer."

Eagledown trotted over to the nymph and the wolf, and stood for several moments, then trotted back to Maggie. Colin heard him tell her, "Say, you know what? Ever since you cut that animal's tail off and Moonshine grew it back, the wolf says he hasn't had to change into a man. Seems our magic cured his ancestral were disease along with growing him a new wagger. And something else, too. He says we can skin him alive if we want to, but spare the nymph."

Maggie shook her head wonderingly, and conveyed the information to the King.

"If ye ask me, everyone is gettin' most awful noble all of a sudden," Rowan complained.

" 'Twas that lovely baff you give us, sire," a bandit offered. "Why, I ain't felt so good since before I stole t'first copper from me ol' mother's purse."

"Aye," another added. "I feel like kissin' babies and helpin' crones up stairs all of a sudden."

"Aw, let 'em go, Sire. They be'nt such bad lads." This was from one of the King's own sergeants-at-arms, a man noted for his severity with miscreants of any kind.

"And beggin' yer pardon, Rowan, m'lad," Prince Worthyman added. "But it seems to me all this coulda been avoided with a bit of statecraft."

Rowan scratched his head in bewilderment. "Speak," he said.

"Before you were King, I promised to help you if you ran into political problems," the former bear reminded him. "Seems to me yer whole problem with Fearchar here is, contemptible as the man is, he's an able, ambitious witch who's had no opportunity to use his power for the good of the country."

Rowan looked to the princess, to Perchingbird, and back to Worthyman. "The Princess suggested t'very same thing," he said. "What I'd like to know is why everyone is suddenly so willing to spare one another now? And why *I* keep listenin' tae this drivel in a most unkingly fashion when I ought to be loppin' off heads?"

Colin surprised himself by kneeling in the mud in front of the King himself and saying, "When you start lopping, sire, I prithee take my head too, for I'm as much a traitor as these others."

The King jerked him roughly to his feet. "Dammit, lad, I've no time for your nonsense. I know very well who stopped those arrows from pricklin' me royal hide, and who took a knife in the back for his trouble."

By then Maggie was kneeling in front of him, too. "Majesty, he's not talking about that, but he's not a traitor, and it's not his fault. It's me who disobeyed you. I was willful and stubborn, and wanted to shirk my responsibility to your trust. I didn't want to be a Princess and marry a Prince. I wanted to run with Moonshine and now—and now, I want something else too. But none of that was Colin's fault."

"I'm going mad!" the King swore. "Silence, dammit! Any more of this and I'll have the lot of ye thrown back into t' river t' soak some sense into ye. Yer bandits and traitors, men, act like it! And you," he pointed an accusing finger at Colin. "Yer one of my ablest men and ye'll be Earl of this place and watch it for me, like it or not, for I need ye.''

"Majesty?" Cyril Perchingbird asked.

"WHAT?" he roared.

"Majesty, perhaps the change in attitudes among your subjects is a byproduct of the unicorn magicks. Perhaps their power cures ill humors of an—er—spiritual nature, as well as of the physical variety?"

"I'll test it. Hillman, you're a good stout dirty laddy. What say you we do with this man?" He prodded Fearchar with his muddy boot.

"Slay him, sire. Slowly, my liege. Let these lads finish the work they started." He jerked an unwashed thumb at the bandits his men had rounded up and added, "And then finish them off as well."

The King scratched his beard as furiously as if it were infested and said, "Hmm. That's a reasonable answer, Hillman, but somehow it pleases me not. Ye stink, man, and all of yer men and prisoners stink with ye. Go bathe, the lot of ye! Now!"

"And the other matter, Majesty?" Perchingbird prodded prayerfully.

"Give me time, man, I'm comin' to it," he snarled back, then straightened his still-dripping tunic and set his hand on the pommel of his sword, and said, "Ahem. It has been brought to our attention that within our midst are some very extraordinary beasties, even for this, our realm, which has never exactly been shy o'magic and t'marvelous. Today we have all, in one way or another, had our lives and limbs saved by t' magic o' these unicorns. At this time, we have been moved to mercy by our own experience with the darlin' creatures, and the lot of you have benefited. We have no way of knowin' how long all this unexpected good will is goin' t'last, but we mean to take advantage of it by seein' to it that you don't take advantage of our unicorns. I want a solemn blood oath from every man and woman, friend or foe, among you that this battle never took place, that you never were healed, that you got religion or fell under an enchantment or any other fool thing you want to tell folk t' explain t' changes in yer own natures. But you're never to tell a soul or mention again to each other what our unicorns did on this day. I command this not to lessen the credit due to them, to which I'm comin' directly, but to protect them from the greed and wickedness of men such as the scalawag at my feet. Do you so vow?"

Everyone did, including Fearchar.

"There'll be no clemency for any one among ye who breaks his vow," the King said grimly.

"There is a surer way to insure silence, your Majesty," Fearchar suggested, so humbly that Colin knew for sure that the stuff of legend was taking place before his eyes, a legend which must never be told at the cost of destroying its source.

"Aside from killin' you all, you mean?" the King asked. Fearchar nodded. "Speak then," Rowan said, wearily, and sat down crosslegged in the mud. Everyone else sat down, too. "Try t'make it simple, will ye?" the King asked.

"Highness," Fearchar said, "I can by my own magic convince everyone here that this day was something else, the forming of an alliance for your Majesty, or any other event you wish it to be. Only withhold salt from those you would have me bespeak, and they will never speak of this event as a battle but will speak of it as they believe it to be, as a meeting, an oath-swearing of fealty, or whatever your wish is."

"My wish is that you didn't take me for such a simpleton I couldn't see you're tryin' tae gain t'upper hand again," the King replied. "As if I don't already have enough problems thinkin' how I'm tae make honest subjects out of two hundred foreign brigands and keep my other nobles from huntin' these wondrous beasties—"

"My Lord, I will speak my spell publicly, in front of yourself and my niece and whomever else you trust to insure my honesty and loyalty to your Highness."

"Hmm. Fair enough. And you've gi'en me an idea too. You'll tell these men here, and this woman," he indicated the brigands and Sally Forth, "That they're to form a new order of Royal Guard. From now on, their job will be to protect the unicorns and to apprehend anyone who tries to poach them. Because here and now I'm makin' all the Royal Argonian Forest a royal preserve for unicorns. These fellas will be called the Order of the Unicorn. And they're not to seek or molest the beasts any more than anyone else, I want that understood, too. What d'ye think of that, Perchingbird? Pretty good, eh? Just to make it look good, see to it that a new crest is designed for our Royal House—put the 'corns on me rowan leaf. We'll let it be known that the beasts are our special talisman, and under our protection. How's that?"

"I will do as you command, sire," Fearchar said. "If these folk are kept saltless today, I will bespeak them this evening. Keep them saltless a day longer, and the spell will be permanent,

335

though if they take salt after that time, they will be immune from my powers of suggestion.''

''Excellent. We'll bind and gag you meanwhile, to make sure you don't turn on us again. Perform this task faithfully and I've got a little job for you, one suited to your powers as to no other man's. You recall that edict of mine about the dragon tax? Thing's deuced hard to collect, and with your magic . . .''

EPILOGUE

Maggie slipped through the door, shutting the maelstrom in behind her. Colin's combination investiture celebration and hearth-warming was exhaustingly successful. All the best people were there, including the King, Winnie, and the baby, Sir Cyril and Princess Pegeen, and the crew from the wrecked *Snake's Bane*, who had stayed on to help Colin build a new hall while waiting for their own new ship to be built.

Wizard Raspberry was in the kitchen with Granny, who poured the ale, assisted by the Brewers from Little Darlingham. The Wizard disguised twenty of the blueberry pies guests had brought to taste like strawberry, apple and peach instead. He had helped Maggie with the decorations, too, several hundred silk balloons bobbling colorfully among the fresh-hewn cedar ceiling beams. Princess Pegeen's splendid cartoon for an ornamental tapestry, featuring unicorns, adorned the wall opposite the main hearth. The faery Trickle had filled a sled with fragrant crimson and fuschia flowers which she and Sebastian Bigfoot had brought across the glacier, along with a load of ice.

Rusty entertained with the new magic tricks her father was helping her learn, most of which involved rabbits instead of simulacra.

The dragons sent warm regards, along with a particularly nice diamond to announce the birth of their new get, Grippeldice.

Xenobia's people camped close by, and tonight the hall bloomed with the hues of their brilliant clothing and jingled with the noise of their jewelry as they danced and sang with the rest of the revelers.

The King had thoughtfully sent for Granny and Father and Aunt Sybil, along with Colin's aunt and uncle. They had all arrived, complete with Maggie's cat, Pem, and Ching, just this morning after spending nearly three weeks on horseback. The knowing looks which had started passing between Granny and Aunt Sybil almost as soon as they saw Maggie, and the guarded way in which they spoke to her, bothered her more than anything else about this evening and sent the confusion in her brain straight to her stomach. She needed fresh air.

The freezing-snowing-thawing-raining-freezing cycle of the last week sheathed the world in a fine gleam of ice, reflecting back the full moon in millions of tiny bright replicas. The snow covering the ground was scuffed and dirtied near the hall, but lay serenely unbroken closer to the banks of the ice-muffled Blabbermouth.

Or at least, relatively unbroken. For on closer inspection, she could see the prints of cloven hooves coming from the woods beyond the village.

Moonshine stood beside the river, his horn half-hidden in the hole in the ice through which the newly-settled inhabitants had been drawing water.

"Fancy meeting you here," she said. "You've been gone so long, I thought I'd never see you again."

"Dearest Maggie, it has been long, but many were the streams which needed our attention."

"I daresay," the river chimed in. "But the young lady is absolutely correct. You've been gone far too long. I was quite going round the bend again before you came along this evening."

"Ah, but now I'm back," Moonshine reminded them. "And my two friends are here to bear me company. How goes it with our good Master Colin these days?"

She shrugged her cloak closer about her and pretended to watch the river running black past the hole. "Don't ask me," she said. "He's been so busy with his new duties as Earl that he's barely spoken to me all this month."

"Do they sit so heavily on his shoulders, then, that he has no time for his beloved?" Moonshine asked sympathetically.

"No more heavily than yours do," she snapped back. "I have work of my own, you know, but I wouldn't neglect YOU because of it. I've been so bloody helpful to everyone I seem to have helped the two beings I love best right out of needing anything at all from the likes of me."

"Nay, Maggie, it is not so," Moonshine said. "Other matters entirely keep me from your side, and other matters also occupy our Colin, I'll vow, for he loves you well."

"He doesn't. And I'll bet those other matters of yours are because I'm not a maiden any longer. Isn't that right? I'm not pure enough for you any more."

"Maggie, your heart is as pure as any unicorn's in your love of justice and goodness, as Master Colin's is pure for love of you. How that may relate to the stricture of virginity laid on unicorn companions is still a matter of mystery to me but—"

"Mystery? Of course, it's a mystery!" the river interrupted. "Though, of course, it was never supposed to be mysterious to unicorns. But with magic like you creatures have, Moonshine, you have to understand that there has to be some mystery surrounding you, and you have to be careful who you associate with.''

"Halt!" Moonshine said. "Do you mean to tell me you understand the Creed? ALL of the Creed?''

"Who better? I've washed the horn tips of generations of unicorns, though just lately I was beginning to think I'd been forsaken. Listen, I've been running through this valley for a long time, and I'm a pretty important drink of water. I knew the first unicorns IN Argonia—though that was long before the witch taught me to talk, of course, which is just as well. I listened better in those days. Your ancestors held their very first council here on my banks, and I can tell you, that entire maidenhood clause wasn't designed so you could meet only PURE people, because there's no such thing. A young inexperienced girl will muddy your waters as quickly as anybody, quicker than most, I'd say. But at least most of 'em are *young*, and impression-able, so that the powerful goodness of your Creed and your magic will stick with her the rest of her life. She's apt to be a better-than-average human because of you, if she's got any potential at all. With any luck at all, she'll pass on a little of what she learns to her family. It's too dangerous for you to consort with the human race as a whole, you see, but with one small, usually harmless segment of it—well, your ancestors felt that a girl like that could be like the first ripple to touch your horn, spreading out to clean up the rest of the river. You see? They'd had experience where they came from, it seemed to me, and they hit on befriending virgins because virgins are young and relatively helpless and the condition is fleeting and swiftly cured. They might have chosen pregnancy, as well,'' the river paused significantly, "But that happens more than once. A girl's vir-ginity flows away from her the way your magic flows from me . . . it's a singular, rare, ethereal time that is clearly the proper period for confronting unicorns.''

"Yes," Moonshine said, his eyes opening wide with inner revelation and his nostrils flaring excitedly. "Oh, *yes*! That's true! That's why! I feel it—I know that is the true message of that part of the Creed! Wait until I tell the others! And oh, does that mean that any maiden who has once been a unicorn maiden may remain always a unicorn friend?''

"I don't see why not.''

"Hurray!" Maggie caught his excitement, and hugged him. "But why didn't your silly Creed say that if that's what it meant? None of you knew it that way.''

339

"Elementary, my dear witch," the river replied. "It was too difficult a concept to put into a rhyme. Thus it was forgotten by the youngsters."

"There's a lot to be said for *noisy* waters running deep," Maggie said. "You are a very intelligent river."

"Thank you. I've always thought so."

"Oh, good river, oh, my dear friend, Maggie, I beg you to excuse me, for I must fly now to Snowshadow and the others to tell them of this wonderful new knowledge. Now then, river, if you could but repeat it over to me, *why* the unicorn may befriend only the virgin but how it is that he may remain her friend after the girl is a virgin no longer. I don't want this to be lost on our foal as it was to us," he added to Maggie.

"Your foal? Moonshine! You?"

"That is the other matter of which I spoke. My Snowshadow is to bear a new unicorn. But how can I pass on this knowledge if I cannot remember it?"

"A song is always a good way," Colin said, approaching them.

"Master Colin! How fine you look in your new raiment! Would *you* compose such a verse, containing the river's knowledge, so that I may pass it truly to my new foal?"

"I'd be delighted," he answered, slipping his arm around Maggie's shoulders. "I know you're not much of a hand with a verse. I've a boon to ask of you, as well, while you're here."

"Ask it."

"Will you use your influence with this lady to persuade her that though she's a Princess and a nobly born sorceress, she should ask the King for MY hand in marriage in preference to those other blokes who are going to be lining up soon? I know I'm just a lowly Earl, and a new-made one at that, but I think that as father of the child her Granny and Aunt have been telling me she's expecting, I ought to have some preference over the others."

But there was no need for Moonshine to answer. Before Colin had quite finished speaking, Maggie threw her arms around his neck and kissed him fiercely. From the chimneys of the new hall, the fire leapt so high that its flame was seen as far away as the capitol of Brazoria, where the preistess Helsinora noted the marvelous ascension of a fiery new star into the heavens.

ABOUT THE AUTHOR

ELIZABETH SCARBOROUGH was born in Kansas City,
KS. She served as a nurse in the U.S. Army for five
years, including a year in Viet Nam. Her interests
include weaving and spinning, and playing the guitar
and dulcimer. She has previously published light verse.

SONG OF SORCERY
by Elizabeth Scarborough

THE WITCHMAID'S QUEST

Maggie Brown was a hearthwitch, good at whipping up banquets and starting fires, not a *true* witch, like her Granny, who could turn men into birds, or her Aunt Sybil, who could see into the present.

But when Maggie's beautiful but empty-headed sister Amberwine ran off with a raggle-taggle gypsy, it was up to unkempt, unruly Maggie to track her down.

So she set out with Ching, the talking cat, and Colin Songsmith, a travelling minstrel who was not so bad once you got to know him, to bring back her wayward sister.

On the way they met a gnome, a unicorn, a mermaid, a lovesick dragon and an enchanted bear, braved ambush, flood and abduction by gypsies, and stormed the lair of a particularly evil sorcerer, in a rescue mission fraught with excitement and danger.

0 553 17282 4

RIDERS OF THE SIDHE
by Kenneth C. Flint

Out of the mists the Fomor came to enslave the isle of Eire, a dread race of twisted men ruled by an inhuman lord: Balor of the Evil Eye. But a champion came from out of the sea, a youth called Lugh, seeking his destiny, sent to Eire by the seagod Manannan MacLir to fulfil an ancient prophecy.

With Gilla, a jesting rogue, and Aine, a spirited warrior-woman he came to love, Lugh challenged the Fomor to restore the True King to the throne of Tara, and summoned the Silver Warriors of the Sidhe to fight in the realms of men.

The tale of Lugh of the Long Arm is among the greatest of all Celtic myths. Now this mighty legend comes blazing to life in a new retelling filled with all the fire and magic of the ancient bards.

'An excellent fantasy adventure'
SCIENCE FICTION CHRONICLE

'Enough derring-do for at least one Lucas film'
LOCUS

0 553 17250 6

STARTIDE RISING
by David Brin

The Terran exploration vessel *Streaker* has crashed on the uncharted water-world of Kithrup, bearing one of the most important discoveries in galactic history. Above, in space, armadas of alien races clash in a titanic struggle to claim her. Below, a handful of her human and dolphin crew battles armed rebellion and a hostile planet to safeguard her secret – the fate of the Progenitors, the fabled First Race who seeded wisdom throughout the stars.

'Not since Stapledon has a writer succeeded so well in conveying a sense of the strangeness of the universe and the infinite possibilities which space and time must hold'
Poul Anderson

'Brin is a scientist who knows how to tell a story. That's a rare combination'
Jerry Pournelle

0 553 17170 4

THE POSTMAN
by David Brin

"TO ALL CITIZENS: Let it be known by all now living within the legal boundaries of the United States of America that the people and fundamental institutions of the nation survive. A provisional government is vigorously moving to restore law, public safety and liberty once more to this beloved land . . ."

In a few years from now, a handful of men and women struggle to survive in the dark days after a devastating war, battling disease and hunger, fear and brutality.

Gordon Krantz is one such man, an itinerant storyteller. One night, he borrows the jacket and bag of a long-dead postal worker to protect himself from the cold. In the next village he visits, he finds the old uniform still has power as a symbol of hope, for the return of an age now gone.

Unwilling to disillusion the villagers, Gordon accepts their letters to loved ones who may or may not still live, and in doing so creates his greatest tale, of an America on the road to recovery. His deception takes on a reality of its own, as others come to join him, supported by the strength of a vision he himself only half-believed.

'It is a powerful novel; a perfect example of a good story told with emotional honesty and depth, resonant with myth'
FANTASY REVIEW

Also by David Brin in Bantam Books
SUNDIVER ● STARTIDE RISING ● THE PRACTICE EFFECT

0 553 171933

A SELECTION OF
SCIENCE FICTION AND FANTASY TITLES
AVAILABLE FROM BANTAM BOOKS

☐ 17291 3	**THE HEART OF THE COMET**		
		Gregory Benford & David Brin	£2.95
☐ 17184 4	**THE PRACTICE EFFECT**	*David Brin*	£1.95
☐ 17170 4	**STARTIDE RISING**	*David Brin*	£2.50
☐ 17162 3	**SUNDIVER**	*David Brin*	£1.95
☐ 17193 3	**THE POSTMAN**	*David Brin*	£2.95
☐ 17398 7	**RIVER OF TIME**	*David Brin*	£2.50
☐ 17247 6	**THE HOUND OF CULAIN**	*Kenneth C. Flint*	£2.50
☐ 17250 6	**RIDERS OF THE SIDHE**	*Kenneth C. Flint*	£2.50
☐ 17256 5	**CHAMPIONS OF THE SIDHE**	*Kenneth C. Flint*	£2.50
☐ 17292 1	**MASTER OF THE SIDHE**	*Kenneth C. Flint*	£2.50
☐ 17181 X	**BELOVED EXILE**	*Parke Godwin*	£2.95
☐ 17280 8	**THE SARABAND OF LOST TIME**	*Richard Grant*	£2.50
☐ 17188 7	**THE BOOK OF KELLS**	*R. A. MacAvoy*	£2.95
☐ 17154 2	**DAMIANO**	*R. A. MacAvoy*	£1.95
☐ 17155 0	**DAMIANO'S LUTE**	*R. A. MacAvoy*	£1.95
☐ 17156 9	**RAPHAEL**	*R. A. MacAvoy*	£1.95
☐ 17282 4	**SONG OF SORCERY**	*Elizabeth Scarborough*	£1.95

All these books are available at your book shop or newsagent, or can be ordered direct from the publisher. Just tick the titles you want and fill in the form below.

ORDER FORM